EXPIRED GETAWAY

LAST CHANCE COUNTY - BOOK 7

LISA PHILLIPS

Publisher: Lisa Phillips

Cover design: Ryan Schwarz

Edited by: Jen Weiber

❀ Created with Vellum

1

Denver, Colorado.

The back door to the accountant's office had been broken and busted into. The keypad smashed up, obliterated by the butt of someone's gun. Or so she assumed.

Bridget had a phone, but 911 was the last thing on her mind.

All she could think of as she drew out her gun and deposited her pack by the back wall was wondering who had been on shift tonight. She'd been out of town for two days delivering a care package to one of their clients. It was a regular enough occurrence, but traveling to Caracas to do so wasn't. Being discovered there by cartel guys while fishing the client out of a dicey situation and running for their lives? Also not so much.

Bridget had very nearly been shot right before stashing the client somewhere safe. Afterward, she flew to Mexico City and met with a doctor, passed out for two days from exhaustion, and managed to miss her meeting time.

Now that she was finally here, she discovered the office had been broken into.

Bridget didn't believe in coincidences. But of all the enemies the accountant's office had, she didn't have the first idea who might be inside.

Or what they wanted.

Bridget cast a longing glance at her backpack. She didn't like leaving it unattended, but it could hinder her if she had to fight.

She eased the door open with her foot and stepped into the back hallway.

A muffled grunt echoed from the main office.

The place wasn't big. A strip mall storefront with a small unused apartment above—a safe house when one was needed. Bridget made up one quarter of the four employees. The boss was currently out of town on vacation with her husband. That left Clarke and Sasha. If someone had broken in while Sasha was working late, they'd be dead already.

That left Clarke.

Her sometimes-on-again/sometimes-off-again boyfriend had made it clear before she left that he wanted things to go to the "next level." Bridget didn't even know what that meant. Or why she was dragging her feet over him.

She needed to tide him over with some sort of excuse until she figured out for herself what her deal was with him.

Bridget crept down the hall to the door at the end, ajar. Beyond, the main office was lit. They'd painted the front windows so no one could see inside.

Another cry sounded, not so muffled now.

Bridget whispered, "Clarke."

She should get in there and save him from whatever was happening. Still, part of her wanted to wait so she had a better idea of what she was getting into. Another part of her—one she wasn't sure she liked—wanted to see what he'd do. How he might handle this. As though his mettle hadn't been tested already in this job, and she needed to put him through the wringer all over again. She didn't need to see the depth of his skills. That was selfish.

"You will tell us what we want to know." The accented voice

held the strain of authority. Someone not used to being ignored, who was accustomed to making someone pay dearly for such lack of judgment.

A shudder began but Bridget locked it down like she always did. She needed steady hands and a calm mind. Something she'd worked on for years, battling her fear to the place she could be strong. Valued.

Not the beat-up, broken-down teen who'd left Last Chance in the middle of the night without ever looking back. The lingering trauma flared on occasion—like when she saw blood. Given the last few days, her history was pretty close to the surface.

But she couldn't let it penetrate. That would only leave her useless.

Bridget kicked the door open. She clocked the two guys in suits right away. Clarke stood behind his desk across from them. Unsure. Debating. He started to speak.

The door behind her hit the wall with a thud. Both suited guys shifted to her. Before they could face the new threat, Clarke pulled a gun from his desk and shot twice.

Both men fell to the ground.

Bridget blinked, but the prominent feeling that settled upon her was relief. It might seem harsh, but in their business, hesitation meant death. And given the last two days, she wasn't willing to take any chances. After the mission she'd just been on, Bridget knew something wasn't right.

She glanced around. "Are there more of them?"

Clarke stumbled back and sat heavily on the desktop before sliding sideways and falling to the cheap carpet. Blood trickled down the side of his face from a nasty gash on his temple. "Bridget. Hey."

"What is going on?" She strode over and held out her free hand. He'd killed those two men. "You good?"

Clarke clasped her wrist way too tight and nearly pulled her over as he stood. Once at his full height, he barely matched hers despite the fact she was wearing sneakers and not heels. She had at least two inches on him. Clarke flung his arms around her and squeezed, her arms—and the gun—smashed between them.

"Oof." Pain sliced through her middle—a bruised rib from yesterday. "Let go, Clarke."

He didn't. "I'm so glad you're here. I knew I'd have to take them out, but the element of surprise..." He squeezed once more and leaned back. "Works every time."

Bridget extricated herself from his arms. "So it was just the two of them?"

She moved to the closest one and took a look. Could be Capeira's goons, but she'd left Caracas two days ago. Had they really caught up to her this fast? There was no way they could've found the accountant's office that quickly.

"You see them," Clarke said. "There are two."

As though she couldn't do simple math, or needed what she'd seen with her own eyes explained to her. Bridget might not have been a particularly stellar student in high school, but she had skills. And a brain.

She tried to figure out what was up with him. "What did they say to you?"

"They wanted access to the computer systems. Of course, I would die before I ever gave them that."

The back door had been busted in to grant these men entry. He'd probably been taken by surprise. Hit over the head and disoriented before they demanded what they wanted. No one who worked here would ever give armed intruders anything. Except for a bullet.

She was just glad it had been Clarke and not her. She knew how to use her weapon, but only did so when it was a matter of life or death. Sneaking up on two men whose intentions she didn't know? That wasn't honorable.

Plus...she'd already killed someone this week.

Bridget walked to the second man he'd shot. A gun lay close

to his hand, fallen from his fingertips. He had a scar just below the base of his thumb. It had been carved there. "These guys are both underlings."

She straightened in time to catch Clarke eyeing the discarded weapon. "There should be a driver or a lieutenant with them."

No way would someone who knew what this place was actually trust a mission like this to two guys who hung on the bottom rungs of the ladder.

Bridget started to turn. Clarke was far too close to her.

He touched her shoulders, but the weight of his arms proved too heavy for it to be considered sweet or comfortable. "I'm so glad you're here." He shifted his body closer, but it wasn't comforting.

It was a threat.

"You probably saved my life." He let out a depreciating laugh. "If I was willing to admit it."

"You just did, but all I did was distract them." She tried to step back, but he didn't let go.

Clarke's gaze shifted over her shoulder. Holding her still.

Someone else was here.

Bridget held back the reaction that wanted out. She still had her gun. She could shoot Clarke right now. Instead, she brought her knee up between his. High enough to make contact, but still like she hadn't noticed it wasn't just the two of them here.

He doubled over.

"Clarke, you let a woman go when it's clear she wants to be free." It was a good point to make, but it became really clear really fast that it wasn't *the* point she should have focused on when a fist smashed into her cheekbone as soon as she spun around. A flash of pain doubled her over. Bridget blinked and stumbled back from yet another suited man.

Ouch.

He pried the gun from her fingers. She tried to grasp it, but by that time Clarke had recovered. He twisted her fingers almost to breaking point. She cried out. With her free hand, Bridget punched him in the stomach as hard as she could.

"Quit messing around and get her secured." Another heavily-accented voice.

Clarke pulled her hands behind her back. "I told you she would come here."

"Mmm."

Bridget struggled, fighting against the man until she found herself staring down the barrel of a Glock, pointed right at her. Beyond it stood a man whose brother she had shot two days ago. She gritted her teeth. Was he here for revenge?

"Your brother nearly shot me." He'd also compromised their client, but Bridget wasn't going to bring her into this. The woman needed a new identity and somewhere to go—both of which Bridget was supposed to figure out tonight. Until then, the client had to lay low. The Capeiras weren't going to find her.

She turned to Clarke. "You're the one who sold her out and told Benito Capeira where she was. Aren't you?"

His expression hardened. "They made me do it. They said they'd kill my mother if I didn't."

Bridget's overblown sense of empathy for the underdog flared to life inside her. At the same time, she tried to figure out if he was even telling the truth.

Capeira laughed. Smaller than his brother, Enrico was still built like a powerhouse. She needed to not underestimate him the way she had with Benito. That only landed her with a broken rib before she was forced to shoot him. Both men's reputations spoke of a ruthless need to be obeyed at all times.

Those who did not? Their bodies were never found.

Until the client discovered their secrets and took that information to the Justice Department. Instead of being given the case, she'd been told to go find "actual evidence." Bridget had heard enough. She was going to help.

She'd also thought Clarke would help.

Guess not.

"A chair, I think." Enrico stepped back and motioned with his gun. "Make it look like she fell asleep exhausted and smoking a cigarette. Accidents happen."

Clarke shoved her into a chair. "I thought we were doing a gas leak."

"Like I said, 'accidents.'"

Bridget looked up at her colleague. Before she could say anything, he ran the back of his hand down her cheek. "I'll be heartbroken. But I'll find someone else."

Before she took her next break, he raised his hand and pistol whipped her with her gun. Everything went black.

The next thing Bridget knew was that she couldn't breathe. She tried to move. Her face was smashed against the carpet. Using both hands, she did a push up and got her knees under her. No restraints. They had to have left her free to make the "accident" look real.

When she lifted up, the temperature of the room registered within her.

Then the smell.

Bridget launched herself toward the back hall. She stumbled, slammed her shoulder against the corner of the wall, and cried out. She didn't have time for more injuries. The building was about to explode.

She braced the wall with one hand and raced the other direction, down the hall to the back door she'd come in.

An explosion ripped through the building. The force blew apart the door and flipped her over. She slammed onto the asphalt outside and rolled. A moan escaped her lips, but she needed to see it. She needed to know it was still there.

Her backpack.

Bridget crawled to the wall beside the spot the door had been just a moment ago. She shifted rubble and tugged over her pack to hold it close as she dug inside for her phone. Relief washed over her, though this wasn't done.

Far from it.

She pulled up her texts and sent one to her boss.

CODE RED.

Nothing needed to be—or could be—salvaged from the building. It was all saved to an encrypted server. They would move on. Rebuild. Once Bridget took care of the threat, and Clarke.

She forced her legs to take her weight and start walking. The last thing she needed was to still be here when the cops arrived.

A second later she got a reply with an address.

GET HERE ASAP.

Bridget sagged against the siding of a neighboring building. Go there? After all these years, that was the last place she wanted to be. But orders were orders. She had to head home.

To Last Chance.

2

Last Chance

"I was hoping you'd be here." The woman who'd sidled up to him lifted a beer bottle and took a sip.

Aiden Donaldson, Last Chance police officer—currently off duty—tried to remember what her name was, but for the life of him, he couldn't. He smiled. "It's good to see you." Then turned back to the group of kids bowling.

His kid was up, so he squeezed through the crowd of moms and children—including the birthday girl—and made his way to where Sydney waited for a ball to come out.

"This purple one will work."

"I'm waiting for the pink one."

Behind them, a group of first grade girls erupted into laughter. The pink ball came out.

"Ready?"

"I want to do it by myself."

Aiden bit back what he wanted to say and squeezed down on his back teeth while he sent her a closed-mouth smile.

His little redhead missed nothing. "I can do it."

"And I'll be right here while you do." Aiden walked with her to the ramp that'd been dragged over. All she had to do was push the ball and watch it sail down the alley.

She hefted the ball onto the ramp that was little more than three bars of metal welded into a frame. The ball started to roll, so he put out his hand. It didn't need to go down before she had the chance to push it.

He lifted his gaze to the face of his six year old. "Ready, Beautiful?"

"Ms. Maggie said you'd like my dress." Her fingers lifted off the ball, and it started to roll toward his hand. "We got the blue one because it's your favorite color."

"That it is." Aiden grinned and saw the next kid waiting. "Ready?"

She nodded. He moved his hand and Sydney pushed the ball, her tongue stuck out from between her teeth in concentration. Aiden didn't watch the ball. He watched her face, garnering enough information from that as to what was happening down the alley.

Tomorrow he would be back on swing shift for the next four nights before he got two days off. That meant Sydney would be with the sitter after she got out of holiday kids club and in bed before he was home.

But he got breakfast, and they tried to live it up with the time they had. Aiden was a pancake artist using squirt bottles and food coloring. He could make a rainbow, and he was working on perfecting a unicorn, though it wasn't going well.

"I knocked down three!"

Aiden picked her up and spun her, even though she said she was too big for that. Sydney slapped his cheeks and blew a raspberry on his forehead.

He set her down, grinning.

"Cake!" Sydney ran off to her friends, and he wandered back to where he'd left his water cup. The mom with her beer watched him. The look on her face wasn't one he wanted to entertain.

Still, as he moved toward the table of kids all eating a slice of pizza before their cake, she also moved. When he reached the edge of the birthday party, she was beside him.

"You're a pretty good dad."

He glanced aside to see her eyeing him over her beer again. "And that's a surprise?"

The woman shrugged a slender shoulder. Too slender, by his estimation. "Single dad, right?"

"What does that have to do with it?"

"Usually dads aren't all that interested is all."

Aiden watched Sydney reach for her cup. He winced as she nearly knocked over another kid's soda.

"It's nice. That's what I'm saying."

He turned. "Which one is yours?"

"Oh. None." She motioned with her head toward the bar. "I just hang out here."

Aiden's stomach turned over.

"They're so cute at this age, aren't they? Then they turn into unholy terrors at the drop of a hat if they don't get what they want. Am I right?"

"Not in my experience."

He wanted to walk away. To stand closer to Sydney like a helicopter dad. Which he pretty much was, but only because he was the only person in the world there to watch her back. The sitter was amazing and he didn't know how he would do it without her and his army of church ladies to help, but at the end of the day, Aiden was alone in this.

"Huh." The woman blinked over her beer.

As a father and also a police officer, he needed to stick near this woman and try to get her to open up about her intentions here.

"It's more like, sometimes, she's not a kid at all. She's a tiny teenager." Aiden smiled, though the precise teenager Sydney reminded him of flashed in his mind.

There hadn't been much of a relationship between the two

of them, and they'd been barely out of high school. A summer romance gone wrong, if they could even say it had gone anywhere in the first place. Months later he'd found out she'd died in childbirth. That he was a father. Social services had asked him first if he wanted to raise the baby. As the father listed, he'd have had to give up his parental rights otherwise.

Give up the chance to pour love into a beautiful, innocent child of his own?

No way.

The woman barked out a rusty laugh. "Welp, I see my friends. I hate to love you and leave you, but I gotta go, gorgeous."

Aiden didn't even know what to say. He kept his mouth shut. He had no intention of setting her straight. There were no sparks between them. He was who he was—a twenty-four-year-old police officer and single dad to a six-year-old daughter.

Not most people's idea of a stellar beginning to adult life. No parties. An online degree. He knew more about assembling furniture and French braids than he knew about fraternities. But he wouldn't have it any other way.

Sydney had healed everything inside him that was broken. Aiden didn't want to know who he would be without her.

She tugged on his hand right then.

He looked down. "Pit stop?"

"Yes." She held his hand until they separated, and then she went into the ladies' room while Aiden waited outside. It still made him nervous to trust other people's goodness, but this was a small town and a lot of people knew their little family unit.

Aiden checked his emails while he waited, most of which were about the police post-holiday bash happening in a few days. No one was free to party during the holidays, so they did it mid-January.

The woman who'd tried to pick him up had chosen a new target, a guy at the bar. Worn jeans and steel toe boots. He wore a faded white sweater and had sunglasses on his head.

As he watched them, she pulled something from the back pocket of her jeans and exchanged it for what the man had. Plastic wrap, bundled up. The contents weren't something he could see, but experience and instinct indicated crack. Whether it was another illegal substance or that one, it didn't matter. It wasn't good.

The man squeezed her hip and she walked off, headed for a door that read, "Employees Only."

Aiden pulled up a text thread with his sergeant who was at work tonight and laid out what he'd just seen.

"Can we play at the arcade before we go?"

He looked down at Syd. "Probably not. It's pretty late, and we have church in the morning." After lunch, he would be on shift until past midnight.

"Donuts for breakfast?"

His phone buzzed. "Absolutely."

She jumped up and down. "Yes!"

Aiden read the text from Sergeant Basuto. An officer on duty was on the way. He eyed the door the woman had disappeared through while they made their way back to the party in time to sing and for Sydney to watch her friend open the doll they'd bought her.

He moved to Sydney and crouched to whisper. "Stay here with your friends. I'll be back in a few minutes, okay?" The birthday girl's mom seemed to have it all in hand, so he went to the Employees Only door and pulled out his badge. Just in case.

Aiden had a weapon on him but didn't get it out. All he needed to do was make sure the woman hadn't left. If she had, he wanted a description of her car. Or a plate number.

If she exited this way, he would talk to the manager about surveillance. Interview customers and staff, find out if the woman was a regular. Methodical actions that would get him in another conversation with that woman—one where he explained the seriousness of her actions. He'd make sure she knew help was available if she needed it, or caution her to get a lawyer if the situation warranted that.

He flashed his badge to the bartender who lifted his chin, then pushed through the door. The hall beyond was empty.

Three doors on both sides. One open. He moved to it, listening for…voices. At the door, he peered in.

"I said I did, didn't I?" Her tone wavered as a sliver of fear crept in.

The man she faced was taller, muscled. He wore slacks, black shoes, and a buttoned white shirt. Still, despite the professional clothing, there was an air of lethality about him.

Aiden cleared his throat.

The woman spun around while the man turned more slowly to find him there.

He decided to just pretend. "I'm totally lost. Is there a bathroom down this way?"

"Get him out of here." The man turned to his desk.

That left the woman to cross and jerk her head toward her shoulder. "Let's go. There's no bathroom over here. This is employees only."

"You work here?"

She led him to the door. "Just get out of here."

He held it open for her. She shook her head at his gentlemanly move and strode off. He spotted the person Basuto had sent and made his way to Officer Frees, at the same time watching where she went off to.

A group of men at the far end of the bar. The woman passed them. She said something low before heading for the front door, pushing it open to go outside.

"That her?" Frees eyed the woman's retreating form.

Aiden nodded.

"I got it. You get back to Syd."

Frees strode after her. He angled his radio to his mouth to speak as he headed out the front door. Aiden went back to the party, compiling his thoughts. Drug deal, and she was affiliated with the bowling alley. Whoever that guy was in the office, Aiden would talk to the sergeant about him. This could easily be a big case for the department. Though, given what they'd been through in recent months—this whole past year, basically—no one wanted to dip their toe into a huge problem so quickly.

Of course, they would if it became necessary. But a shark known as "West" had been swimming in the local pool for years. The result? Near devastation. Months of investigation down twists and blind corners. The cost to the department had been huge.

"Daddy." Syd slammed into him, and he lifted her again because she still let him do it. "Did you get that perp?"

Aiden grinned. "I'm not working. I'm hanging out with you." Never mind that no cop used the word "perp." Ever. "Is the party done?"

She eyed him. "I'm still hungry."

"So we should stop for broccoli on the way home?"

Syd made a mock-gagging noise. "Ice cream!"

Aiden blew a raspberry on her cheek. "As you wish."

He set her down, and they said their goodbyes to the birthday girl before turning to the front door of the bowling alley.

The guy from the office stood by the Employees Only door. Arms folded.

Watching him.

3

Two days after the accountant's office exploded, Bridget pulled into the garage of a townhouse just before two in the morning. The address was the one her boss had given her for the safe house in Last Chance. She waited until the garage had rolled down before pushing open the driver's door and grabbing her duffel from the backseat.

There wasn't much to haul into the house, considering she hadn't had time to go home before she drove north out of Denver, nor was it safe to have done so. All she had with her was everything she'd taken on her last mission, along with her backpack. Plus, she'd had to find a new vehicle, as Clarke knew the one she normally drove.

Exhaustion weighed down her muscles and made her want to flop onto the couch and fall asleep. But she knew rest wouldn't come. She set the backpack down beside her bag and wandered through the rooms to familiarize herself with the layout.

Times like these, when her body was a mess of aches and pains, the nightmares came. And then she'd wake up more tired than before.

Bridget had no intention of allowing Enrico or Clarke, or

the past for that matter, to invade her sleep tonight. It was only a matter of time before one or both of them figured out she was still alive. And then they would come again to kill her.

But that wasn't even what she was worried about.

Bridget brewed a pot of coffee she would have to drink black, as the house was only stocked with dry goods. No perishables. Fine by her. She also dumped two cans of soup into a pan to heat up on the stove.

While the noise of the gas flame and the coffee percolating filled the kitchen, she fired up her laptop. It didn't take long to log remotely into their security system and get a look at Enrico and his men arriving at the accountant's office. They'd been there for more than an hour before Bridget showed up in her car. She fast forwarded through the part where she walked in through the back door, and slowed it back down right before they stepped outside.

Her phone vibrated in the front pocket of her backpack.

Please be Millie.

But it was her other female colleague. Millie was a wife and mother. She didn't make middle-of-the-night phone calls.

Bridget swiped her thumb across the screen and put the phone to her ear. "Hey, Sasha."

"I'm guessing things are about as good as you sound."

"I'm in a safe house." She wasn't going to tell Sasha where it was, or even the connection she had to this town. Sasha knew their boss was from Last Chance. But the less Bridget's colleagues knew about her past, the better.

She'd been trained that way, by them, and it had kept her alive all this time.

"Good." Sasha let out a long breath. "I can't believe Clarke would do this. But maybe I'm not that surprised, you know?"

"I know what you mean." Then again, she would've said the same thing about Sasha if this whole thing was her and not Clarke. "I'm looking at the surveillance footage now."

"And?"

Bridget studied the screen of her laptop. "Enrico doesn't seem too upset that Clarke killed two of his men. They seem kind of chummy. After they knocked me unconscious, they walked outside and had a short conversation. Clarke watched Enrico leave and then walked off down the street."

As though the building wasn't about to explode, and there weren't two dead bodies and an unconscious woman inside.

Her stomach knotted. *What did you get into, Clarke?*

"Toward his car?"

Bridget said, "Maybe. I don't know where he normally parked."

She was still trying to puzzle out the relationship between Enrico and Clarke. Let alone why Clarke had chosen Bridget, of all the people at the office, to get close to.

I'm not a weak link.

Sasha broke the silence. "So who contacted who, and when? Does Clarke work for Capeira number two?"

"Enrico's the number one now." Bridget had been forced to kill his brother just days ago, which meant he'd inherited everything. "I can't tell by studying the video whether he and Clarke were friends, or just in business together. Or who exactly is in charge."

"And we can't get into his phone to find out," Sasha pointed out. "But that also means he can't track any of us or breach our firewalls."

Security went both ways with their system. To access the company information stored on the cloud—not an easy task on remote servers—there had to be two user IDs entered along with both user's passwords.

Sasha wasn't a weak link either.

Which was why Bridget thought Millie might be. As the only one with a family, she was vulnerable.

"You're somewhere safe, right?" Bridget worried her colleague might be targeted, even if it was a long shot and she knew very well that Sasha could take care of herself. And would.

"I'm good. Do you need help?"

Instead of answering, Bridget said, "I'd have thought Enrico would be taking advantage of the power vacuum in the cartel. Though coming after me and getting revenge for his brother's death might be part of assuming control."

"So he could be using Clarke to tie up one final loose end. And you know it's easier to pay someone who'll do anything for cash rather than use threats to force a person who isn't easily bought."

Bridget frowned. "I don't believe he didn't contact Clarke until *after* I killed his brother. I think he and Clarke have had a longer relationship than that because it's the only thing that makes sense. There's no way he could have convinced Clarke around to his way of thinking—even with blackmail—fast enough to get here in time to try and kill me."

"He should've just put a bullet in your head."

Bridget swallowed. "I'm partial to the fact that he didn't."

"Don't get me wrong, I'm glad you're alive. But if he wanted you dead, then he should've killed you, not just blown up the office and assumed you died in the blast."

Her soup began to boil to the top of the pan. Bridget hopped up and got a bowl to dump it into. Only now it was far too hot to eat, and she didn't want to burn her mouth. Her growling stomach just needed to hang tight a little longer while she waited for it to cool.

She slumped back onto the stool. "Staying alive when by all rights I should be dead is about the only thing I'm good at."

Sasha laughed. "You and me both, girl. Let me know when you find Clarke. I'll help you take care of him."

With that last parting threat, Sasha hung up. It was all part of her charm.

Bridget didn't know her all that well, despite working together for years. Sasha kept to herself. What she did know was that Sasha would be an asset in a situation like this. Bridget would be making the right move if she allowed Sasha to help her, and being a team player usually counted as a good thing. Except that she was far more comfortable working alone.

The way she'd always been.

Always would be.

Bridget ate the soup and drank enough coffee to keep her awake for a week. She made notes of everything that'd happened on her mission, right up to walking into this house. Just before sunrise, she made macaroni and cheese and jazzed it up with fake bacon bits from the cupboard. Later she would go out and get some real protein, but she'd had to go without food often enough in her life to be grateful for what she had in any given circumstance.

Who complained about bacon, anyway? Even if it was the shelf-stable kind.

To stay awake, she wandered around the townhouse and even took a shower. Eventually she was going to have to submit to sleep. Resting during the daylight hours, maybe even on the back deck of the third floor while the winter sun shone on her, would be her best chance at negating the nightmares.

All she had to do while she waited for Millie to call her was keep from losing her mind.

If it only were that easy.

Bridget eventually resigned to watching the surveillance footage again.

Every frame with Enrico and his men. Then every minute of the footage she had of Clarke working for the last week or two.

If she wanted to implicate him in something, then she needed evidence. But there was no way a man with his training would leave a breadcrumb for her to find on their computer system or the proprietary phone system they had purchased.

No one could trace any of their cell signals or hack into their phones. Sure, it was a network designed for criminals to keep their conversations from getting into law enforcement hands, but for the right price, they sold phones to good guys too.

Bridget wandered to the front window and looked out through the lace curtain that hung over the glass. A row of townhouses faced this one, and she saw a garage door roll up.

An adorable little girl skipped around the back of a small SUV wearing a big winter coat, gloves, and a wool hat on her red hair. She disappeared to the other side, a backpack dangling from one arm. Seconds later, a guy in jeans and a jacket with a backpack of his own, got into the driver's side.

Bridget had an uncanny feeling she had seen the guy before, but brushed it off. It wasn't like she had a super clear view.

He pulled out and they set off together while the garage door rolled closed again. Bridget looked at her phone. Just after eight in the morning. Two members of a family going about their normal life.

Headed to wherever kids went during vacation from school, and work.

Just another day.

Bridget's entire body wanted to turn so she could look at the backpack. Years of training held her still. Nothing could induce her to give away how she felt when she didn't want to. Not even when no one was looking. She lived her life assuming that someone was always watching, even when she was completely alone.

Not even the burn in her heart over the one thing she would always miss could break that concentration.

Her life was what she'd made of it, and nothing would change that. Everything was fine with her mental state. Her emotions were in check. Pretty soon there would be a ton of work to do, but right now there wasn't. And it was fine.

All she had to do was wait for Millie.

Bridget could try and figure out how to find Clarke or how to get Enrico to let go of his revenge plan.

Now that she knew Clarke was working with the Capeira's, it was clear there was a bad seed in the company. So long as he was the only one. Much better to dwell on that than to start thinking about her personal life. Bridget had plenty to sink her teeth into. The potential for devastation across the accountant's firm and their clients was catastrophic. Clarke could single-handedly destroy the entire business and put everyone's lives at risk. Nearly two hundred clients could be killed because of him. Everything they'd worked on for years would fall around them like the walls of Jericho. The stronghold in ruins.

Just because Bridget was back in Last Chance didn't mean the past needed to creep in. What was the point anyway when there was no way to fix it?

After all, she had faked her death for a reason.

Most people pined over the past. She had changed everything about her life, with no intention of ever wanting things how they used to be. There had been nothing good about who she was back then or the town she'd lived in.

This town.

So maybe her heart's cry was to be like that guy coming out of his garage, just like it was any normal day, taking his kid out for a drive. Going to work. Millie managed to make it—doing the family thing, the spouse thing. Her life's role wasn't the same as Bridget's, but she'd found a work-life balance. Not perfect. Just hers.

But no matter how much she secretly longed for what she'd never had, Bridget had come to terms with the fact her life would never be that fairytale.

Even if she walked away from everything she'd built, the life she had now would continue to follow her to the ends of the earth.

Bringing danger along with it.

She slumped onto the couch and tugged the backpack onto her lap. She didn't pull out the scrapbook, just held the bag. Looking at what was inside would be indulging her feelings. *No way.*

Nothing good ever came from letting her emotions distract her.

Not when there was so much at stake.

4

"Is everyone ready to begin?"

Aiden took his paper plate loaded with a sub sandwich, chips, and a cookie, and hustled to an open chair in the middle of the briefing room.

The chief looked up from the tablet on his lectern. "Good."

Conroy Barnes had been the chief of police in Last Chance County since the previous chief passed away from pancreatic cancer. Aiden had respected Ridgeman as a boss, but now that his lieutenant was the chief, it seemed like the whole department had been closing cases left and right. They'd also had more injuries recorded. And more breaches of the office by gunmen and mercenaries—even a wanted fugitive—over the past few months.

The only officer killed in the line of duty in the last five years occurred during the case where Conroy met his now-wife.

"There's been an uptick in vandalism on the west side of town. Mostly barns tagged with graffiti, but also a couple of fences destroyed. Randall lost two cows on Tuesday. So we'll be spending more time on that side of town for the next couple of weeks."

Aiden pulled out his notebook and wrote that down.

"There has also been a rise in the number of overdoses recently." Conroy gave a few more details, and Aiden wrote those down as well. "And we are currently on the lookout for a blue truck with no rear license plate, driven by a woman. Her description, along with other relevant details, has been sent to your inbox."

Aiden glanced at Officer Frees, who lifted his chin. So that was the woman from the bowling alley. The one Frees had followed outside.

The officer beside Aiden elbowed him in the ribs.

He glanced over at Officer Jessica Ridgeman, the previous chief's granddaughter. Her hair was blonde again, and that wasn't the only thing that'd changed about her life. "How's Ted?"

"Both jobs are going great," she whispered back. "I swear he's able to work them at the same time, and since they're remote and no one has a non-compete, he's going to keep doing it." She grinned. "He makes more money, and he wants to build a house."

"Wow."

Ted had previously worked for the department as their tech specialist, but due to withholding important information from the police—things he'd been involved with in the past—Conroy had been pressured by the Mayor to fire him. Even after the two of them had received kudos for their work uncovering the fire chief's criminal activity.

"Plus, the government keeps calling and offering him classified projects." Jessica shook her head with a roll of her eyes. "Not to mention everyone who's clambering to write a book about his father. Ellie might do it, but he's not sure he wants to tell the whole story outside of grand jury hearings."

Aiden knew Ted had met regularly with the FBI. There was even an agent in town. Eric Cullings had ties to Last Chance and knew Ted personally. Aiden hoped the guy had vouched for him. "Will there be charges?"

She shook her head. "Doesn't look like it. And I think Ted's more bothered about the fact that Basuto still won't talk to him. Even Conroy has to make it look like he's giving him the cold shoulder."

"Something you want to share with the class, Officer Ridgeman?" Conroy's eyebrows lifted. "Perhaps some tidbit you learned studying for the detective's exam."

"I'm working on that."

"Sure you are," Officer Frees muttered. "We definitely need more girl detectives in this department."

Jess crushed her paper cup and threw it at him. Frees caught it before it bounced off his forehead.

"Speaking of—" Conroy ignored the interplay. "—I'm currently interviewing candidates for two detective spots and a dispatcher to replace Bill who, by the way, reports that his sunny Florida retirement community is chock-full of New York Mafia dinosaurs." Someone snickered, but Conroy continued, "I'm also interviewing for Ted's replacement, and will soon be studying each of you under a magnifying glass, looking for the next lieutenant."

Jessica shifted as though she wanted to raise her hand.

Before either of them could ask why they needed a new lieutenant, Conroy explained, "For several reasons I am not required to explain to you, Mia will be transferring to a position at City Hall where she'll be a liaison between me and the Mayor. She'll also be working on community engagement."

Jessica leaned over to Aiden's shoulder. "I bet she's pregnant."

Aiden figured she was probably right, but he wasn't going to give her the satisfaction of telling her that. He had been the new guy on the force in Last Chance when Jess, a police officer in New York City, moved home. The two of them had worked together ever since. He considered her a good friend, even though she sometimes annoyed him with the way she never *ever* dropped any matter until she got to the bottom of it.

Mia, currently their lieutenant and the wife of the chief of police, had hearing damage from a suspect who had shot off a firearm beside her head. She'd already been through several surgeries and had been pretty much reassigned to a desk ever since. Her previous career as an ATF agent made her a solid part of the team here. Now they were losing her to city hall?

Aiden had learned a lot from her. After two good lieutenants, he wasn't excited to have to learn a third. Unless it was Basuto.

Jessica leaned over again. "You should study for the sergeant's exam."

He frowned at her. "Why?"

"Basuto gets the lieutenant's job, right? Makes sense." She shrugged. "That leaves his sergeant position open. And you know Frees is a lifer as an officer. Sergeant gets you more money, better hours, and more time with Sydney."

Aiden didn't quit frowning or considering it as Conroy wrapped up the briefing.

He tossed his plate in the trash and sucked down the rest of his coffee before heading to the parking lot and his black and white small SUV. Snow had been plowed into piles in the corners of the lot. The pure white snow that had fallen from the sky was now marred, practically black with the exhaust and dirt.

Even at midafternoon it was still barely twenty-five degrees out, but completely dry with blue sky overhead. Aiden preferred that it snow in the winter if they were going to have to endure these crisp, freezing temperatures. But not when he was on shift and Sydney would be home from school enjoying the snow by herself with the sitter. Or at Hope Mansion with Ms. Maggie, where she hung out often at their holiday kids' club with the other residents' kids.

As he drove through town, Aiden's phone rang. The screen lit with the word, *Mom.* He stared at it for a second, then figured he may as well get this over with, so he pulled over into a parking lot and left the engine running so the heater would stay on.

"Hey, Mom. How are you?"

"Aiden. How are things?"

He ignored the fact she'd answered his question with a question. "Did you get my card?"

He'd sent her and his dad a holiday card, inside which had been pictures of him and Sydney at the pumpkin patch a couple of months ago. In return, she'd sent a card for Sydney with a twenty-dollar bill in it.

"Those were lovely pictures of the two of you. How was your Christmas?"

Aiden's stomach clenched, but not out of nerves. He tried to tamp down the resentment. After all, they'd left town—and Aiden—immediately following his high school graduation and moved to South Dakota to take care of his aunt. Months later, he'd found himself a single father.

"Christmas was good."

When he'd called to tell them about Sydney, they'd just told him over and over again how happy they were to be grandparents but that he should give the baby to someone else to raise. Never mind that Sydney's mother was dead and Aiden had been given the chance to finally do something good with this life. Over the six years since, they'd met Sydney twice, during visits back into town.

He mostly figured she was only calling now out of a sense of duty. After all, Christmas had passed days ago.

"And everything is…okay?"

"Sure, Mom." Aiden didn't know what she expected him to say. Probably that everything had turned into a disaster and she'd been right all along. "Everything's fine. Thank you."

"After all that West stuff I've been reading about in the news articles, I was afraid the whole town had been overrun by criminals."

"If it had been, then we'd take care of it. I'm actually on

shift right now."

"Oh! Well, I should let you get back to it."

Aiden glanced at the carpeted roof of the SUV. "That isn't what I meant. It's nice to talk to you, Mom. How are Dad and Aunt Lena? How was your guys' Christmas?"

"Oh, it was quiet. Just a few friends over from bridge club. You know?"

No, he didn't know, considering it had been him and Sydney by themselves since the day that lady from social services showed up with her in a carrier and the story about her mother's death in childbirth.

Of course he would take a child who was his flesh and blood. Just because she was the product of a friendship turned disastrous summer fling that ended abruptly didn't mean she deserved anything other than the best life he could give her. Even if he had been eighteen with next to no clue what to do with a baby. They'd learned together, and he'd had a ton of help from church folks.

Aiden's radio crackled, and he heard a call come in. "I have to go, Mom. I need to respond to a call."

She rushed a goodbye and hung up abruptly, not giving him time to say anything.

Aiden grabbed his radio, responded to the report of a car accident on the highway, flipped on his lights, and gunned it out of the parking lot.

Ten minutes later, he pulled over behind a truck that had plowed into an embankment of snow before then barreling into a tree. Given the tree was completely frozen, it had splintered on impact and several branches were now lodged in the windshield.

Aiden winced and headed for the driver's side. No one else was around. It was just the two vehicles and him.

He grabbed his radio and twisted it toward his mouth. "Dispatch, come back."

"What is it, Officer Donaldson?"

"This call I responded to. It's the blue truck we're looking for." He opened the door and saw the driver. "And the woman is inside." He pressed two fingers to her neck, but it was obvious she was no longer living so he explained that as well. And yet, something about this just wasn't right. "I need another set of eyes."

Something about the crash didn't quite add up, and he hadn't been there long enough to figure out what it was yet.

"Copy that. Sending a detective to your location."

By the time Detective Wilcox pulled up, Officer Ridgeman in her passenger seat, Aiden had figured it out.

The two blonde women strode over to him. Savannah Wilcox wore her red coat, gloves, and a hat. Jessica Ridgeman had on long sleeves under her uniform shirt, but no coat—the same as he did. Aiden knew for a fact she had foot warmers in her boots, though.

"Officer Donaldson."

He nodded. "Wilcox."

"This is the woman you saw dealing drugs at the bowling alley?"

He followed her to the driver's door, which was still open. "Shouldn't there be more blood?" That was what was bothering him. The whole interior of the truck just seemed… Clean. "If she died in a horrific crash, there would be more blood. Right?"

"If she bled out after impact, then yes there would be." Wilcox turned to Ridgeman. "Check the passenger side for a purse or any other personal belongings."

As Jess rounded the back of the truck, Wilcox straightened. "Could be she was dead before the truck hit the tree."

"Which could've been what caused the crash. Like a medical event that stopped her heart, leaving the truck to veer out of control."

Aiden wondered if it had been some kind of heart attack or stroke. She looked pretty young at first glance, but he knew from talking to her up close that she was much older. Or, at least, her eyes showed her age.

"There's a purse and a wallet. But no phone." Jess straightened and came back around the car.

Savannah, Detective Wilcox, nodded. "I think you're right, Officer Donaldson. Her heart wasn't pumping when she sustained these injuries. She might've already been dead when the truck went off the road."

Jess stopped beside him. "What do you think caused her death?"

"This is just a guess, of course, considering I'm not a medical professional, but I've seen this many times, and even more recently here in town. It almost looks like the drug overdoses we've been seeing." Detective Wilcox folded her arms. "So what we do now, Officer Ridgeman?"

"Compile everything we have on who she is, contact the next of kin, and talk to anyone who might've seen her before she climbed into this truck today."

Aiden frowned. "That would include the guy I saw her talking to yesterday, right?"

She'd been having a heated conversation in the office at the bowling alley when he found her. Along with a man who considered her someone who should answer to him. That meant he had responsibility for her, whether he liked it or not.

"Good idea." Savanna nodded. "I'll take the scene here, and you guys go to the bowling alley. See if you can find that guy and speak to him." To Jessica, she said, "We can meet up later and talk to the next of kin."

"Copy that." Jessica turned to him. "What do you say, Donaldson?"

Aiden reached for his radio and called in his plans for him and Ridgeman to head to the bowling alley.

Jessica wiggled her fingers as they strode to the car. "I'm driving."

"That will be difficult, considering I have the keys."

She barked a laugh and got in the passenger side.

The bowling alley was open, but given it was midafternoon,

patrons were pretty sparse. Aiden found the first employee he came across and explained they needed to speak with the manager.

A few minutes later, the man found them. "Can I help you, Officers?"

This guy had a red polo shirt that matched every other employee of the bowling alley, though his distended stomach stretched out the front. He also wore matching tan slacks. But it wasn't the man from last night.

"We're looking for a guy who was here yesterday, in an office through there." Aiden pointed at the "Employees Only" door. "Shined black shoes, black slacks, and a white shirt."

Jessica showed him the screen of her phone. "He was talking to this woman."

It had to be a picture of her from the truck because the manager guy paled. "I've seen her around here, but I don't know why she would be in the office." He swallowed. "Is she…dead?"

"She was talking to the man we are looking for." Aiden wondered if the guy was gonna let them look at their surveillance video. "Which means, now that she's deceased, we need to know what your bowling alley has to do with her."

"She was just a customer." He shook his head and sweat beaded on his forehead. "We don't have anything to do with her death. And no one who works here wears black slacks and a white shirt." He flicked out his collar. "We're all dressed like this."

"If we could take a look at your security camera footage." Jessica pointed at a camera high in the corner at the ceiling. "We can figure out for you who was in the office when they shouldn't have been."

The man lifted his chin. "If you think the bowling alley has anything to do with this woman's tragic death, then you should come back with a warrant. Because I don't have to give you access to anything."

"Thank you for your time." Aiden ushered Jessica to the door before she could say something they would both regret.

Now that the woman was dead, maybe they would never figure out if there had actually been a drug deal last night, or if what he had seen had been nothing at all.

It was a case for Savannah, though. And Jess, since she was shadowing Detective Wilcox. But not one that he, as a patrol officer, needed to be involved in.

As he turned, he spotted a familiar man over by the bar. Right where the dead woman had made the exchange with the construction worker.

Not related to the case. But still significant.

What was he doing here?

The man stared at him as he turned. Of course, Jessica caught it. She lightly whacked his arm. "Who is that guy?"

Aiden gritted his teeth and pushed the door open. He held it for her so she could leave first. He didn't look back at the man in jeans, a winter jacket, and a beer in his hand, glaring daggers at him. As though anything that'd happened in his life was Aiden's fault.

"Seriously, who is that guy?"

He said nothing.

"Professional, or personal?"

If he didn't say professional, she would know it was personal whether he admitted that or not. So Aiden said, "Personal."

"You, or Sydney?"

Aiden gritted his teeth. "Both." That man back there was literally the only person in town directly connected to both of them. "Let's go get coffee. We can pick one up for Savannah too."

Jess eyed him. "I will find out who that was. Or you could just tell me, and I'll have more time to study for the detective's exam."

Aiden stared at her over the roof of his cop car. "Fine. He's Sydney's grandfather."

5

The path was more overgrown than Bridget remembered. Even in the dark she could navigate her way to the creek from where she'd parked. Through the frozen earth that cradled spring runoff—dry right now—up the ridge to the farm.

Her childhood home.

Bridget supposed at some point it had been a real farm, not just a rundown house on twelve acres of grass her father never mowed. At one point he'd rented it to the neighboring herd so they could graze it down. But that never lasted long. Even a simple transaction like that, which should have brought income, dried up like the creek sooner or later.

Bridget laid down at the top of the hill and pulled out a pair of binoculars. She set her elbows on the frozen earth and watched.

Light illuminated the kitchen window in a yellow glow. Someone had replaced the curtain that used to hang there with lopsided cardboard. Beside the backdoor was a milk crate, full of mismatched boots. Snow lay in patches on the ground, swaths of earth shaded by the house so they got no sun.

In the same way her parents' lives had shaded her. It wasn't until she left Last Chance that she'd finally known what the sun felt like. Sure, summer had been part of her life here. Literally and otherwise. But there had been no good times in this house.

Nothing good at all until…that final summer.

Then, nothing but pain. So much pain that all the good in her broke apart until she was nothing but a collection of fragments. Millie had helped her put them back together. And Sasha, too. In her own way.

What Bridget had now wasn't much better, though she was capable of finding peace by herself. In her faith. Through the quiet times and solitary places when she could just be…Bridget. No pretenses. It wasn't overflowing with abundant joy the way it maybe should've been. But she was happy enough.

There was still violence in the world, but now she knew how to work through the fear and survive intact.

Unlike what had happened the night she'd left town.

Memory of that pain washed over her. Bridget rolled onto her back and stared up at the stars, millions of them. And here she was. Just one woman down here, millions of miles away. Her tiny life didn't mean much in the grand scheme—nor did her suffering in light of all the pain in the world. In the whole history of humanity.

Bridget breathed until the ache of the past melted from muscle and bone. Maybe someone new lived here now, so she wouldn't have to see her father.

She rolled over and picked up the binoculars in time to see the back door open. A hefty mastiff trundled down the steps and into the grass where he sniffed around for a minute before lifting a leg.

Bridget whimpered. She managed to swallow down the reaction but didn't take her gaze from the animal. All the while her heart raced faster and faster. "Butch."

She'd thought it was a dumb name for a majestic English breed, but her dad hadn't paid her any mind.

An early warning sign if ever she'd seen one. Too bad twelve years old was too young to know. Too young to see the truth of how her father treated her. To her, he'd just been her father.

The dog was old now, and it clearly pained him to walk much. Still, he scented something on the wind.

"Where you goin' dog?" The low rumble of her father's voice drifted to her in the still of night, when sound carried best.

Had Butch heard her say his name? She was maybe four or five hundred feet from them, hidden in a bundle of berry bushes no one ever picked or trimmed.

The dog ambled up the hill toward her. He could definitely smell her, but then she'd wondered if this might happen and had come prepared. Just in case.

Anything but having to face down her father. She wasn't even sure what her purpose was for coming here, except to find out if he was still alive. Not much could be learned about a guy like him from a web search. It wasn't like he regularly updated a social media account, and she had no idea if he even used email.

"Butch." Her father stopped. "I ain't comin' up there to get you, boy."

Bridget's stomach turned over. She hated that voice and everything he represented. She should've brought the rifle Clarke had taught her how to use and taken care of the bulk of her life's problems in one shot.

Except, in the end, it would make her no better than him. Plus, it was, like, illegal and stuff. That never bothered him when he wanted to do something. She didn't know why it should bother her. She'd been raised to do whatever she wanted, whenever she wanted, since that was exactly what he did.

Bridget stared down at the dark figure as the dog sniffed steadily toward her. By all rights, her father should be in jail, or dead. If there was any justice at all in this life, one of the two would have already happened during the years she had been away.

But no.

There was no justice. Not in this life, and not to the true extent of what that word meant. After all she'd seen and done, Bridget had to rely on God in His wisdom and power—and His kindness—to figure that all out. It was part of the peace she'd found.

"Butch."

The dog kept on, while her father kicked a rock or something on the ground. His dark figure shifted, and he set his hands on his hips with an audible sigh.

Bridget stilled. The dog drew closer. Everything in her wanted to reach out and grasp him, hold the big animal in her arms. She'd never be able to heft his hundred-thirty odd pounds over the hill. Not without her father shooting her with the gun he kept on his person at all times.

A tear rolled down her face, but not because of fear.

The dog's snout rustled a brown leaf and crushed it into pieces. He moved closer, and she drew out the bag of leftover chicken from her grocery trip that she'd hung onto just in case. *You wanted this to happen.*

Fine. She shouldn't lie to herself. Bridget wasn't here to check if her dad was still alive. She wanted Butch.

"What's up there, Butch? What do you smell?"

Bridget pressed her lips together.

The dog sniffed her shoulder. She moved her hand slowly, a chunk of chicken in her fingers. He lapped it up with that big fuzzy tongue. She ran her hand over his mushed up, ridiculous face with all those rolls. He sniffed around her neck.

Then licked from her chin to her hair.

Bridget nearly cried her tears aloud.

"Let's go, dog!" Her dad's call rang out.

Bridget ran her fingers through the dog's fur. *You shouldn't have come.* Tears rolled down her face.

"Butch, come!"

The dog didn't leave her.

"Go." Bridget gave him a small shove toward her father. *I love you, baby.*

Her dad had wanted a fierce, imposing animal. He'd gotten one of those two things—Butch lived up to his name, and she'd tried to help him hide how soft his temperament was. Teaching him to growl was about the cutest thing she'd ever seen.

"Someone's here." Her dad called out again. "Butch. Come."

The dog trotted off. After a few seconds, for some distance to grow between them, Bridget lifted up and looked to see who had come.

A dark-colored car pulled down the lane toward the house. Headlights lit up the side of the dilapidated barn, which had been falling down even before she'd left. It probably wasn't safe to go inside it now.

She watched as the driver shut off the engine and climb out with the headlights still on. Probably because her father had no exterior lighting.

Bridget studied the way the man moved and clocked two things—the visitor was Clarke, and he was carrying a gun. She heard the audible inhale of her mouth and had to swallow down a gasp. Once she had herself under control, she crawled down the hill. The risk of exposure increased, but considering Clarke was here, she had no choice. Bridget had to know why he'd come. What he wanted from her father.

Her dad stopped at a distance. Butch took two steps in front of him. When nothing happened, her father kicked Butch's flank. The dog dropped into a low stance and growled at the man approaching him.

"Lovely." Clarke's displeasure was clear. Why he thought he had the authority to cast judgment on her father, she didn't know. Not with everything he'd done lately.

So he was here to throw his weight around?

Bridget crawled closer.

"Seems like it's a night for critters to visit." Her dad shifted.

Maybe he had a weapon in reach, maybe not. "What do you want?"

Bridget wanted to text Millie for help. Ask for backup, or simply commiserate over what was happening. Too bad the light of her phone screen would give her away.

"You seem like a man who gets straight to the point." Clarke folded his arms. A move she'd seen before—because it put his hand close to his weapon, holstered under his shoulder. "I'm looking for Bridget. Seen her?"

Maybe she only wanted to tell Millie that Clarke was here because it would get her fired. She would finally be done with all this. *Free to move on.* That was the only possible reason for having let her guard down so thoroughly and being so stupidly close to giving away personal information.

She'd thought it was good they'd been getting more personal.

But, no.

Clarke was using her need for emotional connection against her. Probably that was why he'd tried to date her—not because he actually wanted a relationship. All he'd been after was a shot at leverage. A way to make her vulnerable and gain an edge since she'd never have let him in otherwise.

So stupid.

And, okay, so that wasn't *all* he'd been after. But given her history and the disaster that was, Bridget hadn't been prepared to give him *that* either. No matter how sweet he'd been in the moment, he'd still been pressuring her for intimacy.

"If you're gonna ask dumb questions, you should just go. Do your homework and come back when you aren't stupid anymore."

Butch growled, then let out a thunderous bark.

She flinched. Her father's harsh words settled on Bridget like a blanket. One that weighed her down with all the fear and pain she'd experienced before she left Last Chance in the middle of the night.

Her life since hadn't been peaceful, but it was what she'd chosen. Not others' actions forced on her whether she liked it or not. And in all of it, what had made the biggest impression was one solitary man. A kid, really. One she'd walked away from because she had been a kid, too. What they'd shared had been a bright spark in the darkness that lit quickly and burned both of them.

Yet another tragedy.

Clarke pulled a gun. "I think I'll take a look around."

Butch barked. His whole body shook with the force of it. The sound rang across the dark of night, and Bridget had to wince as it echoed in her eardrums.

Then came the gunshot.

Her father's sharp cry cut off abruptly as he toppled backward onto the grass. Butch raced at Clarke and was kicked far worse than her father had done.

Bridget lifted to one knee, aimed toward the man lit by headlights, and squeezed off a round of her own.

The crack echoed across the clearing.

But she missed.

Clarke hit the ground, rolled, and came up. Bridget knew he was going to fire even before it registered that he wasn't dead. She dove to the side as another shot answered hers.

Fire blazed through the outside of her left arm, high up. Close to her shoulder. She gritted her teeth, bit back the moan, and rolled. Over her arm. Onto her back. Her front. She shifted and got her legs under her, then ran.

Anything to draw Clarke away from Butch, and her father. If he wasn't dead yet.

Again she wanted to call for help. But the light would expose her, and there was no way to do that and run.

Clarke thundered through the brush behind her. Bridget raced between trees. She used the deer trail, her memory rushing back in a tornado of images. She ran on instinct, relying on the path she'd taken years ago, assuming it hadn't changed.

Up ahead was a descent down into a shallow valley, full of berry bushes. A thorned mass of brush that would shred skin and certainly slow Clarke.

If she could just keep from falling into it herself, getting cut up in the process the way she'd done years ago.

Bridget angled right just before the hill dipped. Her foot glanced off a rock, and she rolled her ankle. The cry that escaped her lips sounded like a scream—far louder than it ever should've been. She was trained. No, she was still a nothing little girl who couldn't handle her life. She would try to save herself only to wind up hurting more. Damaged. Lost.

Clarke followed her cry, and Bridget scrambled for a new plan.

He was gaining on her.

She headed for the road. If she could get to her car, then she had a shot at getting out of here. After she regrouped, she could figure out what to do next.

How to turn the tables on Clarke.

Bridget stumbled down the incline toward the dark highway, the echo of his footsteps right behind her. The berry bush plan hadn't worked. The second she hit pavement she almost collapsed but planted one hand on the grit of the road. She stumbled to her feet.

A car honked.

Bridget twisted away from the oncoming vehicle and tried to turn back, but she wasn't quick enough.

The car clipped her side, and she flew through the air.

6

Aidan slammed on the brakes. His tires squealed as the car came to a halt. As soon as he threw the lever to park, he jumped out. The woman lay on the grass on the side of the road. Unconscious from the fact that he had…

Aidan tried to breathe through the terror as he fell to his knees beside her. He'd hit a woman with his car. Sure, she'd run out in front of him and there'd been nothing he could do to stop it from happening. An accident. A tragic once-in-a-lifetime scenario.

He touched her shoulder, but couldn't look. Instead, he hung his head. As the images replayed in his mind, he saw the flash of her cheek as she turned. Her arm. Past the feeling that she was familiar—as though he'd seen her somewhere before—it seemed like she might've been bleeding. At least, he'd gotten a glimpse of wet and red in the second before he clipped her with this car.

Lord. He whispered a prayer for help.

Aiden didn't do it often. But he needed God right now.

Seeing her fly through the air like that? All he could do was hold back the urge to hurl on the asphalt as he pressed two fingers against her neck. Blonde hair hung over her face, obscuring her features. Did he know this woman? Would it matter? Whichever the case, it wouldn't take away from the fact she was hurt, and it was all his fault.

A steady beat answered the press of his fingers.

Aiden nearly sagged on the ground in a sigh of relief, all of it washing over him in a wave he couldn't control. A whimper escaped his lips.

He managed to grab his radio and call in the need for an ambulance.

"Copy that," came the reply from dispatch. "Help is on its way."

He brushed back hair from her face, though he had no right to touch her after what he had done. There was no excuse. Even if it had been unavoidable, it still never should've happened.

Her hair was so long, it tangled in his fingers. Eyelashes fanned across her upper cheeks, partially lit by his headlights.

He needed to know who she was.

Aiden didn't think he recognized her as someone who lived in town. The EMTs would find a wallet, or ID, if she had one on her. He wanted to look more closely at her face, but he was distracted by the blood seeping through the sleeve of her sweater. She was injured, and he might've paralyzed her for all he knew.

A branch cracked to his left in the trees.

Aiden spun toward the sound. "Who's there?"

He pulled his weapon, just in case, but stayed beside her where he would remain until help came. No way would he abandon her now. Not when it was his fault she was in this condition.

Aiden had messed up again. *Of course, since it was pretty much par for the course of his entire life.* He was dumb to think he could get away with doing good things for this long. All that striving to be better to make up for the ways he'd messed up. Sure, he was young, but he'd acted foolishly and was careless with his actions.

After becoming a father so young, he had to grow up quick and started facing his imperfections.

He'd tried to make amends.

Become a police officer.

Being Sydney's father was a pleasure he didn't take for granted, but he still strove every day to be the best dad he could be. The best man she would ever know.

The woman moaned.

Aiden touched her shoulder, not sure if she would appreciate being woken up right now when it could be extremely painful for her. She was probably better to do that in the hospital where they could take care of her and make her comfortable. Not on the side of the road with the stranger who had done this to her.

Before he could say anything, several rocks and a boulder rolled down the hill from the direction where she'd come. Running. Bleeding. Had someone been chasing her?

Did they hurt her?

They could be watching what was happening, even now.

Aiden was helpless to both safeguard her and take them down. He would stay with her and protect her. That was the most important thing right now. Until backup came, there wasn't much he could do except that.

As soon as back up arrived, he stood. Aiden waved the officer over and saw an ambulance pull in behind them.

It was Frees who'd been sent. As he hustled over, Aiden got up and jogged across the street.

"Stay with her. I need to check out the area."

Frees was the one who normally jumped at the chance to chase down a suspect rather than take care of a victim. That was just how he was wired. And when the job was done, no one complained. Aiden didn't wait around to see his colleague's customary frown. There wasn't time for that. Not when there could be a third party out here who meant intentional harm.

Aiden raced up the embankment and into the trees on the far side, where she'd come from.

There were ranches and farms in this area, as well as a ton of open land. The terrain was rocky and steep, but he raced up the hill anyway. Whoever saw two cops and an ambulance pull up wasn't waiting around to try and get that woman again. They were probably long gone. Which meant he had to catch up, or he would never find who had been chasing her.

In the moonlight, on the top of the hill, he spotted a dark figure moving fast. Aiden called it into Frees on his radio, then raced after the guy as quickly as he could.

Branches whipped his face and clothes. Considering what he had done to that woman, Aiden, almost in relief, took the blows as his due punishment and moved as fast as he could despite the sting.

Elbows tucked, he pumped his arms and legs.

He crested the hill and saw a farmhouse below, yellow light in the window. Aiden didn't look overlong at the light so he'd still be able to make out the route in front of him. *Thank You for the moonlight.* The path was uneven and fraught with rocks, changes in elevation, and possibly a dangerous suspect.

A dog barked.

The dark figure he chased ran for a car parked by the house. Intercepted by the dog, the figure stumbled. Aiden picked up his pace, faster than he would normally run. He nearly rolled down the hill but managed to catch himself before he tumbled.

There had been far too much injury and danger already this year. Aiden wasn't prepared to add to the tally. Things were going to be different from now on.

"Stop! Police!"

The man dove for the driver's door and yanked it open.

"Stop!"

Aiden pulled his weapon and held it. The dog barked. He didn't want to get bitten, something that'd happened to several officers in the department.

The man twisted before he got in. Aiden saw the glint of a gun a second before the barrel exploded with a flash.

He dove to the side and only barely avoided the shot as he rolled. Aiden came to a stop on his stomach with his arms out ahead of him, elbows braced on the frozen ground. He squeezed off two rounds, but the man had already shut the door. Aiden caught the front quarter panel with his round and realized he might be able to disable the car.

Dog tags jingled.

He moved his finger off the trigger as the dog trotted. He didn't want to shoot the animal. The car engine revved and it sped away, spraying gravel as the driver turned in an arc and headed down the driveway road.

The rapid sniff of a dog muzzle neared him.

Aiden held himself still. "Hi, dog."

The animal slowed.

Aiden lifted his hand and let the dog smell it. Then he got up, slowly. He didn't want to startle the dog and kick off something else he'd have to deal with. But the dog trotted off on his own.

Aiden moved over to see what the dog had raced back to. A dark lump lay on the ground.

He grasped his radio. "Dispatch, come back."

"What is it, Aiden?"

"I need another ambulance at my location." He checked his GPS on his phone and told her where he was.

"Copy that. Five minutes."

Aiden knew that wouldn't make a difference. The man on the ground was dead. He pulled the flashlight from his belt and shone it at the face long enough to see where the bullet had entered. "And send a detective."

He knew who it was. He just didn't want to think about who it was.

Aiden called Sergeant Basuto and ran down everything that'd happened while the dog stretched out beside the man. He wanted to call the animal away but wasn't sure it would even leave the dead man's side.

"I'll be there in thirty minutes."

Relief nearly caused Aiden to sink to the ground. "Thanks."

"It's my job." Basuto hung up.

Aiden stared at the phone for a second. Then he stowed it in his pocket. A second later, it rang again. "Donaldson."

It was Frees. "Woman is all loaded up in the ambulance. You need help up there?"

"Did you see a vehicle? Silver compact, driving fast?"

"Nothing like that down here. He fled?"

There was no tone or insinuation, but Aiden still gritted his teeth. "Yes."

"Must've gone the other direction."

Aiden swallowed. "How is she?"

"Banged up, but they don't think there's anything seriously wrong. Other than the gunshot graze to her arm."

So that man had shot her *and* the man up here? He was going to withhold his relief she was still alive until the doctors checked the woman out, though. There could be any number of serious injuries. Or some internal bleeding.

Who was she? He twisted around and studied the trees.

Aiden didn't want to get so close he disturbed any evidence, so he jogged to the back door. "I'll check for mail." Something with an address would give him a name.

The minute he entered the house, his nose wrinkled. He breathed through his mouth and waded through a pile of discarded boots—even a couple of pairs of ladies' shoes. The kitchen table, every inch of counter space, and the sink were piled high. Dishes, pots, mugs, boxes. Open food containers. Only the temperature outside kept this place from buzzing with flies, but in summer it was likely a nightmare.

He found a pile that looked like mail and found the address.

His stomach dropped, faced with the truth. "Thomas Meyers."

"Who is that?"

Aiden squeezed his eyes shut. "He's Bridget's father."

The old man was out there, laying on the grass. Dead. Shot by the gunman who'd driven away in that car.

How many times had Aiden snuck over to pick up Bridget for a date? He hadn't even realized where he was.

Now her father was dead.

His stomach flipped over. He had so many thoughts swirling in his head. For one thing, the condition of the house made him finally realize why Bridget had always refused to bring him inside her house. He would've been embarrassed, too. And also, who was the woman, and how did she fit in with all this? Why was Thomas dead?

"Who?"

Aiden gritted his teeth. "Sydney's mother was Bridget Meyers." He choked out the words. "The dead guy up here? He's my daughter's grandfather."

"Dude."

"Sydney has never met him."

"Still." Frees paused. "And the woman the ambulance took to the hospital? That's her, this Bridget person? Sydney's mother?"

"No. That's impossible." Aiden strode back outside. He shook his head even though no one but the dog could see him.

"Why?"

Aiden stopped and stared at the dead man. "Because Bridget is dead."

7

"Kathryn?" A steady hand shook her shoulder. "Kathryn, can you hear me?"

Bridget pressed her lips together as she came awake. Before she answered, it was necessary to assess the situation and figure out what was happening.

The last thing she remembered? Headlights. Pain.

Her elbow hurt, and her hip. One arm was kind of limp, and the outside of her bicep didn't feel good.

"There you are."

She blinked and clocked the evidence this woman was a nurse. The voice held authority, as though anything less than Bridget coming to full wakefulness was unacceptable.

She cleared her throat. "What happened?"

"You're in the hospital, Ms. Weston. The doctor will be in shortly to take a look at you."

Bridget noted the fact she didn't answer the question. They'd found her wallet, along with the driver's license she kept there for times exactly like this when her real name would raise a flag. It was best to remain…not anonymous. Just well under the radar.

Kathryn Weston lived in Denver, worked for a certain

accountant's firm, and had a social media profile that although showed a social life, was otherwise bland and unoriginal.

"Is there someone I can call for you?"

She shook her head just a little bit. Though she could call Millie, her boss, since they were in Millie's hometown—also Bridget's hometown. Though, doing so could cause problems or raise questions she couldn't give a good answer for. "Where are my things? My phone?"

"Right here." The nurse lifted a paper bag with its top rolled down and set it beside Bridget's hip.

"Thank you."

"I'm sure the doctor will be right in." The nurse turned back at the door. "Oh, and the police will likely want to speak with you about what happened."

"The police?"

The nurse nodded. "Because it was one of their officers who hit you with his car. The young one, not the superhot one with the stripes on his shoulders."

Bridget blinked.

"Probably not professional for me to say that, but I'm not wrong. Am I right?" The nurse chuckled, apparently not requiring an answer. "Sit tight. Hit the button if you need anything."

The door shut.

Bridget tore open the paper bag and dug for her phone. The clothes she'd been wearing were in shreds. Likely from being cut off her. She lifted the collar of the hospital gown with one hand and the blanket with the other and looked down at the state of her body.

And winced.

Maybe she had been given pain killers, and apparently they were doing their job, if how she felt was any indication. Because given how she looked—bruises and road rash mostly—she should be feeling way worse. When they wore off, she'd probably be extremely stiff and sore.

Bridget squeezed her eyes shut. The dark of her father's yard filled her mind. Butch, and his sniffs. The car that had pulled up with Clarke inside.

And the muzzle flash.

Her father, falling back to the ground.

Yet more tragedy in her not-so-long, tragic life. Another blood relative lost.

Bridget set a hand low on her stomach. *I'm sorry, baby.*

She couldn't seem to keep those she loved safe. Nor could she keep safe the members of her family she had an obligation to love, but didn't. Her father hadn't loved her either, so that was mutual. Didn't matter though. Love or the absence of it didn't matter. It had no power to do anything except make her stupid.

Decisions. Actions. All of it was called into question when feelings clouded her judgment.

Now she would have to bury her father, too. If he was dead. Or had the old ox survived? That would be just perfect. He was exactly ornery enough to survive what would kill most anyone else.

Clarke had made his point, so he wouldn't need to come back and finish the job. But her father would still be in danger.

Bridget would continue to kill the people around her—not purposely, of course. But they seemed to die just the same.

She unlocked her phone and called Millie's number.

"Cullings." The voice that answered the phone belonged to a male.

"I think you picked up your wife's phone, Mr. Cullings. Or should I say, Special Agent Cullings?" Bridget managed a short laugh while she prayed there wouldn't be any hospital noises in the background she'd have to explain. It needed to sound like she could actually be in the office. "I have a quick question for Millie about the Penderton account."

"Mill, one of your colleagues is on the phone."

Bridget waited for her boss.

"Thank you." Millie's voice made her sag back against the pillow, but Bridget still said nothing. "Hello?"

"It's me." To her consternation, tears filled Bridget's eyes. She blinked against them as she explained about Clarke. The gunshot and how the cop hit her with his car, all the way to the present, how she'd woken up in the hospital.

"Hang on. I'll get my laptop."

Bridget heard a door shut.

"Are you okay?" Millie's voice jumped an octave. "Bridget, this is crazy!"

"Clarke is here. I think I need Sasha. I don't want to pull you in, given this is your town. But Sasha could help."

Bridget would feel a lot better with backup by her side. Someone like Sasha, who could remind her what was at stake. Why she couldn't let this town, or her emotions, cause her to do something she wouldn't have done otherwise.

Sasha, the only one of them to have been Millie's employee at the time, was the one who'd broken the news to her that her baby had died. It was moments after she'd given birth, while their company doctor worked to stop Bridget's bleeding. So much had gone wrong that day. The complications were just part of it.

Then Sasha had disappeared for days, but Bridget had been too focused on her own grief to ask why. Thankfully, Millie had stayed with her long enough to offer Bridget a permanent job as soon as she recovered. Not just a position at the accountant's office, continuing as a receptionist, but the chance to train as an operative. To learn how to be strong so that she would never have to suffer ever again.

It had seemed fitting to be reborn, in a way, the day her baby girl had died. A way to honor her.

Millie cleared her throat. "I've been out of the game way too long. I'm freaking out."

"You're a mom." Bridget had to swallow the lump in her throat just to get the words out. "And you just had a happy

Christmas with your husband and your boys back in your hometown. Naturally you wouldn't think something like this would land on radar in your backyard."

"The boys are headed to Hawaii with Savannah and Tate tomorrow. They'll be gone until after the new year." Millie paused. "I might have to tell Eric everything if this gets worse."

Bridget didn't know how much worse Millie needed it to get, but she also didn't want Millie to ruin her marriage. Keeping secrets the way Millie had wasn't what Bridget would've done. No one wanted to play the part in every aspect of their life, including the most intimate.

Even so, Bridget didn't want her to blow their whole cover. "Just hang on, okay? It might not come to that."

"The cops will want a statement." Millie's tone turned to one of all business.

"Can you sign me out of here?" Bridget needed help. Not her boss freaking out. It might be justified, but until Bridget was completely alone—and safe—she had to hold her reaction back. Otherwise, everything would get even worse.

"Sign yourself out." Millie paused. "Can you walk?"

"I'll make it. I just want to get back to the townhouse."

"I'll get you a car, have it in the parking lot. Keys in the glove box. This is what you do, right?"

"As long as Clarke isn't waiting for me."

"He doesn't know about the safe house. It's clean, okay?"

"You're sure?"

"A hundred percent." Millie sounded certain. "But the cops here know me. And they'll figure out who you are eventually."

"No, they won't." That was impossible, right?

Bridget didn't know anyone on the police force in town. Not personally. It had been six years since she'd walked the highway out of town, beat up and bleeding. The night she'd witnessed a horrific crime and her father had responded with violence, as though it was her fault for seeing what she never should have.

Millie had seen her walking and picked her up.

After two weeks of recovery Bridget had discovered she was pregnant.

Millie had offered to find the father and tell him, but what was the point? It wasn't like it'd been a great love affair. No, they were two seventeen-year-olds bent on having summer fun, despite how it had felt to walk away from him. Didn't mean they were good for each other, especially when both of them wound up with juvenile records for several misdemeanors.

Much like what happened after, her life up until that point had been nothing but a series of tragedies. She supposed he'd been a spark of light in the middle of everything else. But as with a single star that shone in the night sky, it was quickly swallowed up by the overwhelming darkness. True, both overhead and down here on earth.

One light couldn't shine bright enough to make a difference.

"We'll find Clarke." Millie sounded so sure.

"I think my father might be dead."

The door to the room opened, and the nurse came back in. A plan to get out of there formed. Bridget pretended she was engrossed in her conversation so she could use it. "He tried to kill me tonight. He'll come back and finish the job unless I get out of here."

She hung up on Millie. Didn't bother to wipe whatever feeling had bled through to her expression. Bridget needed to get out of the hospital, and the nurse was her best bet at getting assistance to do just that.

The nurse moved to the side of the bed. "Girl, you talking about the man who shot you or the cop who hit you with his car?"

Bridget could hardly believe the depth of tragedy that was her bad luck. "The one who shot me." She let her eyes fill with tears. "I think he actually wants me dead this time."

"Your boyfriend?"

Bridget supposed that was true. "Yeah." She swallowed. "He shot my father tonight as well. I think he might be dead."

So far she hadn't spoken an untruth. But what she didn't want was to get her fake name on a police report. Bridget didn't need Clarke discovering she was in the hospital—if he hadn't already seen the ambulance for himself.

Likely he was just biding his time and waiting for another shot at her so he could kill her. Or capture her. She didn't know which. Nor did she know if it would be for himself or the Capeiras.

"Oh, hon."

The disparity between this compassionate nurse and the authoritative one she'd met first was a significant switch, but one Bridget needed to use. "He'll find me here. He'll come, and he'll hurt me again."

All true.

The nurse shook her head. "You're safe. We have procedures so people can't just walk in off the street. He won't get to you here." The nurse squeezed Bridget's hand. "Tell the cop that's coming all about your man and what he did. I know they didn't do right by you tonight, but the cops in this town are good people. *And* they're good cops. File a restraining order."

Bridget shook her head. "I have to get out of here. Now." She shoved the blanket back and sat up. "I need your help. Some clothes."

"I know you're scared—"

"Please, just either help me, or leave." Bridget held up a hand. In the bag, her pants were intact. It was only her shirt that'd been cut off her. That was enough. "I have to *go*."

The nurse shifted. Indecision warred on her face with what she knew to be true about hospital security…and good cops.

Bridget had nothing against cops. They were people who made mistakes just like everyone else. But they were also held to higher standards of honor and upright behavior. They were *supposed* to be the best of what humans could be.

She just didn't need to talk to one right now, when it would be about the wrong they'd done. Cops in this town would want to envelop her life. Make sure she wasn't going to sue the officer or press charges for an accident. Try to help her out. Pay her back.

All of which was a complication she couldn't afford.

"Maybe you could wait until morning?" the nurse suggested. "I'll find you clean clothes. After the doctor has checked you out, *then* we'll make sure you can get somewhere safe. There's a house in town, Hope Mansion, where any woman or child is always welcome."

Bridget knew about Maggie's shelter. She'd lived there with her mom for a few weeks right before her seventh birthday. Before her mom got a new boyfriend.

One who had beat her so badly he'd killed her.

Bridget let the tears fall. The nurse didn't need to know she was only crying over the memory of her mother—even though she hadn't done that in years. Of course, the tears were for more than just her mother. She hurt and she was exhausted, but she also cried for the baby she'd lost. She'd shed so many tears after birthing the most beautiful baby and having her die from complications.

Yet another failure Bridget had been unable to prevent.

Her tragic life.

"I have to go."

The nurse bit her lip. "I'll be back in a minute with some clothes. Please let me help you out."

Ten minutes later, they stood at one of the side doors. Close enough to where Millie had left the car for her. Once she got back to the safe house, Bridget would be able to collapse in bed and cry for as long as she wanted. Then pass out. Literally *everything* hurt and her head spun just being upright. Until then, she had to hold it together and not think about every awful thing in her life.

Or that one star trying to shine, though enveloped in darkness. "Thank you for your help."

The nurse nodded. "There's a cab right outside the door.

He'll take you to Hope Mansion."

Bridget had no intention of getting into the cab. "Thanks."

She pushed open the door one handed and let it shut behind her before she bypassed the cab at the curb and strode down the sidewalk.

She brushed back blonde hair from her face. She probably looked like she'd been dragged through a hedge.

A man turned the corner of the building and headed down the sidewalk toward her. Dark hair, lean but toned under his police uniform. He walked with confidence and control in a way that made her…ache. It wasn't the cop, it was the man. Why did she have to fight an attraction *now*? This wasn't the time.

His gaze lifted, and her next breath caught in her throat.

Bridget coughed. The air emerged as a whimper. Tonight of all nights? The past had no intention of letting her go.

"You…" Disbelief warred across his face.

Bridget sidestepped him.

He grabbed for her, taking hold of her wrist in a grip that made her cry out as pain sliced through her wound. He let go as though he'd burned her. "You're the one I hit."

She didn't know what to say. "Aiden…" Even as she whispered his name, she knew she had to walk away.

Bridget stumbled off the curb.

He took a step toward her. "She said you were *dead*." His gaze hardened. She'd never seen him angry before.

"She was right." Bridget took another couple of steps away and put yet more space between them. It had been too long. Her life was a dangerous place, and she couldn't stand the thought of losing anyone else.

No matter how much she might want to stay.

"Bridget." Her name was a moan from his lips. "You—"

She shook her head. "Don't." Then took two more steps. "Let me stay dead, Aiden. It's for the best."

Bridget ran to the car, while more tears rolled down her face.

8

One wheel of his police car bumped up onto the curb. Aiden shut the engine off and stumbled out. He was supposed to be off shift by now, which meant coming back to the office. All the way here he'd been working on autopilot. Text the sitter to stick around. Drive back to the office. Aiden pushed through the front door and nearly fell.

"Whoa, buddy. You oka—"

Aiden looked up.

Basuto hit the button to let him behind the counter and met him at the door. "I got you."

He lifted Aiden's arm over his shoulder and held up his weight as they walked to the break room where the sergeant deposited Aiden into a seat on the couch. Then Basuto sat on the coffee table in front of him.

"What happened, Ade?"

He ran his hands down his face, the first hitch of his breath signaling an oncoming breakdown.

"Sydney?"

What? "No." He blinked. "No, Sydney is fine. Elexa is going to sleep over."

"Then what's up? You look like you've seen a ghost. Is it the woman you hit with your car? We all know that was an accident. You aren't going to get in trouble." Basuto studied him.

He probably thought it was just hitting Aiden now, what he'd done. As though the weight of what could've happened overwhelmed him in a rush.

It was the woman. Basuto had that much right.

Aiden wanted to throw up. *Sydney.* He'd looked up from the sidewalk, and in that moment his whole world changed, which he could admit sounded cliché, even to his own brain. But the supposedly dead mother of his child, the child he'd raised singlehandedly her whole life, had been standing in front of him.

Blonde now, not the redhead he remembered.

Aiden covered his face again. He could hardly process enough to say it out loud. "She's…alive."

"I know. That's a good thing. You just clipped her, right?"

"She walked out of the hospital."

"Already?" Basuto's head jerked. "She left?"

"I saw her coming out. Took me a second to put it together, but the hair…" Aiden made himself stop. Find the right words. "The woman I hit." He couldn't even believe he was saying this. "It was Bridget."

Not dead.

Very, very much not dead. After all this time, and after he'd been told she had passed away in childbirth. That woman—the one who'd shown up on his doorstep—had given him a baby and told him her mother was...gone. That he'd have to do this by himself, or she would hand his newborn over to child services. And who knew what kind of family she would end up in? His mind was whirling a mile a minute.

Aiden knew it wasn't normal for a single eighteen-year-old guy to raise a baby girl by himself. He was her father, so naturally that made it the right thing to do. He'd started going to church a few months before. It had seemed, at the time, as though God had handpicked him for this task.

No one could love a child he'd made—with Bridget—the way he could.

They were all each other had. A family.

Or, they *had been* all this time.

Now…

"She's back."

Basuto spoke quietly. "Who is Bridget?"

Aiden looked from his knees to his sergeant. "Sydney's mother."

"You said she died."

"That's what I was told." He relayed everything that'd happened. His awkward attempt to get her to stay with him at the hospital so they could talk.

He'd wound up hurting her. Then she'd run away from him. As though it was better for him to think she was dead. Or for Sydney to believe that.

He'd told his daughter the truth. In an age-appropriate way, of course. As soon as she started asking questions, he'd let her know that her mother was in heaven. An angel. Even though he'd been a believer at the time and knew Bridget wasn't necessarily up there. They'd never discussed faith like that. Their relationship had been an inferno, burning out as fast as it had ignited. A few passion-filled nights he knew as a dangerous mistake.

Then one day, she was gone.

"I thought I got the best part of her." He took a breath. "That God had given me yet another gift I didn't deserve. I've spent six years giving Sydney everything she needed. Making the world a safer place for her every time I put on this uniform."

All this time.

Aiden pushed out of his seat to pace across the breakroom. "That lady sat across from me with Sydney in a baby carrier and told me that Bridget had died in childbirth. And now I find out she's alive? She doesn't ask how I am. She says nothing about Sydney."

He turned back to Basuto. Ire burned hot in his stomach. "She was probably going to just leave without saying anything. Not a single word about how I hit her with my car, or about her father. Or that guy who fled the scene. Her father is *dead.* Does she know that? Did she even wait around to find out what happened to her dad? Maybe she's the one who shot him. She could've come back to town just to do it, and now she's on the lam."

Bridget couldn't possibly act more selfish than this. Only concerned about her need to run away. Not about him, or the daughter he was raising. What kind of mother was she?

"Who does that?"

Basuto walked to the coffee pot and set a pod in to brew one cup. "Women..." He shook his head with a deep exhale. "Who knows why they walk away? One day you think everything's fine. The next? Her stuff is gone, she leaves her ring on the nightstand, and all you have are questions."

As soon as the light flashed, Basuto removed the cup and slid it over. He inserted another pod, put a mug under the spout, and pressed the button to make another cup.

"Nothing you can do but wonder...for years...what happened. What you did. What she thought was a problem so unfixable there was nothing to do but leave. Quit. Flee. Whatever you want to call it, she's gone and you have nothing. Least of all an explanation."

Aiden stared at his profile. "Sounds like personal experience."

"This woman meant something to you?"

"She's Sydney's mother." How could she not mean something to him when she'd given him their daughter? Life certainly hadn't been perfect...or easy. But it had been beautiful. Painfully beautiful.

"Not to your daughter. To *you.*"

Basuto didn't have kids. Aiden wasn't going to explain that sometimes that was the same thing. "Bridget and I?" He didn't know how to explain it. "No one said, 'I love you.' It wasn't like it was serious. We were right out of high school. Mostly it was fun, or so I thought. Turned out we were just self-destructing and making Sydney at the time." He had to shrug. "I guess."

Aiden hardly liked to say it out loud. Let alone for a man he respected to know what he'd done in the past. God had said that all of it was washed away. In response, Aiden wanted to live his life as though what He'd said was true. That he could do the right thing now, and every day he could choose to act as though he was free of guilt and shame, even when it didn't feel like it.

Basuto slapped a hand down on his shoulder. "Sounds like you got the best part of the deal."

"I just wish I knew why." Why she left Last Chance. Why that woman had shown up to tell him she was dead. What kind of person did that? "I just don't get it."

He'd been working to do the right thing for years, while she did whatever she wanted. And got herself in trouble for it. At least it seemed that way when he factored in the man chasing her. The fact she'd fled the hospital, wounded.

Secrets. Lies.

Sydney didn't need that in her life.

She'd needed her mother. Every day. She still did and would each day to come. But that wasn't what Bridget wanted.

"Where has she even *been* for six years? And why come back now."

Basuto lowered his mug from his mouth. "Let's go find out."

Aiden blinked. He swallowed a mouthful of his coffee, finally able to drink without wanting to throw the mug at the wall.

No, he still wanted to do that.

He was moving from angry to surprised, which consisted of a huge swatch of feeling like a chump. One who'd been duped, ending up on kid duty while she'd waltzed off to do whatever she wanted. Still, he hadn't seen that in her eyes. Or on her face.

She'd been surprised to see him, sure.

Coming back wasn't about reconnecting—not for her. Maybe she'd had no choice and didn't want to see him or Sydney. Too much pain and she couldn't deal.

Aiden grabbed his coffee and followed Basuto out of the room.

It was past two in the morning now. If he didn't get home and sleep, he would be useless on shift tomorrow night. Because there was no way he would miss Sydney getting up in the morning. Eating oatmeal together—only because they'd had donuts once this week already. Packing her stuff to spend the afternoon at Maggie's while he worked, since she had another week off school.

"You look wiped."

Aiden shrugged. "Not like I'd sleep anyway."

The sergeant eyed him. "You can stay as long as you like, but I'll get someone to cover your shift tomorrow. Don't come in for a day."

He wanted to say thanks, but figured he would only end up breaking down again. Looking like an emotional wreck. On the outside.

"What did you mean, 'find out?'"

"I mean run this woman's name. See what we can find."

Basuto typed. It was like pulling up to reports of shots fired, not knowing what he would find in that second before it loaded. Or the night he'd been called to assist the lieutenant—currently the chief of police—to get Mia back. Now she was the lieutenant's wife. They were happy. Life had moved on, no matter how dark it had been that night.

So many of his colleagues and friends had fallen in love and paired off over the last few months.

That wasn't going to happen to him. There was a female in his life, and she would be the only one there until she was in middle school at least. Maybe older. Dating wasn't remotely on his radar. Life always seemed to get in the way, so what was the point?

Now Bridget was here. For however long that was going to be. *No.* There was too much negativity in him. He needed to beat back the anger. The rage. Figure out how he'd managed to get everything about the past so wrong.

No matter what amends he made for his actions it would continue rearing its ugly head in his present. What was the point in trying to have a healthy, respectful, loving relationship in the middle of all that?

"Kathryn Weston."

"Who is that?"

Basuto hit "enter" and glanced over. "The ID that Officer Frees found while she was unconscious. The name she was checked into the hospital under."

His whole world turned a revolution yet again. Faster than it should have. Aiden was nearly knocked onto his butt at the sensation. "That's her name?"

Basuto stared at the screen. "Look at this. The ID is less than three years old, Colorado driver's license issued in Denver. No record." He typed faster than Aiden could absorb. "Social media accounts on the big sites. Look at this one."

He clicked and a post of photos came up. Basuto scrolled through them.

"These are fake."

Aiden leaned over. "Like photo manipulation?" They looked fine to him.

"I would bet money she never posed for these." Basuto stabbed a finger at the monitor screen. "Those women she's standing with? I don't think Kathryn Weston was even there when their picture was taken. She was added later."

"I can't tell." As far as he could see, it looked legit.

"It's subtle, but they're fakes."

"Huh."

"Why would Sydney's mother need a fake ID and fake social media accounts?" Basuto turned in his chair. "Unless she wants more than just you to believe she's dead?"

"Her father? He's dead. That man killed him tonight." Aiden sank onto the nearest desk. He tried to sit and not slump down as his body wanted to do. "I'd be inclined to wonder if she hadn't come back to kill him herself if not for that man chasing her." And the fact she'd been shot before he hit her with his car. "Maybe they planned it together."

Aiden winced. So much pain. It had been clear in her eyes when she told him it was better off that she stayed dead.

He wanted to know why.

He also wanted to be there when she found out about her father—if she didn't know. But that was simply latent care, something he couldn't switch off. Too much empathy. He could care for her the way he cared for Sydney, wanting to make her life the best he could, because it was the right thing to do. But she didn't need him.

No one had ever done anything to make Bridget Meyers's life better than the tragedy it had been.

Then Aiden had used her for his own satisfaction. Yeah, he'd been attracted. Back then he'd have said he cared about her—maybe even loved her. They hadn't hurt each other. They'd both been in it for the same thing. Barely out of high school, high on adulthood—and other, more potent substances.

Now he knew better.

Or so he'd told himself all this time. Tamping down his grief with the reality of the situation. She'd been gone. Dead. What would be the point in overly romanticizing it?

She'd lied, maybe even paid someone to tell him she was dead. He wasn't going to forgive a woman who didn't even seem prepared to *try* and work on a relationship with her child. It was like she didn't care at all.

No, he could never forgive.

Even if he'd never met Sydney, there was nothing in this world that could induce him to pretend she didn't exist.

"There's more to this woman than what you know." Basuto shot Aiden a look. "She's hiding a whole lot."

Aiden was about to answer when the door opened and Officer Frees muscled something in. "What is—"

A dog barked.

Aiden met him at the door and held it open while a huge, wrinkly-faced beast of a dog ambled in. "Butch." More memory came rushing back. Thomas Meyers. The dog at his house. Of *course.*

"You know this dog?" Frees held out his end of the leash. "Here you go. Animal control doesn't open until the morning."

Aiden took the leather cord before he realized what he'd done.

Basuto said, "What is this?"

"It's Thomas Meyers's dog." Frees shrugged. "Couldn't leave him up there with no one to take care of him. Or running loose in the yard where Thomas bled out."

Butch moved to Aiden. The dog lumbered as though he was tired, or feeling lost. He sniffed Aiden's shoes. His pants up to his knee. Then the big dog laid down, his muzzle on the toe of Aiden's boot.

"Guess you just got yourself a dog."

When he whipped his gaze up to Frees, the officer shrugged. "For tonight, anyway."

"I have enough problems right now. I don't need—"

"He's right," Basuto said. "You take the dog. Use your day off to leave him with animal control." The sergeant clapped his hands together. "All done and dusted."

"I hardly think—"

This time it was Frees who interrupted. "I'm sure Sydney would love babysitting a dog for the day." The lightness in his eyes said more, and Aiden had to wonder if he didn't want to point out it was a family dog. *Their* family, given the animal had belonged to her grandfather.

Even if Sydney had never met him.

Now he was dead, and she never would. Another person in

her life she would miss out on the chance to know. And good riddance, as far as he was concerned.

He could say the same about Bridget.

Aiden decided then and there, whether Bridget wanted to meet Sydney, or more than that—something that scared him more than he'd care to admit—there was no way he would allow it.

She had no right to come back now and ask anything of him.

9

Bridget gasped and sat up. Pain rolled through her hip and her arm. She hissed out a breath between clenched teeth and flopped back on the pillow. The blanket had twisted around her as she slept. Fitfully, by the look of it.

Beside her lay the scrapbook.

Bridget laid her hand on the cover of her most prized possession. If she told Sasha about it and how she couldn't go anywhere without it, her colleague and friend would check her into the psych ward. Millie was a mother. She would better understand, though she'd never lost a child.

Between the pages were ultrasound pictures that tracked the baby's growth. Her daughter. Then pictures of Bridget, her belly round. And one single picture of the baby after Bridget had given birth to her.

One photo. That was all she had.

I'm sorry. Sasha's tense expression filled her mind. *She's gone.*

Bridget hadn't even had the chance to name her baby.

She pushed back the covers and headed for the bathroom. Seeing Aiden last night made it worse. Everything had rushed back.

Leaving town. Discovering she was pregnant, and the

emotional rollercoaster *that* had been. She'd loved her baby. Of course, she'd been terrified of what having a child would mean, even to the point of telling Millie and Sasha that she didn't even want a child. *Lord.* She'd gotten her wish, hadn't she?

Bridget took a shower while tears rolled down her face. She hung her head below the spray and worked through the feelings in the way she was taught. Being told she hadn't manifested the death of her baby through careless words was one thing. Believing it was another.

Maybe she would've been a terrible mother, and maybe she wouldn't have. What did she know? And what did it matter now, anyway? Her life was one she would spend alone, always wondering, "what if." She worked with clients all over the world. Made sure they were safe enough to live the happy lives they were building. The kind she could never have.

Bridget shut off the water and immediately heard banging. She grabbed a robe and headed for the front door, though not before retrieving her weapon.

She stopped three steps from the door and stood behind the cover of the doorway to the living room. "Who is it?"

"Millie. Open the door."

Bridget twisted the handle and let her boss in. Millie Cullings was older than Bridget, closer to forty than thirty. A mom of two boys, and the wife of an FBI agent. Her brother was a private investigator in Last Chance County, and *his* wife was a police detective.

Bridget didn't need to get on any of their radars, except for Millie's. That would be okay. Her boss had special training, and Bridget trusted her. Millie—and her brother Tate—had helped her when she'd been broken and bleeding, scared. She would be in their debt for the rest of her life.

"Hey."

"Go get dressed."

Bridget grabbed clothes from the bedroom and left the bathroom door ajar so they could still talk.

"Are you okay?"

Bridget slid pants on. Her hair dripped around her shoulders. "Because of the gunshot, getting hit by a car, or running into Aiden?"

"That's not all that happened yesterday."

Bridget pulled on a tank top and toed the door open. "What else happened?" She grabbed the towel and started to rub her hair dry.

Millie sat on the edge of the bed. Her attention snagged on the scrapbook.

And then Bridget said, "I'm okay."

"You only think that because your baseline is survival and a modicum of emotional stability." She turned back to Bridget with a sigh. "I get the feeling you don't think you deserve happiness, or at the very least, that you don't expect a whole lot of good to come your way."

"Not sure I'll ever have to worry about an overabundance of happiness." Bridget couldn't help the sarcastic tone that showed up in her voice.

"It's part of life. Eventually you'll meet someone and fall in love. You'll have babies. Your heart will be so full you won't know what to do with yourself." Millie's nurturing lectures often came back around to Bridget finding someone to share her life with.

"So I'll die happily of a heart attack." Bridget shrugged. "Besides, I've already met enough people. Most of them I don't like. The rest I can tolerate. A few I appreciate."

She knew she sounded callous. The idea of dying from happiness after finally finding the family she'd always wanted wasn't something that sat well with her. But she could say it to Millie, because she didn't believe it would happen.

Millie just stared at her. "We need to get down to business. Eric is at the police station, and I'm supposed to be grocery shopping."

It wasn't often they were in the same room, given how much

Bridget worked in the field. So she took the opportunity to ask, "Are you ever going to tell your husband you used to be a spy?"

"He knows." Millie lifted a brow. "Of course he *knows*. He just doesn't know that the accountant's office I work at is not an accountant's office."

"You mean he doesn't know it's a front for an international company that protects and safeguards former spies and the like?" She knew she sounded snarky, but she was still coming down from their "happiness" conversation.

Millie shushed her and looked over her shoulder, as if they weren't the only ones in the apartment.

Bridget held back a smile. "No one is listening, Millie. Are you going to tell him you're still in the spy business?"

"He doesn't have clearance to know. Kind of like how there are things about his work with the FBI that I can't know. It's not keeping secrets, just operational security. We both know that."

Bridget wasn't sure it was that simple.

She spoke maybe too much and words were powerful. It seemed like Millie didn't speak enough sometimes. They all had secrets. Theirs was a messy line of work, and not just the fact Bridget was currently nursing several injuries.

The worst was the bruise from being hit by a car. She could handle almost anything from an enemy. She'd proven that to be true enough times. But getting struck unintentionally by a man who was at one time her ally? She had dreaded seeing him again, and yet it had happened, and in the worst of circumstances. She was sure he hated her for leaving. Or maybe he was completely indifferent over the fact she'd simply disappeared one night, never to be seen or heard from again. Until last night, that is.

She didn't know which was worse, but knew she would likely never find out. After all, Bridget didn't plan on seeing him again.

"We need a way to find Clarke."

Millie nodded. "Before he finds us. But what does he want besides carnage? He didn't need to kill your father yesterday…"

Bridget's hairbrush fell from her hand to the floor.

"…but he did."

"My dad is dead?"

Millie started to speak, but stopped herself. "You didn't know."

"I didn't know." Emotion started to swell in her. Bridget pushed it down enough she could say, "Where's Butch? Who has my father's dog?"

"I can find out, but is that the priority here?"

To her it was, but Bridget didn't expect it to be a priority for anyone else. However, considering the dog was now an orphan just like her, it was on the list of things she was going to be concerned about. "Like I said, we need a way to find Clarke. Can we use the phone system somehow? I know it's designed to be completely secure, but isn't there a way somehow to access it where we can get a GPS location for him?"

Millie thought about the question for a second. "The person who designed the system is no longer…available."

"Burned, or dead?" Once the transaction had been paid for, Millie usually kept a client viable for future products. Whatever happened, it had to have been serious if there was no longer a way to get a hold of them.

"The FBI raided the whole operation not long after. But they didn't find anything that would give them access to our system."

"So, you saw how awful they were and decided to tell your husband's people all about them?"

Millie shrugged. "They did a mediocre job, but our phones are secure. I had someone I trust confirm that. Everything else they were into?" She shook her head. "I couldn't let them continue operating in all good conscience."

"If I had a dollar for every time I've had to say that." Bridget returned her friend's expression. Both of them had zero tolerance for people who victimized others. She could only imagine what these guys had been into.

If Millie had made sure they were taken down, then it was because she knew they deserved it.

"I'd love to know what Clarke is after." Bridget stayed quiet a second so she could think it through, knowing Millie would rush to answer. Some things had to be mulled over. Even though she'd spent most of the night already doing that, there were still a lot of unanswered questions.

Bridget leaned against the dresser. "Either he's on his own, determined to find me for whatever reason, or he's trying to take down the whole company. He could be after the database—in which case, every one of our clients needs to be warned."

Millie nodded. "I've already sent the first email in the sequence. They'll know something is happening and be on guard. But until there's a concrete threat on any of them personally, that's all they're going to get."

Their client list was comprised of former covert agents, Special Forces soldiers, or anyone else with a high-risk job who couldn't just walk away. People whose lives would be in danger for the rest of their days. The kind who needed an alias to live under, one that was legit and would withstand the test of time. They needed a support system and official documentation.

It was a lengthy process, but the thanks she'd received from each client she had worked with made it all worth it.

"He could be after you."

Millie was the one who had indicated they were both in danger. She nodded now, probably because she knew Bridget was right.

Bridget continued, "Make sure you watch your back."

"I will. You need to do the same." Millie stood. "I need to get to my real errand, the one I told Eric I was doing. If I find anything out, or if Sasha does, one of us will let you know."

"Any idea how I can get in contact with your guy who verified the phone system was secure?"

They couldn't use satellites to pinpoint Clarke's location. The cell phones they used didn't even show up on the system most people used, with cell towers and GPS triangulation. It would be tricky to get into Clarke's phone, but there were people in the world who knew how to do this.

Surely it could be done.

Millie nodded. "There's a couple people I can call. This town has a private security team that lives locally and runs missions all over the world. You've met them. They have a tech person they use when it's ultrasensitive. And then locally there's a guy as well, one who could probably hack our system if I asked him."

"You think we'd get a location? Or do you think he's already thought of that and taken measures?"

"I think it's worth a try, at least." Millie tipped her head to the side. "And I have something for you to do as well."

Bridget headed for her suitcase and found the boots she hadn't unpacked yet. Bending over hurt a lot, but she tried to hide it. The last thing she needed was for Millie to bench her.

The sooner she got on the move, the sooner she would be back here and safe. The idea of being out and around town, possibly running into Aiden all over again, made her want to crawl back under the comforter and hide.

Not just because she wanted to avoid the emotions that came from seeing him, but also because being nowhere near Aiden kept him safe from Clarke.

And all the other threats she faced.

Bridget zipped up the boots. "Where am I going?"

"Head over to Tate's office. He and his wife took my kids on vacation for New Year's, so he's not there—he's headed to Hawaii. Get on his computer and see if you can pull up the log for our database. Find out if anyone has tried to access it since the office went up in flames. After that, call over to the local police department and speak to whoever investigated what happened at the accountant's office. Make up some story like you're a reporter, or one of our clients. Find out if they might know anything they're not willing to say."

"Copy that."

Millie leaned over and hugged Bridget. After Bridget got over her surprise, she hugged her friend—and boss—back. "I'll call you later."

"Be safe."

Bridget watched her friend through the blinds. Millie jogged to the end of the townhouses and around the corner. She'd probably parked her car in the grocery store parking lot and walked here. Thankfully, it was less than a mile.

Her town. Her *home*town. Too bad all that was left here for her were nightmares and grief.

Bridget drove down Main Street to the private investigative offices Tate rented. She tried to think about him and not her father. There was nothing she could do about the fact her dad was dead.

Tate, on the other hand, had never been anything except helpful and supportive. The night Millie had found her walking along the highway, broken and bleeding, Tate had been the one who helped Millie get Bridget out of town.

She would always be grateful to them for that.

Bridget circled the block three times to make sure no one was following her. Then she parked two streets away and pulled on a ball cap before heading to the back door. Tate hid a key for the times he forgot his, but she also needed the code Millie had texted her. The two used together got the door open.

Knowing what'd happened the last time she'd come in the back door of a building made her hesitate. Even as much as she didn't want to react like that, or at all, she was still wary. Yet another thing she had to work through.

Bridget pulled her gun out, just in case. *Wary and smart.* She let herself in, then took off her cap and waved at the security camera. When Tate saw it, he would know it was her and hopefully not worry.

She made her way down the hall to the office he used just as another text came through. The passcode for his computer so she could log on.

A rustle of movement stalled her forward motion.

Bridget froze, the gun held out in front of her. Angled toward the ground.

She listened. Who could it be? Not only was the private investigator on vacation, but she'd had to use a code to get in.

Considering it would be relatively easy for Clarke to figure out that Millie had a family connection to this local business, she figured he was the culprit.

She crept on toward the office and peered around the door.

She was right. It was Clarke.

Satisfaction was elusive as she watched him bang the keys on the keyboard in frustration. Okay, maybe not so elusive. She had the code. Bridget felt her lips curl into a smile.

"Knock knock!" The call came from the front of the building, but inside. "Are you here, Tate? Your door is open." She knew that voice. *Aiden.* "I need a favor from you."

The rustle in the office grew louder, and she heard Clarke move toward her. Bridget froze in the hallway. Pretty soon the man who'd killed her father would find her here. And the man she never wanted to see again would block her escape.

Bridget was trapped.

10

Aiden unclipped Butch's leash and let the dog go. He shut the door so Butch could roam freely without escaping outside.

The door met the frame and opened again. The lock was busted. *Guess that's why the door was open.* Someone had broken in the front and somehow disabled Tate's security system.

But the intruder didn't need to know that Aiden knew that.

Aiden unclipped the snap on his off-duty gun but didn't draw. "Tate, you here? The front door was open."

He thought he'd heard Tate was on vacation, but with an open door, he'd figured maybe he was wrong. Now Aiden's instincts were going haywire. Instead of a chat with the private investigator about how to find Bridget, he'd walked into yet another situation. At least this time he didn't have his car, so he couldn't maim some unsuspecting person.

He pulled out his cell phone and sent a text to the duty officer asking for backup. A second later, there was a reply.

Before he could read it, Aiden heard a woman cry out. Then a thud. The cry cut off and someone grunted.

He read the text. Two officers would be here within two minutes.

Aiden stowed his phone and headed in. Butch sniffed along the ground, caught a scent, and chased it across the room. Having spent the last twelve hours with the animal, he figured someone must've dropped bacon. Sydney had given Butch most of her rashers this morning, then clapped with delight as Butch lapped up each one and then came back to sniff for more.

Aiden was just grateful they weren't keeping the dog long term. What a nightmare to combat all the bad habits that would no doubt develop.

"Tate? You here?" He moved in slow, measured steps across the open storefront. Whoever broke in could be in the office. The back hall. They could've run out the rear exit already, except that he'd heard a fight.

Butch headed down the hall first.

Aiden waited. Listened. A dent in the wall about the height of his shoulder was the only evidence of the altercation he'd just heard, but he knew there was more than one person here, and he knew Tate wasn't one of them.

Which meant whoever *was* here certainly wasn't supposed to be.

The dog padded to the open door of the office, took a look in, and immediately braced. He barked.

A grunt sounded. With the next bark, the dog's front paws lifted off the floor. Aiden marveled at the massiveness of the animal. Considering the way his fur rose on his back, he was alerting to something serious.

Aiden moved down the hall toward the noise. A struggle. Someone in there was fighting—or continuing their fight. He hustled to the doorway and looked inside Tate's office.

A woman lay on the floor, stirring as she came-to from being unconscious. Blonde hair hung nearly to her waist. *Bridget.* Blood trickled from a spot on her temple.

At the desk, a man slammed down on the keyboard, one key at a time. He completely ignored the dog. The animal braced, about to lunge at the man.

"Clarke." Bridget roared his name. "What are you doing?"

"Something that should've been done a long time ago." The man was muscled under his sweater and jeans. Brow furrowed. His jaw covered with stubble, hair mussed. He'd obviously been having a rough time on the run. After killing Bridget's father, maybe?

"Whatever it is, you're not going to finish." Aiden lifted his gun and stepped in. "Last Chance Police Department. Step away from the computer and put your hands up."

This had to be the man who'd shot her. The one he'd chased back to his car, a man responsible for Thomas Meyers's death.

"You're under arrest."

"You called the cops!" The man rounded on Bridget. He swung out his foot to kick her in the head.

Bridget shifted as his leg swung out. She grabbed his boot and toppled him to the floor with a grunt. Even as injured as he knew she was, Bridget had considerable strength. Maybe she'd even been trained by someone.

He realized then he knew nothing about her or what her life had been like the last six years. Not that Aiden planned to soften toward her. Or let go of his anger. But he could still have empathy. And curiosity.

Butch ran to Bridget and got between her and the downed man.

Aiden rounded the desk from the other direction, determined to secure this guy before backup arrived. He didn't need the situation to get more complicated than it already was.

The man was up. He launched toward Aiden and sidestepped the gun to barrel into him in a full-blown tackle.

His back hit the wall. Aiden's right hip slammed the side of a file cabinet and metal gave way. He grunted, and the man she'd called Clarke reared back to punch him. Aiden slammed the butt of his gun into the man's left shoulder before he could throw the punch. A sickening crack sounded. The collar bone.

The guy cried out. He swiped with his right hand anyway and punched Aiden's cheekbone.

Aiden puffed out a breath on impact, dazed and disoriented.

Then he realized he was on his hands and knees.

Before he could scramble up, the man wound up and kicked Aiden's ribs. The force of it sent him in a roll to his back. He gasped for breath as the suspect ran from the room.

Aiden lay on the floor and Bridget grunted in a way that sounded beyond frustrated. Was that how she dealt with her pain? "Backup is coming."

She huffed out a breath. "They'll be too late."

He blinked in time to see her stumble from the room. Aiden pulled his phone and sent a quick text informing them that the blonde woman in the building was friendly. He prayed the information was relayed fast enough to be helpful to whoever showed up.

A second later, Frees strode in, his gun drawn. "So this is how you relax?"

"Bridget—"

Butch barked. Aiden didn't bother to yell over the dog who padded to Frees for a pat. As though he'd done something worthy of praise.

Aiden tried to get up. His ribs screamed in his chest, so he grunted and laid back down. It wasn't like Bridget was in here to see him act helpless.

"You need an ambulance?"

"Nah." Aiden touched a hand to his chest. "But give me a minute, yeah?"

A second later, there was movement at the door. "He got away." She sounded strong. Not at all frightened as she had seemed when he'd spotted her outside the hospital. In the daylight, he saw her for how she wanted to be seen.

Down, but not out. She'd been bested, but had fought back.

Aiden rolled so she didn't see the pain on his face when he pushed up and stood. His head swam.

"You good?"

He turned. "Yep."

"Good." Frees stowed his weapon. "Let's go." He motioned to Bridget.

"Excuse me?" Her blue eyes widened.

He remembered her eyes as brown. Colored contacts? A woman with training in how to fight. She was nothing like the woman he'd known before Sydney came into his life. "Who are you?"

Her gaze shifted to him. "You're not okay."

Before either of them could speak, Butch padded to her. Seemed like the dog thought this was his best day ever. He sniffed at Bridget's pants until she crouched. Aiden caught her wince. She wasn't pain free, just good at hiding the truth.

Aiden clenched his back teeth and watched as she petted the dog. Butch muscled into her personal space, and she toppled to her backside. Her smile preceded a sound that almost could've been a giggle. He'd heard that same sound from Sydney many times.

The woman she had grown into was…striking. The kind who turned heads, unless she worked to purposely downplay it. A woman he would have looked twice at even if they'd not had such a marred history.

But Aiden didn't need to get distracted by her. What he needed was answers, and a whole lot of them. A million questions warred for superiority in his mind. Meanwhile, she stared at him, and he stared at her.

"Any-who." Frees rocked back and forth on the balls of his feet. "I'm going to go look around. Dog?"

Butch trotted after him.

Aiden yelled, "There's a leash by the front door."

"Copy that!" Frees called back.

Pain rolled through his chest, and he sucked in a breath. *Ouch.* He perched on the edge of the desk.

"Are you really okay?" For the first time today, she looked scared.

Affected by him? Maybe.

Aiden didn't need to get swept up. He needed to focus on the issue at hand. "Who was that Clarke guy?"

"A coworker."

"What does he want?"

"To ruin me. The company." She shrugged one slender shoulder. "Take your pick."

"Are *you* okay?" From the stiff way she moved, he figured she was still in pain. Not surprising, considering she'd been shot and hit by a car. Now a fight. "That guy didn't kill you." Not the way he'd killed her father.

"He could have." She folded her arms. "Which means he needs me alive. I just can't figure out why he didn't try and take me with him. Or what he wanted with Tate's computer. He didn't have the code, and I wasn't about to give it to him."

"You know Tate?" It occurred to him then that she might've come here with that man, the one she called Clarke. The "coworker." Maybe she hadn't come upon him by accident, the way Aiden had.

Maybe they'd been together.

She blinked heavy dark lashes. "Tate helped me out when I left town."

Aiden opened his mouth. He didn't know where to begin asking about that day he thought she'd died and what on earth had happened.

"I wasn't in a good way when Millie found me. She brought me here, and the two of them patched me up before she drove me to Denver." Bridget glanced at the window, though she couldn't see outside because the blinds were currently shut. "After everything that'd happened, I was barely coherent with all the shock. I don't think I spoke for a week."

"Are you going to tell me about that?"

Maybe if she did, he'd have a clue why she ran. Why she

lied to him by not showing up. He figured withholding the truth was as good as lying. It wasn't like she'd bothered to come back to set the record straight.

Then again, maybe that was the point.

She'd have come face to face with Sydney, the person she obviously felt just fine pretending didn't exist.

"What's the point?" She shook her head and glanced at him with a sheen of tears in her eyes. "My dad is dead. So is the fire chief. That means whatever it was, it's over."

"The fire chief?" Aiden frowned. "He was one of the town's founders, doing whatever he wanted to the people who lived here. That guy lorded it over all of us with his criminal activity for *years*, not caring who he hurt."

Frustration burned in his chest. Jessica and Ted had both been injured and traumatized because of the fire chief. Not just them, but so many others as well. And yet they'd come through it healthy and safe. Better, even. They were in love. He was pretty sure Mia was pregnant and figured it wouldn't be too long before Savannah and Tate had a baby.

Dean was happier—lighter—than he'd ever seen. Even Ted smiled these days.

"I read in the paper that he was killed by police."

"Did you know Pierce Cartwright?"

Maybe he'd hurt her, the way he had with Kaylee. The PD receptionist had since married a long-time covert operative who was now a cook at Hollis's new diner. Or, Stuart would be a cook once her fiancé and his father finished rebuilding the place for her. Another pair of couples, moving on with their happy lives.

She shook her head.

More relief moved through him than he was expecting. "But the fire chief?"

"He's dead. Like I said." She shifted her weight from one boot to the other, but what arrested him was the look on her face. Strength and vulnerability. Stubbornness and weakness. She was a puzzle he couldn't figure out.

The fact he even wanted to was the worst part.

After what she'd done to him? No. She didn't deserve him softening toward her. Trying to understand why she'd left him alone to be a single dad, lying, and then having someone tell him she was dead.

Bridget sighed. She moved to the computer. "He was looking something up. Hopefully we distracted him before he was able to find out whatever it was."

"We need to talk."

"I can't read you in on this. Not without authorization."

"What's going on?"

She shook her head again. "Clarke is dangerous. I need to know who he's working for, or if he's acting independently. And I need to know who his target is. When he left me for dead, I figured I was the target, but there's something bigger at play here, and I don't know what."

She shook the mouse and the monitor hummed to life. "Why did you come here?"

"To ask Tate to find you. Have him run your alias. See what I could find."

Instead, he'd found her. Before she split—something he could see she wanted to do—he needed answers.

Aiden continued, "I didn't realize he was on vacation, but when I found the door busted open, I figured somebody was up to no good." But Bridget didn't answer. Her attention was on Tate's computer screen.

"Is that west of town?" Her brows bent toward each other.

Aiden rounded the desk. Standing close was a bad idea, considering her perfume caught in his nose in a way that got his attention. He pushed aside the distracting sensations of her presence right next to him and looked at the screen. A map had loaded, the dot marking the center of a forest.

"That's a cabin." The one Kaylee and Stuart had stayed in.

"Whose is it?"

"Her name is Victoria Bramlyn. Some kind of government director. She's retired, though. As far as I'd heard."

"Millie."

"What?"

She straightened and turned to him. That was when he realized exactly how close they were standing. Her nose flared. "I have to go."

"We need to talk, Bridge."

"Don't." She shook her head. "Millie is in danger."

He could help her, if she let him. Problem was, he didn't think she would. "I'll come and help. Frees too."

"I have to do this alone."

Aiden couldn't hold back the question burning in him. "You're not even going to mention our child?"

How could she not ask about Sydney?

Bridget's head jerked back as though he'd slapped her. "You know about our baby?"

Of course he did. What was she thinking? Before he could ask, she cut him off.

Bridget took a step back, and away. The fear that made her flee was there in her eyes again. "She's dead. What is there to say?"

A second later, she was gone.

11

Millie Cullings rolled over in bed and snuggled up to her husband.

"We should take naps more often."

She chuckled. "Except for the fact you're a busy FBI agent, and we have two boys who are definitely not the 'napping' kind. And haven't been for a long time."

Their boys were eight and ten, precocious and smart enough to get into real trouble when they tried—and when they figured out how to join forces.

His chest rumbled under her cheek as he laughed. Eric traced his hand up and down the back of his shirt—which she wore. "Guess we'll just have to take more vacations then."

"If you're after a life where the impending change is more sleep and not less, you made the wrong choice." She smiled against his bare chest.

He tugged her up so her face was level with his. "I most certainly did not."

"You still look exhausted."

He grinned. "No regrets."

Millie wanted to agree with him. Instead, her head filled with all that was happening right now. Clarke. *Bridget.* Even

Sasha was in danger as she worked things on her end. Millie thanked God their boys were on vacation and nowhere near this.

Who knew what kind of chaos was going to kick off. No point even trying to believe it might not happen. Not when things always seemed to get worse before they got better.

But yet there was more, even beyond all the stuff with the company.

Millie's phone buzzed across the top of the bedside table.

"Ignore it."

She planned to, unless the vibrating continued. Everyone knew that meant an emergency.

Eric's thumb rubbed her bottom lip, and she realized she'd been biting it. "Tell me what."

"What?" They'd been married nearly sixteen years. At this point, it was unlikely he'd be unable to tell something was wrong. Even though he worked long hours—and sometimes didn't come home for days or weeks on end—they were solid.

Except for the fact she'd been essentially lying to him for years.

Eric shifted. "I've broken criminals tougher than you. I'm sure I can get it out of you."

Millie frowned at him.

He smiled. "Or you can just tell me."

Before she could figure out what to say, the phone rang again. Eric rolled away from her and sat up. "You should take that. Probably someone calling about their tax return."

She heard something in his tone. His expression indicated he knew that was a lie. But how could he possibly know that the accountant's office had nothing to do with any of them being CPAs?

She looked at her phone. "It's Bridget."

Her employee—and friend—had called once and sent half a dozen texts. Millie shot to her feet. She choked back a gasp.

"What is it? The boys?"

Millie shook her head. "He's coming here."

"Mill—"

She cut him off. "Get dressed and get your gun." She started for the bathroom, but turned back. "Did you bring a vest?"

"You think I carry protective gear to a remote cabin where I'm going on *vacation*?"

Maybe not. "We can look. Victoria might have something stashed around here."

"Millie—"

The window exploded.

Both of them dove for the floor. Millie winced. That was not good. The last thing she should be doing is jumping around, or landing wrong.

She crawled to the end of the bed where she'd left her suitcase. Beyond it, Eric moved to his own and snatched out his jeans.

When they'd met, Millie had been working the front desk at her brother Tate's private investigation business. She'd only been home to recover from an injury she got on her last mission for her employer.

The CIA.

After meeting Eric, she'd quit but still wanted to do something worthwhile. So she'd started the company she now ran.

"You wanna tell me who is shooting at us?" Eric shifted his hips and buttoned his jeans. Of course, he also caught her staring at him. "I'm not getting killed in my underwear. I'll never live it down."

"That's not…"

"Then what?"

She shouldn't be distracted, but he… "I'm just looking at my husband. It's not a crime."

He blinked. "Did you bring a gun? Because someone is shooting at us."

Millie grabbed her phone. She'd dropped it when the window was shot out. Now it was shattered.

She tossed it aside and moved to her suitcase, pulling a protective vest out so she could roll on the floor and get it on. She didn't dare sit up. Not if Clarke was looking through the window—down a sniper scope.

"You brought a vest?"

Millie hesitated a second, even though there wasn't time. "I need to tell you something."

"It will have to wait." He checked his weapon, readying it. To protect his family.

"Thank you."

"For what?"

"Being here."

Eric shook his head. "Where else would I be?"

Millie pulled on a pair of loose sweats she'd brought with her for lounging, then dug out her gun. Shoes. She needed shoes.

"Who is outside?"

"Clarke."

"Your employee is shooting at us. Why?"

Millie studied the window on her side of the bed. Then the one on Eric's—the one he had shot out. "My guess? He's trying to kill you."

"Jealous rage?"

Millie's stomach rolled. She nearly puked on the rug under the bed. For the first time in a long time, she decided it was best to just tell the truth to her husband. So she rolled to her back and started talking.

"He needs to get to me, so he can get the password to the database. He's going to sell out the company. That will raise seed money for whatever he's going to do next, because he doesn't care that hundreds of people trying to live their lives in peace will be killed if he sells the database. My guess?" She stared at the ceiling. "He ticked off the wrong person and he needs to either make it right or disappear. This is his best shot at leveraging whatever comes so he can stay alive."

"Was he CIA, too?"

"Army Rangers."

Her husband, the FBI agent who'd never met a law he couldn't follow, blinked. A muscle in his jaw flexed. She *hated* that look. Knowing she was the cause of it? "Great."

"Do you…know?"

"That your business isn't a CPA firm?" He shot her a "duh" look. "What I can't figure out is what it *is.* The accountant firm "front" is clever. I'll give you that. But what is it a cover for? Because you don't run covert operations for the Agency." He shook his head, out of answers.

"I'm so—"

"Don't bother apologizing when you don't mean it."

"I—"

"Stay here. I'll take care of this Clarke guy." His gaze drifted away from her, and she saw the flex of his muscles as he prepared to get up. "If you've been out of the game this long, your skills will be rusty."

"That isn't…" She needed to tell him why she'd brought the vest.

"Later, you will be filling me in on the company you run and what exactly you do."

Cold settled over her. Millie should've told him long ago, but how was someone supposed to confess something like this to an FBI agent? "I am sorry."

He was already at the door. "Stay here."

Millie crawled after him. "You have to be careful. He's desperate and dangerous. Bridget is on her way so backup is coming, but she's injured and I—" She stopped herself. This wasn't the time to tell him.

"More secrets?"

"We need to talk. That's why I wanted to come here."

"But you weren't planning on telling me everything, right?"

He sat up in the hallway, then climbed to his feet. Strength rippled through his muscles. Everything she'd fallen for was right there in front of her. Physically he was exactly what she found attractive, and then on top of that? His sense of honor was off the charts.

She *loved* that about him.

Eric was what she'd always wanted and exactly what she wanted to be. The person she'd worked to become since meeting him and giving up her life as an officer for the CIA. Trying to make amends for everything she'd done, even while she got as much distance from her former life as possible.

Millie sat up as well, the gun still in her hand as she leaned her back on the wall. "I don't know what to say. The last few days have been…amazing. I wasn't in a hurry to disrupt that."

His brow furrowed. The same look he gave their boys when he was disappointed in them. "I'll call Conroy. Get some police officers here to help. No disrespect to Bridget."

"She's had a rough few days. Backup would be good."

"And you?"

Millie prayed for him to understand what she couldn't tell him until the danger was over. "I can't face down a gunman right now."

His expression blanked. "Like I said. Stay here."

Eric headed for the front room, which was the whole west side of the cabin. She liked to sit on the porch on that side and watch the sunset. They'd done that last night, snuggled under a blanket together. All the while, she'd tried to puzzle out why Clarke had left Bridget for dead, instead of just killing her there and then.

Unless he'd wanted Capeira to think she was dead. Even while he knew she would probably survive. Now he'd come after Bridget here in Last Chance.

Millie didn't like her and Eric being compromised like that. She'd been having a winter getaway with her husband, time spent together where she hoped they'd be able to talk.

Now Bridget was here.

Clarke had found the cabin.

And that meant he was here for the password because there was no way to get into that database for the client list without one.

But why?

She heard Eric's voice in the kitchen where he'd left his phone. Millie crawled to the end of the hall and looked out at the open-plan kitchen, living area, and farm table with its uncomfortable chairs. The whole place belonged to a former spy who'd married an FBI agent.

Victoria and Millie had gone to high school together and kept in contact sporadically over the years. When Victoria had gotten married, her doctor had told her that getting pregnant could be dangerous considering her age. They'd decided to adopt, and had found four children in foster care—siblings who'd all been orphaned. Two boys, two girls, all under eight.

She'd sent Millie pictures on their "gotcha" day when the adoption had gone through.

Tears filled her eyes even now, just thinking about it.

"You good?" Eric shoved the phone in his jeans pocket.

Millie nodded, even though that was a lie.

"Help is on the way. We just have to sit tight." His expression was still blank. "Tell me about this guy, Clarke?"

"Former Army Ranger, like I said. Thirty-four. No family, no ties. Underfunded retirement accounts. Two gym memberships, and he's been sober six years."

"So basically you'll fall for a sob story. Because this guy is prime sucker material, and he's probably leveraged to the hilt. Now he's desperate and looking to get out of whatever mess he's gotten himself into."

"He's a good guy."

"Is he?"

"I thought so." Millie couldn't believe he might be right. Not because she begrudged her husband his ability to assess people the way he did at work. "Apparently I was very wrong."

"Did you even look at his service record?"

"You think I didn't call in every favor I had before I hired him? I vet the people who work for me."

"And yet he's outside with a rifle, and we're both sitting on the floor waiting for him to kill one of us."

"I'm sorry, okay? I didn't know this would happen."

"Right. That's why you packed a protective vest to go on a week-long romantic getaway." He shot her a look. "Because that's standard operating procedure."

"I'm allowed to be cautious."

"I'm going outside. If I can find him, I can get to him before he gets to you."

The way he said it didn't make Millie super confident. "I know you're mad—"

"You think I'm mad?"

She opened her mouth to argue but didn't know what to say again.

"Okay, fine. I'm furious. You should've told me you had reason to think a threat was in play. You could've put our kids' lives in danger. And for what? That's what I don't get. What does your company even do?" His jaw flexed again.

Millie felt a tear roll down her cheek.

He ignored it. "If I'm going to die for your client list, I'd like to know who they are."

"Please don't die." She swiped at the wet on her cheek and realized she still held the gun.

"Talk fast."

She swallowed, while her stomach refused to quit roiling. "When a spy is burned, they're left wherever they are with no resources. No way home. Nothing to help them start over, or build a life. We help them get where they need to go and give them a loan to get them started. Housing. IDs—driver's license and social security number. They can set up bank accounts and work on getting a job."

"After they're burned."

"They deserve to have lives, even if the CIA doesn't want

anything to do with them anymore. These people have enemies who want to find and kill them and anyone they care about."

"So it's like witness protection. For spies."

She'd heard it called that before.

"I've heard rumors. I just didn't know the mastermind behind all of it was my *wife*."

"Eric—"

"I need to go find this guy before he gets the drop on us." He headed for the living room, where he lifted just barely enough to peer over the bottom of the window frame.

It shattered above him.

Eric ducked as glass sprayed over his skin.

Millie screamed.

"Stay there!"

The scream died to a whimper.

"I'm serious, baby. Stay there."

His calling her that only made her whimper more. *Please don't die.*

The client list was valuable, and if he knew how many spies would be at risk, he would consider his life a worthy exchange to keep them safe. Millie did not. He was her husband, and she needed to be selfish right now. The alternative was watching him die in front of her before she got to tell him her news.

"I'm going to—"

A dark shadow appeared in front of the shattered window. The blast of a gunshot echoed through the living room.

Eric fell to the floor.

Millie lifted the gun, squeezed the trigger and screamed. She kept squeezing it even as she corrected her aim. Again and again, the man's body jerked. He moved then.

Ran off.

Had she hit him?

"Millie!"

Silence settled with the dust falling around them.

She scrambled to her husband, who had both hands on his abdomen. Right side. Blood seeped between his fingers.

She twisted, pulled the blanket from the back of the couch and pressed it against the wound.

Hard.

Eric grunted. "Backup is coming."

Maybe, but would they get here fast enough?

"Is he gone?"

She glanced out the window but could see only trees.

"Mill—" Pain cut across his expression, and he grunted.

She pressed on his wound. When his gaze met hers, Millie said what she'd come here to say.

"I'm pregnant."

12

Bridget gripped the steering wheel and made the turn onto the dirt road that led up the hill to her father's house. She'd seen the map. The cabin was barely accessible, but her dad had dirt bikes. He was obsessive about maintaining them for when the weather was bad—or, at least, he had been.

Hopefully that was still true. Because the cabin was nearly two miles from here and she needed to get there *fast.* This was the quickest way.

Please, Lord. She prayed it would come together like a good plan. Not a spur of the moment reaction.

Clarke better not hurt anyone before she had a chance to get there. Regardless, she owed him for getting the jump on her in the hall at Tate's office. As if running into Aiden hadn't been shock enough. Clarke had nearly knocked her out. She'd pretended to be completely felled, unconscious so he would be more apt to reveal his plan, and she could figure out what he'd been doing there.

How he'd found out about the office, she didn't know. She did know that he'd done a deep dive into each of the employees of the accountant's office so he now knew everything about their ties to Last Chance. Millie. Her family.

Bridget didn't want to know what might happen had Millie and her husband's kids been in town right now. *Thank You.* They weren't.

She parked and had to slow her breathing before panic set in. The last thing she needed right now was to have an anxiety attack that stopped her from helping. Millie and her husband were in danger, and Bridget was going to help.

After all, this whole mess was at least partially her fault.

Another car pulled up behind hers, and she stared at it in the rearview mirror. Of course he'd followed her. She hadn't had enough of him back at the office, when he'd stood too close and spoken too softly. Her teeth gritted. She didn't need the reminder of the potent attraction between them.

Especially not when one of the first things he'd done was bring up the fact she'd lost their baby. How he even knew she'd been pregnant, Bridget had no idea. But right now there was no time to find out.

And right on the heels of him handing Butch over to the other cop? Aiden had to remember how much she'd loved her dog. He hadn't even asked her if she wanted to take Butch. Of course, she'd have had to turn him down, but still. It was the principle of the thing.

She shoved the door open and got out. Aware he could see her, she shook her head as he pulled up, then turned away to the house.

She was better off alone. Bridget needed to save Millie, or Tate would never forgive her. Millie's children would be motherless.

A tear rolled down her cheek. Why did Aiden have to mention their baby? Surely he would know how much that hurt.

"Bridget!"

She headed for the barn, where her father kept his dirt bikes. Snowmobiles. Tools. Whatever he'd collected over the last decade or so since he bought this house. She prayed a working vehicle was in there.

"Bridget." He was closer to her now.

She spun at the door to the barn. "Can you just go?"

"I'm here to help." Stubbornness laced his tone.

"I don't need your help." After all, he had people who cared about him. She didn't need him getting injured. "You've made a good life for yourself. Don't ruin all that today by getting hurt, or maybe even dying."

"You think I'll get killed because of you?"

"This is about helping Millie and Eric."

"He's a fed. Backup is on the way to them." He waved his phone at her.

"Then why are you trying to help him, if he'll be fine?"

"I'm helping you." The intent in his eyes impacted her. "I hit you with my car. Means I owe you."

She turned away, not wanting to think about the deeper meaning she saw there. "You don't."

"Please let me help you."

If she let him help her, she'd have to let him in, and there was no way she wanted—or needed—Aiden to have any part in her life. She would only end up right where she'd been.

Broken and alone.

She was about to tell him "no," when she noticed the door to the house. About twenty feet from her, she spotted what might be a bloody handprint. Also, it looked like the door might be open.

She spun back. "Look in the barn and see if the dirt bike is functional. We need a way to get to the cabin. Fast."

Except she was pretty sure Clarke was here somewhere. Bleeding.

Maybe.

She took a step toward the house. "I'll look for ATV keys just in case there is one."

It was a lame excuse. But instead of waiting for his response, Bridget jogged to the house. Aiden was going to do whatever he wanted. What was the point worrying about him? She had a bigger threat to deal with right now.

Clarke's words played in her mind. Like a stuck record to remind her that he had not only bested her, he'd also told her that he'd deal with her later. As if. Bridget didn't need to be any more irritated than she already was, but it sure served to energize her muscles. Adrenaline born of frustration was the best kind.

She could deal with that.

Bridget pulled out the stun gun she'd grabbed from her duffel. She didn't need to be carrying a loaded weapon when there were cops around—even if she could produce a valid license for it. She didn't like questions.

The mark on the door was definitely a bloody handprint, and it was wet. That meant fresh.

She felt the urge to glance at the spot on the grass where her father had bled out. *I shouldn't be glad, but I kind of am.* He'd never been nice to her, and that was the best she could say. The worst it ever got? That was the night she'd left town. When he'd kicked her out—literally.

Bridget eased the door open. She could hear someone rustling around. If it was Clarke, he wasn't going to get the drop on her this time. And if he'd been hurt? She wanted to shake the hand of whoever had made him bleed.

The living area was a mess, and it smelled. Not the familiar musk of growing up surrounded by dirty dishes he'd yell at her to take care of. Or a rug that needed vacuuming with a vacuum that was broken, and a constant promise that he would fix it when "he was good and ready to fix it." She gritted her teeth as memories swamped her.

Could be an animal making that noise, but she figured this critter was much bigger.

Her old bedroom was nothing but boxes piled up. Her dad should've just shut the door and left it that way—the same way he'd shut her out.

Bridget rounded the corner and found Clarke in the bathroom, where he rummaged through the medicine cabinet. "Who do I have to thank for this?"

Clarke snatched his gun from the counter, raised it at her… and stopped. The second he realized it was her, he lowered the gun. "Get out of here."

"So you can hurt more people." She almost smiled. "Who shot you?"

Blood was running down his side. Too bad it was just a graze and not an actual shot. Bridget needed to get his gun from him so she could subdue him. Aiden could use his cuffs, she supposed. Clarke would be secured and no longer a threat.

"Doesn't matter. They're dead anyway."

Her stomach dropped. "What did you do?"

The corner of his mouth curled up.

"I mean, in addition to leaving me for dead at the office and shooting at me in the woods." Before she was then hit by a cop car.

"Well, I didn't know that was you, did I now?"

She figured that was unlikely. "You need to stand down. Whatever's going on, we can work it out."

He huffed out a breath she figured he intended as amusement, then pressed gauze to his side. Teeth gritted. "Feel free to stick around, but I have stuff to do."

"Like get the password to access the database from Millie?" Which he couldn't do if he killed her. "Then what?"

"Long as I'm clear, doesn't matter. And I have a new plan for that."

"That's how it is? You don't care who you hurt?"

He shot her a look. "What do you think?"

She *thought* it was good he hadn't yet realized how she was edging her way closer and closer. Almost close enough to grab for his gun.

He stared at her. "Whatever you're thinking, don't do it."

The gun was still on the bathroom counter. If she could subdue him, she could grab it.

Bridget lunged at him, tackled his middle and sent them both crashing into the shower curtain.

Clarke roared. She heard his head hit the tile, and they tumbled into the bathtub in a tangle of limbs. The next few seconds passed in a blur of grunts and pain. Her head exploded. There was no time to figure out what she'd smacked the back of her skull into. Bridget kneed him—close enough to his wound that she scored a hit.

He screamed and his eyes rolled most of the way back in his head. Before he managed to pull himself back from passing out.

She launched herself out of the tub, going for his gun. Clarke grabbed her foot. She slammed into the floor, her legs still in the tub, and he laughed. He actually *laughed.* As though he was enjoying this.

She kicked back at him, but he didn't let go. Clarke landed on her back. Her injured hip pressed against the floor. "I've always admired your spirit. Too bad you never showed me just how deep it goes."

His hand ran down her side and squeezed, right over the bruised spot where she'd been hit by the police car.

Aiden.

She couldn't let him find her like this. Clarke would kill him.

Bridget pushed against the floor and moved up into plank position. She shoved him off her and stood. Reached for the gun. He yanked on her foot, and she fell. Her knee slammed into the floor, and she cried out.

"Too bad Sasha didn't show as much spirit as you. But blondes are okay, I guess."

"What did you do to her?"

He laughed.

Bridget spun to hit him. Clarke jabbed the stun gun into her side. She braced and heard the crackle, then thousands of volts surged through her.

Her stun gun. The one she'd brought to use on *him*.

His laughter continued. *Aiden, where are you?* She didn't care now how he found her. Maybe he wouldn't be killed, and he could take down Clarke. Bridget might've admitted then, if only to herself, that she could use the help right now.

"This was fun." His breath brushed her ear. "Let's do it again soon."

He grunted as he stood, and then he was gone.

Bridget only had the strength to breathe. She lay on the floor in the bathroom. All the while trying to muster the energy to get up.

Clarke was gone.

Where was—

"Bridget?!" Aiden called out her name. His shoes thundered down the hall to her. "What happened?"

She gasped.

"Okay, okay. Don't try to move." He pulled out his phone and called for an ambulance, then went quiet for a minute or so. "You're kidding me." Pause. "He was here. Bridget is down, and she needs medical attention." His hand on her shoulder shifted as he turned. "Copy that."

He hung up, and she thought he might be calling another number. It was confirmed when he spoke again.

"Yeah, I need your help. The ambulance is up at Victoria's cabin because Eric got shot." He sucked in a breath. "It sounded bad. But I need you here." He gave them her dad's address. "I don't know what happened."

Bridget managed a breath. "Stun gun."

He repeated that to whoever was listening. "But she's pretty beat up already, and I don't think she's been looked at much since she was shot. And then I hit her with my car. And now this." He blew out a breath. "Okay, okay. I got it. Yeah, see you soon."

Aiden squeezed her shoulder. "Dean is on his way."

"Millie."

"She's with Eric. Apparently, he was shot."

That meant Millie would've responded in kind, right? That had to have been what happened to Clarke. Why there was blood everywhere. But she must've missed, because he'd only had a graze.

Now he was on the run with her stun gun and their fight was something they'd be doing again, "soon." Whatever that meant.

"Can you sit up?"

She groaned.

"Okay, then stay where you are." He shifted and plopped his backside on the floor next to her, his back against the bathroom cabinet. Aiden tugged on her until her head rested on his leg. His very muscled leg.

Bridget shut her eyes.

"Rest. But I need you to stay awake."

"I'm not…" She took a breath. "Pass out."

"Good." He ran a hand over her hair. "I like it blonde. I mean, the red was cute. All your freckles."

She covered those with makeup now.

"This is beautiful."

"Don't."

"Hate to tell you, but I'm not gonna listen to that."

Bridget pushed out a breath. She wanted to get up and walk away, but there was no version of this moment where she had the strength to do that. Or the will.

Truth was, she didn't want to leave him.

She could try and tell herself all day long that getting out of Last Chance as quickly as possible was for the best. But it would be a lie.

Even though the lie was what she'd lived for years, trying to believe she'd done the right thing by never coming back. Being here was making her see the real truth.

Too late.

She could never come home. Not really.

Aiden shifted. "Dean is here."

He didn't know that. It might not be a friendly. "Clarke—"

"It's safe. He's gone."

She shook her head, even though it seriously hurt.

"Time for you to go to the hospital and be seen for real."

"Fine."

"Wow, that was easier than I thought."

Only because she wouldn't stay. Right after the doctor saw her, Bridget would leave. For her peace of mind, and everyone's safety, she was getting out of Last Chance.

As quickly as possible.

13

When Dean walked in the door, Aiden lifted his chin. Even though Bridget had her eyes closed, he didn't think she had lost consciousness. "The list of her injuries is pretty long." Aiden worked to keep the worry from his voice, but knew he hadn't succeeded when Dean clapped him on the shoulder.

The medic crouched. "Guess you guys drew the short straw because you got me."

Aiden tried to smile but, unfortunately, it was similar to his attempts to keep worry from his voice.

Bridget opened her eyes. "Uh, hi."

"So you're the Bridget everyone's talking about."

Her brow furrowed. Aiden's eyes widened, and he shot Dean a look. "Can we make sure this woman isn't in medical distress before we get into the banter, please?"

"What can I say? I'm in a good mood." The former Navy SEAL and town trauma therapist unzipped his duffel and pulled out a stethoscope. While he assessed Bridget physically, Aiden took a look at her from up close in a way he hadn't been able to before.

Her clothes were stylish and not bargain-basement. The

boots she wore appeared to be comfortable and broken in like an old friend. Her dark brown eyelashes were so long he wondered if they were fake. He remembered her eyelashes being short and very red.

"You're staring at me."

Aiden felt his cheeks heat. It might have been six years or more since the last time they saw each other, but he couldn't deny that time had not dulled the attraction he felt for her. Not even when Dean glanced over again.

Aiden met his gaze. "What's the verdict?"

"Given everything you've told me, our friend Bridget here has been through the wringer. But she should be safe to be transported to the hospital."

"Good."

"Your friend Bridget is right here, and legally responsible for her*self*." She sat up with a groan.

Aiden's body temperature dropped from the loss of contact.

She slid around on her behind but didn't get up. Instead, she tugged her knees to her front with a wince and wrapped her arms around them. "I need to know if Millie is okay."

"As far as I know, she is," Dean said. "Eric will be in surgery as soon as he reaches the hospital."

"I should get there. I need to talk to her."

Aiden bit back the urge to argue with the logic of that.

Dean stood and stretched out his hand. "I'm sure Aiden will give you a ride to the hospital. You can talk to her as soon as the doctor clears you."

Bridget took his hand and stood. "Thank you for coming out. I appreciate it."

Aiden realized he was the only one still on the floor. If he wanted a shot sticking around with Bridget, he needed to get moving. "We can take your car if you want. I can have someone drive me back to mine later."

She lifted her chin. "We can take your car. And when we get mine back, I want Butch as well."

"Fine by me."

Dean glanced between them. "Oh-*kay*. Glad you guys have this all figured out. My work here is done, and I get to torture Jess with a juicy story she hasn't yet heard."

Aiden was about to object when he realized it was true. Jessica Ridgeman might be one of his best friends, but he hadn't even told her about Bridget yet. How was that possible? There just hadn't been time.

He checked his watch. He still had a couple of hours until he needed to pick up Sydney. Until then, he wouldn't mind having a conversation of his own with Millie.

When he glanced up at Bridget, he realized she was confused about the interplay between him and Dean. There wasn't time to get into all that right now. "Let's head to the hospital. You look like you're about to fall down."

She breezed past him. "That's what happens when you tackle a man into a bathtub a day after a cop hits you with his car."

He followed her out. "Don't forget the gunshot wound to your arm."

"Or the fact he turned my stun gun on me. Or what happened at the office, and before that."

Aiden shut the door and then trotted after her. "You went up against an armed man with only a stun gun?"

She strode to her vehicle and grabbed a backpack, then made her way to the passenger side of his car. "I learned he isn't here to kill me." She shrugged. "So there's that."

He beeped the locks. "But he shot you the other day."

"He claims he didn't know it was me. He also said we would do this again soon." She hauled her door open and got in.

He did the same, quick enough to see her wince as she tried to sit all the way down. The quicker he could get her medical attention, the better. "What does that even mean?"

"I wish I knew what he still wants with me." She leaned her head back on the headrest and shut her eyes, the backpack hugged against her front as he pulled out. "But I also don't care. Not now that he shot Eric."

"Special Agent Cullings is a strong guy. I'm sure he'll pull through."

Truth was, Aiden didn't know that. He might just be lying to make her feel better, and that was the last thing he wanted to do. Pretty quickly here, he needed to figure out how on earth he would tell Bridget that their baby hadn't died after all.

Unless it was only a story she'd told herself to overcome the guilt of abandoning Sydney. No, he'd seen the look in her eyes when she said it to him. The grief so close to the surface, raw and painful. As though he had taken a knife and shoved it into her stomach.

So how on earth did she not know that Sydney was alive?

There was no doubt in his mind that his daughter was hers also. Not only did the timing fit, but Sydney was a miniature version of her mother. Red hair, freckles. A sassy little package full of love for everyone she met. The kind of child Bridget would've been if she'd been raised by a parent who'd loved her.

Even one good one would've been better than the two who tried to call themselves her parents.

Bridget's mother had been beaten to death by her drifter boyfriend one night. Tucked away in the closet beforehand by her mother, Bridget had heard the whole thing. Her father had grudgingly taken Bridget back to live with him after that. Though, the way he'd treated her, maybe he shouldn't have. She probably would've been better off anywhere else.

But that was hindsight talking, not the reality. To top it all off, he had to see the truth of the woman she'd become. Someone he thought was amazing.

That had nothing to do with her parents and what they'd instilled in her—except the fear he sometimes saw in her eyes. Someone had shaped her, somehow. Or she had found herself. Grown into a woman who was confident and never afraid. Even if every time he turned around, she was hurt. That didn't mean she wanted him to save her.

Aiden had no idea what to do about any of this besides pray. Telling her about Sydney couldn't be rushed. Not when it would probably be the most important conversation of their entire lives.

He parked at the hospital and touched her shoulder. "Bridge, wake up."

That was the second time he'd called her that now. The name he used to call her during their short relationship.

She gasped and jerked in the seat, then swung out with her arm and slammed the blade of her palm into his outer arm.

"Hey. It's just me." He squeezed his arm with his other hand and tried to massage some sensation back into it. "Ouch. That's some strength you've got."

She stumbled out of the car. He rounded it and reached out to help her get steady on her feet. She took a step back against the open door and nearly fell in, but caught herself just before he could reach for her.

Aiden sighed. By the time he got both doors shut, and locked the car, she was halfway across the lot. He ran to catch up with her and spotted her the rest of the way. If she fell, he would be there. But if she wanted to walk on her own, then he would grant her the freedom to do it. Not that he had a choice.

She checked herself in, and a staff member who also spotted her on her other side walked her back to be assessed by a nurse. As she moved away from him, Bridget turned back. "You don't need to come with me."

"I'll go check with Millie and see if Eric is okay. When I know something, I'll come and find you."

She actually looked relieved. "Thanks."

"Right this way, Ms. Weston." The nurse glanced at him. "Officer Donaldson."

He nodded. "How's it going?"

Bridget muttered something about a small town and went

after the woman. He watched her move until she was out of sight, observing the hitch in her stride. Bruises. Those were better to contemplate than the things that drew him to her. Fact was, she had been injured while he was with her.

Looking back, he should have stayed with her. As soon as she'd sent him into the barn at her dad's house, he'd realized the reason she'd given him an errand was to get some space for herself. While he'd been happy to give her time alone, and he'd made a couple of phone calls in the barn, Aiden shouldn't have left her for that long. If he had known Clarke was inside the house, he wouldn't have left her at all.

He should have known something was wrong.

A crowd had gathered outside the room Eric had been assigned. Aiden found his sergeant and walked over. "How is he?"

"Out of surgery. Conscious, but not happy even though they said he'll make a decently quick recovery." Basuto waved him to the door. "This way."

"What's going on?" He needed to speak with Millie, but couldn't if she was sitting with Eric.

"Millie will tell you." The sergeant strode to the door and knocked. "She said if you or a blonde woman showed up that we should immediately tell her you're here."

The door opened and Millie stood there. "Aiden. Good."

"Let him in, Mill." The voice from inside the room was thunderous and extremely irritated.

Millie swallowed and pushed the door open. She stood by it as he strode in, looking like she wanted to run.

"I want to hear this conversation." The man in the bed was pale, but the life in his eyes indicated a serious amount of strength. If Aiden hadn't met him before and hadn't worked with him as a cop, he might be inclined to believe the guy was a threat. Instead, all he saw was someone in pain—both physical and emotional.

"My husband is now fully up to speed with everything

concerning my occupation, among other things. He would like to be involved right now in the case, considering this is time we're scheduled to spend together."

"Plus, I just got shot." Eric glanced aside at her. "That means I get to be briefed."

Aiden figured both her statement and his amounted to the same thing. "I'm not sure about the job thing, except that Clarke attacked Bridget at her dad's house." Since they both looked ready to ask, he said, "He got away. After he hit Bridget with a stun gun."

Millie looked like she wanted to punch someone.

Aiden stepped back. "He's on the loose, and as far as I can tell, coming after both of you. He has a plan, and he wants to do things his way, but I don't know what he's after."

"The database. Our client list."

"So why would he leave Bridget alive and come after you?"

Millie settled on a chair by the bed. "It takes two of us—both passwords—to access the database. But as soon as Bridget called me, I revoked Clarke's access, which means he can no longer use his access as one of the passwords. He'll need both of us to cooperate, which is why he tried to kill Eric. To force me to go with him."

"Thank You, God, the boys are out of town."

Millie laid her hand on her husband's. "Amen."

Aiden put a couple of the puzzle pieces together. "He's the kind of guy who would go after someone's child to persuade them to his way of thinking?"

"I wouldn't have thought so." Millie tipped her head to the side. "I mean, I hired the guy. I knew he was dangerous, but that's a perk in a job like this. You have to be able to take care of yourself." She paused. "You don't need to worry about Sydney or anything. Not if you're not on this guy's radar."

"So you're certain Bridget can take care of herself?" Aiden folded his arms. "Because it seems like she could use a little help from where I'm standing."

Eric glanced between them. "Was this Bridget person a CIA agent too?"

Aiden stared. "Was she…what?"

Millie shot her husband a look. "We don't work for the government. Our company is independent. We help people. As soon as Zander gets back, you can talk to him about the work his team has done for some of our clients. Get a referral."

So this was what Eric was mad about. "Bridget's business has something to do with the CIA, but is not the CIA?"

What on earth had she gotten into after she left Last Chance? This whole thing was turning out to be a whole lot more serious—and complicated—than he'd originally thought.

"It's complicated."

"No kidding."

Millie shot him a look. "You of all people know Bridget is different than everyone else. But the fact is, she *is* one of my best people. If anyone can figure out how to turn the tables on Clarke, it's her."

"And if he wants her for something other than her password? Something more, maybe?"

Millie gaped. "Oh, no."

"What does he want with her?"

"It doesn't matter. He won't get it, no matter how much he tries. No matter how bad this gets."

Millie's husband lifted his hand and held hers.

"There is nothing he can do that will convince Bridget to give him what he wants."

Aiden wished he could be as sure as she was. The truth seemed to lead him down a different path. Millie considered Bridget to be someone who always put the job first, someone who would never allow her personal feelings to cloud her judgment or cause her to not make the right choice.

Eric studied him. "What are you thinking?"

Aiden shook his head, too full of a million thoughts to voice any of them. "I'll let her know I talked to you guys, and that you're okay."

"She's okay too, right?"

"I'm going to find out."

If she wasn't, Aiden would figure out a way to help her until her life had righted itself. That meant keeping Sydney safe. And doing it in a way Clarke wouldn't be able to use her as leverage to get Bridget to do what he wanted.

And that meant he couldn't tell her that Sydney was the baby she thought had died.

But how could he not tell her?

14

"I know, baby." The soft voice drifted to Bridget's awareness, a man. "That sounds like fun." After a short pause he said, "I love you, too."

The low, smooth tone was like a balm. Only it didn't work like medicine. Instead, it intrigued her. As much as it settled within her a sense of peace. She wanted to smile while she heard more of it. That would be better than waking to this stiffness alone. Not pain, as such. But she wasn't looking forward to having to move.

"Hey." The voice was closer now.

Bridget blinked against harsh fluorescents.

"There you are." Weight settled on the edge of the bed, and a warm palm covered the back of her hand. "You were out for a while. Guess you needed the rest."

"How long?" She tried to swallow around the dryness of her mouth.

Aiden shifted and then held out a cup. She sipped from the straw. "Thanks."

"You were asleep for nearly sixteen hours."

Bridget braced to sit up.

"Whoa." He touched her shoulders, gave her a gentle squeeze, and then let go. "Easy. Don't move too fast."

"I need to get out of here."

"Why?"

Bridget had to think about that. The urge to flee was a primal response, but was there anywhere she had to be right now? What she needed was information. "Run down what you know." She figured if it sounded like an order, he might forget he didn't work for her. "Millie. Eric—" She remembered then that her boss's husband had been shot. "Sasha. *The phone.*"

"What phone?"

"Clarke's phone." He didn't know about the phone?

Aiden shook his head. "What about Clarke's phone?"

"You don't have it?"

"No. Do you?"

"Maybe. Find my things."

Aiden said, "First, update. Eric is fine…if you call super cranky fine. Because Mr. Special Agent is *not* happy he just found out his wife has been lying about her job for years."

"Uh-oh."

"They'll figure it out. He's just in pain and irritable, plus the hurt feelings."

"Is Millie okay?"

"She's worried about you. Everyone's out looking for this guy. Millie gave us his photo so the police can be on the lookout for Clarke."

Memories swirled in her mind and she winced. Tackling Clarke into the bathtub. Getting hit by her own stun gun and falling to the floor. That was when her fingers had found his phone before she lost consciousness for a few seconds. Discarded—or dropped—Bridget had grabbed the phone and slid it into…

She sat up suddenly. "My jacket."

"You need me to get it?"

She nodded. "Front right pocket." As soon as he turned

away, she sat up. It hurt. A lot. All the bruises she'd amassed, and the gunshot wound. "Clarke was shot."

"I wondered where all the blood was from. Millie said she tagged him."

"It was just a graze, but he's running hurt." Just not scared. Bridget knew from personal experience that scared people made mistakes. Would Clarke make one that landed him in the hands of the police? She could hope, but she wasn't going to count on it.

"Here."

"That's Clarke's phone."

Aiden's brows rose. He pressed the home button with his thumb. "Passcode. Think you can get in?"

"Not sure I can get the right answer before it locks out." She tried to think what it might be. "Millie mentioned some guy in town who is a computer whiz. You think he can access it?"

"Technically, Ted shouldn't work police contracts. But also technically…this isn't a case." Aiden shrugged one shoulder. "I'll clear it with Millie and Eric, but I don't think they'll have a problem. This could be a serious lead."

"Great. Hand me my clothes and let's get going."

"Pretty sure a doctor should clear you before you up and leave the hospital."

"And yet, somehow, that's never stopped me before."

Aiden barked out a laugh, his expression showed her sudden humor had surprised him. It was kind of adorable.

"I might not want to be here, but it's still good to see you."

"A bright star in the night sky?"

Memory rolled through her. Time they'd spent together, during their summer of disastrous romance. A whisper. A touch.

"Bad memories?"

She thought over everything that'd happened since. Calling it disastrous didn't mean there weren't sweet moments. "Not all of them."

He took half a step toward her. "When the doctor clears you

to leave, I can drive you to Ted's. While you're getting seen by the doc, I'll make a call and set it up. See if he can get us into Clarke's phone."

Bridget nodded. He wanted sweet moments but apparently wasn't interested in dragging them out. Whoever he'd been talking to on the phone when she woke up was probably the reason he wanted nothing more than to catalog those sweet moments as merely memories. Nostalgia, or whatever. Clearly Aiden also wasn't interested in anything happening between them in the present.

That was fine with her, considering she didn't want to be the "other" woman. Bridget had no interest in that.

He'd moved on with his life. The way she'd done—though their paths were very different. He was a good guy who made the people around him care. She saved lives on a global scale, and then went home to her solitude. The place where she worked through her grief and the trauma of it all.

Not just the baby, but everything that'd happened before that.

"What do you say?"

Bridget realized she'd been drifting. "Sounds good. I'm ready to get moving."

Two hours later, they pulled up outside a huge house on the far side of town. Bridget remembered it, though it had been a rundown wreck last time she'd seen it. "Didn't we use to come here on Halloween and pretend this place was haunted?"

Aiden chuckled. "Pretty sure my friends and I were the ones hiding in the closets, wearing horror movie masks, jumping out to scare the cute girls." He laughed for a second more. "Good times."

She stared at him out the corner of her eye. He only laughed harder, so Bridget shook her head and got out. Aiden jogged around the car. "I would've helped you out."

"Like you did with those girls? Scare them so much they fall into your arms…and then what?" One of those middle school party games, no doubt.

"It was a long time ago." He shut the car door for her. "Much has changed, for both of us."

She nodded. "I can't say I ever thought you'd be a cop."

"Me either." He shrugged. "But it's stable work with decent benefits, and I get to feel good about myself. Maybe even make up for some of the bad stuff I did."

Bridget knew what that felt like. She glanced at the trees and wondered if Clarke was out there in the woods. Watching. "That's how I feel about my job. That I get to make a difference." She figured she might as well tell him. "Our clients have served their country, and for whatever reason, that country left them hung out to dry. We help them start over." Something she had first-hand experience with.

"There had to be a reason."

"Sometimes it's just that policies change. A different person —with different priorities—is suddenly put in charge of a task force, or a team. Someone was out sick, a director of some department, and all of a sudden a different call was made by whoever took over."

"That's harsh."

"It's easy to pretend politics don't control us, but the truth is that we're at the mercy of the people in control. Whether we voted for them or not. We're the ones who have to live with it."

"So it's like covert agents?"

He knew. She nodded anyway. "Burned spies. Special Forces guys who need to lay low because of an imminent threat. Even state department employees, ones who were formerly stationed in a particularly hot zone. We can provide protection. We can get someone a completely clean identity and a place they can live in peace with their families. Or off the radar altogether. There are a couple of clients like that. No trace. No ID. No trail to follow."

In fact, there was a guy like that who lived in the woods a

few miles outside of town. At least, she was pretty sure he might still be here. That whole thing had been Millie's idea since he had family in Last Chance.

"You guys gonna stand there all day?"

Aiden spun. Bridget would've drawn her weapon, but she didn't have it. Her stun gun was...wherever. Maybe Clarke had taken it with him, the way she'd taken his phone. Her weapon was...somewhere. Maybe back at the house?

The man at the door was lean and about five-nine. Younger than her and Aiden. Dark hair fell over his forehead.

"I told you we were coming." Aiden made his way over. "You didn't get dressed?"

The guy looked down at his sweatpants and the tie-dye T-shirt he wore. "I am dressed."

Bridget followed. At the door, Aiden turned to her. "This is Ted Cartwright. His fiancé is a police officer."

"Please don't tell my long, tragic story."

Bridget smiled. "If he does, I'll tell you mine. Though, we'll probably both want to jump off the cliff into that freezing river once we're done swapping stories."

Ted shuddered. "Don't even." He held up a hand. "That's part of it." He twisted to Aiden. "Phone?" When Aiden handed it over, he stepped back. "Come in. It shouldn't take long, and there's coffee in the pot. Oh, and Ellie made muffins."

Aiden stepped in, going straight to the kitchen. Bridget watched him over the breakfast bar as he pulled down two mugs from a cupboard. "Creamer? Milk?"

"Whatever is fine." She wandered to the living room. Domestic life wasn't her thing. He might be comfortable making himself at home in someone's kitchen, but she was not.

Bridget moved around the living room. Above the fireplace was an ocean print on canvas. Bali, if she wasn't mistaken. On the mantle were a few framed photos: the medic who'd helped her just yesterday danced with a dark-haired woman. Ted, at the top of a mountain with a blonde, both of them celebrating.

Another man, one with brown hair. He held a curvy woman with dark features.

All of them looked so happy, even the brown-haired man with dangerous eyes.

Beside those was another picture—a group of men. But that was all she could take in before Aiden handed her a full cup of creamy-looking coffee. She took a sip. "Thanks." Then another, as she looked at the farthest picture on the mantel…and choked on her next drink. "Is that Zander and his team?"

"They live here."

She spun to Aiden, careful not to spill coffee on these people's carpet. "In Last Chance?"

"Yeah. In this house, actually."

Bridget lowered the mug from her lips. "Seriously?"

When he nodded, she pulled out her phone and turned. "Selfie time." Aiden looked confused but got in the picture. She shared the grinning image of the two of them in Zander's living room via text. "Seriously. The team lives here?"

Aiden nodded. "Millie mentioned them when I was talking to her and Eric. I didn't put the pieces together, but I'm guessing you both know them."

Bridget set the message. "Small world."

"Do I want to know *how* you know a team of international private security specialists?"

She grinned. "Probably not."

"Yeah." He eyed her.

Never mind that he left the conversational door open, and she didn't go through. Their chat didn't need to move to heavy topics right now. There was already enough of that between them.

"I'll have to tell them about Clarke." Bridget winced. "Zander is going to be seriously mad. I'll never hear the end of it when he finds out Clarke is behind all this. Zander never liked him."

Aiden frowned over his mug. "He's the type of guy to rub something like that in your face?"

"Zander is the law. I just choose to not always follow it." She didn't figure he'd find that too surprising about Zander's method of working. "Don't get me wrong, Zander and his team don't work for Millie the way I do. They're more like independent contractors we employ from time to time if a client needs to get out of a hot situation."

"Like an extraction?"

She nodded.

"Super spy stuff." Aiden frowned down at her, a tiny smile on his face. As though being involved with something like that was a measure of all she'd achieved—and he was impressed by it.

She supposed it did speak to what she'd been doing since she'd seen him last. Still, it wasn't all she was. "Sometimes we don't get there in time. We don't know beforehand that we needed Zander, and I wind up in over my head. Like on my mission last week."

She probably shouldn't even be talking about this.

But it was Aiden. Literally the first person she'd ever been able to trust in her life, the one who'd taught her what that meant.

"What happened?"

Bridget sighed. "The client knew she was being followed. She asked for assistance figuring out who the tail was. By the time I realized it was Benito Capeira stalking her, and he didn't even know she was ex-CIA, he'd already made his move. I rushed in. We fought, and I had to kill him. She and I ran, but a couple of his guys chased us. I got her to the safe house, though."

"So Millie was right, you are amazing."

"It's all her." When he started to object, she held up a hand. "Millie trained me. I just worked at it long enough I could put it into practice instinctively."

"And use it to save lives." He set his cup on the mantel and folded his arms. "It's not Millie out in the field, right? That's all you."

"She has kids. No way should she be putting her life at risk."

Aiden flinched.

She wondered what that was about. Surely it wasn't about the baby they'd made together.

Before she could ask him, he spoke. "Life is a risk. Anytime you go outside, you face down the unknown. Not just outside. You could fall out of bed and crack your head open. A house fire. A gas leak. You could just not wake up one morning."

"Is there a point here, or are you just being terrifying on purpose?"

He grinned, but only a tiny bit. "You never know what might happen. Life is about taking that risk. Otherwise, how do you know you've really *lived*?"

She wondered then if he was talking about her taking a risk on *him*. But he was in a relationship. She'd heard him talking to someone he loved. The care in his tone had been familiar, the way he spoke to this mystery woman.

Like the way he'd spoken to Bridget years ago.

She turned away and heard him follow her to the kitchen. "You're right. There is risk. But I have a battle to fight, and that's my life. Not whatever I think it should've been, or I might want it to be. This is where I've come to. Chasing down Clarke and safeguarding our clients' personal information. Making sure he doesn't come at Millie and Eric again or hurt someone else."

"So you'll just fall back on nobility at the expense of any personal gain?"

She rinsed her mug and found a towel hung on the oven to dry her hands. "It doesn't matter. It's what's right."

"Guys?!" Ted rushed into the room, flushed and breathing hard. "I cracked the password and now I'm in the phone. Who is Sasha?"

She hadn't talked to Sasha in a couple of days, but Millie probably had. Their friend was laying low. "Why?"

At the same time, Aiden said, "Bridget's coworker."

Ted glanced between them. "You need to call her. Clarke told the Capeiras where to find her, and they've called out a hit."

15

"She didn't answer. I left a voicemail and about fifteen messages." Bridget strode into the room that was Ted's office. The one that used to be Stuart's bedroom.

Aiden wanted to tug her over and give her a hug—if she would let him. Instead, he watched her stow her phone with a wince on her face.

"Doing okay?"

"When Sasha checks in and tells me she's all right, then I'll be okay."

That wasn't what he'd meant, but he let her have that and turned to the work station set up—the one that took up a whole wall. "Ted?"

"I'm working on something. Give me a minute."

Bridget seemed amused by the younger man, even though Ted wasn't that much younger than them. Aiden didn't know if she remembered him, or if Ted had arrived on the scene after she left. He'd become a cop later, so he wasn't sure on the timing.

Under her amusement, he could see worry for her friend. Between Millie and this Sasha person, it seemed like she had a decent support system. At least, they were the kind of people

Bridget would stick her neck out for. She would put her life on the line and go all in to save those she cared about.

Like she would for Sydney. If she knew their child hadn't died.

It still didn't make sense to him—at all—that Bridget thought their baby had passed away. And then why had he been given the child? He reached back and squeezed the back of his head. How did he even begin to explain that?

Despite the danger swirling around them, he had to tell her. Even if it pulled everyone into its undertow? No way did he want to put Sydney's life on the line. But she deserved to know. He would want to know if he was in her shoes.

If Clarke was watching, and he saw Bridget with her daughter, he would know instantly who they were to each other. No question about that. Which only made him wonder why Millie hadn't figured it out.

Hadn't she met Sydney?

Maybe not.

He shook his head.

"Are *you* okay?" Bridget pierced him with questioning eyes.

Before he could answer, his phone buzzed. He looked down to see a messenger app notification—one Sydney used to contact him through her tablet. He replied to her gif with a gif of his own, imagining her laugh when she saw it.

"Never mind." Her tone was a little on the abrupt side.

Aiden looked up. "What—"

"Okay." Ted's voice cut through their interchange.

But Aiden still stared at Bridget. What had that dismissal been about?

"Thanks to the magic of technology, I present your guy, Clarke." Ted shot Bridget a pointed look Aiden wanted to ask about.

"Well, I know *now* that it was a mistake. But you don't have to give me grief about him." She held up a hand. "I'm sure Zander will do that enough."

Ted winced. "Good point. You know Zander?"

Bridget grinned. "Unfortunately, in this case, yes. And he warned me about Clarke. I believe his words were, 'Later I'll be saying I told you so.'" She rolled her eyes. "So we already know Clarke is a bad guy. Let's cut to the chase. The phone?"

Ted grinned and glanced at Aiden. "I like her."

Jealousy whipped like a lash through him. "I saw her first."

"Whoa." He didn't know if that was Bridget or Ted. Or both of them.

Aiden shook his head. "Just tell us what you found. Please?"

"Fine." Ted turned back to his computer. Aiden saw Bridget look at him, but pretended like he hadn't noticed. Ted tapped a thousand keys and the TV screen on the wall—the middle of three—flashed to a picture of Clarke.

"This guy is in deep with a lot of people. He owes money to two crime families and is playing them against each other. Like one will retaliate if the other hurts him too badly, that kind of thing. To make them all think he's a valuable commodity. Or at least more valuable alive than he would be if he was dead."

"Is he in Last Chance under orders?"

Bridget settled on the arm of a big, cushy chair. "If he is, it's likely related to the Capeira family."

Ted tapped a few more keys. "They're in here too, but I'll get to them in a minute. What I'm seeing? It's more like your friend Clarke is working all the angles. Getting ready for a double-cross, where he jumps on whoever will pay more and ditches the other party."

"So he walks away and leaves a fallout that will probably destroy several people's lives, if not your whole client list." Aiden glanced at Bridget. "Because he's determined to wheel and deal his way to getting clear of you guys."

"We can't let him get the client list."

"Seems like he should've forced you to go with him." When she started to object, Aiden lifted a hand. "Don't get me wrong.

I'm glad he didn't kidnap you. Or try to. I'd have stopped him. I wouldn't have let him take you."

She bit her lip. "He said let's do it again soon. But why doesn't he need my passcode now? Unless he has to wait for some reason."

At least Clarke didn't want her hurt. And he didn't need her now, but he would in the future.

"No way." Aiden shook his head. He wouldn't allow her to go with Clarke at all.

She had to know he would fight for her. And not just because she was Sydney's mother. They had history that went deeper than that—to the first day he'd met her in high school, in the front hallway.

Ted continued, "This guy is Enrico Capeira."

A dark-featured man popped up on screen. Another picture joined it, and then more until four quadrants of the screen showed his passport photo, another ID, and two shots from surveillance video.

"He's been communicating with Clarke. There's a thread of messages back and forth between the two of them in one of those encrypted messaging apps."

"Anything older than three days ago, or is it all since then?"

Ted scrolled with his finger on the rollerball of his mouse. "First one was over a year ago."

Bridget frowned. "A year."

Aiden waited.

"We were dating then. But early on, you know? Like he was trying to figure me out. Maybe that's why it felt off."

"You have good instincts." After all, she had fought her feelings for Aiden, and he was pretty sure she knew there was something he wasn't saying. Things between them were on a precipice. Pretty soon they'd either plummet, or they would soar.

He knew what he wanted. But what did she want?

She didn't even know about Sydney.

"I can't believe it." She pressed the flat of her palm to her forehead. "A year? Did he sell out the client to Capeira's brother? There had to have been an introduction because this wasn't just random."

"He's playing Enrico off as well, just like the others he owes money to. Looks like things were heating up. He was supposed to deliver the client list to them, and he's past the deadline. They were getting antsy, so he dropped the bomb that you survived the office fire?" Ted glanced over, a questioning look on his face.

Aiden nodded in answer.

"They know I survived." Bridget bit her lip.

"Do you think they'll come after you?"

She glanced at him, eyes wide. "Once I know Sasha is for sure safe, I need to get somewhere off the grid where I can figure this out. Because if Enrico knows I'm still alive, then he's going to want revenge for his brother's death. And he likely won't settle for me dying in an accident that no one can pin on him this time. He'll make sure I'm dead."

"Nothing I have here indicates how Clarke and Enrico know each other." Ted shot her a look. "But I can tell you he's not a good guy. I haven't looked at everything stored in Clarke's gallery, but from what I've seen? I want to scrub my eyeballs with bleach."

Aiden wasn't sure how helpful that comment was. Before he could point that out, a notification buzzed. Ted's screen flashed up with a bunch of messages.

The younger man braced. "Uh-oh. People who regularly use the words, 'national security' just caught onto the fact I searched Capeira's name. In a second, I'm gonna get—" His phone buzzed to life. "A phone call." He swiped it off the desk and answered. "This is Ted Cartwright."

Bridget got up. Aiden followed her to the hall, leaving Ted to his conversation. She leaned against the wall looking wrung out. Or, at least, like someone who'd been in several fights recently.

There wasn't an inch of the wild teen he'd known in this

woman. The girl who'd matched him, stupid choice for stupid choice. Getting picked up by Last Chance officers, drunk at the golf course. After several instances like that, the cop who was now his chief—Conroy Barnes—had sat him down to give him the lecture about how a sealed juvenile record might not follow him into his adult life, but if he kept going down the same path he would end up with an adult record.

Something much harder to come back from.

His teenage self hadn't wanted to listen. Not the first few times. Aiden had been much too self-absorbed to consider the future. But eventually, Conroy had been unavoidable. Aiden got a job on a construction crew that started every day with Bible study, and then he started going to church as well.

Two months later, a woman had shown up with Sydney.

There was a lot for him and Bridget to talk about. Like why she'd left town so abruptly, and the fact their daughter was happy and healthy and needed her mother in her life. Aiden was the best dad he could be, but Syd was six. Later, as she grew up, she would need certain guidance he couldn't give her.

And she would always need her mother's love.

She did that palm-to-the-forehead thing, so Aiden took a step closer to her. He'd like to offer a hug. But she had to make the first move if that was something she wanted. "We'll find him. If he's after you, then maybe you should stick around? Draw him out somehow, like with a cop who can be a decoy."

"You think I'll let someone else take the risk for me?"

Aiden shrugged even though he knew the answer. "We can minimize the danger here. If you leave, you'll be alone with no backup. Can you guarantee you won't end up with the same outcome as in the bathroom?" Not to mention that Clarke could have something much more major than a stun gun next time and kill her before he split.

She might be this great, trained operative. But right now, she was injured. And this whole thing hit her emotions deep. When he told her the truth about Sydney, it would all be a million times worse.

She stared at him.

Aiden couldn't resist. He reached out and touched her cheek, then slid his fingers past her ear into her hair so that his palm rested on her cheekbone. "I want to help. I don't want anything to happen to you."

"And if something happens to *you*?" She grasped his forearm as though she didn't want to push him away, but she tugged and he dropped his hand in response. "I'll still walk away, only with the knowledge you're lost to the people who care about you. The ones who—" She choked up a little. "—*love* you."

"Like the way I was lost after you left?" Truth was, he'd been destroyed there for a while.

Pain lanced through her features, but she said nothing.

"If you tell me why you went, maybe I can understand why it was necessary for you to leave. Without even coming to tell me." He knew he was pushing her. She could shut down instead of telling him what she'd started to tell him earlier, about the previous fire chief. But he had to know, or they would never be able to move on the way he wanted to.

Together.

Her phone rang. She looked at the screen and sagged against the wall in relief. "Sasha." She put the phone to her ear. "Are you okay?"

He waited.

As soon as she looked at him and said, "Good. That's good," to her friend, he headed into the office with Ted.

Two steps in he wondered if she would stay. Or if he would go back to the hall to check on her, only to find her gone.

A shiver ran through him, and he glanced back. She was in hushed conversation with her friend. He had to trust her. They would get there. He believed in that, despite the niggle of doubt. But it would take time. Right now things between them were like a fragile bird.

He decided to trust her.

Ted hung up the phone. "My search was flagged by feds with their eyes on everything that has to do with the Capeiras. I refused to tell them who asked me to search, and it will stay that way without a court order. Or until your friend out there tells me otherwise."

Aiden didn't turn. *Trust her.*

"But they're going to coordinate with Eric since he's the boots on the ground in Last Chance right now."

"As if his vacation wasn't already ruined by getting shot. He's probably raring to get to work on this, if only as payback for Clarke trying to kill him." More than that, Aiden figured Eric wanted to put things right for his wife. Any man would if it was in his power—even if his wife might already be able to take care of herself.

Maybe that was why it hurt so much that Bridget had left him all those years ago. Sure, they'd been young. Barely more than children at the time, but old enough to change the course of their whole lives. Things hadn't been long-term serious between them, just close. Building to…more. And yet, she hadn't sought him out.

When push came to shove, she hadn't trusted him.

She'd simply left.

Ted flipped hair back off his forehead. "This is a case now. They've been watching him for a while, and they know the brother is dead. The two women involved in it have evaded the feds' search to find them and figure out what happened to Enrico's brother. In *Caracas.* They want Enrico Capeira, since they know his brother is dead, and there's not much they won't do, now that he's on radar in the US."

Much like the chance to take down Capeira, this was Aiden's shot to make amends for everything in his life he needed to undo. No more striving to go above and beyond. It was his chance to live clean and clear, with everything he'd ever wanted.

And he wouldn't have to convince anyone to testify to do it.

"Chatter suggests he's mobilizing for something big." Ted stood. "Which is why we're headed to Tate's office now for a meeting."

Aiden turned to the hall. "Last time I was there…"

Bridget wasn't in view.

He strode out and found her down a ways, just out of sight. She paced as she spoke on the phone. When she saw him, she said, "Call me when you get there," then stowed the cell in her back pocket.

"Meeting at Tate's. All of us and the feds." Which probably meant Eric was out of the hospital. "We're headed there now."

"Copy that."

"Everything good with your friend?" He reached to touch her cheek again.

She stepped back and blinked those long lashes. Lifted her chin. "You don't need to worry about it. I can take care of myself."

After that, she brushed past him, and he heard her talking to Ted. While he just stood there and wondered if he was going to have to watch everything he wanted slip through his fingers again.

Just like last time.

16

Millie glanced over at her husband, sitting in the passenger side while she drove. So pale. He looked like he wanted to pass out—or hurl. "Maybe leaving the hospital wasn't such a good idea."

"I'll be okay once I get out of this car."

She should drive back to the hospital and convince them to readmit him. But she didn't. Millie drove to her brother Tate's private investigator office.

"They gave me medicine. I'd rather be useful, not just lying in a bed for two more days."

Millie groaned. She was going to *kill* Clarke.

Eric squeezed her knee, his voice as soft as his touch. "What?"

"I should've seen it. I should have known he was betraying us." She gripped the steering wheel. There was no point in him trying to make her feel better. She shouldn't get to feel better when it was all her fault he'd been shot. And Bridget had nearly died—more than once.

Now Clarke was in the wind, and they needed to figure out a plan for what to do next.

"Do you really want me to tell you that, yes, you should've known?"

Millie wasn't sure what she wanted. Unless she could just say, "none of what's happening." Because that was pretty close to her wish right now. Their five-day vacation to reconnect was toast. He knew now she'd lied to him for years, and now he'd been shot because of the secrets she'd kept.

"Does being a CIA agent years ago somehow give you special mental powers?"

"Maybe it should have. And either time, or life, killed them."

"So having the boys made you soft? Or at least, distracted."

She shot him a look. "I've done the best I could."

"Maybe it's because you're pregnant. It probably fried your brain cells."

"That actually might be true." Ugh. Why did he have to be so reasonable? "At least be mad that I got you shot."

"I've been shot before. It's a hazard of my job—and apparently, it's a hazard of being married to you as well." He didn't shrug. More like a scrunch of his nose that meant the same thing.

Millie pulled onto the side street so hard he let out a moan. She pulled into Tate's reserved spot and shut off the car before turning to him. "A hazard. Of being *married to me*?"

"Do you drive like that with our boys in the back?"

"I *knew* you were mad about getting shot."

"My whole stomach is on fire. Of course I'm mad. But not at you. I'm mad at the guy who shot me."

"Ok, so you're not mad at me?"

"I knew you were CIA before I married you. The accountant's office was more of a mission to you than a job, so I knew it was important. I might not have known you were helping ex-spies, but it wasn't illegal or immoral. So why would I be mad about it? Things that are important are worth doing, even if the cost might be high."

"Even if it risks the kids?"

"It hasn't. Not yet." He studied her. "Right?"

Millie looked out the windshield at the brick wall of the building. Eric covered her hand with his. Given how much pain he was in, even with the meds they'd given him, she was surprised he had the energy. *Things that are important are worth doing.* She squeezed her eyes shut.

"Hey."

Millie twisted. She laid her head on the headrest and stared at the man she'd loved since the first day he'd walked into Tate's office. She'd been working the front desk then, providing her brother with admin help and intel she could gather using her skills. Eric had come to ask Tate for help. The two had known each other in the FBI years before that and kept in touch.

She'd married Eric just weeks later.

"I counted the cost of doing it, even knowing we would have children." She swallowed. "The gain outweighed what I would sacrifice—or might have to give up—in the process. But now there's a traitor after us all, and I didn't see it coming. It makes me question everything."

"He fooled all of you."

"Clarke knows we have children. If he wants to get to us, he could use them to hurt us." Fear was like swallowing a gallon of ice and feeling it settle in her stomach. "I'm sorry you got hurt."

"You think I was gonna let some guy kill me and take you?"

She shook her head. "You didn't."

"I understand why you never told me what your job really was, but that doesn't mean I have to like that I was kept in the dark."

"How do I make this right?"

"Let me help you. We stick together, and we get as much help as we can. That's our best shot at keeping everyone in one piece. Right?"

She nodded.

"The boys are with Tate and Savannah. You've warned

them. Do you think they're going to let anything happen to our kids?"

"No."

"Right." He had that look in his eye. The one he got when he thought about kissing her. Eric tugged on her hand.

Beyond his window, another car pulled into the spot beside them.

Eric grunted. "Raincheck."

Aiden sat in the front seat, Ted in the passenger side. Millie didn't think there was anyone in the back—until Bridget sat up.

Millie got the back door unlocked and turned off the security system—the one Clarke had disabled, but not broken, thank goodness. Tate was already mad enough about the break in and the fight. He wanted to come back and help, but protecting his nephews was priority.

For all of them.

Bridget refused help, though she walked like she was sore. Like maybe she needed help. Millie had seen that before. She figured her friend wouldn't want Millie involved in this because of her boys. Did she not know Aiden had a child? Millie hadn't met the kid but was pretty sure he had a young daughter he raised by himself.

She should ask Eric about that.

But needing to help her husband inside the building put her question on hold for the moment.

She walked Eric all the way to Tate's desk where he could sit in her brother's expensive chair. He took her hand, so she stood beside him while Ted found a seat for himself on the couch in the corner. Aiden directed Bridget to a chair at the desk. Aiden sat beside her, and Ted pulled out his laptop and booted it up.

Eric squeezed her hand. "This is a federal case. Capeira has been on the FBI's radar for a while, but his activity in the US is limited. Until now."

Millie started to twist toward him.

He sounded every bit like she imagined he did when he led

whole teams of Special Agents into dangerous situations. "The bureau wants to bring him down along with his entire operation. They are aware the brother is dead and would like to speak with the woman seen fleeing the scene and the companion who was with her."

"So they can question me for days about what Benito did and everything I knew before I killed him." Bridget folded her arms. "Or they want to set me up as bait to draw out Enrico when he tries to get revenge?"

Aiden glanced over at her.

Eric didn't back down. "What about the woman you were with?"

Bridget lifted her chin. "I have no idea who you're talking about."

Eric sighed. "Make sure you're never in my interrogation room."

"I'd take that as a compliment, but it implies I'd allow myself to get caught."

Eric laughed, his body jerking. The sound quickly dissolved to a groan, and Millie leaned down. "You might want to consider letting someone else take point on this."

"I'm okay. It just caught me by surprise is all."

Bridget waved a hand. "I get that the FBI wants Capeira, but this isn't about him. It's about Clarke and the potential of our client list getting out. If he gets the password, the fallout will be bigger than all the harm Capeira could do in his lifetime."

Millie sat on the edge of the desk. "She's right. It could be."

"Will be and could be are two very different things."

"But neither is what we want, right?" Aiden glanced between them. "So maybe we can use Clarke to reel in Caperia and snatch up both in one fell swoop. Everybody wins."

No one spoke. The others were deep in thought. Millie ran through half a dozen scenarios that might work before she realized they'd all drifted into brainstorming mode. "We need Sasha here as well."

Bridget nodded. "Agreed. Once the three of us sit down, we can hash out a plan."

Ted held up a finger. "You'd have to get Capeira to Last Chance. From the last few messages between him and this Clarke guy, I'd say he's aware Bridget is alive but doesn't know about her ties to this town."

"Right." Millie nodded. "He may not know where to look. Especially considering Clarke is the one who told him about the accountant's office, and when Bridget would be there."

Bridget shifted in her seat.

Millie eyed her. "You had no idea he was setting you up."

Eric turned his head to his wife. "Neither did you. So if Bridget can't blame herself, then…"

She couldn't either. "There's no time for guilt anyway. We have work to do."

The door flung open and Jess strode in like a tornado. "You guys didn't start yet, did you? What did I miss?" She moved right to Ted and flopped down beside him. "Hi, babe."

Ted gave her a quick kiss. "We need a plan to draw him—them—out."

"I'm blonde again. I could be the bait if I borrowed some of Bridget's clothes." She barely paused. "Hi, Bridget. I'm Jess."

Bridget just blinked. Aiden said, "Jess is a cop, like me."

Jess grinned. "Aiden and I go way back."

"Probably not as far as Aiden and *I* do." Before anyone could react to Bridget's statement, she coughed. "I mean, no one is going to pretend to be me. If I need to draw out Clarke, then I'll do it myself." She glared at Aiden. "I thought I said we weren't going to put anyone else in danger."

Bridget shifted. To Millie, it looked like she was trying to hold back the urge to run from the room.

Millie dipped her head. "I agree. This is our problem, and we're going to be there when it gets taken care of."

"We're cops." Aiden probably figured that should be an

asset. "We're in danger every day, and we're trained to face down guys like this."

Eric tapped the desktop. "This is a federal case. If Clarke is selling out former spies, that's a national security problem."

Millie shifted. "Maybe, but it's my business. The one I built from the ground up and put my heart and soul into. You can't just dismantle it for a case. Especially when all parties involved signed non-disclosure agreements. No one is going to tell you anything. And we definitely won't be handing over access to our computer system, I'll be out of business."

He shot her a look. Millie paced away from the desk, not wanting to see his real thoughts about her future career plans. Maybe most of it was about the pain he was in. But he had to know shutting her down wasn't what she wanted.

Jess was the one who spoke then. "I thought taking down this Clarke guy was the point. Arresting him with enough evidence he spends the rest of his life in jail."

Millie glanced at Bridget. Her friend shrugged, just barely enough she saw it. They were in agreement. "If it comes to that, it's one thing." Millie leaned against a file cabinet. "But you're banking on the fact a jury would convict him, the judge will issue a decent sentence, and nothing else gets screwed up in the process."

She didn't have all that much faith in the government or the judicial system. Even though her husband represented both. That was just how she'd been trained—to work alone for survival.

"So neither of you will let the police take the lead on this?" Eric lifted his brows. "You want to dispense your own form of justice."

"I plan on doing what's best for my clients, the people who work for me and the company. The rest of the world is number four on the list." Millie figured he would glean from that whatever he wanted, and it would be pretty accurate.

She wasn't about to say in front of a bunch of cops that she planned to kill Clarke. He'd shot her husband. What other reaction was appropriate? Not that it would happen unless he forced her to do so. Like Benito Capeira, and the way he'd provoked Bridget. Forced her to defend herself and take lethal action. Clarke would go down.

The manner in which that happened was entirely up to him.

"The expression on your face is pretty scary."

She shrugged in response to her husband's comment. "You have to know I'll do what I think is right."

If he didn't respect her need to safeguard her clients' lives *and* their privacy, then what kind of relationship did they have? Sadly, after nearly ten years, Millie wasn't sure. She'd held back for so long. Maybe she'd done irreparable damage to their marriage. And now she was pregnant on top of all that?

She blew out a breath.

Bridget glanced at her. "Clarke first. Then Capeira."

"Sasha first," Millie countered. "Then those two."

Bridget nodded. "Once she's here, we can brainstorm." She still squirmed in her chair.

Things had to be bad if Bridget was displaying her emotions this much. She'd been trained to give nothing away, which meant either pain or fear—or both—were overriding what she'd been taught.

Millie saw again that bruised and bloody teen walking along the highway. The story Bridget had told wasn't something Millie could fix, but she'd been able to help the girl. After all, that was what Millie had been called to do.

She rescued the wanderers and gave them a place of safety.

A refuge.

"Maybe that's what Clarke wants." Aiden glanced between Bridget and Millie. "What if getting the three of you together is playing right into his hands?"

Millie couldn't argue that very real possibility. After all, they'd been blindsided by Clarke so many times already.

"This time we'll be ready." Eric glanced at her. "Right, Mill?"

She thought she might have seen affection in his eyes, despite everything, and had to nod. "Right."

As long as the FBI can keep from railroading everyone around to their way of thinking.

Millie's phone beeped in her pocket. Bridget reached for her phone, and Millie realized they'd both received a message simultaneously.

"Something's coming through on Clarke's phone." Ted snapped his fingers. "An emergency?"

Millie looked at her phone screen. An alert that went to all three phones at the same time? That meant one thing.

"Sasha is in trouble."

17

Bridget used the app through which Sasha had sent the emergency notification and backtracked to the GPS location it was sent from, a feature they'd specifically requested. Her skin itched to get moving. But unless she had more information, she'd be useless.

Not yet.

Aiden closed in on her side, his presence a comfort even when she was about to freak out with nothing to stop it. He squinted at the screen.

"Sasha was on her way here." The GPS location loaded. "That's a rest stop just outside Cheyenne."

"Wyoming?"

Bridget glanced up at the woman's voice. Jess. A cop, like Aiden.

Aiden nodded. "That's what it says."

Affection was clear between them. They cared about each other and were friends. Maybe even dated once? Before she got together with Ted? Just a guess. And why was Bridget's mind going there? What did it matter who Aiden had dated—right now, or at all?

It wasn't like they were starting up anything again, so it wasn't like he was cheating on whoever he'd been on the phone with. But it was still frustrating whenever he got close and tried to comfort her. He obviously had someone in his life. Why was he being this way with Bridget? Just for old times' sake, or something else? Whatever the case, it made her uncomfortable.

Millie frowned. "It'll take hours to get there."

"In a car, yes." Bridget needed faster. Like a friend with a chopper.

She was about to mention Zander and his business assets when Aiden's phone rang. The second he looked down to read the screen, his whole face changed, softening in a way she'd seen before.

Because he'd looked at her like that. A long time ago.

"What are you thinking?"

Jarred by Millie's question, she blinked at her boss.

"How are you going to get to Sasha before she's picked up and long gone? She might've dropped her phone there."

Bridget didn't want to imagine her friend in trouble. Though, she had to admit that the word "friend" was a pretty strong word to use in regards to Sasha. She wasn't sure anyone could claim to be truly close to her. True, Sasha could take care of herself. Then again, Bridget would've said the same about herself. And yet, when it came down to it, Clarke had bested her.

Let's do this again soon.

Eric and Aiden were both on their phones, Ted on his computer. Jess and Millie waited for her to spit out what she had to say.

Bridget needed to get to Sasha before it was too late. If it wasn't *already* too late. "I need to make a call."

"Zander?" Millie asked.

Bridget nodded, pulled out her phone, and called him. He'd replied to her text—the selfie of her and Aiden in Zander's living room. She didn't want to get distracted by the picture and his comment, but she'd look at it later. Probably while eating a pint of ice cream.

Zander had replied to the text with, "Small world." The man should really use emojis. He'd be able to be a whole lot more expressive.

"Hey." His normally rough voice sounded like gravel.

"Sasha's in trouble, and I need a favor."

"What's up?" His tone changed. If there was something he could help with, Zander didn't hesitate. But Sasha? Take that willingness to help and multiply it a hundredfold like a shot of the protein he probably drank. Distilled. He was huge.

Bridget explained the present threat—Clarke—and the fact Sasha had triggered a call for help. Then she told him the location. "I need to borrow your chopper."

"No one flies it but me."

"That's good, because I don't have a pilot's license."

"We're on our way back, thirty minutes out from the airport. Soon as we land, I'll make us ready."

Bridget glanced at the time on her phone. "I should be there by then."

"See you soon." Zander hung up, probably so he could brief his three teammates on the situation. Or so he could take a power nap and wake up ready to jump on this new mission. She didn't know which, but she was grateful for him anyway. The kind of guy you called when you headed into danger, and who you also sent a gag Christmas gift to.

Only it was his teammates who'd sent her *several* videos of them making fart noises with the little tub of glow-in-the-dark slime. Not Zander, who the gift had been for. If she had time, she'd ask Ted where the slime was now. Maybe he knew. She could steal it and send them a bunch of videos.

Her boss said, "Keep me posted."

Bridget gave Millie a quick hug and accepted her car keys,

then headed for the hall. She needed her car back, but this would do for now.

"Bridget?"

She glanced back at the door. "I need to go help my friend."

Jess strode down the hall toward her. She walked like a cop. They didn't think that was a thing, but she'd always been able to tell. "He cares about you."

Bridget figured she was talking about Aiden, though Jess didn't say.

"I have to *go.*"

"I can tell he cares, even though I barely know your guys' history."

"Well, it's complicated."

Jess said nothing.

"I knew your grandfather." Alan Ridgeman had been the chief of police before Conroy Barnes. "He knew not to poke his nose into things that weren't his business."

She was out the door before Jess could say anything. The woman knew nothing, so why did she even feel the need to comment? It didn't seem to Bridget that Aiden needed to be protected from heartbreak. He was capable of doing that himself. Strong. A good guy. Possibly two-timing someone he claimed to love. He made her want to swoon and managed to infuriate her at the same time.

A man in a relationship.

She stewed on it all the way to the local airport. She got there early and leaned against the side of the car while the plane landed. Trying not to shiver and wondering where her coat even was. The plane taxied toward the hangar where she'd parked. Inside was the chopper. Zander's chopper.

Where the man got money for a helicopter *and* an airplane, she had no idea. No one checked into Zander's background. If they did, he quickly found out and they were persona non grata forever after that.

Or so the tale went.

As the four men descended the plane steps and into the night, lit only by the airport street lamps, she wondered what was myth and what was fact about each of them. Considering their team was legendary, it was hard to piece out the truth. Except what she'd seen with her own eyes, of course.

Zander strode right past her car. "Let's go."

The four of them were all dirty and exhausted. Badger had a smudge of blood on his cheek. She glanced between them. "You guys okay?"

Zander was already out of earshot.

Two of the guys were the jokesters and Badger was one of them. She had no idea where he got his moniker. He was blonde and California-surfer tanned. He cracked a smile while the youngest teammate, the stoic one, headed for an SUV. "Fun was had."

"So...you got in a firefight and almost died?"

Badger lifted one finger. "Almost is the fun part."

Bridget shook her head. "I need to get to Sasha."

"I know." He slung an arm across her shoulders. "We're all coming."

She started to object.

"You know that don't work, darlin'."

They were exhausted, fresh off a mission, and still rolling out to help her. "I think I'm gonna tear up."

Badger cracked a laugh. She elbowed his side, and he hopped three steps. "Ow. Broken ribs."

"You should've told me!" They all climbed into the helicopter, and she was handed a headset. "You and me both, though."

Badger raised a brow.

"It's been an interesting week."

Zander called out, "Everyone ready?"

The youngest team member shut the door and sealed the five of them inside. Zander lifted off, and they were in the air.

Bridget stared out the window. "Thanks for doing this."

"Nowhere else we'd rather be." Badger squeezed her knee.

"I can't believe you guys were able to get here just in time to help me."

Zander was the one who said, "That's what God does. You know that."

She did. Still, there were so many more questions. She knew she was supposed to have simple faith but hadn't been naïve and given over to blind faith for years. She'd left childish notions behind and now was far too aware of how the world worked to just allow herself to believe without question.

"Why would He dangle in front of me everything I ever wanted, and at the same time let me know there's no way I'll ever get it?"

Badger nudged her. "What's going on?"

She thought of Aiden, and the soft look that had come over his face when whoever had called—or texted—him. Then she thought of the night she left town. Discovering she was pregnant two weeks later. Then, giving birth to a beautiful daughter only to have her snatched away in tragedy. Bridget visited the grave regularly. It was her only concession in a world where she had to carefully guard everything she was about so as not to risk the security of the work she did.

"Doesn't matter." She brushed off the thoughts and tried to smile. "Sasha is our priority right now."

"We are going to talk later."

She rolled her eyes at Badger. "Make me."

He grinned, allowing her to move the conversation to a lighter place. "Challenge accepted."

As soon as the chopper set down in the parking lot of an elementary school—thankfully it was past midnight, and a Saturday—they piled out. She hoped no one was woken up by the noise.

"Your location is half a mile west of here. Let's go." Zander handed her a bulletproof vest, and they jogged as a group.

Soon as they rounded the corner, a gas station came into view. Bridget checked her phone. "Behind the building."

Two of the team members broke off and went around the north side. One headed into the gas station, and she and Zander rounded it to the south. The back alley held an overflowing trash bin and a bike against the wall.

She glanced around. *Where are you?* If Sasha had been attacked, then they'd find a dead body here—either Sasha's or whoever had come after her. Someone would have died in an exchange like that. Sasha lived that kind of life.

Alternatively, Sasha could have triggered the emergency notification just before being kidnapped, and then dropped the phone so that it registered her as still being here. But Bridget didn't see how Sasha would let herself get kidnapped. It just wasn't in her nature to allow something like that, at least not without some bloodshed or evidence of a scuffle. There weren't even any tire marks on the asphalt.

Bridget pinged Sasha's phone. On a normal day, it would light up and play a tune, kind of like the "find my phone" feature on her smartwatch.

She heard the sound.

Zander twisted first. "Over there."

Around the back of that huge, stinky trash bin, the phone lay on the ground. If Bridget's heart hadn't already hit rock bottom, it would have sunk even lower.

"She's not here." Bridget swiped up the phone and turned.

Zander just looked mad.

"Are we even going to find her?"

Before he could answer, Badger waved them to the back door. "Guys!" The others met them there, and all five traipsed inside the building.

The tension in Bridget grew worse as the minutes went on. It was like one of those wild goose chases—though she had no idea what one looked like. Probably a lot like hunting deer, something she didn't remember with too much fondness. It meant extended time spent with her father, who only brought her along because she'd been too young to leave at home alone for five days straight. Instead, she'd had to miss three days of school.

"Hey." Badger nudged her.

She blinked her way free of the memories. "What's going on?"

Zander spoke to the cashier. The man nodded. Zander turned to them and said, "Four guys, blue van. But he doesn't think they left with her, and their whole surveillance system is down but don't tell anyone."

Bridget didn't like the sound of that. Had the attackers known no one would be able to get footage of them?

"There's a blue van parked on the far side of the building." The youngest teammate motioned with one hand.

Bridget hit the door first, pushed the glass, and ran outside. She rounded the corner and saw the van.

"We looked in the front windows, but it's clean and you can't see in the back."

Zander pulled out a lock pick kit. She held out her hand and he actually gave it to her. Bridget swallowed her surprise and worked to get into the back of the van. It took a minute, but she got the back door open.

Zander motioned for her to back up.

She didn't begrudge him taking the lead when there was a possible threat. She might be armed and wearing a bulletproof vest, but they worked so well together they could sometimes make a simultaneous move without even saying anything. Just by reading each other's body language.

The door swung open.

Zander braced at the sight inside. Bridget peered around his massive shoulder and gasped.

Four men inside. All dead. Two had obviously been piled into the van after the fact, loaded on top of each other. The others had been shot where they were.

Sitting with her back to the side wall, Sasha was pale and unconscious and bleeding from her shoulder, just below her collar bone. The blood had soaked into the front of her shirt and down to her lap. A gun lay just beyond her fingers. She'd passed out and let go of it.

"Sasha." Bridget wasn't going to touch her, but she did reach for the gun. Just in case. Her friend's eyes flung open, and Sasha grabbed the weapon. "Easy."

Sasha's gaze flashed with pain. Bridget laid her hand on the top of the gun, along the barrel. Thankfully, Sasha let go without too much prompting.

"Doctor Reece or a hospital?"

Sasha shook her head in the barest of movements. "Zander."

"No. No way." Bridget knew what he would do to cauterize the wound. The man was a barbarian, and she would never let him near a wound of hers. "He's not treating you."

"What?" Zander cut in. "I have field medical training."

"We're not in the field. We have access to proper medical care."

"Fine." Zander laid the back of his hand on Sasha's forehead. "We need to move out. Now."

Badger leaned in. "I'll make an anonymous tip about these guys."

"Do it fast." Zander leaned in and lifted Sasha into his arms. "Why do I always have to save you, huh?"

"Pretty sure I saved myself before you got here."

Zander grunted.

Bridget followed while the others wiped her prints from the lock of the van and closed the door. Badger made his call as they strode down the rear alley and headed for the elementary school at a fast clip.

As they approached the helicopter, Zander turned. "Badge, call the doc. Tell him to meet us at the hangar in twenty minutes. And bring a few pints of A positive."

Bridget pulled open the helicopter door. "You know her blood type?"

"Let's just go." Actual fear moved across his expression. Before she could ask if her friend would be okay, he yelled, "Now!"

18

The address that came over the radio from dispatch directed Aiden and Jess to a ranch on the outskirts of town. Considering everything that had been going on lately—from the suspicious drug overdoses, to Bridget's father's murder, and the man on the loose in town—Sergeant Basuto had ordered them all to double up tonight.

That meant Jess had commandeered the keys to their squad car, and Aiden sat in the passenger seat, continuing his conversation with Sydney, the one that had started before Bridget left to go save her friend.

Though it was more like she'd walked out the door without a single look over her shoulder. Probably what she had done the night she left town, considering the fact she hadn't told him she would never be back.

As they climbed out of their car, the owner made his way down the front steps of the house. The older man gripped a metal railing as he descended.

Aiden reached him first. "You called in that there might be a prowler out back?"

"My grandson installed one of those security camera things. A floodlight comes on when someone sets it off. Might've been one of the barn cats, but he called me and said there was a dark figure on the camera."

Jess drew close to their huddle. "You haven't seen it?"

"I don't have one of them newfangled smart phone thingies. I wouldn't know what to do with it." He pulled a flip phone from his pocket.

"I didn't even know they still made those."

Aiden ignored Jess's comment. "Mind if we look around out back?"

"Knock yourself out. Just watch out for animals." The old man flashed a toothy grin. "The four-legged *and* the two-legged kind."

Before Jess could ask him about two-legged animals, Aiden said, "Great, thanks. We'll knock again before we leave and let you know what we find. If anything."

He led the way between the house and the barn. When he reached the back corner of the home, he stopped and gaped. "Whoa."

"I can see why the need for security," Jess said. "This is a treasure trove of old junk. You know, the kind they pick through on TV shows and discover stuff worth thousands they can buy off the owner and then go on to flip for a huge profit."

"You watch those shows?"

She shrugged as they wandered toward a rusty, old fifties model Ford. "Ellie lives in my house. My sister watches all those shows about old stuff."

"You should ask the homeowner if you can bring her out here to take a look. I bet the history professor could find something interesting."

"I'd rather find the guy everyone is looking for."

Before Aiden could respond to her snide comment about being on the lookout for Clarke, she continued, "Which is an interesting segue into talking about Bridget. How do you guys know each other?"

He snorted. "Interesting segue my foot."

She just about managed to stop herself from asking more questions than that. Aiden shook his head at her antics. He could see the restraint cost her. In a way that made him want to laugh. When she got a bee in her bonnet about something and couldn't find out everything there was to know, it was liable to build in her until she exploded.

"Can we just look around for this prowler?" He glanced at the stuff and saw a lot of old farm equipment piled up. Beyond it, he could see one of those metal trailers, a camper that looked like a bullet, dented from years of being banged around.

That could be the perfect hideout for a person hiding from a town full of cops all looking for them.

He headed for it.

"So you're just going to avoid the whole Bridget thing?"

He said nothing.

"When you're clearly into her, and she's clearly into you, and neither of you is willing to put your egos aside to say something. To the point that she walks out to save her friend and doesn't even ask if you want to help."

"You know I had to work."

"Did she?"

Aiden shrugged. "Who knows? Millie probably told her. You don't know. And besides, she has a lot more serious things to worry about than my feelings."

"I know you did *not* just tell me this girl doesn't need to have care with your emotions. You have Sydney in the mix. Are you going to take that stance when it comes to her?"

"You're assuming that's where it's going when you have no idea, and neither do I. Maybe I knew Bridget a long time ago. We're two completely different people than we were then."

Jess just grunted. That was what she did when she didn't want to admit he had a point.

There was no way he could tell her that Bridget was Sydney's mother. Not when Bridget not only didn't know yet but also thought that her baby had died. If Jessica discovered the truth, she would find a way to make Bridget realize it as well. *Before* Aiden was ready to tell her.

And when he considered the fact there was a man in town looking to hurt people—including Bridget—there was no way he could put Sydney at risk.

Aiden was already concerned over the level of involvement he'd had so far. If things got worse, he'd have to figure out a plan. Like sending Elexa and Sydney to stay with Tate and Savannah on their vacation with Eric and Millie's kids. Sydney would have fun, Elexa would be with her stepdad, and he would have the peace of mind she was safe. So long as Aiden could figure out how to make sure they got there without risk.

But send his child to Hawaii with friends?

Even if she was in danger here, it would still be hard to let her go.

"You think someone is in there?"

He realized he'd stopped in front of the trailer. "It's worth checking out." He pulled his gun and grabbed the handle to swing the door wide, then sidestepped.

Jess entered first. "You called it."

He stepped in behind her. "Clear the place first. Then tell me how I was right."

When they were sure there was no one inside hiding, he turned to look at what she'd seen first. Piles of bandages covered in what looked like dried blood lay in the kitchen sink and on the counter. Pizza boxes. Empty cans of a drink Aiden hadn't touched in years since he decided he didn't need that kind of temptation with a child in the house. In his life. Some people could handle more than he could, but he knew himself and it wasn't worth the risk.

"You think this was that Clarke guy they're all looking for?"

Aiden continued to assess the living area of the old trailer. The couches had no cushions and there was only threadbare carpet where the bed should've been. "If he's been staying here, then he's been sleeping on the floor."

"We've seen worse than this."

"True." He turned again. "There's nothing here that will indicate who it was. Unless we set up a stakeout and wait for him to come back. Which he may never do."

"I'll radio in and see what Basuto wants. Maybe evidence collection to get DNA samples so we can ID who was here."

She wandered outside while Aiden thought over the possibility of this Clarke guy actually going to trial. It had seemed, back at Tate's office, that both Millie and Bridget were perfectly okay with the man targeting them never having to answer for himself in a courtroom.

Whether that meant he ended up in a body bag or somewhere else—like, disappeared altogether—Aiden didn't know what he was supposed to think.

He knew what he was supposed to do as a cop. The question was what he was supposed to do as Sydney's father and the man who couldn't let the idea of her mother go.

Bridget needed to know her child was alive, and that he had raised her this whole time. That he was fully committed to continuing to do that. The fact she could take him to court and demand restitution for the wrong done to her, even though it hadn't been his fault, worried him. A sympathetic mother who had missed six years of her child's life through no fault of her own, who was desperate to raise her now, would likely win considerably in a custody battle.

He could be completely selfish and never tell her, but that would make him no better than whoever did this to her. He might get what he wanted. Only, through that, everyone else would lose. And in the end, he would realize he'd lost as well.

It was absolutely not the right time to tell her. But he would.

As soon as he was able.

"I got a bag from the car. Basuto says get the evidence we need and get back to the office. We're supposed to sit down with the feds and go over everything. Eric is going to get caught up to speed later."

After Aiden and Jess made sure there was no one hiding anywhere else in the old man's backyard, they chatted with him for a few minutes and then headed back to the station house via the gas station to grab coffee and snacks.

By the time they walked in, the place was in full nighttime mode, with only a few people on the premises. Most of whom were gathered with Conroy and Basuto in Conroy's office.

Conroy waved them in. Aiden deposited the majority of his snacks onto an empty desk and took his coffee with him into the room.

"Donaldson and Ridgeman—" Conroy indicated which of them was which. "—these are Special Agents Nicholson and Turner from the Denver FBI field office. They are working with Homeland and the Marshals in a joint task force, looking closely at the Capeira family. Or, what's left of it."

Aiden and Jess shook the hands of the agents. He opted to lean against the wall while she sat.

Nicholson was around forties and female, with dark features and a dark complexion, while Turner was at least a decade younger and probably had a side career as a heavyweight champion. If the FBI allowed that kind of thing.

Nicholson turned her attention to Aiden as he sipped his coffee. "Benito Capeira has been on our radar for almost two years. Now I hear through the grapevine that you might know who killed him, handing over his empire to his younger brother."

"You heard he's dead, or you found a body?"

"We have a DEA agent in Venezuela on the taskforce. I'm sure you understand that's a dangerous position to be in. Still, he took the time to inform us Benito's body turned up."

"So he's dead. For sure."

"Which means Enrico inherits everything legitimate and illegitimate." Nicholson eyed him. "Or, at least, he would if he was anywhere to be found." She stared him down for a full second, all that federal authority on her face. "Do you know who killed Benito?"

"On official record?" Aiden didn't know if they were recording the conversation in here, or if the plan was to possibly subpoena him later. He needed a life with less complication. Not one where he could be called on to testify against the mother of his child.

Added to that, he had no idea who the second woman was. All he could give Nicholson would be considered hearsay.

"Humor me."

Aiden said, "No offense, but I barely know who you are, let alone any of these guys you're talking about." It wasn't a good excuse, pleading ignorance. But he was going to go with it since it was hard to argue without insulting his own intelligence. "So, I'm sure you understand I can hardly speak to this with any level of authority."

Conroy shifted in his seat. "And your friend?"

Nicholson said, "I'd like to talk to her."

Aiden didn't take his gaze from Nicholson. He knew it was unlikely Bridget would voluntarily surrender herself for questioning. Even if she'd done nothing wrong, she wouldn't risk getting tied up in something formal that exposed her to official record.

He didn't shift out of his purposefully lazy stance, though it was getting harder to hold. "That's up to her. Last I knew, she left town to go do something."

"So tell me where to find her."

"I have no idea where she is at present." That was true enough.

Nicholson twisted to Conroy but said nothing. Aiden couldn't see her face. Whatever happened there resulted in a shrug from the chief. "Officer Donaldson has been forthcoming."

Nicholson let go a tiny snort.

"If, or when I'm able to tell you more, I'll do that. Right

now, I have nothing more to say." Aiden nodded to Conroy and strode out to his desk.

Too many people in a small space made him antsy. Sydney might be a whirlwind sometimes. Eventually she crashed and he'd usually get some peace and quiet. Both were enjoyable—peace and quiet—but when he needed to think something through, it took space.

Jess followed but didn't strike up a conversation. She logged onto her computer while he drank his coffee and stared at the front door of the police station.

He needed to do right by Bridget, someone who hadn't had many people in her life treat her that way—except for the people she worked with now. Over the past few years, she'd found a family of sorts. When she showed up here a short couple of days ago, he'd thought of her as his ticket to final redemption. A way to truly make amends for all his bad decisions by giving her what she should have had all along.

The family that'd been taken from her.

Even being a cop hadn't given him that deep sense of satisfaction. Saving lives. Taking down West, or the Founders. None of it had filled the void in him.

Then Bridget ran in front of his police car, and everything changed.

Making up for hitting her had come first. Then the realization she could use his help. Then the bomb had dropped. She didn't know about Sydney. Things had gone from bizarre to downright crazy in a matter of days, and he'd been trying to find redemption through helping Bridget get what she was after, or rather, what she needed.

What if he could do one better and make it so she wasn't involved, while the FBI still got their result?

If he could find Capeira, he could turn the guy over to the feds and Bridget wouldn't have to be put at risk. Aiden would finally do something that had a more widespread effect for good than catching vandals or writing speeding tickets. Sure, he'd saved lives before, but this would be so much bigger.

"I'm not sure I like that look on your face."

He glanced at Jess.

"I'm seeing trouble on the horizon."

"You like trouble," he pointed out. "You jump right in the middle of it and work full speed for what you want."

"To get Clarke and save Bridget?"

"Not just that."

"You want to take down Capeira as well?" Jess smiled. "I'm in."

19

"I can't believe you asked Zander to just cauterize it." Bridget turned into the townhome complex and glanced at Sasha in the passenger seat.

Her face had a little more color, but not much. They'd met up with Zander's doctor in the hangar, and the office had become a treatment room. Sasha had been stitched up and given a prescription. Bridget was supposed to watch for signs of infection, like a fever. Bullets were dirty and one had traveled through Sasha's shoulder, out the back, and into the wall of the van.

It had been removed by one of Zander's guys when the van was "cleaned," so that no physical evidence of Sasha's presence was left behind.

Bridget pulled into the garage while her friend's lips curled up at the corners.

"Tell me you're not serious."

"I wasn't delirious. I knew what I was saying."

Bridget opened her mouth to speak. Instead, she shoved the lever into Park and shut the car off, trying to figure out why on earth her friend would want that instead of real medical care.

This wasn't a war zone—something she was seriously thankful for.

As the garage door rolled down, a dark figure ducked under it, causing a stutter. The light overhead flashed. Bridget reached under her arm and snatched up her gun from its holster before she realized it was Zander.

He pulled the door on Sasha's side open and leaned in to stab at the button of her seatbelt with one finger. "Come on. Let's get you settled."

Bridget stared.

"I didn't get shot in the legs." Before anyone could comment on that, Sasha said, "You followed us?"

Strategically changing the subject away from things Zander had no doubt seen in war. Though, he'd probably seen a lot worse than double leg injuries. Sasha too.

Bridget's hair-raising experiences were few and far between —a good thing considering she occasionally didn't react so well to blood. Traumatic memories rose at will—the same ones that had kept her from ever giving serious consideration to joining the CIA. She'd thanked God after Benito died, which of course the client thought was bizarre.

But she wasn't thanking Him that Capeira had died. Or that she'd survived. Just that her memories hadn't sent her hurtling back to the trauma of all she'd seen. By all rights, Bridget should be a basket case in any intense situation—especially ones involving blood. Right now, she was overly tired and everything was much too close to the surface.

She'd stayed outside the office while the doctor saw to Sasha, and leaned against the wall with her eyes closed. Images of those guys, piled up in the van, swam in her mind. She didn't like anyone making compensations for her shortcomings. But the truth was, when it hit…it was bad.

"You think I'd let you go without protection, Sash? I thought you knew me better than that." Zander reached in and lifted her out.

Bridget had to wonder if that was a commentary pertaining to her ability to care for someone when there could be blood involved. Before she could mention it, Sasha let out a cry. She wasn't able to hold back the moan as he jostled her.

"So you didn't take a pill, then." He started for the door. "Because if you had, you'd probably be passed out right now. Resting, instead of in pain."

Bridget got there first and opened it for him, moving into the hall so she could hold the door for the two.

Zander gave her a small smile, but he didn't look grateful. Instead he looked like he wanted to punch a hole in the wall—or tear someone's head off.

Had something happened? Bridget looked hard at Zander. "What is it?"

Zander ignored her question and strode in. "Let's get you settled, Sasha. Then we can talk."

"Uh-oh."

Bridget figured Sasha's assessment wasn't far off the mark. "Talk" sounded ominous the way he'd said it. "I'll check in with Millie."

"Don't leave me with him, Bridge!" Sasha would've said more. Normally. It was a testament to how much pain she was in that she stopped there.

"I'm not going anywhere."

Instead of calling, she sent Millie a text to let her know they were at the safe house. Not that she was going to tell Sasha that's what it was. The woman would walk out the front door if she thought they were trying to protect her—as though that was an assessment of whether she could protect herself. Which, of course, was a valid question, considering she had stitches and her arm in a sling.

But those men hadn't taken her.

Zander laid Sasha on the couch. She immediately sat up and frowned at him as she leaned against the back of the couch.

Getting mad was preferable to acknowledging pain. Everyone knew that.

He folded his arms, standing like a glacier in the middle of the room. You could cut the tension in the room with a knife.

Bridget didn't want to get in the middle of the two of them—and whatever was going on between them—so she headed for the kitchen to make coffee. It was nearly breakfast anyway, so what did it matter they hadn't had any sleep? She planned on taking a nap right after Clarke was taken care of.

"You're just gonna abandon me?!" Sasha called after her.

Bridget smiled at the can of coffee grounds. "You're a big girl, Sash. Time to face the music."

"Hey, I took care of those guys by myself."

Bridget wanted to hear that story. But before she could ask for it, Zander spoke, "I'm glad you mentioned them, because I had my guy do some digging and all four had ties to the Capeira cartel. Care to share why they might be targeting you?"

As if he didn't know. Or at least, he should be able to connect all the dots. But she knew what he was asking.

She just didn't know why he was so up in arms about Sasha getting hurt. Were there feelings between her two friends she didn't know about?

"Spill, Sasha." He didn't move a single muscle. "Why did they come after you?"

"Ugh. Fine." Her friend sounded drained, though she attempted to keep that from bleeding into her tone. It still did, and Bridget figured Zander heard it too. Sasha huffed. "I put the word out that I was headed to meet up with Bridget."

"You *what*?!"

Bridget winced at Zander's roar and pressed the button on the coffee pot. After it came to life, she headed back to the living room where Zander and Sasha glared at each other. Definitely feelings. Neither kept the truth completely out of their expressions. They liked each other, that was now obvious, but now they were at definite odds.

Bridget tried to be the voice of reason. "You put yourself out there as bait?"

Sasha didn't respond to either her comment or Zander's, she only shut her eyes. "I spotted the tail shortly after. When I never met up with Bridget, they decided to grab me at the next stop. But Enrico wasn't with them. They were gonna torture me into telling them where Bridget was so they could inform the boss, and then they were gonna dump my body. Probably in the desert. Somewhere only the birds know about."

Zander said nothing. On his face was written plenty, though Sasha didn't seem to notice. He was furious.

Bridget walked to the window and looked out at the same spot she'd first seen two members of that family, thereby finding the peace she was after. This was her life. Trauma notwithstanding, these were her people. The kind who provoked a dangerous group into targeting them.

"I knew they'd have to put me in the van, so I played along when two grabbed me. The others were inside. I waited 'til they thought I was subdued and so shut the door, then I pulled my gun from my ankle holster and shot them all. One got off a shot and then landed on me, so I shoved him onto the other guy."

Bridget stared into the street. The rear garages, an alley between. All in a row. *Crack.* The sound of a shot fired reverberated through her and she flinched. It was only in her mind. Her gunshot wound, the graze on her outer arm, hurt. She covered her sleeve, under which was the bandage.

Clarke had shot her. Even if he hadn't shot to kill, he had probably intentionally wounded her so he could take her. He had treated her like a trophy animal for his collection.

"You forgot the part where you were shot." Zander's hard tone rumbled over the sound of coffee percolating.

Bridget inhaled espresso-laced air. The calming scent that always seemed to make everything better.

"I wanted to draw him out." Sasha huffed. "What else was I

going to do? You got their phones from the van, right? Call Enrico yourself. Take him down."

Zander still didn't move even one muscle. "I'll hand whatever information I obtain over to the authorities. They're the ones who are going to take down Enrico."

"Et tu, Brutus?"

Zander didn't even raise an eyebrow. "That's not how it goes."

"You think I don't know that, *Brute*?" Sasha raised hers. "I was being facetious. Do you even know what that means?"

"*Nooo.*" Zander drawled the word out in a sarcastic tone.

Bridget's lips curled up. These two were incorrigible.

"But you did get the phones." That was Sasha.

Zander came back. "My guy is taking care of it."

Bridget turned back to the window to watch a huge, tan-colored dog wander around the corner of the end townhouse. No leash. She couldn't make out the breed from this distance, but it seemed to be all alone. Like someone had let their dog out, not realizing it was out running loose. The dog looked so much like her dog, Butch, that she became homesick for him.

"So we have leads we didn't have before." Sasha was determined. "Thanks to me."

"You got yourself shot."

"Psh. You're gonna tell me a shot to the shoulder would even slow you down?"

"It's not me that got shot." It sounded like Zander was moving around. Bridget heard a cupboard close and mugs being set on the counter. "So that point is moot."

Bridget twisted to her friend, interrupting. "Do you need anything? Food? Medicine?"

Sasha lifted one hand and signed, using the other in her sling as best she could. Bridget wasn't as well versed in sign language. Sasha had taught her enough she got the gist—most of which was her unique way of expressing concepts and definitely not any kind of official use of the language, apart from the basic phrasings most people knew.

Bridget shook her head and mouthed, "No." She wasn't going to get rid of Zander when he might be able to talk some sense into the woman.

You're taking his side?

"Not likely. Considering I'd have done exactly the same thing." Bridget sat on the arm of the recliner. "And you're right, we've got leads we didn't have before. Though, I'm more concerned about Clarke and what he has planned than about you purposely drawing out Capeira. By yourself."

"So you agree with him."

Bridget shook her head. "It's not that simple. And I'm not an operator like you."

"Yet you took out Benito."

Bridget pressed her lips together. "You know what I mean."

Sasha stared at her. "Tell me right now."

Even Zander quit pouring coffee and came over. "Bridget?"

Great. She was never getting out from under their scrutiny. Not until she spilled. "He was attacking—" She nearly said the woman's name. "—the *client*. I killed him."

Sasha cut her off. "Explain better than that."

"I don't—"

Zander interrupted. "Start from the beginning."

Bridget didn't want to do that. With all the blood she'd seen recently, bringing up additional memories wasn't going to help anyone. It would only make things worse, and she would be on edge instead of focused on their problem.

There was a scratch at the door to the garage. Bridget started for it, but was called back by Sasha's yelling, "Don't make me get up and drag you back in here."

Bridget turned. "What?"

"Time to talk."

"I was helping the client pack."

She closed her eyes and imagined the scene. She'd been in the bedroom, gathering clothing from the closet and stuffing it into a suitcase so they could get out of there. The residence had been compromised. Instead of dropping off a new packet with a fresh ID, she'd found herself facilitating a getaway.

"Bedroom?"

Bridget nodded.

"So he came in but you didn't know until things kicked off."

A sick feeling welled in her stomach. She swallowed it back down and stared at the carpet. "This isn't about me. You're the one who's had a rough day." She didn't like being the one they had to baby. Not when they were both elite as far as operations were concerned. Bridget felt like a rookie compared to them.

"Talk," Sasha ordered. "I need a distraction from my rough day."

"He was on top of her, pulling at her shirt."

"If he wasn't already dead, I'd kill him myself."

Zander nodded. "I'd help."

Bridget wanted to smile, but all she could see was the scene in her mind. "I pulled my gun and pointed it at the back of his head."

"And pulled the trigger," Zander finished for her.

Bridget managed to nod.

"So you sprayed blood all over her." Sasha shrugged her healthy shoulder. "I'm guessing she was grateful you saved her."

"You should stop now." Zander stared down Bridget. "She looks sick."

The scratch at the door happened again. She jerked in her seat and twisted toward the door. She didn't need to respond to Zander's comment, even if he was right. The last thing she needed was to talk more about this.

"You saved her. You killed him."

Bridget sighed. "And now his brother is coming after me, Sash."

"Which exposed Clarke for the true slime he really is. Something we'd have never known otherwise." Sasha sighed. "I should change my bandage. It's seeping."

Bridget still had had to help the client out from under the man she'd killed. The woman she'd sprayed with Benito's blood and brains. She'd been slick with it…she stopped.

There was that scratching again, louder this time.

If there was ever a time the notion "saved by the bell" came in handy, it was now. She headed to the door.

Zander called out, "Hey, wait…"

The second she opened the door, the loose dog she'd just seen bounded in. Bridget gasped. *Distraction achieved.* She crouched. "Butch!"

He bounded onto her knees and licked her in the face.

Bridget laughed. "So it *was* you—you big rascal!"

The door behind him opened. "Excuse me—" Aiden stepped in. "Butch." Relief and frustration warred on his face.

She glanced up. "You had him?"

"He was…let out accidentally. I saw him come in your garage."

Back in the living room, Sasha muttered a few words. Zander headed back there, leaving Bridget alone with Aiden.

"You found your friend?"

She nodded and stood before Butch could lick off every scrap of makeup she had left. The dog trotted around her, off to explore.

Bridget followed him.

Sasha had unbuttoned the shirt she wore, exposing her shoulder and the stitched-up wound. Bridget could smell the blood—mixed with the antiseptic and iodine the doctor had used.

Zander peeled open fresh gauze.

Bridget heard the tearing sound. She stared at the blood and got lightheaded. Aiden bumped into her. Or maybe he grabbed her as she stumbled back, swaying into him. She didn't know which it was.

Everything came tumbling back, and her legs gave out.

"Whoa. I got you." Aiden shifted her, and she felt his warmth. The strength in his arms. Until he froze, nearly solid behind her. "You."

20

Aiden had two problems. First, Bridget's collapse into his arms and making sure she was okay, and second, the woman on the couch. He trained his gaze on her. "What did you do to her?"

"Me?" Yeah, she pretended to be totally innocent. He knew better.

Bridget stirred, her breath coming hard. "She didn't…"

He waited for her to say more, but she had trailed off. Aiden helped her up since they were essentially on the floor with his leg bent at a weird angle. He didn't let go of Bridget's elbows. "What happened?"

"She has issues with blood."

He shot a look at the woman on the couch. "I'll deal with you in a minute."

"Hold up—" That was the big man present.

Sasha huffed. She muttered something under her breath that sounded like, "You can try." Only, at that moment, Bridget turned in his arms and he found himself looking into her eyes, those long lashes blinking. "She didn't do anything."

"I assume you're referring to this moment?"

Bridget wasn't part of this, was she? Was this some kind of

conspiracy? He shoved the thoughts away to revisit them later. He was going to ask *all the questions* and demand the woman on the couch explain herself. But for now, Bridget needed him. "Are you okay?"

"I need a minute." She stepped away from him and moved on unsteady legs toward the hall and the bathroom or bedrooms beyond. Aiden stood up to go after her but stopped as she held out a hand to the man standing by the breakfast bar. His arms, once crossed over his huge chest, reached out to steady her by clasping her forearm with his. Aiden had seen him in town before, so he was obviously a local.

The man held her steady for a second longer as she passed. "Okay?"

She nodded, not stopping. Butch padded after her. He sniffed at the knee of the other man's cargo pants. "Sit."

The dog carried on down the hall, following Bridget.

"Huh." The man said, "Sasha, you know this guy?"

The woman on the couch turned and looked at the window. "It was going to come out, eventually."

The man turned to him next. "Donaldson, right?"

"Aiden." He nodded as the man strode to him.

"Zander." They shook.

"Right." Aiden had seen his photo at Ted's house. "Explains a lot. But not everything."

"What's going on?"

Aiden turned to the woman. "Your name is Sasha?"

She glanced at him. Unremorseful. Determined not to break.

"Funny. That's not what you told me when you came to see me six years ago." He took a breath, hardly able to process the truth. "You told me you worked for *child services*."

Aiden couldn't believe it. He wanted it to come out, but not like this. Not when Sydney was on the couch across the alley, watching her favorite show. He'd been out looking for the dog so she wouldn't worry about Butch. Keeping Butch in the backyard was proving to be a full-time job by itself. Had the dog been trying to get to Bridget the whole time? Once out, he'd come straight here.

Zander said, "Child services, Sash?"

She had the decency to shift on the couch. Aiden realized she wore a sling. She'd been injured.

He didn't let that soften him. "Does Bridget even know?"

Sasha glared at him. Before she could say anything, Bridget reentered the living room with Butch right behind her. She pulled out a breakfast bar stool and sat while the dog laid down at her feet.

Guess he knew whose dog it was now. Unfortunately, he was going to have to break that news to Sydney.

"What's going on?" Bridget glanced around.

Sasha didn't answer her. She was looking at Aiden. "Did I do the wrong thing?"

"Is this about my freak out?" Bridget chuckled, but it sounded hollow. "I have a problem with blood, okay? I can handle it most of the time. Until I'm exhausted and one too many memories creep back in." She looked nervous.

"This isn't about that." He sent her a soft smile. She was a trained operative who didn't like blood?

Zander leaned his hips back against the breakfast bar. "You knew about this, Sasha?"

The woman on the couch shot him a look.

"You should be more careful with your friend." Zander then motioned in Aiden's direction with a wave of his hand. "Now tell us the rest of what's going on."

Bridget glanced between them, a frown emerging on her forehead.

"I did the right thing."

Aiden pressed his lips together. Sasha was going to keep thinking that? Convincing herself it wasn't a serious violation of whatever relationship she and Bridget had. Unless it was spiteful. And yet, she'd done Aiden the best favor he could've asked for.

Sasha pushed at the material of her pants and shifted it over her bent knee. "The right thing for everyone." She glared at Aiden.

"Sasha." Bridget shook her head. "What?"

She said nothing. Aiden wasn't about to let her get away with that. "Tell her how you lied. Tell her how you betrayed her."

"Betrayed?" Sasha shot off the couch to stand. "I did what she wanted! What was best for all of you!"

He couldn't look at Bridget. He'd need to eventually. In the aftermath, he would be there for her. He'd have to figure out how to navigate this in the middle of everything else. And take care of Sydney.

"What is he talking about, Sasha?" Bridget's expression turned cautious. Because she knew what her friend was capable of? "What was best for everyone?"

Aiden folded his arms. "Six years ago, Sasha here knocked on my door." He didn't even know how to say it. Bridget was going to be *devastated.*

"I protected her!" Sasha yelled. "Did I do the wrong thing? She's safe, right? She'll continue to be safe, regardless of what happens with Clarke or Capeira. I protected her. *Both of them.*"

Bridget said, "What did you do?"

"That guy was dogging you."

"Six years ago." Bridget nodded. "So the fire chief?"

Aiden twisted to Bridget. "This is still about him?"

The fire chief was dead. He'd been killed a couple of months ago after he'd tried to hurt Jess and Ted. He'd been a definite bad guy. One of the town founders.

"I saw him kill a woman." Bridget swallowed and her face paled. "Before I left town. It was..." She shook her head. "I went home and told my dad what I saw. He said to keep my mouth shut. When I tried to walk out and go report it to the police, he…"

Aiden knew exactly what her dad would've done. "Beat you." He said the words carefully. Quietly. Thomas was dead as of only days ago. Aiden couldn't find justice.

Bridget nodded. "He left. Before he came back, I got a bag and started walking. I was on the highway, headed to your house, when Millie found me. I was about ready to pass out."

"But why did you leave with Millie?" Aiden was trying to follow.

"The fire chief sent some men after me. My dad must have told him because we were being pursued. The car was shot at."

"Exactly!"

They all spun to look at Sasha.

"I did the right thing. It was too dangerous."

Aiden stared at Sasha. "You didn't know she was pregnant until after that."

Sasha lifted her chin.

Bridget glanced between them. "What does this have to do with my baby?"

Aiden waited, but Sasha didn't cave. He wanted to say it. Finally get everything out there. Instead, he said, "What happened with the fire chief?"

"We faked my death. He backed off, and I never came back." Bridget paused. "He'd have hurt everyone I cared about. None of us would've been safe."

Aiden closed his eyes.

"There's more isn't there?" Bridget asked. "Why do you two know each other? Why did she knock on your door?"

He opened his eyes and nodded. "Sasha wasn't alone. She—"

Aiden's phone rang. Knowing Sydney was alone across the way, he had to answer it. He swiped his thumb across the screen and lifted it to his ear. "Yeah, babe?"

He realized what he'd said when Bridget stiffened. She moved to go somewhere, but Zander touched her shoulder.

Sydney was on the other end of the call. "Dad. My show finished. Can I watch the next one?"

"Yes. I'll be home soon, okay? Just sit tight."

"Did you find Butch?"

"Yes."

"Can I have a cookie?"

Aiden smiled to himself. All was right in the world, so it was time for a cookie. "Yeah. Save one for me, okay?"

"Okay, Daddy. I love you, bye."

"You, too. Bye." He lowered the phone.

Sasha still didn't back down. "Tell me now that I did the wrong thing."

"Someone had better explain."

Beside Bridget, Zander's jaw flexed. "I'm thinking that's a good idea. I wanna hear firsthand from Sasha what she did."

Sasha shot him a look.

"Now." Zander's tone invited no argument.

"Fine." Sasha didn't manage to hide the hurt from her face as she turned to Bridget. "He was sending people after you. Looking for you. You were pregnant, but you wanted to be part of the accountant's office. We were going to train you. How, with a baby, I have no idea."

Bridget frowned.

"You had so many doubts. How you were going to take care of her. What your life would be like. That was all you wanted to talk about." Sasha shifted her stance, winced, and touched her elbow in the sling. "Until the bathroom."

Bridget winced, remembering. "I told you I didn't want the baby. That I didn't want to have any part of Aiden, and I wanted a clean break. To build a life of my own, by myself." She sucked in a breath and blew it out. "I know it didn't—it couldn't have—but it always felt like maybe I caused what happened. That I willed my baby to die because I said I didn't want her."

Aiden's vision blurred with tears. "You let her carry that for six years, Sasha. Since the day her baby was born. What kind of friend does that?"

Bridget held out a hand to her friend. "I'm sorry you had to be the one to see it happen."

Sasha's face fell. She didn't take the hand. "Bridge."

"No." Aiden pointed his index finger at her. "You did this." He wanted to throttle her for all the destruction she'd caused, so he stayed where he was and worked to get his anger under control. "You made her believe she caused her baby to die. *All this time.*"

"She got the life she wanted."

Aiden said nothing.

"She's been good. Moving on. Happy. Right?"

Zander shifted.

Bridget covered her mouth. "Sasha." Her hand dropped. "What did you do?"

Aiden needed this done. "Sasha showed up at my house. Me, an eighteen-year-old kid doing construction, living in a one-bedroom apartment. She had a baby with her."

Zander's arms slid around Bridget.

"She told me you were dead. Which, I suppose, was the story she was going with all the way around." A tear let loose and rolled down his cheek. "Told me that if I didn't take the baby, she would wind up in foster care."

Zander caught Bridget before she hit the floor.

"I set you up."

"You think I care that you handed me fifty thousand dollars and a *child.* My child. The one I made with Bridget."

Sasha waved her arm at the window. "Seems like you've enjoyed the fruits of it."

"The money is in a trust. For Sydney. Because I thought her mother was *dead,* so I figured she might want something to remember her by. Like college paid for, or a down payment on her first house. Not guilt money because you *lied.* To both of us."

"She's alive." Bridget whispered the words.

Behind Bridget, Zander glared at Sasha. "Are you serious?"

"It was a dangerous time. That kid would be in danger even now if it wasn't for me. She could've been killed!" Sasha's expression turned desperate.

Bridget let out a deep sob. Her face crumpled.

Zander didn't let go of her. "You're the one who took her family from her."

Sasha stared at the two of them.

Before she could make more excuses, Aiden said, "You did this."

Bridget had Zander help her to her feet.

Sasha's face reddened. "It was too dangerous for a child. You'd have had to go into hiding, and you'd have been all alone."

"So you tore everything apart. All so Bridget could be who you thought she should be." Aiden swiped the moisture from his face.

"Get out."

"Bridge—"

"Get. Out."

Zander looked mad enough to spit fire. "Sasha. You need to go."

Aiden didn't know what would happen next but he prayed. He *prayed* that God would make something beautiful out of the ashes of what their lives should've been.

Bridget had missed so much.

Sydney's life had a hole in it that only her mother could fill.

"You stole her mother from her. Lied to all of us. Took from us." Aiden could go on, but it would be redundant. She knew what she'd done.

Bridget lifted her chin. "Get out, Sasha. I never want to see you again."

Sasha strode to the door and walked out. As though dismissing them, though she had nothing with her but a sling.

The other man in the room glared at the door. "I should go too. Let you guys talk." Zander gave Bridget a hug. He whispered something in her ear, and she nodded. Then he was gone.

And they were alone.

"Bridget." Her name was a moan.

He needed to get back to Sydney. Aiden didn't like leaving her alone normally, let alone when there was a dangerous man in town. Was she going to come with him? They should go slow. Meet each other. Not overload Sydney with the sudden news her mother wasn't dead, an angel in heaven.

How were they going to do this?

"You should go, too."

Aiden frowned. "Bridget—"

"I need to think." She looked haggard. Destroyed, the way life had left her. Struggling to put the pieces back together. "Clarke…"

She'd been through so much. It was unlikely to get better without things getting worse first. Things were seriously complicated. The road ahead would be rough going, but they would walk it.

Together.

"Do you want to meet her?" He motioned to the window.

Bridget glanced in the same direction, and he saw tears swimming. "Sasha was right about one thing."

"No. She wasn't."

Bridget shook her head. "She's not safe with me." Then she turned to him. "Clarke. Capeira. I can't be in her life." She gasped a breath. "What is her name?"

"Sydney."

Bridget's face softened into the smallest of smiles, probably at the mention of the name she'd put on the birth—and death—certificate. Just a second, and then it was gone. "I can't see her. I won't put her in danger."

"Bridge—"

"You need to leave, Aiden." Her expression blanked, and

she glanced at him. Her eyes might as well have been dead. “Just go.”

“This isn’t done.” She deserved a relationship with her daughter. Both of them did. They could even be a family if that was what she wanted.

Anything to heal that pain on her face.

Tears rolled down her cheeks. “Please, just go.”

21

The front door closed behind him, and Bridget almost sagged onto the floor. She pressed her palm against the wall instead, breathing hard.

Sasha. She was so angry.

Sydney. My baby.

Bridget had so many emotions rolling through her, she didn't know what to do.

Butch stood at the opening to the living room. Not aggressive in his stance, just alert in the way dogs were when they knew everything wasn't all right.

She patted his head as she passed. Still unable to speak, even to reassure him. It wouldn't be true.

She wasn't okay.

Bridget pushed away every thought as it tried to enter her mind. Taking it captive and dismissing it until she was ready to process. It had taken a long time to master the skill of keeping her mind free of errant thoughts, but she used it now when everything in her wanted to fall apart. To rage. Scream. Ugly cry. Scream some more. Lay in the fetal position—which just made her have to force away thoughts about babies.

Sasha.

She'd forced Sasha out of the townhouse, but she should have killed her friend instead. It was the only reason she'd kicked her out. Bridget had been mad enough she could've done it.

Bridget stumbled across the living room to try and catch a glimpse of Aiden before he moved out of sight. Into his house. *Her* house. That little girl. She was Sydney. A six-year-old girl he called, "Babe." One who made him smile like that? Bridget would have loved her already, just for that, even if the child wasn't hers. But she was.

Her child.

Her baby.

Nearly seven years, stolen from her…so she could have this? Blood. Pain. Fear. The tools to be the person she should've been. A life outside Last Chance, not stuck here where the threat was real.

But the fire chief had died.

That threat was over.

Now there was a new one, and she couldn't afford to let down her guard. Not when even a second of distraction meant Clarke, or Capeira, showed up and took her. Or took her out.

Aiden had his phone to his ear as he strode to the garage door of his townhouse, across the way, confirming her suspicions that he was the man she'd seen that one day with the little girl. Living their normal lives.

Until she drove back into town and tore it all apart. Or flipped it upside down. Which was the better of the two scenarios. Either way meant irrevocable change, and there would be no going back.

He glanced over his shoulder, back toward the window she was standing at, still on his phone. Bridget realized he could see her. He even lifted his hand to wave.

The garage door rolled up.

Butch padded over and sat, leaning against her leg. She touched the top of his head for support while the lump grew in her throat and bands that felt like steel tightened around her chest until she could barely breathe.

A little girl in leggings and a T-shirt bounded out, barefoot. Red hair flew behind her in a mass of curls that was probably a nightmare to tame.

The first sob emerged from her throat.

Butch whined, and she watched Aiden lift the girl into his arms. He held her up, and they spoke with their faces close. She loved him. Aiden was her family—and she was safe with him.

In a way she would never be with Bridget.

The first tears fell then. Even though she was overjoyed and so grateful Aiden had given her this gift, she turned and sagged onto the floor beside Butch. Bridget grasped handfuls of his fur while great sobs wracked her body. Until she could barely breathe and bile rose in her throat.

Bridget didn't care.

She had missed that little wonder's whole life so far. Nothing would get that back. Time had been stolen from them, and it would continue to be—until the threat was gone.

If it was *ever* gone.

Minutes later, she vaguely came aware of a knock at the door. Bridget didn't move. She had no strength. She felt as though someone had shattered her, leaving her destroyed on the floor of this living room. No one. Nowhere to go. Nothing to do but just get on with life.

And how could she, when there was a little girl across the alley with her hair. That leggy build she'd hated so much when she'd shot up in seventh grade, suddenly taller than all the boys.

"Bridge." Millie practically flew across the room.

Butch lifted his head and growled at the intruder.

Bridget didn't have the strength to even tell him, "No." She couldn't lift her head when Millie settled beside her. She could only lay there with her cheek pressed to the floor.

Someone else was in the room. Butch actually lifted his front from the floor, up into a sit. She had to let go, and the sudden absence of the dog's fir between her fingers felt like a scab ripped from a wound.

She cried out.

"Millie." It was a man, his voice more than a moan, but not by much.

"I know." Millie ran her hand over Bridget's hair, from her forehead to behind her ear. "She wasn't even like this when I found her on the highway." Millie shifted closer and spoke quietly. "Bridget, what happened?"

She inhaled to gather the words. Her entire face crumpled, and Bridget rolled so her nose was smashed into the carpet and her body curled further in on itself.

"It must have been Clarke. But this… Why did Sasha tell us to come over if she's not here?"

"I don't know, Mill." Eric's boots squeaked as he crouched, and the movement caused a hiss of pain. "Stupid gunshot wound."

"Go sit down, then."

"You think I'm not here to help, just like you are?"

Bridget squeezed her eyes shut.

Millie petted her hair again and kept doing it. Imparting strength into Bridget when she had none left. She had nothing.

But she found the strength to say enough that Millie understood. "Sasha…" Neither said anything as she explained. When she was done, there was total silence.

Then Eric said, "I'll go talk to him."

Millie shifted. Her hands slid under Bridget's waist and her shoulders. "Okay, here we go." She sounded like she was trying to coax a feral cat from under a bed.

Bridget wanted to laugh, but her face wasn't working. She sighed, and it emerged as a series of sobs.

"I know." Millie sounded like she was holding back. Bridget heard the strain and spoke up. "I'm going to kill Sasha." Millie leaned Bridget back against the wall.

Her body kind of sagged.

"We're going to fix this. I know it seems like it will never be okay, but that's a lie."

Bridget started to shake her head.

"It is. Listen to me. Sasha did the wrong thing. I also want to stab her for what she did, and it might make us feel better for a second. But in the end, it would be a bad choice."

Bridget pushed away thoughts of Benito Capeira that wanted to fill her mind. She didn't need to be attacked by the same bout of lightheadedness that she got when she first saw Sasha's wound, so she focused instead on Millie.

"There's a lot here, but we'll work through it. All right?"

Bridget still said nothing.

"I saw the baby. She looked...gray. After Sasha took her out of the room, I went with her. Because you were so distressed. She actually did stop breathing." Millie swallowed. She looked uncertain. "You screamed, so I ran back to you. I had to choose. I thought the baby was good with Sasha. I had no idea she would do something like this."

Bridget lowered her head and touched her friend's shoulder with her forehead.

"I wonder, did she plan it, or did she react in the moment? Trying to free you from having to care for a baby. It's a big thing, and she had no right. But maybe she just made a really, really, astronomically-bad judgment call. I'm not excusing it, but there has to be an explanation."

Bridget wanted to be sick.

Millie was all about managing the fallout. It was what made her such a good boss—the way she always knew how to control any kind of breach. To mitigate pain for the client. At the same time, she managed to neutralize the threat, whether through misdirection or having the client simply...disappear.

Often for a second, or third, time.

Sasha? She'd always been a wild card, but this? Bridget would never forgive her. She lifted her head. "She was supposed to be my friend."

Millie's expression softened. "It's possible that she thought this was her way of being exactly that for you. I hate what she did, but people can convince themselves of all sorts of things under duress."

"You think she was coerced into it?" Had Clarke worked to undermine them, even back then? He hadn't been hired on until later. But it was possible. Just the thought made her even more fatigued than the already drained feeling she was battling.

Millie tipped her head to the side. "I want Ted to look into Sasha and find out what else she might have done. With the FBI on board, and the police here in Last Chance, I have plenty of help. You can just concentrate on Aiden, and working things out with him."

Before Bridget could respond, Millie continued, "I knew he had a daughter and that she was young, but I never expected this. It's unbelievable that Sasha took the baby from you *alive.*"

Bridget swiped at the tears on her face. That was about all the movement she could handle right now. She probably had her entire face of makeup running down her cheeks and looked similar to a drowned raccoon, so it was a good thing she wasn't meeting Sydney right now. She would think her mother was unhinged.

"No wonder she didn't come back into the hospital room." Millie shook her head. "I thought she was grieving like the rest of us. I knew staying with you was the right thing, so I let Sasha deal with the child. Or, her body, so I thought."

Bridget shuddered.

"All this time, she's been lying to us."

"If I see her again…" Bridget didn't want to finish. A hot, tight sensation curled low in her stomach. Rage. Pure, undiluted fury burned in the core of her being. If she ever saw Sasha again, she was liable to lash out and try to kill her.

There was no forgiveness for this.

No justification.

No coming back in the fold.

They were done.

Millie touched her shoulder. "All you need to do is keep Clarke from finding out about Sydney. Do what you need to do, but make sure you guys aren't seen together outside. Lay low, somewhere Capeira can't find you, and let me take care of both while you meet your family."

The fire in her banked a little.

Sacrifice their safety, potentially. Put them in harm's way. Make them upend their lives, just so she could meet her daughter. Finally.

Yes. *Yes.* She wanted to say it. To jump up, and run out the door—after she fixed her makeup, of course—and start her life. For real. But that could put a target on their backs. Aiden was a cop. He would want to protect them. She would be focused on Sydney. Bridget could wind up getting all of them killed. And then, everything she'd lost? It would be gone for good.

Forever.

Life had already taken everything she'd ever wanted. That hole in her where she'd grieved for her dead baby was empty. So empty. It could be filled to overflowing. If she was prepared to be selfish and go after what she wanted, at their expense.

But if she took out Clarke and took down Capeira? Then she would be free and they would be safe.

Just the thought of what Clarke—or any of them—might do to Sydney in order to hurt her?

No. No way.

Bridget scrambled to her feet and locked her knees so she didn't fall back down. She was going to track them down and put the world to rights. Then, when it was done, she would fight harder than she ever had in her life to get back everything that should always have been hers.

Red hair. That leggy build. Jumping into her father's arms.

Millie frowned up at her. "Where are you going?"

"Hunting."

22

"So her friend told you she was dead, and then told Bridget the baby was dead." Jess shifted in her seat and sipped from a paper cup of coffee. "Is that what you're saying?"

Aiden twisted his grasp on the steering wheel. "Yes."

He also gritted his teeth. Of course, Jess immediately figured something was wrong the minute he'd shown up for his shift. Even talking to Eric for an hour while he made dinner, Sydney eating hers while she binged another show, didn't help. Not to mention needing to put the kibosh on the whole binge watching—he'd deal with that soon. He wasn't going to pretend it wasn't helpful right now to have Sydney occupied as he was dealing with all this emotional distress.

There was a slim chance he'd be able to come up with answers now, talking to Jess. But like everything else, she didn't drop it. Because she cared.

He needed to remember that.

"This is unbelievable."

"I know."

"I *know*." She swung her coffee cup around the inside of the squad car. "This is Last Chance, and it's been crazy. Like *crazy-town* crazy. And I can say that because I was trapped in an underwater facility that was set to detonate, so I know what crazy is. Now this? It's like super-spy stuff."

Aiden took the turn for the house. "Let's just focus on this call, and then we can figure out what on earth I'm going to do about telling Sydney the news. And what Bridget and I are, or will be, with each other. I have to navigate the two of them having a relationship. And they've never even *met.*"

He pulled over in front of the house. Behind a pickup that presumably belonged to the manager of the property, or the owner, who'd called it in.

"Sorry." Jess unclipped her seatbelt. "But you are going to figure this out."

He pushed open the car door. "I hope so."

They hit the front walk together, and he ran it down in his head. Owner called the non-emergency line. Failure to pay rent, so he wanted to go inside and talk to the tenant. See if there was a problem. Start the process of eviction by informing them of his intentions.

Aiden understood why the man wanted an escort. Desperate people could react in a lot of different ways. It could be completely peaceful, or they could end up having to arrest someone.

Jess led the way inside, and the owner followed behind Aiden. Working usually served to calm whatever was restless in him. Tonight he hadn't gotten the usual stress reprieve, and since it was barely six in the evening, they still had hours left on their shift. Hours spent out in the dark, where he would try and work toward redemption—if only in the eyes of those who put their trust in him.

He'd let down everyone in his life. Becoming a police officer had been a move designed to give him that sense of honor he hadn't felt outside of being Sydney's father. A chance to be good, instead of just trying to convince himself he was good—when he didn't feel like it at all.

God wasn't likely to argue with hard work, was He? After

all, He'd given Aiden the strength to do it. The drive to be a "good" Christian or at least an authentic one instead of a hypocrite.

Like his father.

Aiden pushed out a breath and shoved the thoughts aside. No matter that his father wasn't perfect, lots of people had much worse parents. He'd simply seen a difference between what his dad said and what he'd done. Professing one thing, but clearly believing differently.

That hypocrisy had kept him from church for a long time until he realized his old man's faith life didn't have to impact his own. Aiden had found a relationship with God for himself. For the man Sydney's father needed to be, to teach her that perfection wasn't the standard. After all, it was unattainable. What she needed to be was humble. Kind. Upright. As good as they could be with what they were given.

"Ugh."

He glanced at Jess just as the smell hit him. Aiden turned to the owner and held up a hand. "If you could wait outside."

"What is it?"

"Step outside. One of us will return in a minute." Aiden unsnapped his gun for precaution, and they cleared the rooms in the house. Walked through each one while they worked to find the source of the smell.

"In here."

At the bedroom door, Aiden peered over her shoulder. "Yep." He reached for his radio and called in the deceased man to dispatch, so they would, in turn, inform the sergeant. Basuto could figure out getting the medical examiner, and possibly a detective, to process everything and get the paperwork done.

"This seems familiar."

"All the overdoses?" He skimmed his gaze over the man's jeans. Bare upper body, distended belly. Disheveled hair and the first growth of a beard, as though it had been a few days since he'd shaved. Aside from his physical features, there were not many signs of drug use. Just the paraphernalia he never would've come across in his life if he hadn't been a police officer.

"It does fit what we've seen so far. But..."

"What?"

"This guy." Aiden realized. "It's the manager we met from the bowling alley."

"Oh, you're right."

Aiden grasped his radio and updated dispatch. That meant a detective would be sent, if this was tied to other open cases and could prove to not be an accidental death. A man connected to another death. To what he'd seen at the bowling alley.

If these proved to be murders, that would be huge.

Savannah was on vacation with Tate and they were with Millie and Eric's kids. Protected. The way Sydney was not. Aiden dismissed that unhelpful thought. He didn't need to push his daughter off on someone else just to make sure she was safe.

That was his job.

And plenty of cops in this town could investigate in Savannah's absence.

"I'm gonna go talk to the owner." Jess strode out.

Aiden nodded and pulled on a pair of gloves. He walked around the room and looked for anything immediate he'd need to secure. Or evidence. The first impression of a crime scene was always a key piece of evidence later, and he would be required to write detailed notes.

"Okay, he's getting me all the info he has on this guy. Our bowling alley manager."

"Good." Aiden's phone rang. "It's Basuto."

Jess shrugged. "I guess he's on this case tonight."

Aiden stared at the room as he answered the phone. "Before you ask, yes, we do think it's one of the OD cases we've been seeing lately."

"I'm on my way, but I haven't left yet."

Something caught his attention. "I found a phone. I'll see if it's locked and take a look."

"You need to take a lunch."

"We're good here." Even if Jess had decided to tell the sergeant where Aiden's head was at right now, that didn't mean he needed special treatment. They weren't due for their break for at least two hours.

"A woman came in. Bridget Meyers. She asked to speak with you."

His stomach clenched. "Kind of in the middle of something."

It was possible she only wanted to speak with him to inform him she was taking him to court to get custody of Sydney. A judge would—he hoped—not tear a child from the only parent she'd ever known. But they might award her mother shared custody. A fifty/fifty split.

Not exactly what he wanted, especially when it was clear his feelings for Bridget were still there. More mature. More responsible. More passionate. She was amazing, and he wanted her in his life. To help her through the grief and betrayal and rediscover what they were to each other. He wanted more than just the few minutes it would take to hand off Sydney.

God, this is what I want. Not just because we have a child. Last time they'd made a mess of the relationship. This time it could be a real God-thing. The kind Conroy talked about all the time.

Maybe they were too far past that ever being a possibility. The obstacles between them seemed insurmountable—and he wasn't even accounting for the inherent dangers going on right now.

"She insists."

Aiden wanted to squeeze the bridge of his nose, but that would require removing his glove. "Tell her I'll be at Hollis's diner in an hour."

"Copy that. And I'll see you soon, so maintain the scene."

"Will do, Sergeant." Aiden hung up.

"What was that about?"

He swung around. Jess lifted both hands. "Whoa. Easy."

"I have a lunch date in an hour."

"Bridget?"

He nodded.

"Wow."

Aiden lifted the phone from the carpet beside the bed. By the look of it, someone should've vacuumed several weeks ago. But he tried not to judge that stuff when he saw it, since he'd been the recipient of all that the church ladies had offered him when they first discovered a nineteen-year-old with a newborn.

When to change the sheets on a bed. How to make lasagna. When to clean a toilet. Where to store things. Baby proofing. Then there were the thousand child-related things. They'd resorted to weekly lessons until he could've passed as a fifties housewife any day of the week—just without the floral dress, thanks.

Still, even with all that had gained him—a clean house, a healthy child. It never got him what he really wanted.

A complete family.

He knew people lived without that "normal" every day. Either by circumstances or by choice. God had blessed the two of them. It hadn't been bad being by himself with Sydney. There had simply been something missing the whole time.

Now that Bridget was back, and he knew the truth of what'd happened to her, he knew why he'd always had that hole in his life.

God *could* give her back to them. Not just Sydney, but him too.

The question was, *would* He do it?

Aiden scrolled through the phone's message and call history, then the contact list. He came up with a few possible ideas for who the dealer might be. Hopefully that would lead them to the source of the drugs. But it still didn't make sense. Why take out your customer base? No one selling drugs wanted to get rid of those who bought them. There had to be another reason.

Someone else had tainted the drugs being sold, and likely, the dealer was unaware.

Or they weren't random but targeted deaths. Revenge. Money. Passion. Whatever the reason, they'd get to the bottom of it.

"Do you need backup for this conversation?"

Aiden shot his partner a look. She didn't laugh in response, or look remorseful. "Let's talk in the hall."

"Good." Jess grinned. "Cause this guy smells."

"You gonna tell the next of kin that?"

"Obviously not."

"Good."

She opened an evidence bag. "I don't have to be all empathetic to be a detective, you know."

Aiden dropped the phone into it. "It probably would help."

"Nah. That's what I have you for."

He wanted to roll his eyes, but she would notice it and give him grief for being dramatic. "No, I don't need backup." The last thing he wanted was for Jess to wade in and scare off Bridget. "I'm going to hear her out, and if she lets me, then I'll state my case."

"Which will be what?"

"Depends on what she says."

Jess sighed. "I'm trying to help you, and you're just gonna roll with it? Say whatever, in response to her?"

An hour later, parked outside Hollis's diner, he still didn't have much more of an idea than what he'd told Jess. Just a few possible answers to whatever Bridget might say. Worst case scenarios were what cops worked every single day.

A car door opened across the lot, and he saw Bridget climb out. Aiden made his way over, assessing how she seemed as she moved. He tried to get a read on her body language so he could guestimate how this was going to go.

Stiff. She still seemed like someone in considerable pain, curled in on themselves. Her long hair was pulled up into a messy bun on the back of her head, through the back of a ball cap that shaded her face from him so he couldn't see her expression.

Car tires screeched. The sound dragged him from his study of her, and he spun to the sound.

The crack of gunfire echoed against the outside of the building as he was simultaneously punched in the chest.

His legs crumpled underneath him, and he fell. Bridget cried out.

Aiden hit the ground, only then realizing what had happened.

He'd been shot.

23

Bridget's world slowed to incremental movements that stretched between breaths. Between each beat of her heart.

Aiden was on the ground. She'd heard the impact of the bullet. She'd heard him hit the pavement with all the force of dead weight. She didn't want to look—couldn't chance seeing blood and freaking out again. Not when there was a threat that required her to be alert.

A shooter.

Above them, stars shone between clouds. Streetlights. She scanned the area and saw a pickup careen away from them down the street. She blinked. Where was the shooter? Aiden was dead. She just knew it. The same way she knew that if she kept breathing like this, she would pass out.

This was all her fault.

Black spots blinked at the edges of her vision. *Get a hold of yourself.* This was the end. She'd destroyed everything good in her life and left Sydney with nothing. The child had no family—Bridget had taken it away from her.

She knew what it was like to have nothing. Now she'd done that to the person in this world she cared about the most. More than anyone, or anything. A person she'd not even had the chance to get to know.

Bridget would always know she'd cost Sydney *everything.*

"Ow." Aiden groaned.

Bridget turned so fast her whole body nearly toppled over. *Aiden.* Her knee hit the asphalt as she half landed on him. She willed herself to look at his wounds. To accept the inevitable mess of his body. She wanted to cover her ears so she didn't have to accept that his rattling, labored breaths might be his last.

No blood.

She blinked. There was no blood. She shook her head. It didn't make sense. It should be everywhere. He should have already knocked at death's door.

Bridget sagged on the ground and leaned more heavily into him, relief flooding her entire being.

Aiden groaned again. He touched her arms and one hand slid around her back. "Whoa. You okay?"

"You were shot." She gasped in more oxygen so her brain would quit spinning. So she could think. A shooter. "You were dead."

His arm, the one not around her back, slid to his chest where a bullet was lodged in the front of his shirt. "Ouch."

Bridget breathed. "You wore your vest."

He inhaled, coughed and groaned again. "That hurt a lot."

Bridget whimpered. His uniform and his good sense to wear a protective vest underneath. They'd protected him. Saved his life, Sydney's father.

"Hey." He touched her face. "I'm okay."

"I thought you were dead. I couldn't look." She gasped, her head bent forward, she planted her face over his police shield. "I didn't know. I'd have left you bleeding out on the ground and gone after him."

"Bridget."

She wouldn't look at him. Too ashamed.

"You were trying to find the shooter, right?"

She shook her head and moved away because she had no right to be cared for the way he was doing. The way she could hear in his tone. Not when she had just about left him for dead to search for the threat.

"Do you see him?"

She was grateful he let the subject go, so she stood to search around some more. "It was only one shot. He hit his target, and I think he ran off. Or he was in the pickup I saw drive away."

Aiden shifted. "This is Officer Donaldson. I need backup at Hollis's diner."

She turned back to see he had his radio to his mouth. Lines on his face gave him a strained expression. "Do you want to sit up?"

He shook his head. "Keep your eyes open. I don't want to get caught by surprise again."

She stood and had a look over the top of both their cars. Clarke? Or Capeira? Right now she wouldn't be surprised if it was Sasha who'd shot Aiden, especially considering he wasn't dead. It would be just like her to make a point like that about real danger, and how she'd basically done them a favor by warning them to be careful.

"Hey!"

She spun to see a huge man race out of the diner. Bridget moved to grab her gun.

"One of the construction guys heard a shot. I was in the back. You okay?" The big man breathed out huge lungfuls of air.

"There's a cop down. He got hit in his vest."

The man barreled past her. "Who is it?"

"Aiden."

"Donaldson?" He passed her and knelt. "You okay, bro?"

"Yeah, Will." He sounded pained. "Help me up."

Bridget gave him a pointed look. "Oh, I see how it is. Reject my help, but jump at this guy's offer."

Both men looked at her in surprise.

She scanned the area and gritted her teeth while she tried not to feel hurt. Maybe she deserved that. He probably hated her for the way Sasha, her supposed friend, had dropped a baby in his lap and lied to everyone, ultimately changing the course of his life. He'd probably never wanted a child. Especially not one with Bridget.

And yet, he'd made that into something beautiful. At least as far as she could see from the way he looked while on the phone with their daughter. The way he'd been with her outside, lifting her into his arms. He loved Sydney, and she clearly loved him back.

"Who's that?" The newcomer spoke in a low voice. "Friend of yours?"

She glanced back and tried to smile.

Aiden leaned against the side of his squad car. Before he spoke, another black and white vehicle pulled in. "Will Briar, formerly with the FBI, this is Bridget Meyers, a longtime friend of mine."

"And the shooter?"

Neither noticed she'd completely frozen up at the mention of the FBI. Another one? Whether he was an agent now, or not, didn't matter. Not when she had a target on her. Getting tangled up with law enforcement in any official capacity was going to hamstring any chance she had of taking care of this problem. And making Sydney safe.

She winced. "The shooter is likely a colleague of mine."

The guy, Will, scratched at his jawline with one hand while another cop strode over. This guy had dark features, tanned skin, and sergeant stripes on his shirt sleeves.

All Bridget had wanted was to talk with Aiden and keep Sydney safe. Now she was mixed up in official business, and her name would land on paperwork.

She strode away from the cars toward the front of the building, unsure where she was even going. On the way past Aiden, he reached out. Their hands clasped. Instead of stalling her momentum, he pushed off the car and joined her. Walking beside her, he shifted to her right side, moving to drape his left arm across the back of her shoulders.

The way he used to.

The way they'd walked so many times, years ago.

She sucked in a breath.

"Talk to me. Don't run."

She managed to stop, and he stayed close to her.

"Easy."

She glanced back and saw Will talking to the Sergeant, their attention partially on her and Aiden.

"Don't worry about them. Stick with me."

She squeezed her eyes shut, focusing on the warmth of his body. She slid her hand to the side of his neck and put two fingers on the underside of his jaw, just to feel the steady beat of his heart. It was racing. Because of her, or the lingering adrenaline, she didn't know.

He was here. Alive.

She held on tight. "I thought you were dead."

"And I'm supposed to be upset that, instead of dissolving into a puddle of grief, you kept yourself collected so that you could get justice on my behalf?"

She sucked in a breath that emerged like a choppy laugh, but then it turned into a sob. "That wasn't quite it."

Aiden turned her into his arms. Where she wanted to be.

Until she saw the bullet. Bridget sucked in a breath. She grasped the sides of his shirt. That tiny smashed piece of metal embedded in his chest. Right over his heart. It would've killed him.

"Don't touch it. We need the evidence to see if we can ID the shooter."

She wanted a hug, not a bullet smashed into her face. A reminder of what she'd almost lost. "You could've died." She barely got the words out. All those trauma tactics she'd learned, ways to breathe through the anxiety and try to calm herself, had gone out the window. Now she had no idea what to do, or say. How to focus.

"I didn't die, I'm right here. I was wearing a vest."

Bridget felt the tears gather. Aiden touched her cheeks, his face close. "It's okay."

She shook her head. "Sydney."

"Elexa is with her, and there are extra patrols in our neighborhood. If we need it, there will be an officer assigned to sit with them. But so far, Clarke hasn't targeted her. Right?"

"We can't wait until he does. It will be too late."

"Sydney will be fine."

Bridget sucked in a breath. "She has to be."

"I know." His expression softened. As though he really did understand. "She will be, but you have to trust that I can handle this."

"He shot you."

"Now we know he's still here. But probably he was just trying to warn you off about involving the cops. He doesn't know about us."

Was there an "us"? Whether there was or not, Clarke had to be kept in the dark. "He can never know." That was why Bridget had asked Aiden to meet her. "You have to leave town. Take Sydney, and go off the grid. Somewhere Clarke and Enrico Capeira can never find either of you."

His body stiffened before she even finished. "You think I'm going to run?"

"I think you don't want to." He wasn't that kind of guy. "But you have to see the truth."

"I thought I *was* looking at it."

Whatever that meant, she didn't get it. "Take Sydney and go somewhere safe. Just until this blows over."

"I'll repeat my question." His voice hardened. "You think I'm going to run?"

"It could save her life."

"God saved mine. Not any plan, or any person. Just God."

He lifted his chin and loosened his hold on her. That warmth slipped away. "He's the one who will keep Sydney safe. Not a plan to escape. Unless He tells me to go. And until He does, I'll be right here. Helping you."

"Putting her in danger."

"Come over to the house. Meet her." He let go to fold his arms loosely. "Then tell me a life on the run is what's best for her."

"It's just until I find Clarke and the FBI takes down Capeira. You know it's for the best that she's under protection."

"She has that here."

"Listen to me—"

"No." He cut her off. "Listen to me. Go do your job. If you're so worried about the collateral damage that you don't even want to meet her because...because... you think you'll wind up losing her all over again? Then just get on with—whatever. Come find me when it's done." He was nearly spitting.

She stared at him. Would he wait that long?

"You're scared." Aiden stared her down. "We're all scared, Bridge. But we move ahead, and we do that together. Standing with courage. Not running out of fear to hide."

"It's the smart thing to do."

"Guess I'm dumb then." He shrugged. "Because this is my home, where I've raised *my* family." He paused. "A terrible thing was done to you, and it stole years from you. But you have the chance to get that back, and you won't take it because you're too scared."

"Of course I'm scared!" She knew they were drawing attention, but Bridget had to get him to understand. "I can't put her in danger. Clarke will use her as leverage."

"Only because you're too scared to protect her yourself."

"I can't do that and find him at the same time. I have to work."

"So you keep everyone at arm's length and save the world all by yourself. Alone."

She huffed out a humorless laugh. "Why would this be any different than any other day of my life?"

He winced. "Guess I know where I stand then." He took a step back. Away from her. "I have to get this bullet out."

Aiden strode away.

Two more cars pulled in. A black SUV and another silver car. Millie's. Before the cars even parked, Bridget raced for her own and climbed in.

Someone yelled, but she turned the key as fast as possible and peeled out. Probably spraying them with gravel in the process.

It didn't matter.

She couldn't be here. Not when her presence meant death.

24

He didn't even look back when she peeled out of the parking lot. A crowd had gathered, mostly cops and federal agents who'd shown up, along with patrons of the diner. Aiden even saw Millie with Eric at the edge of the crowd.

"Ambulance?"

Aiden sagged against the car but held up a hand. "I'm good."

The sarge drew near with a pair of tweezers and an evidence bag. He tugged out the bullet from Aiden's vest and dropped it in the bag. "I don't need to tell you…"

"I know." Aiden fully understood what would have happened if he hadn't been wearing protective gear. Or if the bullet caliber had been higher. The shooter closer. "I'm good."

All this would probably hit him later. When he got home and looked in on Sydney in her bed. Sleeping, innocent of all the things that happened outside the safety she lived in. He didn't want her to know the truth. Especially considering the heightened risk right now.

He still thought Bridget's suggestion was overly drastic, considering the pool of people who made up his support system here in Last Chance. Leaving that group, and the eyes and ears of people in town who knew who they were, would be foolhardy. But he could see why she would think running was the best choice.

He wouldn't deny that her tendency to flee from danger frustrated him, as though safety came from anonymity. But he did understand it.

"Okay." The sarge patted him on the shoulder. "You're done for the night, though. Soon as we wrap up here, you should go home. Tomorrow when you wake up, and you feel like you were hit by a truck, don't be surprised."

Aiden nodded but said nothing. He should go explain all this to his boss. Conroy had arrived and was headed over. There was no reason he shouldn't tell them both how Bridget had witnessed the former fire chief, the now-deceased final member of the founders, murder a woman years ago. The victim was likely buried under a stack of cold cases on someone's desk.

It needed to be closed.

Conroy shook his hand. "How do you feel?"

Aiden made a face. Conroy chuckled. "Been there."

"I was wearing a vest," Aiden pointed out. "And I'm pretty sure it was not a sniper who tagged me. Not like what happened to you."

Conroy shrugged and turned to the sergeant. "Are we searching for the shooter?"

Basuto nodded. "Will headed out, and Frees caught up with him as soon as he showed up. They are out to a one-mile radius now, but haven't seen anyone that matches this Clarke guy's description."

Aiden winced. "We should also be looking for a tall, dark-featured woman wearing a sling on her arm. Ask Zander. He knows her." Sasha might have ditched the sling, but he couldn't imagine she would choose to go without it, considering how injured they had told him she was. "Her name is Sasha, and she works with Millie and Bridget."

Conroy's eyebrows rose. "This Clarke guy has an accomplice?"

Aiden shrugged. "We don't know yet whose side she's on. I'm guessing Millie could fill you in about that."

Sergeant Basuto rocked back on his heels. "Speaking of filling us in, are you going to let us know why you let a person of interest who might be a material witness drive off in her car?"

"She isn't going to leave town. That's what she wants me to do."

Basuto snorted.

Aiden shot him a look and saw Conroy do the same.

The chief frowned. "Doesn't she know you'd never leave town willingly? I mean, you might go on vacation or whatever. But you're way too much like me to uproot yourself and go live somewhere else."

It was probably the pain in his chest, but Aiden almost passed out right there. The chief thought they were alike?

Sergeant Basuto clapped him on the shoulder. "I do believe our boss just paid you a compliment, Donaldson."

Conroy shook his head. "I've liked Donaldson since even before he saved my wife's life. Back, what was it? A year ago, or however long that was?"

Aiden shook his head. "I think I've fallen into a parallel universe."

Conroy laughed. "Probably just the pain scrambled your brain. I'm sure I just said you're so much like Basuto. Not me." He held out his hand, and Aiden shook it again. "Go home, Donaldson. Hug that daughter of yours good night, and we'll see you in a few days. Maybe a week."

They wandered off and left him there, wondering if he could manage to drive himself home.

"Come on, I'll give you a lift back to your place."

Aiden spun to find Millie beside him. "It's not that simple. I have to change at the police station. I have to fill out all the paperwork that goes with having been shot before I go home. I can't pack up my life and leave town just because Bridget thinks it's the best thing for Sydney. The daughter she hasn't even met."

Behind her, Eric winced. "To be fair, I don't disagree with him. Bridget really needs to meet her daughter."

Millie glanced back and forth. "Neither of you understands the pressure we feel as mothers. And you understand even less what it's like to know you're putting that child in danger just by being around them."

"I have no interest in arguing with you." Aiden needed to sit down, not get into another heated debate with a woman who lived in danger and thought that meant she had to hide from everyone. Not to mention that he was also at risk daily because of his job. It wasn't like he sold donuts for a living.

Millie had withheld the particulars of her job from her family. No one in town knew how dangerous her occupation was. She had taught Bridget to compartmentalize her life in the same way. To keep everyone at arm's length in order to minimize the risk.

He was going to be who he was. Risks and all.

That meant doing his job and not going home, even though he'd been ordered to. Aiden needed to find Clarke, or whoever had shot at him, and get this whole thing put to bed. Case closed. No more problems that dragged on for years on end and caused pain for everyone who came into contact with him.

He strode toward the end of the parking lot and across the street. After a quick text to Frees, he got a location and headed out after the officers on the search.

Aiden paced down a side street about a quarter mile from where Frees looked for Clarke.

The hair on the back of his neck rose on instinct. He didn't slow his pace, though, or do anything to indicate he was aware that danger lurked. In mere seconds, he could have his gun out and be already to fire if that was necessary.

The dark-clothed figure stepped out from behind a rusted-out car dumped in the alley.

Aiden pulled his gun. Before he could bring it up to aim, a woman said, "Easy. I'm not trying to get shot again."

Sasha.

"Tell me why you're sneaking up on me. Because I don't want to get shot again either." He wanted to rub the heel of his hand across his front where there was no doubt a bruise rising. But doing that would probably make him pass out. "And you can tell me why you shot me just now."

"You think that was me?" Sasha set one hand on her hip and cocked her foot out. "Ouch. I forgot that was going to hurt." Her hand dropped by her side. "I didn't shoot you just now. That was Clarke, and it's not even why I'm here. I just want to know what you know, so I can get on the search for him."

"Clarke is the one who shot me?"

"Of course. You think he would let Bridget meet with the cops and not try to take one of them out in a warning? He knows if he shoots you dead, he'll be hunted forever. That's why he shot you when he knew you'd be wearing a vest."

"Well, it felt *great*."

Sasha let out a sharp laugh.

"None of this is funny." He frowned. "Bridget thought I was dead." That should make her reconsider. If she had a conscience. "I think you've done enough to try and help any of us, considering you destroyed any chance Bridget and I had of making a family."

"Two nineteen-year-olds and a baby?"

"Like people in that situation don't make it work every single day? Relationships don't always last forever, but we won't ever know, will we, because you took that chance away from us. You took Sydney's mother from her life."

"I saved Sydney, and I saved Bridget." Sasha huffed. "And

there's nothing you can say that will convince me I'm wrong. That's how right I know I am."

"Because the fire chief was such a bad guy? That's true enough." Aiden stuck the fingers of his free hand into one pocket. "But you didn't even let me try to protect them. You're just assuming I'll do it now so you can continue to believe you're right."

Sasha shrugged the shoulder he knew was uninjured. "I'll also be right here, working with you to protect them."

"No one wants you to do that. And I don't need you."

"Sure, that's why you have a bullet hole in your shirt right above your heart. Because Clarke wasn't trying to make a point about how close to Bridget he can get."

Aiden didn't like the sound of that. "I'm supposed to accept your help because you're so all-knowing?"

"Look, I'm not saying I need to move into your guest room —"

"Good. Because I don't have one."

Sasha sighed. "I did what I thought was right. They can all hate me for it for the rest of their lives, but that doesn't mean I was wrong. Does it?"

He pressed his lips together, deciding not to answer that. "Do you know where Clarke is holed up?"

"Why, am I supposed to call you if I find him?"

"I don't suppose you would do that."

Sasha laughed.

"The FBI is looking for Capeira. Do you know anything about that?"

"Yeah, I wasn't going to tell you if I find that guy, either. But I'll call and let you know where to find the remains."

Aiden realized he wasn't going to get anywhere with this woman. He had no idea what her intentions were, or how to convince her to work with him inside the bounds of the law. It was clear she had more of a renegade work ethic. Something she had likely tried to train Bridget on.

He didn't think it stuck entirely. With her aversion to blood and the clear stress response he'd seen in her, he doubted Bridget would respond as aggressively as Sasha might. After all, a woman like Sasha would never suggest running and hiding, even if it involved protecting a child in the mix.

He needed to get back to work. "You're gonna call and give me intel?" He walked past her as he spoke. "Do you even have my number?"

Aiden continued down the side street to the tune of her laughter bouncing off the sides of the buildings.

No matter what she'd done, or the decisions she'd made, Aiden would accept her help if it meant protection for those he cared about. The ones who wanted it, and those who thought they didn't need it.

After all, he knew what it was like to want absolution for your past choices.

Aiden made it to Frees, but the search yielded nothing. Clarke had made his statement. Now he was gone. The question was, when would he strike next? Aiden planned to be ready, now that he knew what he was up against.

Who would be the target?

25

The little redhead girl wobbled on rollerblades down her drive while a teen looked on. A couple of times, the girl's arms swung like two windmills and she nearly went down on both knees.

Bridget gasped. Her breath fogged up the window, so she used her sleeve to wipe it away.

Having caught herself just in time, the little girl adjusted her knee pads and skated on while the teen kept a close eye out, though she clearly knew she was capable enough.

Butch leaned against her leg. Bridget reached down and touched his head. She buried her fingers in his fur while everything in her wanted to run out there. To introduce herself. Even if she only waved and called out a generic greeting in the process.

Sydney would look at her. She might even smile.

Everything Bridget had wanted for years, and she would have it in a matter of seconds. Even if the girl didn't even know her name.

But she didn't go outside. Instead, she contemplated the likely consequences of deciding to venture out instead of staying holed up in here with myriad injuries—fear her only company.

What would happen? A gunshot, maybe. Just like those seconds when Aiden had walked to her between the cars. One moment she was getting ready to say what she'd called him there to say. The next second, a shooter.

And he'd been hit.

He was down. His life, ended.

Okay, so he didn't die, but at that moment, she hadn't known for sure. She was allowed to be a little bit dramatic—okay, a lot. And it could happen again. With Sydney. The little girl outside wasn't wearing a vest. Neither was the teen with her. That meant a round would tear through flesh. There would be nothing anyone could do to stop it.

The child she'd thought had passed away from complications would then die in front of her. Torn apart by Clarke's bullet.

Bridget let the blinds snap back together. There was no point torturing herself with what she couldn't have…yet. Right now there was too much danger. She couldn't be swayed by her emotions, that visceral draw to know her child. To hold her child. She'd barely thought beyond that first moment.

What she needed to do was keep her daughter safe. Right now, Sydney was content with the situation as she knew it to be. She'd grown up thinking her mother was in heaven. The possibility that her mother could be a tangible part of her life just didn't exist in her world. Sydney didn't need to know she was here but choosing to not be in her life. Not when the little girl felt safe. Letting her know would take that peace away.

Bridget turned from the window. She wasn't going out to her daughter. She repeated that twice to herself, a whisper in the quiet of the room. She had to convince herself she *wasn't* going to just walk out there and bombard her.

She couldn't.

Clarke was a threat. Capeira was a threat. She had to take care of both before Sydney would be safe, and that wasn't going to happen while she stood here, peeking through the blinds at her child.

Bridget grabbed her keys and headed out. The second she pulled open the door to the garage, she hit the garage door opener also. Out of habit, mostly. Before she could stop him. Butch wedged past her leg and ducked underneath the rising door, to the driveway beyond her car.

"Butch!"

She raced after him, suddenly remembering the very thing she'd been avoiding. Bridget skidded to a stop before the end of the garage. She peered out, and her world flipped upside down.

Even from this distance, she knew she'd been seen.

But Bridget didn't go outside. Her body swayed. *No. Don't.*

She needed to stay where she was because she was sure Clarke, or anyone else who was on the radar, was watching She knew it would be obvious in an instant, the connection she felt about the little girl across the alley. Bridget knew she didn't have it in her to react like she was just any other child.

Sydney stared at her. Bridget did the same, her eyes unblinking until she was forced to close them to ease the burn.

Tears rolled down her cheeks. She swiped them away and tried to focus better on Sydney, despite the sheen of moisture in her eyes.

"Sydney!" The teen called her back.

Whoever the sitter was, she stared warily at Bridget. But Sydney was distracted by the dog. Butch sniffed around her legs as his big body leaned against her. She landed on her butt, knees bent. Big inline skates in front of her, legs splayed out. She erupted with giggles.

The dog practically sat in her lap while the girl petted him and laughed at the tongue swiping her face.

Bridget felt the sob well up and swallowed it back down. *Don't lose it.*

"Syd." The teen wanted the child to come with her.

Either she'd been warned there could be trouble, or she was

naturally wary of strangers. Whichever it was that made her call the child back, Bridget was glad for it. She had good instincts. A tiny amount of the fear in Bridget eased.

Bridget lifted a hand, palm out. She wasn't going to be a problem for them. In fact, she called out across the alley, "Watch him for me. Please?"

The little girl squealed. "Yay!"

Bridget spun to her car, fell into the driver's seat and backed far enough out of the garage to watch the three of them head inside. Then she drove away, even though that was the last thing she wanted to do. The farther she drove away from Sydney, the more she felt incomplete, and the more she thought about what that beautiful little girl represented.

Her. Aiden. The product of a love they'd shared. Certainly no enduring epic romance, but they'd had their moments of real affection. She would never consider Sydney to be a mistake. Not even after she'd been told her baby died.

At the sign, Bridget pulled into the restaurant on the highway. She didn't know how she ended up there, considering she hadn't purposely headed anywhere in particular.

The sign outside read, "SAME PIE, NEW MANAGEMENT."

Whatever that was supposed to mean.

She flung the door open and fell out, landing on her hands and knees on the gravel. Bridget hissed. Her whole body bucked, and she realized she was sobbing. Rather than curl up on the gravel, she clambered high enough up to set her behind back on the seat. Bridget laid her head in her hands and let it all out. She'd learned years ago it was better to get the emotions out than make it worse by bottling it up.

When it was spent, she got up and stretched. The memory of her little daughter playing in the driveway stuck with her. A treasure. The greatest gift she'd ever received.

She should have told Aiden thank you for the wonderful job

he'd done raising her so far. Sydney was happy. She laughed easily. She appeared healthy and energetic.

God, You made sure she was in good hands.

Bridget would be forever grateful for the care her daughter had been in. Sasha had essentially gambled with the circumstances she'd placed Sydney in, but the reality was that God had it all in hand. Even with the disagreements between them, He had never—would never—let her daughter down. God had turned her life into something beautiful.

Without Bridget.

That hurt, if she was honest about it. And it was going to be hard to forgive Him for choosing Sydney's best life as one without her in it. She couldn't change the past, but Bridget could ensure a good—if not better—future for Sydney.

But she wasn't going to just barrel into Sydney's life, selfishly assuming *she* was what was "better" for her daughter. The time and circumstances had to be right.

And that hurt more than everything else.

A truck pulled up beside her, the window already in the process of rolling down. Somebody needed to speak to her?

She probably looked like she'd been dragged through a hedge and a stream. Backward.

A gun appeared first. Behind it, a shadowed face in the passenger seat. "You're getting in." The accented voice wasted no time before saying, "Or I shoot you where you stand."

She realized what this was. "If Enrico wants me, then he should come here and fetch me himself."

"He did not say you should be unharmed. Just that you're still alive."

Bridget left the car door open, her phone still in her coat pocket. One gun. A knife in her boot—though she'd never used it outside of training because of her aversion to blood. Could she take out the occupants of this vehicle before they left with her?

Sasha had done it.

She'd trained Bridget, as had Millie. That meant Bridget had components of both their skillsets. *Help me do this.* It seemed strange to ask God to potentially help her kill someone—more than one person. Especially when she'd just admitted she might not forgive Him for her recent hardships. But if she didn't get past this situation, then she would never get to speak with Sydney. She would never be able to thank Aiden. Or possibly hear him apologize for the way he'd yelled at her for suggesting he protect their daughter.

"Now!"

Bridget started. She needed to not get off track, distracted by her thoughts. These guys meant to end her life—probably after their boss tortured her for a while first.

She took half a step forward. Once they were on the road, she could find out what arrangement they had going with Clarke. Maybe they had a deal in the works, like the intel Ted had found on his phone.

Police sirens whirled. Two big, black SUVs bumped the curb into the parking lot from different directions. Bridget stepped back.

FBI agents poured out of the vehicles. They took cover behind open doors, yelling for the truck's occupants to get out.

The first shot came from the truck. Aimed at her.

Bridget dove to the side and rolled for the rear corner of her car. She scrambled up onto all fours and raced around the back of the car, while gunshots volleyed back and forth between the truck and the two SUVs.

Someone cried out from inside the truck. More shots. Then another cry, this one from one of the feds.

"Turner is down! He's been hit!"

More shots were exchanged.

Bridget slid out her cell phone and called 911 for backup to help the feds and an ambulance for whoever had been hit. Each second of time that passed stretched out, until heartbeats felt like minutes and dragged the moments out in excruciating detail.

A gunshot blew out the window above her. Glass shattered down over her head.

She clapped her hands over her ears and stared unseeing at the trees beyond the restaurant parking lot. The sound of shots echoed around her. It was like a constant barrage of fireworks with little breath between them. Her ears eventually stopped working, unable to handle the sound any longer.

She didn't lower her hands, though. Each breath whistled under her hands, and she realized she was hyperventilating.

At the tree line, a dark figure caught her gaze. Two tree branches parted, and he came into view. Watching.

Clarke.

He'd set this up. Capeira's men were here to take her, and he was going to watch the whole thing.

No.

Bridget ducked her head and ran straight for him. At the tree line, Clarke's eyes widened and he turned to move out of sight a second later.

She wasn't about to let him get away. Not again. She ran full out, pumping her arms and legs as fast as possible, the way she had during track competitions. The ones where she'd come in yards and yards ahead of everyone else.

She flew toward the trees, nearly stumbled over a downed branch, and hurdled over a tree stump.

There.

She angled toward him.

Seconds later, he disappeared out of sight. Bridget slowed. She had to not run in so fast that he took her off guard and got the drop on her. She pulled the gun from the back of her waistband and flicked off the safety with her thumb. Pain sliced through her chest. *Ouch.* She scanned the area and tried to ignore her body's protest.

She listened for footfalls. A noise that signaled the disturbance of brush. Out here was mostly berry bushes. Huge, thorny masses she would not like to fall into by mistake, kind of like the night she'd run from Clarke. He'd grazed her. Aiden hit her with his car. So much had happened since then, but she couldn't allow thoughts of Sydney to distract her.

Where had Clarke gone? She spun around.

The branch came out of nowhere and slammed into her head. Her finger flexed on the trigger of her gun. She squeezed.

The blast sounded just as Bridget hit the ground and everything went black.

26

The ambulance pulled into the diner parking lot. Millie pressed hard on the wound with the sweater someone had given her. "Help is here."

Special Agent Turner was pale. Too pale, probably. He'd been clipped in the neck, above his vest. Likely he would be all right once he got to the hospital. But with the way it was bleeding, it looked bad.

A gunshot rang out.

Everyone braced. Several people ducked to a crouch, and even the cuffed Capeira soldiers were pulled behind cover. Or shoved into cars that would take them to the closest FBI field office for questioning.

"What was that?" Eric's question preceded a rush of movement. The sea of agents all glanced around to find an answer to their group leader's question.

One of them pointed. "It sounded like it came from within the trees."

Eric glanced at Millie.

"Bridget."

The EMTs reached her side and dumped their gear by the bleeding man. The second one took over with the pressure she had on Turner's wound. As soon as she was free, Millie jumped up and raced for the tree line.

Eric ran right behind her. He called out for a couple of agents to go with them.

Eric had seen Bridget head for the trees but had insisted they help the other agents first to make certain the situation was settled before they went after her.

Now a shot had been fired without a specific location of where Bridget had entered the forest.

"I knew I shouldn't have waited." Her friend could be dead by the time they found her, and it would be all Millie's fault for not going with her instinct.

"But Agent Turner is going to live, thanks to you."

"Your people should've thought to search for the source of the bleeding." She raced into the trees in the direction the agents had indicated and followed a line of fresh footsteps to a small path that hadn't been used much. "Why would she come this way?"

Something had to have drawn Bridget into the forest.

It hadn't been but several minutes, but it only took a moment for someone to be killed.

Even seconds could make it too late.

"Bridget!"

"Shhh. Someone could be out here." Eric's voice sounded strained.

"There!" One of the agents spotted something and took off in that direction. The other one went with him.

Eric stayed with Millie. Probably so he could "protect" her, even though he was the one who looked like he was about to fall over.

"You should have ordered someone else to help me and then stayed with the vehicles." Millie glanced left, then swept her gaze right. Repeat. Repeat. Scanning for Bridget. A flash of her hair or a piece of clothing that might be visible wherever she was.

Don't be dead.

"I'm fine."

"And I'm terminally pregnant? Is that it?" She rolled her eyes. "You were shot. You're *not* fine."

"If you think I'm letting you go off alone and—" He grunted. When she glanced back, he'd slowed and now held his stomach with his free hand. The other one held his gun.

"You can stop. I'll keep looking."

Eric shook his head.

Why he insisted on coming, despite his injured physical state, she didn't know. Unless he really did think he needed to protect his pregnant wife. The agents had told her about the incident with the dog and the rollerblading little girl at the house, though they didn't understand the significance of it all, or why Bridget had been hiding in the garage. Or why that had led to her breakdown in the restaurant parking lot. All they knew was that the woman they'd been charged with watching had drawn out Capeira's men and then run off.

Something Bridget would never have done without a good reason.

A flash of blonde hair caught her attention.

"Bridget!" Millie crashed through the brush to where she lay. Her clothing snagged on sticky prickles of berry bush as she ran. She swiped at them and felt a sting across her palm. It didn't matter. She tugged on her friend's arm, unwilling to concede that the worst had happened.

"Let's lift her." Eric knelt beside her.

Bridget was out cold. A huge knot had formed on her temple, clearly the blow that had knocked her unconscious. The gun she carried lay beside her.

"She must've squeezed off a round." Either accidentally, or to draw attention to herself.

They started to lift Bridget. She came awake with a cry, thrashing against them.

"Whoa. Bridge. It's me." Millie grasped her arms in a loose hold. "Eric is here. It's okay."

Bridget pushed down on both their shoulders and stood. So fast she nearly toppled over. "Whoa." She straightened. "Ouch." Bridget blew out a breath and touched the sides of her face. "That's gonna leave a mark."

"Clarke?"

Bridget started to nod. "Yes." She gritted her teeth.

Millie reached to help Eric to his feet. Her husband shot her a look. She lifted both hands. "Sorry. Do it yourself, then."

"I know when to sit down. And I can stand by myself."

Millie pressed her lips into a thin line. He kept pace, but only barely. He wasn't likely to admit even an ounce of weakness to his colleagues. No, he was going to just pretend he was raring to go, despite the fact he was seriously pale and a strong wind would probably blow him over.

Meanwhile, Millie wasn't allowed to comment on his physical injury, or she would be "mothering" him. She turned to her friend. "What happened, Bridget?"

"Clarke was out here watching those Capeira guys try to take me. He saw me and ran. So I chased him."

Eric glanced around. "Let's head back to the parking lot."

Millie could take whoever came at them. She was *mad* and prepared to fight for these two injured people she loved and cared for. In the same way she would defend her two boys if she had to. Why would Eric be mad about that?

Bridget nodded. "Ouch. Bad idea." She turned and started walking. "I could use an icepack."

Millie said, "There's an ambulance there. If it hasn't left with the agent already."

"Is one of the feds dead? One got shot, right?"

"Right." Eric nodded. "He was nicked pretty badly."

Millie didn't need Bridget to freak out about the possible blood. "Not too badly. He'll be okay."

Eric glanced at her. She didn't meet his gaze. How she helped her employee was her business.

"I get it," Eric said. As though that was some kind of consolation for her. "I want to help her as well. After everything she's been through? I barely know her, and I want to take down Clarke." He lowered his voice to say, "What I don't get is why you kept Bridget and her personal life a secret when she means so much to you."

"It would have put the boys at risk." She shrugged one shoulder and followed Bridget, not knowing if her friend could hear them or not. "You don't bring your work home, so neither did I."

He did that side-glance again. They needed to talk about this later, so she stayed silent while they crossed the parking lot. She'd never imagined this level of mess would come out of something she'd built—not to mention Sasha and what she'd done to Bridget.

Millie needed a plan. If those two feds didn't catch Clarke tonight, she wanted to go after him tomorrow. Catch him unawares.

Eric frowned. "If he was here and aware of what Capeira is up to, then maybe we can take them down at the same time."

"The way your agents tried to tonight?" Bridget turned, and they all had to stop. "They jumped the gun and Clarke got away."

Eric lifted his chin. "They stopped you from being kidnapped and then killed. After Capeira would have done who-knows-what to you. That means you owe the FBI."

"I had it handled. They blew in too fast and someone got hurt." Bridget folded her arms, swaying slightly. "Capeira wasn't here, right?"

"One of his guys will talk."

Millie motioned to an EMT, who was packing up already, and asked for an ice pack.

"Do you want to see a doctor?"

"Not especially." Bridget shot her a sardonic look. "But that doesn't mean I shouldn't go anyway."

"Good idea." Millie figured she wanted to be fighting fit to take down Clarke. If she pushed too hard, she might face complications to injuries previously sustained that would only make things worse in the long run.

Bridget turned to Eric. "I had the chance to find out the details of their agreement with Clarke. They would have told me one way or another, and then I'd have worked out a way to get free."

"There were four of them."

"She's done it before." Millie needed him to know. Which meant she probably should've told him about Sasha in the van, and the four Capeira guys. "That's what we do. We go into situations where the odds are stacked against us. Alone. With no backup. There's *never* any backup except for what we have in each other. And help is usually a continent away."

Eric turned a dark expression her way. "I guess you don't need my help then." He strode toward his people, and she saw the two agents emerge from the trees. Without Clarke.

They hadn't found him.

"He got away."

Bridget touched her shoulder. "He'll crawl out of the woodwork soon enough."

"Ma'am?"

They both turned to the EMT. Millie ushered Bridget toward them. "Go. I'll stop by later."

Bridget gave her a quick hug and then walked off with the EMT, a whole lot less steady on her legs now that the adrenaline had dissipated. She nearly fell into the ambulance but managed to get on the bed and lie down.

Millie turned back to her husband. He leaned against the hood of an SUV and directed his people from there. That strong, commanding man she'd always adored. Since the day she met him, Eric had brought his strength and resilience to a world of uncertainty. He was like the strong, tall mast on the ship. The one central part that held everything else together.

And yet, his people had jumped the gun tonight. They hadn't trusted Bridget's ability to aid them, because they didn't know her. Instead of formulating a plan ahead of time, they had followed and then moved in when the bad guys played the first card—rather than waiting to see their whole hand.

Now they had the chance of a lead, but nothing concrete.

Millie pulled out her phone and called Sasha.

"Mill."

"Sash." She stared at the trees, as though her friend watched, even though that was unlikely.

"You want to know if I'm sorry. But you also need help. Will you still want help if my answer hasn't changed?"

Millie gripped the phone. "Yes, but I want to understand as well."

"You know my past. I told you all of it."

"Maybe that's true." Millie didn't wait for Sasha to object. "Everything you told me is true. I know that." She'd cried over all Sasha had been through. But she knew her friend probably still held some things sacred. Things that were only between her and the Lord.

"There was a baby."

Millie squeezed her eyes shut. "You lost a child?"

Sasha said nothing.

"And you still think removing Bridget from her life was the right choice?"

"You've seen her. Sydney is happy. She loves her father, and she loves her life."

"I know you believe that. But you also have to know she needs a mother." Millie had to try and make her see that point. "There's a reason Aiden never found someone else."

"He's been waiting for Bridget to come back?" She snorted. "He thought she was dead."

Because of you. "And yet, now things can be set right. Bridget can have what life should have given her all along. She can have everything she's ever wanted."

Sasha was silent.

"You have to have hope."

"I thought it had died. It felt like that."

Millie gripped the phone. "You believe you made the right choice before?"

Sasha answered without having to think over it. "Absolutely."

"Then make another one now. Help me get Bridget her happy ending."

A shuffle came over the line. Someone cried out.

A low voice that sounded like a man, moaning.

Millie frowned. "Sasha, what—"

Sasha cut her off. "What do you think I'm doing?"

Then the line went dead.

27

Aiden strode down the hospital hallway. He'd been here less than a day ago, getting an x-ray on the bruised spot where the bullet hit his vest. Now Millie had texted to say Bridget was here. A blow to the head, she'd said, and Clarke had escaped despite FBI pursuit as he fled from the scene.

His pace picked up.

The second he realized he was practically running toward her room, he slowed. Rushing in on instinct and full of emotion wasn't going to endear him to her. The last time he'd seen her, she'd been consumed by her fear. Determined to push him away, telling him to take Sydney and run.

Of course, he'd reacted badly. Probably because of the searing pain still in his chest, but also partly because he didn't know how to dampen his temper sometimes.

He understood that. Of all people, he understood the need to do whatever it took to protect the ones he loved. But not on a gut reaction. Running scared. That urge to flee was all her, and he wasn't going to accept that for him or Sydney. Aiden just wasn't built that way. Not only did he need to protect his daughter, but he also had to keep her mentally healthy. Freaking out only meant she'd freak out, too. It was a balance. Physical and mental safety went together as far as he was concerned—one without the other wasn't healthy.

The door was ajar. Someone moved around inside, and he spotted a suit. A federal agent, maybe? Where one was, another would be also, so he figured there were at least two in there. Maybe Nicholson, who he'd met at the police station. Turner had been nicked, so the second agent wasn't him.

Questioning her. Arresting her. Was she some kind of informant? They absolutely should ask her to provide information, if she was amenable to it. If Aiden wasn't an officer but a higher rank in the police department, he would definitely discuss that with her.

Bridget had valuable information that could help two cases right now.

She could potentially save lives, as well as help capture a man on the FBI's Most Wanted list.

The agent moved, and he got a look at Bridget through the crack between the door and the frame. He'd seen that look before, and it wasn't good. Bridget wasn't about to back down. And they were steadily pushing her into a corner.

Her face reddened. Her knuckles white as she clenched the blanket over her lap. If they pushed her far enough, she would erupt. Something he wouldn't mind seeing. Every time she'd ever been angry, it had only lit more passion for her inside him. She was a force to be reckoned with, a well of deep emotion and strength he was seriously attracted to.

He was starting to get the feeling he always would be.

Aiden pushed the door open, so he didn't have to later explain why he was eavesdropping. Neither agent turned. They were facing down the woman in the bed. Bridget noticed him but didn't react at all. He saw a slight lift of her finger—the only way he knew she saw him.

"I assure you, I'm not joking." Special Agent Nicholson, who'd confronted him before, determined to get him to hand over Bridget, stood by the end of the bed with her back to him.

The other was busy, his nose in a tablet—a guy Aiden hadn't met yet.

Nicholson stared her down. "Whether you like it or not, you're in the middle of this. That means, as of now, you're my new best friend. Or you're my pet project and I stop at nothing to pin charges on you. No doubt it won't be hard to find something. Collusion. Attempted murder. Terrorism. You pick."

The amusement Bridget had been fronting dissipated. "So it's like that."

Nicholson shrugged like she didn't care either way. "Cooperation means you do something for me, so I respond in kind. Either you're helpful so I can be helpful to you, or you're a criminal with something to hide. In which case, that's exactly how I plan to treat you."

"Wow." Bridget rolled her eyes. "All so you can get Capeira in cuffs. Never mind that there's more to taking down his operation than just one guy. I should know."

Aiden figured she did. After all, she'd been forced to kill one in order to defend herself. Now the brother was after her, along with the men at his disposal.

The agents said nothing.

"Which means—" Bridget eyed them. "—you have to be seriously desperate and in need of new evidence. Can't find him yourselves. No one's talking, right? You're stuck and you're going to try and coerce me into giving you something fresh because I'm supposed to be...what? Scared of you?"

"I could arrest you right now. Obstruction of justice."

Aiden didn't figure Bridget would simply allow them to detain her. She seemed like a woman who'd slip out from under their grasp. And why was that? She'd done nothing wrong, and she could stand on that.

She was right. Nicholson was fishing and willing to turn up the heat to get Bridget to tell them what they wanted to know.

"The judge will grant me access to your phone and your whole life. I'll have everything I need." The agent straightened.

Even with her back to him, Aiden could just imagine the stubborn look she had on her face. Probably even lifted her chin. Given their previous conversation, he could picture it well enough just from her tone.

"So that's what you want."

Aiden leaned against the doorjamb and watched Bridget figure it out the same time he did.

"My phone."

Nicholson waved it off, but the line of her shoulders displayed the tiniest amount of tension she couldn't hide. "I'm sure there's absolutely nothing on there that could incriminate you in illegal activity, right?"

"Guess you'll never know, since you aren't getting it. And even if you did—by the way—it's set up to erase everything if someone other than me attempts to gain access."

"A court order will force you to cooperate. Or compel the phone company to get us in."

Bridget grinned. "I might have believed you, but now you just sound desperate. You clearly know nothing about me or the company I work for."

"International…what? Couriers?"

"Something like that."

"You killed Benito Capeira. That's why his brother tried to kidnap you." Nicholson leaned closer to Bridget. "If you want to stay alive, you'll need our help."

"I have help." Bridget motioned to the door, where Aiden stood.

When she met his gaze, he gave her a small smile. "How's your head?"

Bridget gingerly touched the edge of the bandage. "Not as bad as the headache standing in front of me."

Nicholson stared down Aiden. The other agent stood.

He shifted so the doorway stood open. "This conversation is over. Bridget will let you know later what she decides to do."

"The clock is ticking." Nicholson strode out.

Her colleague followed.

"Well, that was enlightening."

Aiden moved around the bed and settled in the chair on the far side. "How is your head really?"

"It hurts. A *lot.*"

He chuckled, then pressed a hand against his breastbone. "Ouch."

"Quite the pair, aren't we?"

He smiled. "She wanted your phone."

Bridget nodded. "I nearly didn't catch it, but I'm glad I did. They might want Capeira, but they really think they're going to get into everything the accountant's office is privy to? All our clients. Everywhere I've been." She shook her head.

"I'd have thought Eric could just ask Millie for that."

"She would never give it to him."

"So, is Eric trying to get it through other means," Aiden said, "or was Nicholson working independently without Eric's knowledge?"

"I guess we should find out." She shifted, and he saw her wince. "Or stay out of it."

Aiden studied her. The pale tone of her skin, and the dark circles around her eyes. She looked like someone who needed support.

Probably if he offered to take care of her, she would balk at the suggestion. Still, it was clear she could use a friend. Maybe more. She'd been alone for so long, like him, that melding their lives wouldn't be easy.

But it could be worth it.

"Rolling my eyes hurts. Blinking my eyes hurts. Anything other than darkness *hurts.*"

He winced. "Ouch."

"They gave me meds, but I don't like that foggy feeling. You know? I need to be able to focus, and I need to think critically. Otherwise?" She shrugged one shoulder.

"Getting caught off guard is never good."

"How about you?"

She didn't seem to feel guarded with him. Not that she was particularly open, but there didn't appear to be a grudge over the fact he'd yelled at her and she'd run off. "The bullet didn't crack anything, but it hurts anyway." He touched the back of her hand. "I'm sorry I yelled at you."

"But you don't think it was wrong."

"No, not necessarily. But, it is wrong if the delivery causes you hurt. The kindest truth shouted at someone, or spewed with a hateful tone, isn't kind anymore. It's just spiteful and mean."

"Thank you for apologizing. I'm sorry I let my fear get the better of me. I know you do your best, and I can tell how good it is because Sydney seems…wonderful."

"She really is." He held onto her hand and would for as long as she'd let him do so. "Sometimes I look at her, and I still can't believe it. It's so amazing to have her."

"Thank you for taking care of her."

Aiden didn't like the past tense of that, as though he might be done taking care of her anytime soon. "It's been my absolute pleasure. I know you're still scared, and to tell the truth, I am as well."

She squeezed her eyes shut and pressed a hand to her forehead, next to the bandage on her temple. He waited while she sucked in a choppy breath. "Nothing can happen to her."

"I know." He gave her other hand a small squeeze and still didn't let go.

"Was she scared you got hurt?"

"I didn't tell her. I usually don't, unless—God forbid—it's bad enough I'm hospitalized. But if I get checked out and cleared to go home the same day?" He shrugged. "I don't say anything. She'll probably figure out I've got a bruise the size of Saturn on my chest the first time she hugs me too hard. But I don't like her to have to face the dangerous reality of this job. Not yet. It was my choice to be a cop. She doesn't need to suffer because of it. Maybe when she's a little older, but not at six."

Bridget stared at him with something that looked an awful lot like wonder. "She's so beautiful."

He leaned close. "That's because she looks like you."

Bridget blinked those crazy long eyelashes. She leaned in a little as well, and memory flooded back. More of the nostalgic sensations. Some meant trouble, but most made him want to smile.

Their lips were a hairsbreadth apart when the door clicked open.

"Oops." It was a woman. *Millie.* "Sorry."

Aiden froze. Bridget's lips curled into a self-effacing smile. He kissed the smile, adoring the lightness it brought to her expression. But he didn't linger there, despite the fact he wanted to. Aiden leaned back. "You want me to let her in?"

"I do need to talk to her. But I was also enjoying um…*talking* with you."

He chuckled and felt his cheeks heat. "Yeah. Talking is good." Then he pushed off the side of the bed. "I'll go—"

Out in the hall, a woman screamed. Seconds later, a gun discharged.

A single shot, and then silence.

28

A woman screamed. Bridget's consciousness seemed to crystalize from paralysis to decision, until she knew what to do. She pushed back the sheet and blanket and slid her feet to the floor on the side where they'd stuffed her clothes in a cupboard. Thankfully she'd remembered to ask them to tie her hospital gown at the back because otherwise this would be seriously awkward.

Another shot rang out, and a low voice yelled. Bridget couldn't make out what was said. Aiden was at the door. She saw him reach for the handle. "Wait for me."

"I'm just looking."

She tore open the bag and slid her jeans up her legs while she sat on the edge of the bed, teeth gritted. Her head pounded, despite the meds they'd given her. Nothing could touch how bad it hurt. Not unless she was willing to dance with narcotics which, for her, was out of the question—even if the pain was excruciating. She planned to out-stubborn this headache until it was healed.

"Are you getting *dressed*?"

"Don't turn around." She tucked her arms inside the gown and pulled her sports bra on, then tugged the gown off and slipped her shirt on. As soon as she had her boots on and zipped over her calves, Bridget stood. She only needed to lean on the bed for a second. "I'm ready."

He turned, and she pasted on a smile. Aiden didn't buy it—because he knew her better than that. "Stay behind me."

"Do you have a gun?"

"Two." He nodded, twisted the door handle and pulled it open a fraction.

"Then give me one, 'cause I gave mine to Millie." She hustled to his side and leaned close to see out. He stiffened, but she ignored whatever made him tense.

"What do you see?" She couldn't make out anything through the tiny gap between the door and the frame. Who was out there?

"Sounds like a fight." His voice was terse.

She lifted her gaze to his. The fire she saw there threw her back years, and she had to take a half step back to put some cool air between them. "I need a gun."

Aiden crouched and pulled one from his ankle holster. He handed it over, and she could see the training he had in each move he made. She reciprocated, hoping he would see and realize she could also handle herself. He could trust her. Even with a weapon, in a hospital, as they faced down an unknown threat.

"You're still gonna stay behind me." He reached for the door handle.

She pressed her lips together because he was right. Aiden was a cop in this town. She was a person of interest in a federal investigation. Even though she hadn't done anything wrong, the FBI was still looking at her. Mostly for help, but she didn't doubt Agent Nicholson would tangle her up in it if she didn't cooperate. Some feds didn't care who they took down as collateral damage. Just as long as they got the person they were after.

Aiden pushed the door open all the way. Bridget could hear the scuffle.

"Let her go! Now!"

Bridget whispered. "Eric." She pushed out beside Aiden and spotted them. Special Agent Nicholson had Millie in front of her. A gun to her head.

Bridget gasped. "Let her go!" She stepped out, gun raised. Pointed at a fed.

Eric was across the hall.

Aiden muttered something she didn't catch and stepped in front of her. He covered her body, so she aimed around his arm. She didn't lower her gun, all the while knowing she'd never actually fire while her gun was right in front of his face.

Nicholson dragged Millie away from them. "Stay back!"

"It doesn't have to go like this." Eric's pale face looked strained. "We can work things out. Don't make it worse for yourself."

Nicholson didn't seem to know where to settle her glassy gaze.

"You made a mistake and got in with Capeira. Or you were forced into it." Eric's voice was breathy, but then he *was* watching the mother of his children being held at gunpoint. "That means we can work it out."

Bridget saw a flash of white teeth as he gritted them. Probably tempted to yell at her to let Millie go—the way she wanted to do as well. This was her friend. Her boss. A woman who had saved her life seven years ago.

This agent had a connection to Capeira? That explained a little more of the tension behind their conversation. What about the male agent, though? Where was he? Just then, a shape on the ground in front of her snagged her attention.

She'd been so focused on Millie that Bridget hadn't even seen the other agent. He was sprawled on the floor, surrounded by a pool of blood but still sucking in gasping breaths. Down. But alive.

"Things aren't too far gone yet." Bridget peered over

Aiden's shoulder. "Don't make it worse for yourself than it needs to be."

At least, she assumed there wasn't anyone else dead.

Nicholson hauled Millie with her as she turned. A security guard approached from behind her. Pretty soon more cops would show as well, and then she really would have nowhere to go. The question was whether she would take Millie with her. Force the cops—and Eric—to kill her instead of them seeing justice. They'd lose the chance to prosecute Nicholson *and* they would lose Millie.

Bridget had to figure out how to take down Nicholson and get her friend back. Eric looked pale, Aiden was injured. Her head pounded. All three of them alone couldn't do it, but if they worked together, it was possible. Then again, Millie knew all this. She would likely be accounting for it.

If she was Millie, she would—

While she watched, Millie brought both hands up between her body and Nicholson's grip. She broke the hold, side-swiped the forearm of the hand where Nicholson held the gun, and then spun. Millie slammed her fist into the Special Agent's stomach.

Nicholson doubled over.

Millie got her gun and walked backward as the FBI agent was swarmed. Cuffed.

Eric grunted. "Okay then."

Millie rushed over and hugged him, then turned to Bridget. "She shot the other agent."

Medical staff rushed to the guy on the floor. Bridget glanced between them all. "You guys knew she was dirty."

Eric nodded. "We just got intel, so we headed over as soon as we realized she was here."

Bridget gave them a rundown of her conversation with Nicholson.

Eric shook his head. "She was hedging her bets. Tried to play both sides and still manage to come out on top."

"Well, she didn't."

Aiden stepped closer to Bridget's side. "Do you want to go lay back down?"

"No." Her friend had nearly died just now, and he wanted her to take a nap? There was far too much work to do.

"Uh-oh." Millie winced. "I know that look. Bridget—"

"Don't bother talking me out of leaving the hospital. I'm done doing nothing when everything seems to be against us. This won't get solved by sitting around."

"Your headache will."

She rounded on Aiden. "And who else will get shot while I wait for that to happen?"

"Were you always this stubborn, or was I just too in love with you to notice?"

Bridget had to close her mouth. She thought she heard Millie giggle but didn't look to check. She just stared at Aiden. Had he really just said that?

"Excuse me." Eric stepped away. "I need to deal with this."

"I'll go with you." Millie followed her husband. The two of them moved more like partners right now. Which wasn't surprising, considering they were both in their element. Working.

"You're sure you don't want to go and lay down?"

"As sure as I'm standing here fully dressed." She lifted her gaze to meet Aiden's. "So I might as well get the doctor to clear me so I can get back to work."

"That might be cute if it wasn't also completely frustrating."

She wasn't prepared to feel guilty about it. "I'm ready to get to work. Save that feeling for later."

"Mmm."

She didn't know what that meant but also didn't have time for it.

"I should get home."

The sensation pierced her like being stabbed with a knife.

He winced. "Sorry."

Bridget said nothing.

"I know it can't be easy that I get to go home to Sydney. But I do need to do that."

"It's not a choice I make lightly. You know that, right?" Bridget countered. "I'm not going to put her in danger just because I want to see her. That would be selfish."

"I'm still sorry."

"I know." She grasped his hand, the way he'd done with her when she'd been in the hospital bed. "And I don't take that for granted."

He pulled her close for a hug, and then she had to watch him walk away. Bridget didn't want to go back into the patient room. She hung out at the nurse's station until the doctor finally showed up. It took some persuading, but he signed off on her going home. They'd had her under observation for hours to make sure there was no lasting damage from the head injury. Though she had so many bruises and scrapes—and bandages—right now that the doctor didn't want her to leave. Bridget didn't really blame the woman.

"I promise I'll come back if I don't feel good."

The doctor rolled her eyes. "I wish I believed that. But it's on you now. I did what I could." She walked away muttering about Last Chance. Worst job she'd ever had. Most stubborn patients ever, always signing themselves out against medical advice.

Bridget headed for the crowd of feds.

Millie saw her coming, broke off, and met her partway.

Bridget held up a hand. "Don't ask me if I'm okay."

"Because you don't want to lie to me?"

Bridget was willing to concede she might be right.

"Before you ask, the intel on Nicholson came from Sasha."

"Seriously?"

Millie nodded. "She grabbed one of Capeira's guys—" She glanced at Eric, but he wasn't paying them any attention. "—worked him over."

Bridget winced. "I feel sorry for the guy." Sasha's methods

could be extremely effective. After all, that had been her specialty as a CIA agent.

Bridget might not like the fact the US government trained people in enhanced interrogation techniques, but it was a reality of war.

"She might've been uh…motivated. Because she wants to make up for what she did."

"I'm supposed to believe she feels bad, or even guilty?" Bridget made a face. "More like she doesn't want me to be mad at her, and she's trying to make up for it."

If that got them Clarke, and Capeira, she wasn't going to complain. It also gave Bridget time to work through her feelings. When she was ready to face it all, she planned to talk everything over with Sasha.

"I'll call her." Bridget palmed her phone. "Find out what she knows, and see if pooling resources will get us further."

That way she could ensure Sasha was still around when Bridget decided she was ready to talk.

Millie nodded. "Good idea."

Even though her friend's actions had wrought serious damage in Bridget's life, she wasn't going to cut Sasha out until she had satisfaction. Neither of them had a big social circle. They'd been family for years. Bridget didn't plan on giving up on her until she got what she needed, and maybe even then she wouldn't cut the other woman out entirely. Even though it hurt to think of seeing her now.

If Bridget wanted Sydney, Aiden, and Sasha all in her life, then she needed to finish this. And even if there were issues between her and Sasha, they could be dealt with later.

Right now, it was time to get to work.

Bridget headed for the lobby. The more they were together, like she and Aiden had just been, the greater the threat for them all.

Eric could take care of Millie. And vice versa.

She sent a text. As she approached the main entrance, she

got a reply. It only took fifteen minutes for Sasha to pull into the parking lot.

Bridget strode out as her colleague slowed in the pickup lane. The second she climbed in, Sasha eyed her. "I'm surprised you called."

Bridget was too but knew Aiden wouldn't appreciate their methods. They worked faster and more effectively without the cops and all their red tape. "Are you working on taking down Clarke?"

"Of course." Sasha drove through the parking lot to the exit. "You just might not like my plan."

At the red light, Bridget retrieved the gun from the glove box. "You really should find a new spot to hide that."

Sasha let the car slow to a stop. "You're going to shoot me?"

"You stole my child from me." Bridget pointed the weapon at her. "Tell me why I shouldn't."

"Because I know what Clarke's next move is."

29

Aiden wandered back to the kitchen after tucking in Sydney. Something about coming home to her every day settled him like nothing else. Except maybe being with Bridget.

Though, that was, at the same time, wildly different.

"She okay?"

He nodded and headed for the sink. It was empty. He spun to Jess who was sitting on a barstool. "Did you do my dishes?"

She grinned. "A kitchen fairy showed up."

Jess and Ted had both come over for dinner, right as the sitter left. At any other time, he'd be at peace with all of what was happening, and the level of precautions he always took. But Bridget's fear had begun to resonate with him, building up over time, until Aiden found himself on edge in his own home.

Waiting for gunshots to invade his world the way they had more than once recently.

For the door to be busted down.

Or the phone to ring.

Jess's smile dropped and she shook her head, asking without words if he was all right.

Aiden shook off the thoughts and tried to focus. "Next time

the kitchen fairy comes, tell her the counters are supposed to be wiped down, too."

"She doesn't do counters."

Beside Jess, Ted grinned. "Ain't that the truth?"

Jess gave him a playful shove. Ted's laptop was open in front of him, and he typed while listening to them chat more.

Aiden appreciated their company. "Sydney is mostly asleep, listening to an audiobook."

Jess's expression softened. He had to wonder when these two were going to get married and have kids of their own. Though there was no rush to do that, he could tell she wanted to have children someday. And she was a fantastic surrogate aunt to Sydney.

Jess was one of his best friends. He was anxious to know if she'd get along with Bridget. Instead, she was off saving all their lives from a threat she'd brought upon herself and, consequently, everyone she was around. Not that it was her fault, but still. He wanted her here with them. Meeting Sydney. Spending time with Jess.

Aiden grabbed a clean rag from under the sink and got to work instead of allowing himself to succumb to the spiral of melancholy thoughts. It was more constructive to finish the kitchen clean up. "You and Sydney made a mess."

Jess bit into a cookie they'd made. "Worth it, though."

Aiden had put a dozen in the freezer to keep. Otherwise, between him and Sydney, they'd have finished the whole batch in just a few days, and then they'd have to go to the nearest trampoline park to burn off the extra calories. He wasn't all about the focus on guilt over food choices—and especially not teaching that to Sydney. It was more about the ebb and flow of life, doing what you enjoyed and balancing that with decisions that also made you feel good.

He wiped down the counters while he thought through everything going on right now. Since Sydney was in bed, they could talk about work stuff without having to worry about her overhearing something scary. And there was plenty of that going around. "Have you heard anything about Nicholson?"

"The traitor?"

Aiden glanced over. "You didn't hear any more about that, then?"

"Who cares about the 'why,' when she betrayed the badge?" Jess frowned. "There's no excuse for turning on your oath, or being disloyal to the people you work with."

"I'm glad you feel that way because I do too." He leaned his hips back against the counter. "But I can't deny she had a good reason."

Jess's expression remained hard as she waited to hear more, her arms folded in front of her.

"Nicholson's sister was on a trip with two friends in Venezuela. Capeira grabbed all three of them. The friends' bodies were found, along with an undercover DEA agent in their organization. All three had been killed and buried in the desert. But the sister was never found. So Nicholson contacted Capeira herself."

"So she sold out the bureau."

Aiden couldn't speak to that. But it was possible the reason the FBI hadn't yet caught Capeira—either Benito or Enrico—was because Nicholson had subverted their efforts.

She could have delayed their investigation and tried to work both sides. He'd likely have purposely messed up so someone would've noticed. If it was Aiden. Once discovered, he'd have asked for help from his superiors to get his family member back. Hoping that all happened before they were hurt.

He figured Bridget would have gone under the radar and got the sister back herself if it was *her* in Nicholson's position. Something Aiden would've been tempted to do as well. Only, he knew the value of a team. The cops in Last Chance worked best together. And everyone could use someone to watch their back.

Bridget might have Millie to watch hers. She also had Sasha in her life, though that was complicated at best. But Aiden wanted her to be in Sydney's life like that. To support their daughter and watch *her* back. He also wanted to look out for her himself.

If she'd let him.

"What Nicholson confessed to Eric is that Capeira used her job as leverage, promising she'd get her sister back if she did what they wanted."

Ted lifted his head. "That's terrible."

Aiden figured that, given everything he'd been through in his life, Ted understood that kind of fear. The relationship he had with his brother was a close one. If anything like this happened to Dean, Ted would do whatever it took to get him back. But considering Dean had been a Navy SEAL, Aiden figured he could take care of himself.

Jess glanced at him with a soft look on her face. "They never would've let her go."

Aiden nodded. "That's why Conroy called Zander. They're on it." The team of private security experts based right here in Last Chance took contracts all over the world, and they were very good at what they did.

Ted lived in a shared house with them. "Then it won't take long now. Zander has *serious* issues with women in danger."

Aiden figured everyone should, but that wasn't the reality of this fallen world and the selfish humans who inhabited it. They saw plenty in their role as cops. Zander could be far more effective, but his sphere was a lot wider. He'd do what he could, as would Aiden—just on a local level.

"What about Clarke? Where are we with him?"

Jess angled toward Ted. "Whatcha got for us, babycakes?"

Aiden nearly barfed. "Wow."

Ted shot her a look. "Say what now?"

She shrugged. "I'm trying stuff. To keep things fresh."

Aiden's nausea didn't go anywhere. "Maybe you could keep it fresh when I'm not around to hear about it."

"You're just jealous."

Ted cracked a smile.

Aiden nodded. "Probably. Still…"

Ted motioned to his laptop. "I've been looking at Clarke's phone since Bridget gave it to me. So far the FBI just wants to know if there's anything related to Capeira, so I'm handing that over. But everything else is going to Conroy, who is coordinating between the two."

Aiden nodded. "Have you found anything that can help us locate him, or give us a heads-up about what he's up to?"

Bridget was on the case. If he could help, she'd be done faster.

"We already know he was playing off people he owes money to and pitting them against each other."

Aiden couldn't remember all of that. "Including Capeira?"

"It looks like it." Ted tapped a couple more keys. "I also found an indication he's planning to chop up the database and sell it in batches to the highest bidders. The location of hundreds of former spies and special operators from all military branches. Former feds. Government staffers. They all have bounties on their heads, and they'll be outed to whoever has a grudge against them."

Bridget had told him enough about their company for him to know that Clarke getting his hands on their computer client list was a bad thing. "He doesn't have it though. Not yet?"

"Right."

"It takes two of them to access it, or something like that? For their passwords."

Jess shot him a look. Aiden didn't know what that was about. So what if he knew specific details?

"That's what Bridget told me. They were worried about Clarke capturing one of them. Or getting leverage that would force them to meet with him and hand it over." Aiden blew out a breath. "Eric and Conroy wanted them in protective custody—separately. Millie didn't agree. She let Bridget leave the hospital before anyone could stop her."

He was still mad about that. And the fact she hadn't answered any of his texts since.

The only saving grace? Millie had planted a tracker on her. Eric's wife refused to share the details with Aiden, so he couldn't find her unless she wanted him to, but at least someone could.

Jess blinked. "So that's why she's staying away."

"To keep Sydney safe."

Aiden didn't figure Jess needed to understand Bridget. However, it was good that she did. He wanted them to eventually be friends. "Bridget would never do anything that might put Sydney's life in danger."

"Good." Jess nodded.

Aiden blew out a breath. "Is it going to be like this until I get to the end and everything is settled?"

She worked her mouth for a second. "What if it's never settled? What if it's just one thing after another for the rest of your life?"

"What are you talking about?"

"Life is life, Ade." Jess shrugged. "It doesn't 'settle,' it just changes. You get into a new season, or Sydney does. Things move on, and then you have new challenges. New joys, and new griefs."

Aiden stared at her. "What's even happened to you?"

"Christmas." She lifted the cookie and took another bite. "Duh."

Ted cracked a laugh. "My girl. She's wise *and* she loves the holidays."

"I don't even know who you guys are right now."

Jess hopped off her stool. "We're two people who should head out because it's late. Where's Butch? I wanna say bye."

Aiden tried to figure out if she was serious. "In Sydney's room, so don't wake her up." She didn't need to know he'd cracked the door so the dog could get out whenever he wanted to roam the house. Still, Jess shouldn't be going back there when the jingle of his dog tags would wake Sydney.

"Fine." She pulled on her coat with extra attitude.

All he could think about was Sydney's first words when he had gotten home.

How a blonde woman who was *so tall* let her keep Butch. How she was *so excited* to spend more time with him. And how she *so badly* wanted to know *everything* about that woman, why she'd just give up her dog like that, and how she was connected to Butch.

Aiden had told his daughter Bridget's name, how she was Butch's owner—though nothing about what happened to her dad—and how she'd asked for them to make sure Sydney took very good care of Butch. His daughter was ecstatic about the whole proposition. She'd been asking for a dog for most of her life, ever since her best friend got one.

The mysterious woman was the cause of a good deal of interest in his daughter's life. And why not? She'd been without a mother her whole life.

Until now.

Aiden hugged his friends. "Be safe, okay? Be careful."

Ted nodded. "You, too."

He watched them pull away from the curb and closed the front door. Bridget's house was behind his, where their garages backed up to each other, the alleyway in between.

If he went into his bedroom, he could look out between the curtain and the blinds. Like a total creeper. She probably wasn't even there.

Aiden drew out his phone and stared at it. She still hadn't replied to any of his messages. Was she even okay? He wanted to ask. To find out where she was and what she was doing. But he just flipped the phone end over end against the side of his leg instead.

Better than looking desperate.

To distract himself, he boiled water with the electric kettle and made decaf coffee in his French press. He called Basuto and got an update on the overdose they'd worked—the manager from the bowling alley. It still didn't sit right with him that a regular guy had been caught up in this. Everyone else involved had been regular drug users, except him.

It made no sense. But the theory that each death hadn't been accidental definitely held a whole lot more weight now. That was for sure.

Aiden pushed the plunger down on his French press, feeling the satisfying give to it. He poured his cup and turned to the living room.

A tall guy stood in the entryway, the front door closed behind him. He lifted a gun. "Put that down."

Aiden wanted to throw it at him. His gun was on top of the refrigerator, in a lockbox with a PIN. He studied the man. Took a sip of his drink to convey calmness. Nothing inside him was calm, and the coffee was far too hot for sipping. He hid the fact it burned his tongue and tried to figure out who this guy was.

Not Clarke.

This was the guy from the bowling alley. White shirt and dress pants. Red tips to his ears, though given he had no coat on, didn't give Aiden any idea how long he'd been outside. Watching. This was the guy he'd seen that woman talking to. The one who'd later turned up dead in her truck.

"You're here to kill me, too?" Aiden eyed the gun. "It won't look like an OD if you use that."

"Put the mug down and we can do this with little fuss."

"So you get your way?" Instead, he planned to give it as much "fuss" as possible.

Sydney was upstairs. This man would never know that if Aiden could help it.

Aiden reached back and pulled out his phone. "I don't think so." He held it behind his back while he pressed the power button five times to make an emergency call to 911. Without looking, he had no idea if it went through.

"I knew you'd be a problem. That's why this is necessary. Whether you like it or not, you're going to die tonight." The silk shirt guy pulled out a pouch from his pants pocket and tossed it onto the counter. "You're about to go on the ride of your life. Too bad you'll wind up dead at the end of it."

And if he didn't, he'd get shot?

Either way, Sydney would be fatherless.

"Don't do this."

30

Bridget crawled on her elbows over the hill and looked down. "In position."

Sasha's reply crackled through the earbud of their comms. "So, you're still mad."

"Uh, duh." Bridget tugged binoculars from her backpack and looked through them at the warehouse below. It had once been a big box store. Even back when she was a kid, this had been the place to get everything. On the edge of town, it had been touted as a sign the big city was encroaching on their small community. Now it was out of business. Someone should've bought the empty building years ago. Turned it into a gym, or a play center for kids. Even an indoor park would be cool, or a library. Or a coffee shop slash play center slash bookstore.

"Great." Sasha mumbled something about it being better if Bridget had just killed her.

Bridget frowned. "Stop whining." She couldn't make out any movement below. "I don't see anyone."

"Look." Sasha sighed. "Sydney is happy and healthy—and safe, right?"

"What more do I want?" That was the inference. Bridget wanted to argue with her. To state a case that *she* wasn't happy or safe. Bridget hadn't been either of those things for years. Meanwhile, Sasha would contend that she'd done the right thing for the baby—and Bridget. She would then argue that Bridget couldn't have become the woman she was without these experiences.

As if that could ever justify her actions.

Sasha didn't see the need to seek justification. She was already thoroughly convinced she'd done the right thing.

"Do you want to meet her?"

The answer came quickly. "No."

Bridget caught the tone in her voice. "Are you scared of a kid?"

Sasha scoffed audibly. "Please. As if."

She totally was. Her gut reaction over a child was to freak out? Sasha was more complicated than anyone Bridget had ever met, and spending time with her meant peeling back those layers. When Sasha allowed it.

Bridget spotted a truck pull up at one end of the building. The occupants got out and moved inside. "Two males, coming in on the east."

"She is happy, right?"

Bridget detected a slight note of worry. "Definitely. Aiden has been wonderful. That's plain enough to see."

"Then what's the problem?"

Bridget clenched her back teeth. Sasha really didn't know? No one could be that ignorant, surely. Sasha frequently decided how the world was, and that was what she believed. A form of denial—she could convince herself whatever she wanted. For example, her belief that tearing Sydney from Bridget's life was the best thing for everyone. Including Sasha.

"Your issues regarding babies, and potentially being around one, hardly excuses what you did. I believed she was dead, and Aiden thought I was as well. All because that's what you told us."

"It was necessary."

Bridget had to wonder if there was any point arguing with her logic. Sometimes she questioned if Sasha even had emotions. The truth was more that she felt deeply and had to work twice as hard to keep from being sucked down by her feelings. Her grief.

"I need you in my life." Bridget could admit that much. "I think we need to work toward a place where I can forgive you, and you can accept it."

"That's the worst idea I've ever heard."

"Sash, I know you think—"

"I'm in position."

"Move in." Bridget dropped the binoculars beside the backpack and palmed her gun. She jogged down the side of the hill toward the loading bay of the empty building.

A total of six guys inside. No idea where they were, or how to navigate the interior. There had been no time to pull up old blueprints for the layout. She hit the side of the building, forgetting about the gunshot graze on the side of her arm. Or her other injuries.

She hissed out a breath.

"Okay?"

Sasha heard that? Instead of answering, Bridget turned the tables. "How's your gunshot wound doing?"

Her colleague snorted. "Just get inside."

Bridget figured that meant she was in considerable pain, but chose to ignore it. Or, who knew, maybe she was hopped up on pain meds. Maybe it wasn't super advisable they were about to breach a building in full operational mode…but these were extenuating circumstances. They could debate the particulars of it later.

She picked the lock on the side door and eased it open. Inside smelled like what you might expect an abandoned building with thirty years of old boxes strewn everywhere would smell. Bridget flicked on her flashlight and held it under her gun hand. She braced the weight of her weapon as she moved through an empty hall.

"Center room. Three guys."

"Copy that." Bridget's voice echoed down the hallway.

She figured Sasha would move in before Bridget got there, since that'd happened basically every other time they worked together. Putting herself out there first. Part of her had thought Sasha might be trying to make up for what she'd done to Bridget, as though she felt some guilt for it. Maybe not, though.

That sent a fission of doubt through Bridget that caused a shudder in her step. They were here because Sasha had intel that Clarke wanted to take out Capeira's guys. It was a long shot they'd be able to convince Enrico they had a common enemy, but saving his life would go a long way toward doing that.

Assuming he was here, these guys belonged to his organization, and Clarke really did plan to take them out.

Bridget found the door to the main room, the huge area at the center where the store floor had been. She flipped off her flashlight before moving through the doorway to find cover.

Somewhere along the line, all those rows of shelves that lined the store had been cleared out. Pallets were stacked on one side, and the floor was littered with trash and leaves. Above her, Bridget figured birds nested in the rafters.

Breath puffed out of her mouth as a cloud. Bridget crouched behind a pile of broken-down boxes and stacked wood.

Light flashed at the far end, and the overhead bulbs flipped on.

"You!"

She couldn't see anything from here. Not until Sasha strode into the room. Then a man emerged from a side office, flanked by two men. All armed. Capeira's guys. Neither was Enrico, but that didn't mean he wasn't here.

Bridget grasped her gun and watched Sasha sway her hips across the room. She stopped fifteen or so feet from the Capeira guys and stuck out one foot, cocking her hip. Bridget nearly snorted but didn't dare make any noise. She did roll her eyes, though. So much drama.

"Yeah. Me." Sasha lifted her chin. "What about me?"

She was going to get killed, waltzing in here like this.

"You killed my cousin!" The man started forward, but one of the others grabbed his arm.

Bridget figured he was referring to the guys in the van.

The second man nudged his friend. "Capeira told us not to kill them."

Sasha didn't even react. "Speaking of Enrico. Call him. I have something for him."

Bridget stiffened. That didn't sound like information. More like a package to deliver, which could very well be her and not what she thought they'd been here to do.

She came out from behind her hiding spot, ready to do what was necessary. Even if that meant protecting a woman who'd betrayed her trust.

She crept forward but stuck to as much cover as she could find.

"What do you have that you think Enrico will want?" The man waved one hand at her. "Unless it's your head."

"Oh, I have something for him."

Bridget almost thought she was here to kill Enrico. It certainly had crossed her mind also, but Clarke would disappear if that happened. What they needed was to turn the tables on both. Catch their underhanded coworker while the feds brought the hammer down on *their* suspect.

"It really is too bad I can't kill you." The man leaned toward Sasha, just a fraction. "Yet." He dipped his chin and looked Sasha up, then down. "Doesn't mean we can't have fun while we wait, though."

Bridget rushed toward the closest man and slammed her gun down. She aimed for his head but he turned at the last second, and the butt of her weapon smacked onto his shoulder. He yelped and his knees gave out. Bridget hit him again in the head.

The other one had turned to see the commotion. Before Bridget could get shot, Sasha pulled her weapon out and shot the guy first. Thankfully, Bridget didn't catch it except out the corner of her eye. She didn't glance over after the man hit the ground.

That left the mouthy, leering one between them.

"Pull your weapon slowly," Bridget ordered. "Set it down on the ground. Or you die."

He didn't move. "Thought you weren't here for that."

Sasha shrugged. "Your choice. Die now, or die when Clarke sets off a bomb and kills your boss."

Bridget didn't much care, either way. But she didn't want to see it happen. Her trauma had been way too close to the surface lately. She didn't think she'd get through it unscathed. "Or, you can call your boss and let him know what you've learned. Save his life so he knows he owes you for it." Bridget paused. "Up to you."

"But it needs to happen quickly." Sasha didn't let the guy get a word in. "Or Clarke will be here with his device, and we'll all get blown to bits."

Not how Bridget wanted to end this season of her life. So close to knowing Sydney and finally being a mother to her daughter.

The fire chief had been killed months ago. Her father was dead. She was about to take down her enemies. The end of this terrorizing time in her life was so close, she could almost reach out and grasp it. Even she and Sasha would figure out their differences. Despite the other woman's actions and the anger that still burned in her, Bridget didn't want to lose one of the few true friends she'd had in her life. They wouldn't get through this easily, but they would get through it.

Bridget wasn't going to settle for anything else.

"Fine." The guy huffed. "I'm getting out my phone. I'll call

Enrico."

He had the conversation in Spanish. Bridget knew enough to get by, but he spoke too quickly for her to make any sense of what he was saying. Sasha, on the other hand, was fluent. Still, while he conversed with Enrico, Bridget decided to make him think they didn't understand him.

She caught Sasha's attention behind his back and silently mouthed enough of her plan for Sasha to understand. The corner of her mouth twitched.

Bridget shifted and glanced around. "How long until Clarke gets here do you think?"

"Dunno." Sasha shrugged.

Enrico's man shifted. He said a few more things in Spanish, and Sasha gave Bridget a tiny nod. An indication he believed they didn't understand him.

"I'd rather not be here when he gets here." Bridget figured she'd go for it all. Make him think she was scared. "Either of them."

"Up to you."

Enrico's man said more. Bridget watched Sasha's very subtle reaction. "After what we did, you shouldn't be here either. We should just let this guy convince Enrico, and then do what we can to be far from here when he reaches out to contact us about a deal."

Make them think Bridget and Sasha were expecting concessions.

"We can get Clarke, too. That will help."

Enrico's guy turned to the side, still speaking. Sasha mouthed, *They think we're idiots.*

Bridget nearly smiled. Problem was, that was the idea.

Enrico will be here soon. I don't know how long. His man shifted and Sasha blanked her face, as though they hadn't been talking. But he didn't even notice their exchange. Sasha continued to mouth her findings to Bridget. *He doesn't believe us. They want to capture both of us so they can…*

Bridget didn't need an explanation. She wanted to slam Enrico's man with the butt of her gun midsentence and watch him drop to the floor.

Instead, Sasha grabbed the man's phone before Bridget could do anything.

"Hey!"

She pointed her gun at him, held the phone to her ear, and spoke in Enrico's native language. Then she hung up on him. "I told him we're going to kill him just like you killed his brother."

Bridget swung around. "You said *what*?"

Sasha motioned Bridget forward. "Come on. We got what we need from Enrico, and we need to get out of this place before Clarke gets here to set the bomb."

Bridget blinked. "He…we…*what*?"

"Let's go."

Bridget took one step but then someone grabbed her foot, and she hit the deck on all fours, crying out. A heavy weight landed on her and smashed her face into the dirty tile floor.

Sasha screeched. The sound cut off mid-way through but was quickly followed by a loud exclamation considered uncouth in many circles.

Bridget didn't have time to offer commentary on her friend's choice of language. She planted one foot on the floor and braced. She rolled all her weight to the right and deposited the heft on her back and to the side. Then she moved in the opposite direction and scrambled around for her gun.

He kicked at her knee. She moved just in time, and he slammed his shiny shoe into her thigh instead. Bridget grunted. Her entire leg went numb.

Sasha screeched again. She sounded *super* mad.

This wasn't turning out well.

Before Bridget could get her fingers around her gun, she spotted the glint of a knife as it swung through the air. He swiped out to stab her. The second she realized it, Bridget was already rolling.

She heard the thud as the blade hit the floor behind her. She did her best to get out of reach but came up against an unconscious man.

The gun. She needed to get to—

"FBI! Freeze!"

Multiple people raced in. Boots thundered across the floor, bringing the squeak of tactical belts and rubber that hadn't been broken in yet.

Bridget didn't move. She kept her hands in plain view, fingers spread.

Her gun lay discarded between her and Enrico's guy.

He let go of his knife.

Sasha shoved her guy away with a cry. He turned to his back and Bridget spotted a bloody nose. She flicked her gaze in the other direction and saw Millie bringing up the rear of the pack of feds.

She set one hand on her hip. "Sasha. What did you do?"

Bridget felt her phone buzz in her jacket pocket. One of the agents helped her to her feet, and she had to hop a few times until the feeling returned to her numb leg. She pulled out her phone as Millie approached.

Before she could see what it was, Bridget asked, "GPS tracker?"

Millie shrugged. "Clearly I was right to be concerned." She glanced around. "Enrico isn't here?"

"That guy knows where he is." She pointed at the one who'd tried to stab her. "And that is on his way."

"Great." Millie turned away. "Eric! Capeira is on his way here!"

Bridget had enough energy left in her only to sit and watch the FBI run a sting operation. She looked at her phone and saw a text, a photo of a little girl she'd only seen from a distance.

She read the message under it.

And froze.

31

Aiden played along. All the way to being forced into his armchair recliner while he watched the guy take out a syringe. How long was it going to take the PD to send a couple of officers? Even one unit would do. Just a distraction, so Aiden could rush this guy and tackle him for his gun. It would hurt however he did it, so he wasn't too worried about the methodology of his plan.

As long as Sydney remained safe—and preferably unaware she'd ever been in danger—he hardly cared how he fared.

Aiden started to worry his emergency call hadn't gone through. That no one from the Last Chance Police Department was coming to help him.

As the guy prepped the syringe, he loosely held his gun pointed at Aiden. Aiden's mind raced to figure out a back-up plan. If no one from the department showed up to distract this guy, then he had no idea how to…

With a low growl, Butch ran into the room. His whole body shook as he lifted his front paws off the ground and landed in time with each reverberation of his throaty woof.

Aiden didn't hesitate to utilize the distraction.

He ran at the guy and slammed into his middle, head

ducked. Arms in. The guy landed first, Aiden on top. The second his breath expelled from his lungs, Aiden got his forearm across the guy's throat. With his other hand, he grasped the wrist holding the gun. "Drop it."

"I'd comply if I were you." Frees stepped into the room.

Basuto showed up right behind him. Both had their guns raised, questioning looks on their faces.

"Took you guys long enough."

Butch got ready to bark again. Aiden sent him a sharp glance. "Butch, go lay down."

The dog turned, walked to the corner where Sydney had insisted they set down a blanket for him, and lay down with his muzzle on his crossed front paws.

Aiden exhaled and his whole body sagged as he fought the urge to collapse. "You're a good boy. Yes, you are."

"Are you talking to the dog?"

He glanced at Frees. "Considering he did your job? Yeah, I am."

Basuto cracked a smile.

"You guys wanna secure this man for me?"

Basuto's smile grew to a chuckle. "What do you think, Frees?"

"Meh." The officer ambled forward despite his vocalization and kicked the gun from the guy's hand.

Aiden flipped him to his front and held the guy's hands while Frees secured them with a set of cuffs. Thankfully, he didn't struggle. Aiden wasn't sure he had it in him to contend with a man who didn't want to get arrested.

Given the guy's face when Frees hauled him to his feet, Aiden figured he was simply biding his time and planned to renew his fight later. Aiden patted him down, found a wallet, and handed it to Frees.

"Save that energy to fight your case in court." Aiden didn't need to wind up in witness protection. He could hardly plead with Bridget to go into WITSEC with him, though maybe she would now that she knew about Sydney. For the sake of not losing her again. Still, the last thing he wanted to do was be moved across the country where he'd have to take an assumed name. Not to mention he'd never be able to work in law enforcement again.

The guy glared at him.

"You tried. You failed." He didn't need this guy making it personal.

"You heard him." Frees gave the guy a slight shake from the grip he had on the man's elbow. "Nothing more for you to do but wait for your day in front of a judge."

Aiden planned to be there so he could explain to everyone present exactly how close he'd come to being this guy's next deadly target.

He ran his hands down his face. This was a man who took out everyone who opposed him. He didn't want to hear any more about him or what he had going on with the drug trade in town.

"Get him out of here, Officer Frees." Basuto moved past Frees, coming into the living room. "You okay?"

Aiden ran his hands down his face again. He scrubbed his hands over the growth of stubble on his cheeks and chin.

"He won't target you. There's no way Conroy would let that happen, and none of the rest of us are willing to allow a scum bag who thinks he has power to hurt one of ours."

Aiden nodded. The sergeant knew it was what he needed to hear. "Thanks."

"Go check on Sydney." Basuto motioned to the hall. "Then we should talk over everything."

Aiden wasn't sure if Basuto thought it was necessary, given the threat, or if he knew that was exactly where Aiden wanted to be right now. He patted the dog's head as he passed and then headed down the hall to Sydney's room.

She was asleep. Aiden paused the audiobook before Aslan's voice could boom through the room and potentially wake her. If she hadn't woken up when Butch had barked, then she had to be exhausted and he didn't want her to be disturbed. He closed the door silently and returned to the living area.

He went to the alarm panel beside the front door. The windows were all still armed. No one could get into her room without serious noise erupting.

He usually only set the door alarms when he went to bed, but that might change now that he'd faced down an intruder. The idea his mistake could have cost his life and Sydney her father, or even cost Sydney's life, made him want to punch a hole in the drywall beside the alarm panel. That, or scream at someone.

He could see now how Bridget might feel that same way. The powerlessness of knowing he'd brought danger right to the home of the person he cared about most in the world made him want to be sick. Or run away.

Even though he wanted her in Sydney's and his life, he also knew she wanted to never bring intentional threat to them.

He could say now that he thoroughly understood why she'd stayed away.

And why she had left Butch.

"You done fussing yet?"

Aiden didn't glance over, though he wanted the sergeant to see the look on his face. Instead, he strode through the living room and righted the end table that'd crashed over when he tackled that guy.

"Leave the rest. I need to take pictures for the report."

Aiden slumped down onto the couch. "So why are we talking instead of working."

There was a minute or two of silence, then Basuto's phone buzzed. "Frees ran his driver's license. His name is Simon Dempsey."

"Anyone we know?"

Basuto settled onto the opposite end of the couch, one foot up on the lip of the coffee table. "Two outstanding warrants,

Washington state and Oregon. Drug trafficking for one, and the other is distribution of narcotics. This guy is big time and the heat was on. I think he's here to lay low, and then you fingered him as connected. Your instincts about him and the woman in the office were right on, and it paid off."

"Because he killed the woman and the bowling alley manager, and then came here to kill me?"

"Tell me what happened."

Aiden ran it all down for him. From the moment he turned and saw the guy to when Frees walked him out. To jail. Where he wouldn't be able to lash out, or come back at Aiden with deadly intent. Again.

Basuto shrugged one shoulder. "You're the one who pointed him out. For that reason, no one else was harmed and we got him."

"Okay." That was good. Basuto was right, though Aiden wasn't going to say that aloud. As soon as the adrenaline rush of what happened bled off—after he totally freaked the rest of the way out and probably shed a couple of relieved tears in the shower—he would realize it was a pretty good outcome. Just not yet. He was still stuck on freaked out and angry.

"Take the sergeant's exam, Officer Donaldson."

Aiden blinked. After everything that had just happened, Basuto wanted to talk about this? If he took that exam, he would be the same rank as Basuto. "You want me to work you out of a job?"

Basuto's lips twitched. "Maybe I do. But you know Frees will be an officer forever. He's content to walk a beat until retirement. Jess is gunning for a detective's shield. You need to take the exam. Being a sergeant means more steady hours, better pay. You'll have more time for…family stuff."

God-willing, Aiden planned on having a whole lot of that "family stuff" going on very soon. Bridget would be here, and things would settle. She and Sydney would spend time together. Sure, he was scared she would shut him out and fight for custody of their daughter, instead of the alternative—getting to know both of them and maybe becoming a family for real. But he would wait to find out.

He knew what he wanted. But what he needed was time to find out what she did.

Aiden figured if he had to take a test, Basuto could too. "And you?"

"I'll take the lieutenant's exam." He paused. "If you sit for the sergeant's."

Aiden stared him down. Both of them would get a promotion. Did Conroy agree, or was this just the sergeant throwing out ideas to see what stuck? "I'll think about it."

"That's all I ask." Basuto stood, closed his notepad and pocketed it in the cargo pocket of his pants. "I have to go catch up with the feds now." He blew out a long breath. "Some hubbub at the old warehouse store building tonight involving their case."

"The Capeiras?" If that's what it was, it would be where Bridget had gone. He hoped she was all right. Given her friend's presence, he was worried.

Basuto nodded. "Apparently the feds found your girl and her friend fighting off the Capeira foot soldiers they had located."

"Is she okay?"

Basuto shrugged.

"Are you still on duty?" He might be working, but that didn't mean he was still on shift.

"No." Basuto checked his phone. "Technically, I clocked out half an hour ago."

Aiden stood, all that adrenaline surging anew. He grabbed his keys and phone. "Stay here with Sydney."

"Donaldson."

"I need to know she's okay." He told Basuto the alarm code. "Lock up behind me."

He raced around to the garage. He needed some of the

erratic sensations to dissipate a little, otherwise he'd wind up driving like a crazy person.

Aiden headed for the warehouse and found an ocean of cars with red and blue flashing lights. An ambulance. Cops everywhere, feds, and a few from Last Chance PD, like Conroy and Mia. He shut off the car but didn't get out. He'd have to fight the ocean of people in order to find Bridget. Instead, he sent her a quick text letting her know he was here.

Exhaustion rolled over him like a wave crashing on the beach as adrenaline dissipated. He was safe. Sydney was safe. There were so many cops here. Of course Bridget was safe as well. She had to be.

Thank You, Lord. Aiden didn't pray that enough, and he should. Mostly he tended to hold on for dear life while expecting the worst. But that wasn't what'd happened today. They were okay. The man who tried to murder him tonight, while his daughter slept in her room, was in police custody now.

His hands started to shake more and more until his whole body fought the tremors. He gripped the steering wheel and sucked in long breaths until he could think again. But what filled his head was more of that sense of relief and gratitude. Knowing what could've happened, hadn't.

Once the feeling passed, he climbed out of the car.

The first familiar face he spotted this time was Millie. Aiden made his way over. "Hey."

She nodded, every bit the authority figure that any of these feds were. And given her position as Bridget's boss, that didn't surprise him. Bridget had huge amounts of respect for her. "Things aren't going well right now. Capeira was supposed to show up, and we were all set up for a sting operation."

"Didn't go as planned?"

"He never showed. We think someone tipped him off."

"And Bridget?" He didn't want to sound too needy, but it was what it was. Millie probably already knew that her employee was the only reason he was here.

"I heard you had a fun night." She lifted her brows.

Aiden shrugged. "We got the guy who has been killing people, making it look like they OD'd."

"Donaldson!" Conroy jogged over.

Millie waved and walked away. Without ever telling him where Bridget was.

His chief slapped him on the shoulder and left his hand there. "Are you okay? I heard what happened."

Aiden nodded. "I'm good. Basuto and Frees got there in time."

Conroy squeezed his shoulder. "I was tied up here, or I'd have come over too and made sure myself."

"No worries." He tried to spot Bridget. Wherever she was. "It's all good. How about here?"

"The feds want Capeira, but he's proving to be one step ahead of them at every turn."

Aiden nodded because he knew how that felt. Bridget seemed to slip through his fingers. Not that he was trying to capture her. Still, it seemed as though she had some elusive quality to her. As though, if he didn't hold on, she would suddenly be gone.

Again.

Maybe for good this time.

Aiden spotted her. She headed through the gathered crowd, away from him. "Can you excuse me?"

Conroy nodded. "Go. But don't stay long. You should be at home."

Aiden just wanted to talk to her, make sure she was all right. Her body language was stiff. As though something was wrong. He jogged after her while all the fatigue of the day weighed down on him and slowed his steps.

She looked at her phone, which lit her face with the light of the screen. Yes, there was definitely something wrong.

"Bridget!" He jogged faster.

She kept walking, scanning the crowd in the other direction, not seeming to have heard him.

"Bridget! Wait up!"

She moved fast, headed for a vehicle parked at the road. As she approached the van, the side door slid open.

Aiden saw a gun.

"Bridget!" He reached for his weapon but felt...nothing. No gun. He hadn't brought it.

He ran faster, uncaring that he was headed, unarmed, into danger.

She climbed into the van, swinging a glance over her other shoulder. But Aiden was too late. The door slid closed as she was forced in at gunpoint.

Just as he neared it, the vehicle drove away. Aiden wasn't going to catch up to it on foot. He needed to get back to his car and—

Sharp pain jabbed the side of his neck.

Aiden heard a crackle, and everything went black.

32

She'd heard her name. In the middle of everything, the van and the photo—focusing on what she *needed* to do—Bridget had heard Aiden call her name. Sydney's life was in danger. That had already been true. Add to that now, a more direct threat.

If she didn't go, Sydney would be hurt.

From the first time she'd heard her name, she'd tried to find him. Desperately, she'd looked for him. Somehow she'd have communicated to him there was a problem. That she needed help, and Sydney needed extra security.

"Get in." Clarke had sent her that photo. He'd used a tone she had never heard before, and then pointed a gun at her.

At first Bridget hadn't moved, but sought Aiden in the crowd instead by looking over her shoulder. Searching for some kind of commotion, and then just for his face when she realized he'd been calling her name. The way he stood. The way he moved. But, no Aiden. Where was he? She was banking on him showing up just in time.

"You know what happens if you don't."

She'd had no choice but to climb into the van. As the door closed, she'd heard her name again and caught a glimpse of someone running. She was sure it had been Aiden. But who were those men coming up behind him? And why had Aiden suddenly stopped?

Bridget blinked awake, out of the dream. Though it was more like a nightmare of true events. She lay up against the side of the van. One knee ached as if she'd smashed it on something. It sure didn't feel as if it had happened an hour ago. Right after seeing Aiden. Being forced into the van by Clarke at gunpoint while he threatened to hurt Sydney.

Bridget winced and shifted. *Ugh*. Her head was groggy, as though she'd been zapped with a stun gun. She tried to shake off the sensation and pushed herself to sit…though it was difficult with bound hands.

The van turned a corner and her body swayed with the movement. She nearly fell back to her side, but caught herself by planting her hands on the floor. Right by her phone.

She snatched it up and flipped it over in her hands so she could—

The screen was shattered. Bridget tapped the screen to try and wake it up, but nothing happened. It was completely busted—of course, the only reason Clarke would have left it back here with her. As an operator and former military, he had serious skills. In a fight between them, there was no way she would win while injured, especially since he had all the firepower. That canceled out the fact he was injured, too.

She had to get the drop on him before he realized the fight had started. Utilize the element of surprise and get the upper hand that way.

She looked around for a weapon of some kind she could use. Not that she thought he'd left her one after already going to all the trouble of taking off her jacket, shoes and socks. Her knife was nowhere to be found. It was freezing back here, while no doubt he had the heater running full blast in the front where he drove.

Her breath was visible in the chilled air.

She slumped against the side and fought a sense of despair. No, that was what he wanted for her. She still had hope.

Bridget knew with all certainty that she *always* had hope.

No matter how bad things got, she could always count on the fact God was in control. After all, her daughter was alive. She knew God would grant her peace and help calm her fears. That was what He loved to do with His children, the ones who believed in Him *and* looked to Him to supply their needs.

Without Him she would have given up a long time ago.

And maybe she wasn't the best Christian. God knew she didn't always focus on the right things, or do everything she should. But she was honest about herself. She'd long since figured there was no point lying to Him when He knew everything anyway.

Please don't let Sydney get hurt. And please, help me too.

All she could think about was that photo. The one she'd received in her texts.

Her little girl. She knew it was Sydney from seeing her earlier, and she'd studied that face on the text message photo. The first time she'd been able to do it up close. Her daughter was gorgeous.

The picture was one of her looking at something to the side of the camera, in a place lit up by colored lights. Given it was the middle of the night, it might not be from today. The expression on her face wasn't terror, but still serious concern. She'd been upset by something. Which, for someone wearing a unicorn headband, should not ever have to happen.

Darkness overcame the back of the van until she could no longer see her bare feet. They'd pulled off somewhere? From the way the streetlights that had illuminated and bounced off the windows above where she sat had now stopped, she assumed they had pulled off the road, onto some sort of side street.

Or they'd gone into a tunnel.

A building.

Where was he taking her? Though she had no idea, her

mind was happy to provide possible answers. Mostly images from thriller TV cop shows and the few horror movies she'd seen.

Bridget needed a solid plan so when he opened the back door, she could…do something. Rush out. Jump him. Launch up and tackle him to the ground.

All sounded great, but her body was losing energy fast. The longer she stayed put against the side of the van, the heavier her limbs got—and the weaker she felt. *Lord, I need help.* She immediately thought of Aiden, then remembered what she'd seen right before the van door shut her in. Aiden *and* those men coming up behind him. The way he'd stiffened and stopped so suddenly.

The van door made a clicking sound, causing her to jump, and then began sliding open. Bridget winced against the glare of fluorescent light. She'd fallen into unconsciousness when she should've been readying herself to attack. "Sydney."

Clarke stood in the open doorway. "What?"

She spoke louder this time. "Sydney."

"Who? You don't even know the kid in the photo. So don't pretend to know her name." He frowned, and then sneered. "Or is that the name of your dead baby?"

Bridget said nothing. She tried to process what on earth he'd just said, what it even meant and what he knew. He believed…her baby had died? He thought she didn't know the girl in the photo.

Also…*what?*

Clarke sniffed. "I figured it was close enough. She even kind of looks like you." He shook his head. "Sasha spouted all that nonsense about lying to you over the whole dead baby thing. I figured you'd care about any kid...even some neighborhood kid you've never met. Maternal instinct and all that."

Bridget blinked. Her brain spun as she tried again to figure out what he thought he knew. He didn't believe that Sydney was her child. He had no idea.

He had no *idea.*

"You threatened her." Bridget barely got the words out. "All to get me to go with you."

"So you'll jump through hoops for some random kid, but you don't care enough when I'm the one who needs you?" Clarke made a face. "Figures. Doesn't matter, though. You have your uses, and now I know I can use that little neighbor girl against you." He lifted a gun and motioned with it. "Get out of the van."

"You sent me her picture. She looked scared."

He shook his head. "I sent what I could find. Hacked *so many things*. And you came here, didn't you, thinking I was gonna hurt her?" A smile curled the corners of his lips. "I guess it wasn't a total waste of time."

Relief flooded her. Sydney was still safe.

"Now get out."

"For what? Why kidnap me?" And she'd seen Aiden. Had he been taken, like she was? Hit with a stun gun before he could run after her. To help her as he'd been about to do.

Did Clarke have anything to do with that?

"You're going to help me."

She lifted her gaze to him. "Why would I do that? You shot me." Among other things, but she didn't think it was worth rehashing their bathroom fight at her dad's house.

"Because I hold a mean grudge."

"And I rejected *you*? You killed my father. Maybe that makes us even."

Seriously, she couldn't believe this was all about the fact she'd spurned him. She'd had no idea Clarke even cared that much about her.

He made a pfft sound. "Too preoccupied to see what's in front of your face. Always clutching that backpack and your precious scrapbook." His brows lifted. "You think I didn't know about that?"

She pressed her lips together, still leaning against the inside wall of the van. Trying to gather more of what Clarke knew—or thought he did.

The doctor might've said she didn't have a concussion, but Bridget thought she may have developed one since she'd left the hospital. Right now, the wall behind her was something solid, while the rest of her world twisted and careened. Not a solid foundation. *Lord.* He was her real foundation. God and, well, Aiden's eyes when he looked at her.

She could kick that gun out of Clarke's hand. Or grab something from inside the van and swing out with it as she closed in on him. Her mind couldn't settle long enough on one thing to figure out how to make it worth the risk of failure.

"Of course I looked into you." His tone flattened and he shook his head. "I wouldn't date someone I hadn't thoroughly checked out. Took some doing, but I found the death certificate. After that, it didn't take long to get ahold of your medical records. I even have your high school transcripts. And your arrest record." His teeth flashed in a facsimile of a smile. "That caught my interest. Made me want to meet *that* girl. You know?"

He grasped her ankle. Before she could figure out what he was doing, he dragged her across the floor of the van to the open door and let go so her foot hit the ground.

"We're in a hangar?" She'd been in one recently and this looked familiar.

"Not for long. Let's go."

"I need my shoes." Bridget twisted around. She rummaged in the van, needing the time to think all this through. She pulled them on with her bound hands. "What are we doing?"

The better she cooperated, the more chances she'd have to overpower him and run away. It might be difficult since she had no idea where she even was. But not impossible—and certainly easier while wearing shoes.

He studied her as though he knew exactly what she was thinking. Maybe he did. Maybe she had a calculated look on her face. "Two-person job. That means you're helping me."

"Couldn't get Sasha to do it with you?"

"Ha."

"Seems like you've been talking to her."

"I don't trust her though." He reached out to touch her hair. Bridget ducked out of the way, frowning. "Not the way I trust you."

Bridget wondered if she'd ever really trusted him back. And yet, with Aiden, she implicitly handed over her thoughts and emotions without even thinking whether he would care for her feelings. The trust she had for him was instinctive.

Clarke's jaw flexed. He just needed to deal with how she was. They weren't going to get close.

She lifted her chin. "Just tell me what you want."

"Two-person job." He said again as he pulled out his phone and checked the time, never once wavering with the aim of his gun. "Breaking into the server farm."

"You're still after the database?"

"And you're gonna get it for me." He took a step back. "Now get out. The chopper is waiting."

33

"You're supposed to be following them!"

"We can't get in there without ID. It's an airport. They have security."

The first man, the one in charge, muttered under his breath something in Spanish.

Aiden's hands were bound. The car stopped and his body swayed, constricted between two guys. One on either side of him in the backseat of the car. The two in conversation sat in front, driver and passenger.

Between the five of them, someone needed to roll down a window.

"Find a place where we can see." That was Enrico Capeira, the boss. The ones responsible for the predicament he was in—having been stunned, tossed in their vehicle and bound, his hands stuck together with those plastic ties that cut into your skin and *hurt.*

Aiden gritted his teeth. Why did they even want him? "I can get in there. I still have my police shield in my pocket."

All they had to do was snip off the plastic tie and set him free.

The guy beside him shoved a hand to the back of Aiden's

head and slammed his face into his knee so fast he wasn't able to stop it or pull back on his momentum. Pain exploded in his cheekbone.

Enrico continued as if Aiden's face hadn't just about imploded in the back of the van. "Stop right here."

The driver jerked the car to the side and pulled over on the street outside the tiny nearby regional airport. Aiden swayed against one guy, then the other. He gritted his teeth and tried to contain his frustration.

"You need in there?" He braced for the retaliation this time. "I can get you in there."

Enrico Capeira turned. "You think I need help from a cop? You're gonna prove useful, eventually. But until then, we'll see how this plays out."

Aiden figured that meant they would kill him. But if all this wasn't because he was a cop, then why did they grab him? The only reason he could come up with was that they'd heard him calling Bridget's name right before. That he was apprehended because he was meddling in what they had planned for her.

Had he drawn attention to himself by causing a commotion? Yelled so loud the feds had realized the danger—and wound up getting himself snatched up in the process. Had no one seen?

God, please let someone have seen what happened.

Maybe they were right behind this car. They could have already figured out a way to get Capeira and rescue Aiden.

"Once we figure out what they're doing here, we'll kill both of them." Enrico's voice held a thread of dark violence.

Aiden had to wonder what all Capeira had planned. Sure, he intended to end the lives of both Clarke and Bridget—and no doubt—his life. But it sounded like there was more to it than a simple death.

Sickness rolled in his stomach. *Sydney.*

This was the second time his life had been threatened tonight.

The only saving grace was the fact he'd left Basuto to care for Sydney in his absence. The sergeant would take care of his daughter. And if Aiden and Bridget were both killed, then his will stated very plainly that Sydney would be raised by Conroy and Mia. He'd emailed over the update earlier today to request Bridget's name be added. It needed to be signed off on to be legal, but her name would at least be on record. After Conroy and Mia's wedding, he'd sat down with them and asked for this favor.

It would be okay.

Things might be bad, but God would be there after the dust settled.

"Why'd you guys grab me anyway?" He wanted them distracted. To delay whatever move they'd planned in order to deal with him. "I don't know you. I've got nothing to do with whatever this is."

"No? You don't got nothin' to do with Bridget in there? Or her boyfriend?"

Aiden held back his reaction to that.

"You probably know all about what they're up to." Enrico lifted a gun and pointed it at Aiden. "Or you don't, and you're nobody she cares about. In which case, I don't need you."

That statement left Aiden with exactly two choices. Tell them he meant nothing to Bridget and get shot, or tell them he did mean something to her and get used as leverage over her… and then get shot.

Enrico seemed to think that was amusing, given the way the skin around his eyes crinkled.

Aiden knew plenty. Like how they'd been too late to get to Bridget, so they'd grabbed him instead. Probably just trying to salvage whatever plans they had. It was becoming clear Enrico didn't know what Clarke was up to.

The Capeira boss chuckled. "That's what I thought."

The driver used a Spanish word Aiden didn't know—one that got Enrico's attention, and a frown. "They're coming out."

Aiden watched the open doors of a hangar. Clarke and Bridget strode out, walking like a couple. They might be close, but he could see the tension in both of them. If Aiden had to guess, he'd say Clarke likely held a gun pointed at Bridget's ribs.

And they were headed for…

Aiden glanced at possible options of where they might be going.

"The chopper." Enrico muttered a curse word and pulled out his phone.

Sure enough, Clarke walked Bridget to a helicopter. The rotors were already turning. Ready to go.

But where?

"Their phones are still in the hangar." Enrico slammed his palm down on the dash. "No way to track them if they fly away in that thing. We need to get in there."

"If we do that, airport security will come gunning for us."

The guy next to Aiden shifted. "I thought we were following them so we can grab whatever they're after?"

Enrico's expression turned thunderous. "I don't pay you to think. Good thing, too, because you'd have been *fired* a long time ago." It was clear the implication of "fired" meant "dead."

The guy stiffened. The driver spoke next. "I can try and follow the chopper?"

Enrico flashed gritted teeth while the driver flinched.

Aiden wanted to be amused by the fact Enrico had clearly inherited his brother's less than stellar lieutenants. Or, given all the men he'd lost recently, he was now scraping the barrel with who he'd brought along.

However, given the number of guns in this car? Aiden decided not to laugh at Enrico's misfortune. He'd only wind up getting shot.

Instead of being easy to dispose of, Aiden needed to figure out how to be useful. "You want to track her?" He asked it while his mind raced, and then he remembered something. Thankfully, he thought fast enough to not give away the fact he was stalling. Which, of course, he was. "I know for a fact she's wearing a GPS tracker."

"So track her."

Aiden shook his head. Then he found himself staring down the barrel of a gun. "I'll get her location. Just give me a phone to use, and I'll call the person who *can* track her. I'll get them to tell me exactly where she goes."

As he spoke, the helicopter took off and they watched Clarke and Bridget fly away.

Everything in Aiden wanted to bust out of the car and run after her. He would probably call her name like he'd done before. Looking like a lovesick fool—which was how he'd ended up in Capeira's clutches in the first place.

"Give me a phone." Aiden knew this was his chance to stay alive *and* get Bridget back from Clarke. "You want to know where they're going? I can find out for you."

Since the only number he knew by heart was the non-emergency number for the police station, Aiden called it and got Eric's phone. When the fed answered with, "Special Agent Cullings," all four of the men in the car stiffened. Enrico tried to play it off, but he wasn't immune to being in such close proximity to a fed. Even just over the phone.

"It's Officer Donaldson. I need to speak with Millie." Desperation leached through his tone, and it wasn't a lie. He could admit to himself he was desperate to get Bridget back. He didn't like the idea of her being in Clarke's clutches. What did that guy even want with her, anyway? Surely not the database still. He'd had the chance to get her password before and hadn't taken it.

"Aiden?"

Relief washed over him at the sound of Millie's voice. "I need you to look up Bridget's GPS location and tell me where she is—where she's headed."

He didn't have a "duress" phrase with Millie. The Last Chance PD had a code phrase, a generic sentence that, said over the phone or radio, meant the officer was in a situation where they were being forced to do something against their will, unable to say that in plain terms. A way to ask for help.

"Is everything okay, Aiden?"

He had to reply as though nothing was wrong, except his responses to the details of his request. The fact Bridget was missing.

"It will be when I've found her." He tried to sound exasperated, not knowing what Millie knew. He assumed she was aware that at least one of them, if not both, had been kidnapped. He also had to play this in a way that was unsurprising to Enrico.

"Agreed. One sec, I'll look it up."

Aiden prayed the whole time as he waited for Millie to get him what he needed. Meanwhile, Enrico's driver pursued the chopper by first heading for the highway and then turning east, following signposts in conjunction with his phone's maps app.

Soon Aiden was out of things to pray for, and Millie still hadn't come back. "Can we crack a window or something?"

Enrico twisted in his chair and brought up his gun.

Aiden should have compassion for their souls—or something like that—and be inclined to pray for them. Maybe he should even take this time to evangelize before they murdered him. But Aiden just didn't have that in him right now. Not when Bridget was in danger, his daughter might lose them both, and he had no way to take down four guys on his own.

He was outmatched, out of options, and out of things to pray for without sounding like a broken record.

"Got it." Millie's tone was different now. Guarded.

He hoped she'd heard at least the one voice of someone with him, giving some sort of indication of who he was with. Then again, as long as she got Bridget back, that was all that mattered, right? Sydney could have the parent she'd never gotten to know, and he could hope they would help each other through what happened to him here because of Capeira.

"She's moving, but not along a road."

"Chopper," Aiden said only that one word. Trying not to lose it and break down in front of these guys.

"She's headed for Denver…" Her voice trailed off. "Zander is calling me. But if she's going into the city, they could be headed for the accountant's office."

He saw Enrico shift. Aiden ignored it. "Wasn't it destroyed?"

"There's another issue. But they'd have to…"

Aiden tensed. "Millie."

He heard someone in the background with her, a low voice. Maybe Eric? She came back. "Denver is also where the server is."

"And that means what?"

"Get access to that, and you could *potentially* get your hands on our entire database." She paused. "But the only way to do that is with two people and, of course, the access code."

"Okay." Aiden sighed. How was this supposed to help?

"That's moot now. I deactivated external access. You can only get to the database from the source. The server." Millie gasped and then hung up.

Aiden watched the phone illuminate. He felt a little more peace knowing that Millie would do everything in her power to track Bridget down before Capeira's guys did. The driver punched down on the gas pedal, and they sped up. It was going to take time to get to the building where the server was located if it was in Denver. By then, he figured the FBI would be all over that place.

Tactical. Snipers. Their whole armed division, HRT—the Hostage Rescue Team that was their SWAT division. Aiden approved of all of that.

Enrico patted the shoulder of the driver. He pulled off.

"Where are we—"

The guy beside him reached for the back of Aiden's head.

He ducked out of the way and smacked into the guy on the other side of him. "Okay. Okay, chill."

Enrico chuckled.

They pulled off the highway and headed for a ranch out in the middle of nowhere. Beside the barn was a small plane.

"*Vamanos.*" Enrico shoved his door open. "Bring the dead cop walking with us."

Aiden was pulled from the car and shoved into the plane.

Dead cop walking?

That didn't sound good at all.

34

Bridget stumbled and nearly fell. "You need an access code to get the data from the server."

Clarke hauled her along with a bruising grip on her arm. The one he'd grazed with a bullet only days ago—though that felt like weeks now. The night Aiden hit her with his police car.

"Your plan has flaws."

Clarke pushed open the front door to the office building while he chuckled low to himself. About what, she didn't know.

"That's all I'm saying." She planned on being belligerent right up until she figured out exactly how she was going to stop him.

She needed a screwdriver.

And a lighter.

Not necessarily in that order.

"Hey!" A uniformed security guard stood up from behind his reception desk. "You can't—"

She knew what was about to happen. Bridget saw it coming. "No—" Too late. Clarke lifted his gun and squeezed off a shot.

Blood blossomed on the security guard's chest, and he fell back onto the seat of his rolling chair before tumbling to the floor.

Bridget screamed. Either she managed to be louder than she'd thought possible, or there was an echo in here. Whatever the case, she thought it was a pretty good attempt to draw attention to herself.

What she needed was to get behind that desk and find useful supplies.

Clarke's grip on her shifted. She took the opportunity and wrenched her arm out through the gap between his thumb and first finger.

It hurt.

She ran to the security guard and collapsed beside him. "He's dead! You killed him!" As though she'd have even the slightest shot to save the guy after a wound like that. Even EMTs wouldn't have been able to do anything for him. But let Clarke think she was distraught. That would slow him down.

Darn. He had nothing useful in his pockets.

Clarke grabbed her elbow. She let him pull her, then used the momentum and shoved him back. He stumbled away, and it was then she knew for sure he wasn't planning to kill her. Clarke might threaten pain, and he'd probably follow through if it didn't slow either of them down. But kill her? No.

She scanned the desk as quickly as possible while he scrambled to his feet. A lighter sat on top of a packet of cigarettes. *Bingo.*

Bridget swiped it up and pocketed it, then raised her hands. "Enough!"

"That's my line." Clarke closed in. Pointed the gun at her face.

"You think I can't get that gun from you before you have time to pull the trigger?" More likely he'd fight her for it. But he wouldn't pull the trigger while it was aimed at her forehead. She'd have precious seconds while he re-aimed for something not so lethal.

His eyes narrowed and he stepped back, out of reach. "Let's go."

"I can't believe you killed that guy."

Clarke shoved her in front of him. She moved along, not wanting the gun to go off accidentally somehow. He propelled her at a fast pace to the elevator. "Hit the down button."

She did it, then glanced at the window out the corner of her eye. Red and blue police lights lit up one corner of the frosted pane.

Cops.

FBI, maybe.

Whichever it was, she was glad. And assumed they were here to safeguard the database and capture Clarke. Or they thought Capeira would be here and wouldn't move in unless they saw him on the security feed. Then again, they could be responding to a call nearby, and those lights weren't even headed here. *Please let them be coming here, Lord.*

The elevator doors slid open.

Bridget headed for the far corner and huddled against the wall. Out of reach—until Clarke hit the button and closed in.

She clenched her jaw and held still as he moved in. That gun remained pointed at her. Clarke's breath on her neck. He pressed his body against hers.

Bridget grasped his wrist with her thumb and index finger and pressed on the nerve.

He yelped and dropped the gun.

"If you want to continue walking without assistance, don't come near me again."

He stepped back to glare fiery daggers at her with his expression.

"I'm only here because…what? You need someone to blame all this on?"

Clarke's expression shifted to amusement.

"So bringing me here to slow you down and make things more difficult was…what? Just for fun? You're just going to leave me and make your daring getaway."

He flashed a smile. "Maybe you are smarter than you look."

She didn't like it, and he didn't explain. He had a plan.

Bridget should've kneed him where it would seriously hurt and *then* asked the question. It didn't matter who held the gun when Bridget had questions that needed answers.

The elevator doors opened.

Beyond them stretched a windowless hall, like a basement. At the far end was a door to a server room she could see through glass windows. Rows of server racks housed information backups. Like their database.

This whole building was supposed to be high tech and secure. "Looks like a keypad entry." She motioned to what looked like a computer keyboard as he walked her to the end of the hall. "Got the code?"

Behind her, Clarke chuckled. Then he stopped her in front of a locked door and keypad. His pinched grip caused her to yelp. "Type this." He rattled off a series of numbers, letters, and punctuation characters until she was dizzy.

The light turned green.

"Get in."

"Why the hurry?" She pulled down the door handle and heard the air seal release. What she needed was static electricity. No, that wouldn't work. There needed to be total destruction. Somehow she had to utterly damage all the server racks in the room.

With the lighter in her pocket.

That could work.

She'd grabbed it to use against Clarke, but she could take away the thing he wanted instead.

If she was going to use fire, then she'd have to disable the fire suppression system first. Places like this were high tech, and it was their business to protect the information stored here. They made sure it wasn't going to get damaged. She'd have to get to the control panel. Shut it down, somehow. *Lord willing.* She needed Him on her side for this to work. After she got that done, she'd have to set the fire without Clarke stopping her.

Watch the whole place burn down.

Make sure it was all destroyed.

This was the backup of their system, so if there was no way to recover the data here? It was gone.

For good.

Forever.

Clarke shoved her forward.

The room was wider than it was long, filled with row after row of server racks. At the end was an office, probably where the staff kept an eye on things. Where the fire suppression control would be. Maybe in a closet, inside the room.

"Walk."

Bridget kept her hands in view. She ran down a few possible scenarios as she moved, then finally settled on a decent one by the time she reached the office.

The second she hauled the door open, Bridget twisted and kicked Clarke square in the stomach. Before he could recover, she shut the door in his face and threw the lock.

"Bridget!" He pounded on the door.

She ran to the metal panel on the wall and tugged the latch open. Score. The fire suppression system.

And apparently whoever worked here wasn't worried. They'd left the key in when they clocked out for the day. She twisted it to OFF and closed the panel.

"The cops won't make it in here before I get what I want!"

He thought she was using the phone? "I don't care!" she called back, then followed it up with, "As long as they catch *you*!"

She grabbed a bundle of papers from the printer tray and drew out the lighter she got from the security desk. Then she scrunched the paper into bundles, one or two sheets each, so she could set fire to them easily.

Now she had to get out there again, with enough time to start a blaze that would fill the whole room. Without him stopping her.

He banged on the door. She heard him start to kick it in, and ran to the desk where she went for the side panel. It was open. Whoever worked here had installed an extra fan in their computer tower, leaving the side open. She stuffed paper in there and lit it on fire.

The door smashed open, flung back to hit the wall, and bounced off it. As it came back, Clarke kicked it open and rushed in.

She rounded the desk in the opposite direction and headed out with her lighter and an armful of papers. He needed the computer in here to access the system that would let him retrieve their files. That would keep him distracted while she set the server room on fire.

Bridget set the papers inside the server racks. She didn't have enough to ignite a quick blaze that would engulf everything all at once, but she'd do what she could to—

Clarke tackled her.

Her head bounced off the floor, him on top. Everything she held skittered across the tile. His elbow jabbed her ribs. She kicked out trying to dislodge him from her. Clarke still had the gun. The second she spotted it in his hand, she tried to grab for it.

The gun went off.

Both of them flinched. She jabbed at his eyes with her fingers. He cried out. She managed to scratch his cheek.

Smoke permeated the air.

Clarke's attention drifted for just a second. Things were beginning to catch fire in a way that made her not want to be here too much longer. Just long enough to make sure the destruction would be complete, and no one would ever be able to get into the database.

His hands circled her neck and squeezed. Bridget gasped, which was about the worst thing she could've done. Now she had even less air in her lungs. She would die of asphyxiation caused by surprise—and Clarke's vice-like grip.

Bridget's vision blurred with spots as she started to lose consciousness. He would leave her for dead.

She grasped with her fingers and felt around the floor for something to use. A way to disable him.

She wanted the gun.

What she found was the lighter.

It took a few precious seconds that felt more like minutes. Bridget got the flame to ignite and held tight as she swung it at his face. Clarke cried out and fell to the side. Bridget sucked in a few free breaths, then rolled and scrambled to her feet. Each inhale felt like trying to drag a thousand pounds toward her. She found a few bundles of paper and set more fires randomly around the room, so it burned as evenly and thoroughly as possible.

Then she went back to where she'd left Clarke—

He was gone.

"Yes, police? I need the police!"

She ran to the office where he had the desk phone to his ear.

"My coworker kidnapped me! She's trying to steal our company's sensitive data and destroy the backups!" His gaze came to hers, calculated and determined. He gasped a few times to work up hyperventilation, making it sound like he was scared. "I think she's going to kill me and make it look like I did it!"

He lifted the gun and fired it at her.

Bridget dove out of the way and hit the floor. She tried to blink and get her thoughts into a semblance of order. He planned to blame all this on *her*. She ran for the exit door.

If she could just get out of here before the police showed up, she'd be fine. It would be her word against his, and she had no proof. Just hearsay. She reached for the door.

He slammed into her back.

Her cheek smashed against the door and she cried out. His hot breath brushed her ear and his body pressed hard against hers, bruising her hip bones on the door. "Not so fast."

He hauled her back and pressed the gun to her temple.

On the other side of the glass, three men stood. Enrico, one of his guys.

And Aiden.

Clarke's arm banded around her middle. "No one comes in, or I kill her!"

35

His eyes drank her in. Maybe that was hokey, but who could blame him? It had been hours since the last time Aiden had seen her. He couldn't decipher whatever it was that Clarke was saying because of the thick glass. But it didn't look good, the way Clarke held a gun pointed at Bridget's head.

Both had most definitely been in a fight recently. With each other, if he wanted to take an easy guess. She'd gotten some good licks in. And given the server room was on fire, he *also* figured Bridget was aiming for complete destruction.

As long as that didn't include the loss of her own life, he was okay with it. Sydney needed to meet her mother. If Bridget died here, he wouldn't be able to bring himself to even tell her that her mother had been in Last Chance. Much less, *alive.* It would be cruel to expect her to understand that level of unfairness.

Bridget needed to live so he didn't have to keep that secret from his child. As if he needed just one more reason to keep Bridget alive.

That guy had better not hurt her any further. Aiden realized he'd started to let out a frustrated growl. He needed to get ahold of himself, or he would do something reactive and the consequences wouldn't be good.

Beside him, Enrico started to chuckle. His man's grip on Aiden's bicep pressed on the tendon on the inside of his arm and started to numb his fingers. Aiden winced and tried to shift the man's grip. It didn't help.

Enrico moved to the control panel beside the door, hit a button and strode back so he could see through the window. A rushing sound emerged from a speaker, set high in the wall. "You think I'll care if you kill her?"

Clarke's gaze shifted from Enrico to Aiden and the man next to him. Erratically, as though he was scrambling to figure out what to do. Bridget, on the other hand, had an emotional mask over her expression. She looked cold. Calculating.

Aiden knew the cold façade she put on wasn't the truth. It was what she used to hide behind. A skill learned so she could deal with her father. And the aftermath of her mother being killed by her mom's boyfriend. The day she'd fled town. The years she'd worked with Sasha and Millie. Dating Clarke. Coping with the loss of her daughter. Or, so she'd thought.

The only person she showed the truth was Aiden. Seeing him again these last few days made it clearer to both of them.

Clarke didn't back down. He held the gun against Bridget's ear, his other arm across her waist. "You'll never get revenge for your brother. You'll get nothing."

Enrico said, "I'll get the database you promised me."

Bridget gasped. "You'll never get our client list! Your brother was the worst excuse for a human I've ever met, but you don't care who he hurt or any of the other horrors he took part in. You care about nothing but power."

Enrico laughed.

Clarke shook Bridget. "Shut up. This isn't your bargain."

She shook her head, restricted in her movement by his hold on her. "Don't tell me to shut up. I'm not part of this bargain." She looked at Enrico. "Let Aiden go. He's not part of this."

Enrico shifted. "Then you won't care if I kill him?"

Bridget's jaw flexed. Her high cheekbones accentuated as she chewed on her response.

"That's what I thought."

Clarke glanced at Aiden. "You seriously care about *him*, Bridget?"

"Uh, *yeah*."

Aiden looked at the smoke as they talked back and forth and tried not to let her words affect him. It was hardly a declaration of affection, but it still made him want to smile. Unless it put either of their lives in danger.

Aiden pressed his lips together. The information could be used against them.

No matter what arrangement they made, the fire in the server room was going to be a problem. Surely an alarm would trigger. Emergency services would come.

He spotted sprinklers in the ceiling. Why hadn't they come on yet?

"Let them out." Aiden turned to Enrico. Or, he tried. The other guy still squeezed his arm. He then tried unsuccessfully to yank his arm out of the guy's grip. He didn't budge. "It's on fire! Let them out!"

Whatever agreement they were going to make, they could do that out here. Where Bridget didn't have to breathe in smoke. He'd seen people die before from smoke inhalation alone. It could be deadly.

Enrico ignored him and continued his conversation with Clarke. "You want out? Get me that database."

"She turned off the fire suppression. I should just kill her now."

"Turn it back on and get the fire under control," Enrico said. "Then I'll think about not killing you."

Enrico was on the verge of walking away with nothing. If Clarke played this right, he would be able to get out of here. Or, he'd lose everything. Enrico would kill him—and probably all of them—before he left.

Clarke shoved Bridget away and pointed the gun at her face. "Go turn the fire suppression on before we die in here."

One way or another, Aiden figured they would likely die in there.

Everything in him revolted against the idea of her going back in, deeper into the building but, in reality, this could go wrong so many more ways than it could go right. Smoke inhalation. Enrico. Clarke.

Bridget could fall, and Aiden would have to watch her die through a window with no way to get to her.

Clarke's arm wavered, but he held his aim steady enough. "Then we'll see if there's anything to be salvaged."

Bridget eyed Clarke. Then she turned back into the room and walked down a row of servers. Aiden watched her go, moving until he could see where she was headed. To an office at the end. She stepped inside and disappeared for a moment. The longest few seconds of his life.

A phone rang. "She's calling back again."

Aiden held still while Enrico turned to his guy who had the phone. Millie had called every half hour since they'd left Last Chance. Now they were hundreds of miles away, and Aiden wanted to answer that phone.

Millie knew where they were. At least, he hoped so. Even if the server room blocked whatever GPS signal emanated from Bridget's tracker, this would be her last known location. Had she called in the FBI yet?

Enrico had brought them in through a side door and, though Aiden looked, he hadn't seen anyone watching. Surveillance was pretty easy to spot, and he knew what to look for. It made his stomach roil with nerves at the idea Enrico might get away with this.

Clarke could skate out from under the consequences of his actions the past couple of weeks.

Sydney. Aiden needed to get home to his daughter. Bridget needed to get her real life back or start a new chapter. He wanted to take Bridget out for dinner and ask her what she wanted her future to look like. Regaining what she should've had, or creating a gift of something new? Or both those things.

God, I want the chance to do that. Please help us. He didn't like telling his Heavenly Father what to do. But some prayers were born of desperation, a plea.

The FBI could bust in at any moment, although that would be a bad idea. They might have already broken into the surveillance cameras, watching everything. Maybe even listening, too.

A second later the sprinklers overhead turned on.

Aiden winced. If they wanted information from these servers, he wasn't sure they would get it with the electronics waterlogged. Someone with technical know-how—like Ted—could probably answer that question. But given the fact he'd dragged in Millie already, he didn't want to offer up anyone else. Not if it aided Enrico.

He saw a flash of Bridget's jacket at the end of the hall. Just a second, and then she was gone. To the right. She raced out of the office and snuck out of sight as quickly as possible.

Aiden's lips twitched. He managed to keep from laughing aloud as he realized she was never going to back down. *Good for her.*

If she wasn't going to back down, then neither would he, though the man's grip on his arm was starting to get seriously frustrating. He decided to use that to his advantage and swung around to the guy. "Will you ease up on your grip for *one second*? I'm not going anywhere while Bridget is in there, okay? You can quit squeezing my arm."

The guy glanced at Enrico for direction, then let go a little.

Aiden twisted his hips and whipped out with his fist as fast as he could to throat punch him. The guy bent double and coughed for air. Aiden shook out his arms, one hand numb and the other hurt from the punch.

Enrico chuckled.

Aiden turned to him. Enrico pointed his gun at Aiden's face.

"You should shoot him," Clarke said through the intercom. Still waiting for Bridget. Seriously? The guy was clueless. He'd lost all sight of Bridget.

This might be fun. Except for the fact there was a gun pointed at his face.

Clarke narrowed his focus on Aiden. His expression darkened. "Get rid of him."

Aiden wasn't going to let that go. "Because Bridget prefers me over you?"

Clarke's eyebrows rose. "That's what you think?"

Aiden just stared at him. *So cocky.* That was going to get the guy in trouble.

Even so, Aiden didn't back down. He knew better than Clarke, and he was confident in what they would be to each other if they all got out of this alive and in one piece. After all, they had Sydney connecting them. Even if it took a lifetime, he'd be able to convince her that she was the woman for him. Always had been and always would be.

If she balked at the idea of them together, he would simply spend the next however many decades they still had to live, proving to her that it was the truth.

He loved her.

If it didn't take long, he planned to ask her to marry him. He wanted to settle down, finally. Then he'd see what she thought about having more kids exactly like Sydney. Or maybe a passel of boys. Butch could get a younger sibling too. He wasn't going to last many more years. They would need more dogs in the house.

All this went through his mind as he stared at Clarke, aware of the gun pointed at his head by Enrico. Funny what you think of when your life could end in a blink.

As he watched, Bridget came up behind Clarke. She hit him over the head with something. His eyes widened half a second before he dropped to the floor. She doubled over and coughed.

Smoke inhalation.

Aiden needed to get her out of there fast. He needed to call Millie back and get the EMTs here to help Bridget. He didn't care at all about the database everyone wanted so much. Only her.

Enrico's guy recovered from Aiden's punch and moved to the door. He jabbed at the control panel. "How do you get this thing open?"

"Like this." Enrico strode over and fired his gun at the panel. The light went red, and Aiden heard metal clank as a lock engaged. Enrico roared. He fired his gun at the window, over and over. Until it clicked empty.

Aiden ran toward him. He barreled into Enrico and sent him careening into his guy. They all fell to the floor in a tumble.

Aiden started punching.

His arms tired quickly, and it was hard to get any real power without actually being on his feet. He grabbed the sides of Enrico's head and slammed down on the floor once. Enough to daze the guy.

He kicked out at the second man and rendered him unconscious.

Aiden grabbed the phone and took Enrico's gun, even though it was out of bullets. He could still hit someone with it. He shoved it in the back of his belt and patted down Enrico's guy, but came up with nothing.

He found the other gun on the floor across the hall, where it had skittered in the commotion.

"Bridget!"

She turned at his call.

"Can you—"

She pushed open the door. Relief nearly sent him to his knees.

The Capeira guys were down. Clarke was down. Aiden wanted a hug, but the phone rang again right at that moment. "Millie?"

He was vaguely aware of the rustle behind him, but they desperately needed help from Millie. That was the top priority.

"What's happening up there?" Millie said, "I can't see the hostiles on the cameras."

"All clear up here. Send in the cavalry."

Through the phone, Aiden caught Eric's voice. "You heard the man. It's go time."

The line went dead.

"They're coming to—"

Bridget lifted her gun.

She aimed it at him and pulled the trigger.

36

Beyond Aiden's shoulder, Enrico fell to the ground. Bridget stared into the vacant face of the second Capeira brother she'd killed. She blinked.

Exhaustion weighed on her shoulders, and she lowered her arm. Every breath was a rush of air she could hear in her ears, until the whoosh filled her whole world. Rushing wind. What was..?

Aiden said something. She couldn't hear it. He frowned and turned to Enrico, then back to her. He said something else. She stared until her thoughts coalesced and the rushing sound stopped. "You thought I was going to shoot you?"

His expression turned sheepish, and she saw a flash of the little boy he'd once been. "Only for a second." He blew out a breath and glanced once more at Enrico. "Thank you."

"You're welcome."

"Are you going to move?"

Bridget realized she still held the gun. She glanced around. Clarke was unconscious. The man Enrico brought with him was also. Enrico lay on the floor… She didn't need to look at the blood. Not when she was like this. She was self-aware enough to know that wasn't going to help her wrap this up and get out of here.

And then there was Aiden. "You're really here."

Standing in front of her, tall and strong like he'd always been. She wanted to fall against him. Collapse in a desperate need for comfort. She'd just killed a man. One bent on revenge for the fact she'd killed his brother.

Her entire body shuddered. And then he was close enough she could feel his breath on her face. "Of course I'm here. Where else would I be?"

"You were kidnapped just like I was." She'd seen it happen.

Aiden's arms wrapped around her. "As if that would make a difference."

She almost wanted to laugh. Instead, Bridget pressed her cheek against his chest and squeezed her eyes shut. She pulled in a long breath and let it out slowly. Felt it break a few times intermittently as tears gathered in her eyes.

"Hey. You okay?"

She felt his voice rumble in his chest and she squeezed even harder with her arms before she realized what she was doing. Cracked ribs.

"Whoa. Easy."

She leaned her head back to look at his face. "I'm good. I'm okay." Aiden needed to know she could handle herself. That she was strong enough to be a good mother to Sydney.

"You don't have to be." He touched her cheek. "It's okay if you want to freak out. Though, I'd do it quickly before the FBI get up here."

"I'm fine if you don't want them to see." She could hold it together until she was alone. Just as long as there was no stirring from Clarke or the other guy, she figured she'd be all right.

She could hold out until she was alone.

If this really was over.

"Bridge." He held her tight in a way she loved. "We don't

have long right now, but I feel like this is a needed conversation. So listen up. You're safe with me, however you want to react. I just figured you might not want to freak out in front of your boss and a bunch of FBI agents. That's all."

That was true enough. Bridget nodded.

"But I'm not in that category. I'm me, and you're you. And I figure it's always been 'us.'"

"Because Sydney—"

He shook his head. "Hold up. Sydney does connect us, and that will be true forever. But what we have is a separate thing also. It was just you and me in the beginning, and we still share that same connection."

The one that gave them a daughter in the first place.

Bridget felt tears roll down her face. "I want to meet her."

He nodded. "I know this isn't the time, but I also don't want to wait any longer. You're back, right?" Before she could nod, he said, "There's a lot to talk about and figure out with you meeting Sydney. I'm so nervous about the uncertainty of our future, but I also know it'll be fine. She's going to love you. And I want to ask if you'll go to dinner with me. Just us." He smiled, and it was kind of a nervous smile. As though he had reason to be unsure of himself. "There's so much to say, and I feel like if I don't get it out now, I'll lose my shot."

Bridget lifted on her toes and pressed her lips to his.

Delight lit in his eyes as she lowered her feet down, flat on the floor. "Let's talk. Soon." Relief took away all the tension in her. All the emotion pent up from everything that'd happened today. "I know Enrico dragged you into this, but I'm really glad you're here. I wouldn't want this to happen without you."

Aiden gathered her close again and pulled her into another hug. She loved the feeling of being in his arms. The memory of it was so strong, and yet this also felt far different. She recalled the time they'd spent together as teens. The feel of it was so familiar, yet they were both different now—in all ways—and there was a newness to it.

It was probably selfish that she was happy he was here with her. After all, he'd been kidnapped as well and she shouldn't be wishing that on anyone, least of all someone she cared about as deeply as she did Aiden.

He was her port. The safe harbor God had given her as a place of peace when the rest of the world swirled around her like a storm. He was a gift God had given back to her now, at a time she finally knew how to responsibly handle those feelings.

In a way, she'd always loved him, though for years she'd denied the strength of what they'd had. She'd always thought of it as a summer fling. She wasn't going to tell him how she felt right now, though. It wasn't the time or the place. Neither was ready for confessions of love, and she wanted to meet Sydney.

She'd be praying this time around that she could handle the feelings that developed with Aiden—feelings that had led them both into trouble before—and that they'd be new this time. The last thing she wanted was for this to turn into a disaster again—especially now that they had Sydney to consider.

She didn't regret what they'd shared, though she knew their actions had become a sin—and the emotions that came along with the sin made her feel the need to leave town without telling him all those years ago. She knew that now.

Bridget had abandoned him. In some way she knew she would be fighting the need to make up for that for the rest of her life. Even though he would likely tell her it was unnecessary. The urge to overcompensate for her shortcomings would be strong. *God, help me do this right.*

He kissed her this time. Not long, but with conviction. "I'm glad I'm here too. And that we're both in one piece."

Bridget opened her mouth to respond in kind when someone shoved her back from behind. She stumbled against Aiden, her head slamming into his chin.

She heard footsteps rush out to the hallway. Over Enrico's dead body.

Dizziness overwhelmed her and her legs gave way. Aiden caught her in his arms. "Clarke!"

She tried to look but couldn't get the dizziness to settle. "Go."

"He ran off down the hall to escape before the feds get here."

She shoved at Aiden. Not hard, but with enough force he'd know she was serious. "Go after him."

"Are you—"

She didn't need him to ask if she was sure. "*Go.*"

"The FBI is on their way up."

She grasped his elbows. "Don't let him escape."

Aiden didn't look convinced, but he went.

He didn't like leaving her. Not after everything that'd happened. Still, he did it. Mostly because she'd asked. Although Clarke had kidnapped, hurt, and used her, Aiden would rather stay with Bridget and let the FBI grab the guy on his way out.

Clarke disappeared around a corner at the end of the hall.

Aiden sprinted faster, though the feeling in his chest wasn't good. Cracked sternum, or ribs. Something. Enough pain he didn't want to think about it at least. A fight, or even getting shoved against something, was going to hurt in a serious way.

He'd much rather be back there hugging Bridget. Talking quietly in sweet words to each other. What they'd been denied for so long. *No, don't think about the past.* It was what it was. Sasha's actions and their consequences weren't something they could change.

He reached the corner and braced before turning, just to make sure Clarke wasn't waiting to jump him.

No one.

Aiden heard a clang and ran to the source. No way. It

seemed like... He opened a hatch and heard a muffled grunt at the bottom.

Clarke had thrown himself down a trash chute, or maybe it was a mail chute for packages. Someone had removed the labeling, but it was obvious it was no longer in use.

Clarke must've known about it. He could've even set it up beforehand, just in case he needed a quick escape.

Aiden heard the elevator ding at the same moment a door flung open and the metal exit bar slammed the wall. Stairs. Multiple entry points.

Booted feet rushed to Aiden. Before they could do or say anything, he pinched the hem of his shirt with two fingers and lifted both hands. It pulled up his sweater and jacket far enough his police shield would be visible. The other hand he held open, palm out, as he turned.

FBI.

HRT.

"Hands!"

"Don't move!"

Vests and ball caps. Assault rifles. He was slightly disappointed not to see a K9 unit dog with them. He'd never seen one before outside of training and conferences, and the Last Chance PD didn't have a department animal.

No one told him to get on his knees, so he figured they'd seen his police shield. Likely along with the giant bruise on his chest. He didn't look down but was pretty sure it wasn't attractive.

Eric and Millie emerged from the elevator, vests over their normal clothes. Both carrying Sig Sauers. Why they'd never put it together that they should work together both at home *and* in their occupations, Aiden didn't know. They moved like a team as solid as any he'd ever seen or been a part of—having dealt with the conflict between them. Or, at least they'd put it aside for later.

"Cullings!" It didn't matter which one of them responded to his call.

Aiden waited for one to glance over, and wound up getting both their attention. "Bridget's inside the server room. She needs an ambulance."

Millie rushed ahead of her husband into the server room. Eric headed his way instead. The agents around Aiden stood down. He held out his hand, and Eric shook it.

Aiden didn't hesitate to fill him in. "Clarke headed down this mail chute, or whatever it used to be before they shut it down." It certainly looked like it hadn't been used in years. "I heard him at the bottom."

Eric turned to the closest HRT guy. "Take a team. Check out wherever this goes." Then he turned back to Aiden. "We have the perimeter surrounded. He won't get out of our barricade."

"If you guys catch him, this will finally be over." Until then, there was still a present threat. Which meant they'd have to continue to keep Bridget separate from Sydney to keep her safe.

He drew out his phone and sent a few update texts to both Conroy and Basuto. The replies came fast. Sydney was still asleep, and the house was secure. The sergeant would be there until Aiden got back. He didn't need to worry.

Aiden appreciated them saying so, but neither knew what it was like to be a parent. Worry was a default until the moment prayer and God's peace entered the equation.

Until they had children of their own, they weren't going to fully get it.

"Sydney good?"

He glanced at Eric, a father himself, and nodded.

"Okay." Eric clapped him on the shoulder. "Let's go make sure our women are, too."

Aiden nodded. Millie and Bridget were in a hushed conversation when they walked in. The dead man and his unconscious friend were still on the floor, though armed HRT agents stood over them.

The two women stepped out of the server room and met them in the hall. Bridget came to Aiden's side. He lifted one arm, and she walked under it.

"I'm sorry." He gave her a small squeeze. "Clarke had a prearranged plan. He got off this floor, but the FBI will catch him. He won't get away."

Millie stood beside Eric. "We got Enrico Capeira's phone."

The special agent's eyes widened. "That's a huge gain for the bureau. We could get intel on a whole lot of his contacts with that. People he works with and transportation routes, as well as potentially his entire network."

Millie nodded.

"And your client list?"

Bridget lifted her chin. "We'll need the company who operates the server to confirm what we think, but the fire I set did substantial damage. If it hasn't been destroyed, then we can rest assured it wasn't accessed either."

Eric tipped his head to the side, studying his wife's face. "Might be for the best if it was destroyed. Given the sensitive nature…" He trailed off and shrugged.

"Why would I not need the client list for my business?" Millie set one hand on her hip. "If it's destroyed, then my company is dead. I'd have to start over again."

Eric shifted. Everyone caught the wince, but given he'd been shot recently, Aiden was surprised he'd been working this long tonight. "Maybe that's for the best. After all…" His voice trailed off, and he waved at her midsection.

Aiden realized what was going on.

"Excuse me."

Eric followed her. "Mill—"

Bridget turned to Aiden and hugged his waist. "I think there's more for them to figure out. What with Millie being pregnant and all."

Aiden felt the pull of a smile on his lips. "I caught that as well."

She lifted one brow. "Are you going to tell me what to do in my career?"

Alarm bells blared in his mind. He had to tread carefully or things could go very badly. "Am I your husband in this scenario?"

"If you were, would that give you carte blanch to decide whatever you want, with me abiding by it whether I agree or not?"

"I'd hope that respect and trust would be mutual." He hugged her back, their faces close. "I would also hope that whatever bump in the road we came across, we'd sit down and talk through together. There are bound to be things we disagree on. That's just life."

"So how do those things get resolved?"

"Wisdom. Prayer. Trust. Compromise. Humility."

Bridget nodded, eyeing him with an expression of amused study on her face. How she managed to have such expressive features, he didn't know. And yet, no one else seemed to be able to read her the way he could.

"But the first step after Clarke is caught is getting out of here. We have a breakfast date with our daughter."

Her eyes lit.

"Hey!" An armed HRT agent yelled. There was a scuffle of clothing and a dull thud. Someone moved.

Aiden looked over Bridget's shoulder. She turned, which put her in front of him as the unconscious man rose. Metal flashed in the air. A blade.

Aiden shoved her away as it flew through the air toward them. With a sickening sound, it sank into flesh at the spot where she'd been standing a mere second ago.

Bridget screamed.

Aiden stumbled back. Fire tore through his abdomen as he fell. Hands on his stomach, and a knife embedded in him.

His tailbone hit the floor and the knife shifted. Aiden cried out.

The HRT agent tackled Enrico's man to the ground and cuffed his hands behind his back.

Bridget screamed his name.

He looked down at his hands, wet with blood.

37

Bridget fell to her knees beside him. "Move your hands." She whipped off her jacket and gently situated it around the entry point of the blade. She couldn't pull it out. Despite the raging instinct to get rid of it, the reality was that the blade currently plugged the hole in him. *Lord.* There was so much blood. "Jesus, help us."

Aiden blinked at her. Bridget pushed the jacket closer around the wound. His breath hitched, and she had to wince. "Sorry. I'm sorry." For so much. For everything. "Hang on."

Behind her, Millie cried. Eric yelled into his phone. "We need medics up here, *now*!"

Aiden's eyes glazed. Bridget stared at him. "Hang on."

He had to hang on. He *had* to, there was no other outcome she would accept. *Lord.* She wanted to make a bargain. To plead with God to save him, promise anything. Everything. There was nothing she wouldn't hand over or change to try and convince the Lord not to take him right now.

"Bridge…"

"Don't try to talk."

Eric touched her shoulder. "They should be up here in seconds."

She nodded but didn't take her attention from Aiden. "You heard that, right?" She knew he had, but needed to say something. "Seconds. They'll be up here in seconds."

She tried to sound reassuring. Maybe it didn't work, but aside from prayer, that was all she had to give. Taking the knife out of him would only cause him to bleed more. A doctor should do that. Something Bridget knew, despite the fact everything in her made her want to grab it and pull it out. To get that blade as far from him as possible.

She knew the Capeira guy had been aiming for her. Aiden had shoved her out of the way and taken the knife for her.

He could die.

For her?

No. No way should he have risked being torn from Sydney's life. *Please, Lord. Don't let her lose her father.* Bridget should've been the one stabbed. Not him. Sydney couldn't grieve what she'd never had—at least, more than she already might.

"Why did you do that?" Tears rolled down her face but she ignored them. He shouldn't have done that. No way was that fair. "You shouldn't have done that."

His expression shifted. She could read enough there he didn't need to try and speak.

She touched his hand, both of their fingers slick with his blood. "Okay. Okay." She shook her head. Maybe nothing would ever be okay again. "You still shouldn't have done that."

She gasped in a breath and tried not to break down. She needed to be strong for him, so he would know everything was going to be okay. If she could also convince herself, too, that'd be great.

Two EMTs pushed a rolling bed off the elevator. Within a minute, they had him loaded and on his way back onto the elevator. Millie walked with her as Bridget's stomach rolled. They ducked into the elevator before the doors closed. He was so pale. Sweat beaded on his hairline.

As the elevator began to move, she reached out and held his hand.

"Are you family?"

She wanted to tell the EMT yes, but it wasn't true, even though Sydney would forever connect them. Bridget shook her head, even while realizing it was the very thing she wanted.

If there weren't five people in this elevator, she'd have told Aiden right then and there that she loved him, even though he wasn't all the way conscious. It didn't matter that they hadn't seen much of each other over the last few years. She knew she still felt the same as she always had, and maybe even more now.

Adding in Sydney to the mix?

Bridget wanted her daughter in her life. She wanted this man in her life. She wanted it all—the three of them as a family.

Forever.

"You're not family?"

This time it was Millie who answered the EMT's question. "It's complicated."

"He doesn't need complicated right now."

Aiden stirred on the bed.

What was this guy trying to say? Bridget shook her head while the second EMT looked on, an unhappy expression on his face.

The first EMT adjusted the strap that secured Aiden. "You can meet us at the hospital. We need to move quickly. He's losing blood."

Translation: this guy didn't want her—and any drama she might bring—getting in the way.

As much as Bridget wanted to argue with that, she kept her mouth shut. After all, the danger wasn't past. Aiden needed to be seen by a doctor as quickly as possible. No way did she want to get in their way just because she was distraught.

She nodded at the EMT, let go of Aiden's hand, and turned to Millie. "Did the feds catch Clarke yet?"

The elevator doors opened and Millie and Bridget waited until the EMTs wheeled Aiden out before following.

"I'll find out from the scene commander when we get outside."

Bridget planned on being there when he was brought in. She wanted to see it with her own eyes, so she would know Sydney was finally safe. She was done dealing with Clarke and his inclination for revenge. She'd had enough from Capeira and his men, resulting in Aiden being wheeled through the lobby on a stretcher with a knife still in his gut. They walked out the doors where a group from the Hostage Rescue Team gathered. An ambulance pulled up, causing the group to move. Millie headed for the scene commander, while Bridget trailed Aiden and the EMTs the rest of the way.

She watched them load him into the ambulance and seconds later they headed out. Bridget prayed until they were out of sight. Then she found Millie. "Update?"

Millie frowned. She was surrounded by several HRT guys and an older man in a suit. "No sign of him."

"So he's still inside then." Bridget figured that was true.

One of the men frowned. Another shifted. The older man said, "If I knew your name and why you were asking, I might be inclined to explain we're currently conducting a full search of the building and the surrounding area. If he's here, we'll flush him out."

"Good." Bridget didn't feel the need to explain who she was.

These guys needed to concentrate on finding Clarke, not going over everything she knew for their reports. All that could come later. Bridget would've preferred to get in on the search, but the FBI would never allow an unknown civilian to join their team for an operation. They had no idea who she was, or exactly how personal this was for her.

"I need to go speak with Eric." Millie squeezed her elbow. "He'll be okay."

Bridget nodded. "Yeah, he will."

She didn't want to consider the fact Aiden could die from the injuries he'd sustained. Because of her. She knew he'd never blame her for it. But it was just another way she had ruined his life. That was the core of it.

The FBI personnel broke off to their own conversation, leaving her standing around by herself. Her phone rang once. She looked at the screen. *Sasha.* Bridget looked around until she found her colleague in a sea of people and jogged over.

"You don't look so good."

Given everything she'd been through? She figured she probably looked pretty good, all things considered. But there was no point arguing with Sasha who never had a hair out of place. "Clarke is going to look worse when they find him. That's what I'm focusing on."

Sasha studied her.

"What? Why do you look like you're up to something?" Never mind the fact Bridget usually regretted asking Sasha what she was up to. And she would *definitely* regret participating. "Don't tell me you have Clarke stuffed in the trunk of your car."

She wouldn't put something like that past this woman.

"Let's go for a wander around." That meant no. "See if we can be useful."

Bridget walked with her, even though she'd have to argue with her sentiment. "Every time you try to be useful…"

"Are you going to expect me to apologize for keeping Sydney safe for the rest of our lives? Because that's already old."

Bridget took a few seconds to try to be honest with herself. What exactly did she want from Sasha? Did she want remorse? Bridget had to wonder if remorse was what she was seeking in exchange for her friend's forgiveness. Correction: *supposed* friend. She knew full well, though, that remorse wasn't a prerequisite for forgiveness. Her ability to offer what God commanded her to do didn't depend on Sasha's feelings, whether she felt guilty or remorseful. But she still needed more time to digest these whirling thoughts.

"I can't talk about this right now."

She walked with Sasha around the corner of a building, onto a dark side street where Sasha beeped the locks on her car remote. "Why don't you go to the hospital? I'll take care of things here." The trunk popped open. She reached in and pulled out a case. "I have stuff to do."

Bridget stared her down. "You're not letting Clarke leave here, are you?"

A sniper rifle. Sasha was going to park herself on the nearest roof. And when the FBI brought out Clarke, she was going to take the shot.

Kill him.

Problem solved.

She'd known her friend long enough to piece it all together.

Sasha set her hand on her hip. "I need the FBI to capture him, and I need time to set up. So whatever you're planning to say because you disagree with the choice I'm making, do it fast."

"Don't kill him." She *had* to have known that was what Bridget would say. A mark like that would leave an indelible stain on Sasha's soul. Knowing Sasha was doing it for Bridget meant there would be one on Bridget's also. "Please, don't do this."

"You'd rather he lives so he can continue to plague you and your *family*?"

"You're doing it all over again. Making decisions that affect me because you think it's the right thing to do, but neglecting to loop me in."

Sasha rolled her eyes. "What do you think this conversation is? Because it's not for my enjoyment, that's for sure."

"I'm supposed to be thankful you're telling me? I could turn you into the FBI. Tell them it was you."

Sasha's eyebrows rose. "You'd do that? Clarke would be left alive. You know he's going to be questioned. Everything we do will be exposed. That puts all our lives—and the lives of every client he knows about—in danger."

"So the answer is to kill him?"

Sasha just stared at her.

"I don't want him to expose our clients any more than you do." Bridget could handle any threat against her. She was worried about what Clarke knew about Sasha. This had to be about more than just their clients. He had to have sensitive information. Something Sasha didn't want getting out.

There had to be an underlying reason.

"If he lives," Sasha pointed out, "you can never be in Sydney's life. You'll always be looking over your shoulder, wondering who'll come at you next. And if Sydney will tragically be in the way when they do."

"I can't let you kill him." Bridget didn't know how to solve this problem. "Maybe Eric can—"

"Time's up." Sasha lifted the rifle case and strode away. Those long legs ate up the sidewalk at a rapid pace until she was practically running.

Bridget stared at her friend. She wanted to yell after her. *If you kill him, you're no better than the bad guys.* Life wasn't always black and white, but that didn't mean Sasha could take vengeance into her own hands.

Bridget was adrift. She didn't know how to find her place to land. Swept around by everything that had happened to her. She didn't know where to find a safe harbor. Aiden had been that for her for the past few days, but he wasn't here now. He'd been hurt because of her and was fighting for his life in the hospital. Their daughter could be fatherless. Bridget might never have with Aiden what she'd always wanted.

And if that happened, she would lose the one person who had always anchored her.

Bridget felt a stirring in her soul.

God needed to be that port. The One who called her home, to come and anchor her life in Him. She couldn't be swept around by every wave and battered by all the storms that left her adrift. She would be tethered to Him.

Safe, in Him.

Bridget ran back to the office building and grabbed the first FBI Special Agent she could find. She practically shook him, she was so desperate to stop her friend from making this mistake.

"Where's Millie Cullings?"

38

Twenty-four hours later

The door to Aiden's hospital room opened and Conroy stuck his head in. The chief started to lift his chin and say something when Sydney wriggled between his hip and the door frame and ran across the room toward him. He didn't like the expression on her face. She looked scared.

"She's been kind of freaked out." Conroy opened the door far enough to walk in and then let it close against his heels. "We told her you were all right, but…"

Aiden nodded. At the same time, he held up his hand so Sydney would see he was moving and functioning, hoping she would stop tearing toward him before she jumped on his stomach.

Conroy frowned at the other person in the room. "Is that who I think it is?"

Aiden ignored the question. Sydney hadn't yet noticed the blonde woman sitting upright in a chair on the other side of his bed with her head dipped. Fast asleep. She'd been like that ever since he'd woken up a while ago. Long enough he was considering having a nurse take a look at her. Bridget was injured and exhausted, and he could admit he was worried about her.

Plus, he wanted to hear what had happened since he was put in the back of that ambulance.

"Whoa, Syd." He held out one hand for her and used the other to protect his stomach just in case. "Climb up but do it carefully, and don't lean on my stomach, okay?"

She scrambled up the side of the bed, her lip quivering. Tears filling her eyes.

"Hey." Aiden didn't like the word "crooned" but that was what he was doing. "Hey."

She burrowed into his shoulder and stuck her face in his neck.

"I'm okay," he murmured.

Her little body bucked.

"You good?" Conroy asked from the door.

Aiden nodded. After the chief shut the door, he held onto Sydney for a while. His stomach hurt, but in an abstract kind of way where he felt kind of disconnected. Floating on whatever medicine they'd given him. Later he would have to deal with the reality of the pain. Right now, he was content to be able to ignore it. The alternative was the sheer agony of the fact he'd been stabbed in the stomach.

"Kick off your shoes, Syd."

She toed them off without lifting her head.

"You okay?" He paused a second. "Did Sergeant Basuto feed you peas again?"

That got her to lift her head. "The Sarge made me a unicorn pancake."

"Is that right?"

She sniffed and nodded. "It looked like a goat."

Aiden wanted to laugh, but it would hurt.

"I'm okay." From her expression it was clear she didn't believe him. "I can't go to work for a while. I have to be on vacation until I feel better."

She eyed him.

"Now tell me more about this unicorn pancake." Aiden would also have to remember to ask Basuto about it, knowing he'd likely get a request to recreate it—only better—sometime in the very near future. He could do a rainbow pretty good. So far, animals had been disastrous.

"He tried to make a horse, but it just looked like a llama. That was what Mia said, anyway. And it was pink. Conroy didn't want any because he doesn't like colored food. Jess had four purple ones and we put whipped cream on them, until Frees stole the can and squirted it straight into his mouth. Conroy took it away from him and threw it in the trash." She pressed her lips together.

"We can get more."

Her eyes lit.

"So basically, everyone came over." He muttered it, more than making a statement.

Apparently, nearly the entire police department had eaten breakfast in his kitchen. Probably while they had their morning briefing. Doing double duty to comfort his daughter while still doing their jobs.

In the chair on the side of the bed, he spotted a shift in Bridget's fingers. He wanted her to wake up. There was so much to talk about.

This wasn't how he'd imagined introducing the two of them, but he'd take it. Aiden wished he could simply tell Sydney that Bridget was her mother. That would freak her out, though. She would be confused, upset, and overwhelmed. And right now, she was already feeling all of those things.

It wouldn't be fair to Bridget to wait too long, but he wanted to ease Sydney into the idea of a woman in their lives.

Because that was what Bridget would be, if he had anything to say about it.

"Taylor got a turtle and her sister wants to call it

Ermagerd." Her face scrunched up in a way that always made him want to chuckle. "But that's just weird."

"Weird isn't always bad. Sometimes it's just interesting because it's different."

"It's still weird."

Before Aiden could say anything, she continued, "Who's that?"

He spotted a slight flex in Bridget's fingers and wondered if she was awake, just bracing for what was about to happen. She was going to meet her daughter. And she would immediately have to face how he chose to play the situation.

"That's Bridget. When I was in High School, she was my best friend."

"I thought Jess was your best friend?"

"That's true, but Jess has Ted." He watched for the flex in Bridget's fingers out of the corner of his eye. "I have Bridget."

Simple enough Sydney would understand, despite the complexity of the situation.

"At least, I'm hoping she'll stick around."

Bridget stirred then. She sucked in a breath and blinked awake with far too much awareness for someone who just woke up. She'd been listening. Aiden didn't blame her. This first meeting would be huge.

"Hey."

Her gaze shifted to him.

"You were asleep a while. I was getting worried."

She winced and touched her temple, where the bandage was tattered now. "Oof."

Sydney climbed over his legs and sat on the edge of the bed on Bridget's side. "Hi." She'd never been shy, something he was massively grateful for right now. *Help this go well, Lord.* So much was riding on this first conversation. They had years ahead of them, but this would set the tone.

Bridget's gaze drank in their daughter and she smiled. "Hi. I'm Bridget."

"I'm Sydney, but everyone calls me Syd mostly."

"My friends always shorten my name, too, and they end up calling me Bridge." Aiden could see the tension in her. He could only imagine how hard this was for her. How nervous she was, and how desperately she wanted it to go well.

"Why would you want people to call you a bridge?"

Bridget's expression lit with amusement, and she shrugged. "I like it."

Sydney's head tipped to one side. "Are you my dad's girlfriend?"

"I used to be. A long time ago, before you were born." Her voice hitched. She looked sheepish and completely adorable. "I want to be again, because I really like your dad. I have ever since I first met him. But I'm not his girlfriend yet." She paused. "I wanted to meet you first to see how you'd feel about it."

Aiden stared at her.

She'd laid it all out in simple terms for Sydney, but for him it was everything he needed to hear. Everything he could have dreamed of. She wanted the same as him, but Sydney had to be on board.

It couldn't ride on the fact Bridget was her mother. It would be like they were forcing a relationship on her whether she liked it or not. Sydney's feelings needed to be taken into account.

Aiden said, "What do you think Syd?"

She just shrugged, twisting to speak to him over her shoulder. "You need a girlfriend, Dad. And she's *super* pretty."

Faced with that flash of the teenager she was going to become, which happened on occasion, he blinked.

Then he burst out laughing.

Which made his stomach hurt.

He groaned. "Ouch."

By the time the door shut, Bridget could have literally slumped to the floor in exhaustion. "That was… She's…"

Aiden watched her.

"Thank you for that." She had to take a second and process it all. "Just…thank you."

He smiled. "You're welcome. I hope it was okay that she went with Mia to get a drink."

Bridget nodded. She touched a hand to her front and shook her head. "She's *so* sweet. And *so* beautiful."

"You forgot precocious." His smile turned to a grin. "I think she has the chief wrapped around her finger. She'll probably come back with candy from the vending machine even if he would never eat it."

Bridget wanted to chuckle. "That was your boss?" She swallowed.

He nodded. "What happened with Clarke? I assume he was taken down."

"Since I'm here?" She hardly wanted to bring all that into the room with them, figuratively, but since Sydney had gone, it was time.

Bridget's heart and mind were full of her daughter. She'd met Sydney, and the little girl was everything she could have imagined. Bridget took a second and closed her eyes, recalling everything about the animated little girl. The shape of her face. Her presence and personality. It was like she'd filled the room with it, absorbing all of Bridget's attention.

She was *everything*. And Bridget couldn't wait to get to know her better.

"You okay?"

She opened her eyes. "Yes. I just… Sydney. You know?"

"It's easy to take kids for granted when you see them every day, but it's good to remember how much of a wonder they are."

"Not that I want to take her for granted, but I want to get to the place where I see her so much that I could. You know?"

"I know." Aiden nodded. "What I don't know is what happened to Clarke."

She stood, smiling. A wave of dizziness crashed over her. She stumbled into the bed. "Sorry."

"Are you okay?" He touched her arm, then slid his hand down to her fingers. She turned her hand in his and held on as she leaned against the side of the bed. "Should I call the nurse?"

"I'm good. Just stood up too fast." Although, not having to talk about Clarke and everything that'd happened was worth being poked and prodded all over again. He didn't look convinced. Before he could argue, she conceded, "The FBI took him into custody. He's been detained, and Millie and Eric both assured me there's no threat. They'll make sure he doesn't target…any of us."

They'd spoken about Bridget, Aiden, and Sydney as though they were a unit.

A family.

His thumb stroked across the back of her hand. "Why does it seem like that's not all there is?"

She supposed she had to tell him. It wasn't like she wanted to start…whatever this was…by lying to him. "It's Sasha."

His jaw flexed. "What did she do this time?"

Bridget didn't want to provide a cop with information that got her friend in trouble later, but she also wasn't going to lie either. "In another effort to do the "right thing" by making irrevocable decisions in the name of what I should or should not have to deal with—"

"Bridget. Just say it."

"She had a rifle case when I saw her last. I have no idea if she was in possession of an actual weapon. I never saw one."

"This isn't an interrogation. I'm in the hospital with stitches in my abdomen."

She winced. "I'm sorry you got stabbed when it should've been me."

"I'm not."

She blinked.

"Tell me what happened with Sasha."

"I told Millie what I'd seen and heard, and Millie made sure Sasha had no opportunity to do something she might regret. Or be arrested for later."

"By taking out Clarke. From a rooftop."

Bridget shrugged. "We didn't let her do it. But then Eric's boss got ahold of the intel, and he had the FBI search for Sasha. They never found her though."

"Why does that not surprise me?"

"I have no idea where she went, or what her plans are."

"Plausible deniability?"

"I have no idea if she's even safe." Bridget figured he was probably right, whether she liked it or not. "She's a good person. Or, at least, I've always thought so. Now I have no idea. I mean, she lied about Sydney. But she's right. She saved her life and probably mine in the process."

Part of her hated saying that.

She had lost years of her child's life.

Bridget thought for a moment. "I wasn't okay back then. I loved carrying Sydney, but the fire chief was asking around about me. There were a couple of near-misses. Until we faked my death and got me a new ID, I knew I wasn't going to escape it."

"I'm glad you're okay." His gaze darkened. "If the fire chief wasn't dead, I'd be having words with him."

"I was walking home through the woods. He was—" She couldn't even describe what she'd seen. "It was violent, and more than that. I'll never forget it."

He watched her, quietly.

Bridget was grateful he didn't want to pry the details out of her. That might come later, but for now she could set it aside. "The woman. I think I need to go out there and see…" Bridget shrugged. "I don't think she's still there. It's been years, and no one found a body?"

"Do you know who it was?"

"No." Had there been that many missing persons during that time? Surely she could find out. "I didn't see her face well enough to be sure if I knew her or not."

"We can talk to Tate when he's back, and maybe contact a K9 officer with the state police. Or search and rescue. See if there's a cadaver dog." He almost looked proud of her.

"I think I need a job in Last Chance." She shrugged one shoulder. "Maybe the grocery store is hiring."

The corner of his mouth curled up. "That would be sweet having you around. Permanently."

"I think so, too."

"Will you go to dinner with me?"

Bridget nodded. "I'd love that."

"It feels strange to start with a date, considering everything we've gone through."

"I know, but I agree—I want to go slow." She didn't like admitting this but needed to. "I'm so scared I'll mess this up. That something will go wrong, and we'll lose everything for good this time."

"I want to do this right, too." He squeezed her hand. "That's why I want you to know that I've always loved you. I want it all because though it might be different now, that feeling is still there. If anything, it's more now."

Affection soared in her. "I love you, too. I probably always have."

"I'm sticking this out. No matter what." He looked so earnest. "So, don't worry about messing up. We both will at some point, so promise me you won't quit. And neither will I."

Bridget leaned in. "I won't quit, and I won't leave."

Joy lit his expression. "Good."

She closed the gap and touched her lips to his. Bridget was vaguely aware of the door opening and then Sydney's voice.

"See, Uncle Conroy. I *told* you she was his girlfriend."

EPILOGUE

Four months later

Cold wind whipped the trees. Aiden flipped up his collar against the breeze and stood watching the clearing. "This is where it happened?"

Bridget's hand slid into his, her fingers covered by a pair of gloves. She leaned her shoulder against his. "Don't make me tell it all over again."

In the aftermath of what had happened with the fire, and the servers, both Bridget and Millie had been interviewed for hours by the FBI. Over a number of days.

Then Bridget had asked to speak with Conroy. She talked to him for three hours while he recorded the conversation. Aiden would never forget the shell-shocked look on her face when she'd walked out of that room.

He'd since read all the notes and the recording of their conversation. Meanwhile, Bridget had been going to counseling twice a week, and he sometimes joined her to talk about things that involved Sydney. They'd settled into a rhythm as a family since he married her only three weeks after he was stabbed.

Neither of them had wanted to waste any time—and Bridget wanted to be there with Sydney as much as she could. That meant being a family.

As for the business Millie ran, it was purchased by an unknown holding company. If anyone knew who was now running the accountant's office, no one was saying. All Aiden knew was that occasionally Bridget's phone would ring, and she would promptly leave the room for privacy. Still, she never left town or went on a job. And she never seemed upset by what she learned. So he let her do what she had to do.

Across the clearing, a German shepherd wearing a K9 unit vest sniffed around the grass beside an overturned tree. Probably downed by a storm.

"Do you think we'll find her?"

He lifted her hand to his mouth and kissed her gloved finger, right over the spot he'd slid the ring on that one perfect day, in front of a small group of their closest friends. Sydney had giggled the entire time, though likely only because she'd tied a halo of ribbons to Butch's head, and he'd licked her little white gloves the entire ceremony. Aiden knew for a fact she'd had candy in the palm of her hand, tucked under the glove.

The dog barked, jolting him out of his reverie.

It sat at attention.

"Sergeant Donaldson!"

Aiden lifted his head. "What is it, Officer?"

"He found something."

Shortly after, the remains of a young woman were unearthed.

"ARE you going to tell me where we're going?"

Bridget grinned to herself, but waved a hand. "Just keep driving east. Toward the edge of town."

In the backseat, Sydney giggled. "Mommy, we should tell him."

Bridget turned to her daughter, all buckled up in the backseat. She'd grown so much since the New Year, when they'd met. Now it was the height of summer, and they'd gone shopping for flip flops, right before getting pedicures. Spending time together was amazing. Bridget was still bursting with the emotion of it all. And still, she had to balance the sheer joy with the need to not give in to whatever Sydney wanted. She had to temper the urge to try to make her happy buying everything she wanted.

As though one day it might suddenly all disappear.

Bridget felt the car slow. "Turn here."

"The warehouse?"

"Pull in. We have an appointment."

Aiden frowned. She stared at his profile. Those same huge, overwhelming feelings rolled over her. These two were like a rip tide. Normally a bad thing. Swept away, unable to fight the current. Bridget was drowning in family.

And she loved every minute of it.

"Care to share what this is all about? Aside from this being the spot where..." He trailed off and glanced at Sydney.

Yes, this was where Clarke had kidnapped Bridget. Where he'd been stunned and grabbed by Capeira. But that time in their life was over.

This was a new season.

"Welcome to Sygnet. Which might sound like a fancy tech company, but is actually a joint venture by business leaders in Last Chance to bring the community together. And the blending of Sydney and Bridget. Kind of. I'll probably change it." She winced. "When I think of something better."

"What are you—"

Sydney shoved her door open. "Come *on*, Dad!"

Bridget got out. He held her hand to the side door of the

warehouse. Had he parked around the front, he'd have seen the spot where she had been kidnapped—now an ocean of cars. The press conference started in two minutes.

"Syd, you—" Aiden spotted the crowd. "Are we supposed to be here?"

Bridget grinned. "Go sit with Sydney. I'll catch up to you in a minute." She lifted up on her toes and kissed him.

"What are you—"

"I'm pregnant." Bridget lowered her heels to the ground but didn't move her hands from his shoulders. "That's not part of this. I just wanted to tell you."

"I know you're pregnant."

"What—"

He kissed her. "Go. Do what you need to do." He strode toward Sydney, who waved him to a chair in the middle.

Bridget swiped away a tear and strode to the podium. Cameras flashed. Local and regional news were here, but she hoped to get some serious attention. Even with the money she'd saved from years of extremely low overhead and the fantastic wage Millie had paid her, there was still a funding gap.

"Thank you all for coming today. I'll cut to the chase. My name is Bridget Meyers, and I grew up in Last Chance. It wasn't always easy."

She spotted Millie and Eric at the back of the room. Her friend's belly was round with the baby she wouldn't birth for another three months at least.

Meanwhile, Bridget still didn't look pregnant. Yet.

She met Aiden's gaze. *I know you're pregnant.*

"I lost people I loved. Many of them. Recently two very special people have come back into my life, and every day we make the most of it. Never taking for granted even one moment together."

She took a breath. "That's why I'm pleased to announce the renovation phase of the Annabelle Filks Memorial Center."

At the back of the crowd, Maggie sucked in a breath. The owner of Hope Mansion lifted her hands to cover her mouth. The body discovered in the woods had been identified as her daughter, missing since the night Bridget left town. Killed by the Fire Chief, she was now laid to rest, and her mother could finally find peace.

Beside Maggie, her son—the town vet—put his arm around her shoulders.

"In conjunction with Hope Mansion, the local church, and the community of Last Chance, this warehouse will be repurposed into community center. A coffee shop and bookstore. A VR lounge and gamer wing are part of a drop-in center for teens. A computer lab. A full gym. An arcade. We will house two dorm rooms and full facilities that will make up a youth shelter for anyone under eighteen needing somewhere safe to go.

"Classrooms with counselors and teachers who sign up to volunteer. The warehouse will also feature a trampoline wing and—or so I'm told—an "epic" kids play area where moms can watch from coffee shop tables while their kids tear it up all the way to the rafters." She lifted both hands. "Safely, of course."

Several people chuckled.

Bridget pointed to the easels on one side. "All the plans have been laid out. I'm happy to announce we have all our permits in place and are ready to begin the work first thing on Monday."

Sydney jumped out of her chair and lifted her fist into the air. "Yes!"

"For a long time, I thought no one in this town saw me. That no one cared what happened to me. Or who hurt me." Bridget grabbed the edges of the podium. "That's not going to happen anymore. In Last Chance, no one falls through the cracks."

She met Aiden's steady gaze and watched his lips move. Forming three simple words she would never get tired of hearing.

I love you.

I HOPE you enjoyed *Expired Getaway*, please consider leaving a review, it really helps others find their next read!

Turn the page for the first 2 chapters of the 8th story in the Last Chance County series: *Expired Betrayal*

U.S.A. TODAY BESTSELLING AUTHOR

LISA PHILLIPS PRESENTS

EXPIRED BETRAYAL

LAST CHANCE COUNTY BOOK EIGHT

Publisher: Lisa Phillips

Cover design: Ryan Schwarz

Edited by: Jen Weiber

❀ Created with Vellum

1

Lieutenant Alex Basuto knew something was wrong the second he stepped out of the gym. Spring air chilled the sweat on his skin. He scanned the parking lot under the glow of streetlamps but saw no movement in the dark.

The jump would no doubt come when he bent to toss his duffel into the backseat of his car.

Alex pressed the unlock button on his keys and popped the trunk instead. Dressed in sweats, sneakers, and a T-shirt, he had no weapon on him. It was in the duffel, tucked in the side pocket.

He shifted the bag and, as he walked toward the trunk, tugged the zipper down.

That was when they approached.

Alex heard a rush of movement and the shuffle of clothing approach him from the back. He swung the duffel backwards and pulled the gun in one movement.

It fell to the pavement with a thud, leaving him holding the gun on the guy behind him. Three others approached. Two on his left, another on his right.

The guy who'd been behind him had a knife.

"Gonna stab me in a parking lot?" Alex didn't lower the gun. He also didn't recognize the guy or any of his friends. Unusual, considering how long he'd worked as a cop in this town. "Start a manhunt, because you killed a police lieutenant?"

He saw the first flicker of unease in the guy's face. Week-old, unwashed hair, and a growth of stubble on his chin from longer than that. He wasn't in charge, Alex figured, when his eyes flicked to the guy on the right.

"Not here to kill me?" Alex looked over each of them.

"You think I want that hassle?"

"So what do you want?" There might be four, but Alex was the one with the gun. Still, it would be a shame if he wound up killed by these troublemakers. Off duty. Three weeks after he'd been promoted to lieutenant.

His mom had thrown a big party in her backyard and invited basically everyone he knew. She'd tried to set him up with a pretty, dark-haired schoolteacher she knew from church. He'd spent the whole party at the grill, hanging with his nephew. Strategically ignoring both his mother's attempts to introduce him to a woman about five years too young for him, and his boss's side glances. Conroy had been far too amused by Alex's predicament. Not to mention as was everyone else he worked with. Including a bunch of FBI agents present.

A whole group of people who'd find out he couldn't cut it as a lieutenant. Forget being cut down in his prime, or never making it to chief. Alex would die, and they'd finally figure out he didn't have what it took to succeed and be the best cop he could be. And he'd never be rewarded, the way he wanted, with a good woman, even though his mama kept saying it would be, "any time now."

Never mind that it seemed to happen to everyone else but him. To which she always replied, "yet."

After his disastrous first marriage, Alex wasn't so sure that was what he wanted. Still, it was like his heart wouldn't listen to him.

The guy took a step closer. If he had a gun, he didn't get it out. The guy just kept both hands by his sides, thumbs hooked in his pockets. "Where's your brother at?"

Javier.

Of course, this was about Javier. Alex glanced aside slightly, keeping the other three in his peripheral vision. "You think I know?"

"I think you're gonna call him and ask. You can come with us and, when we have him, you can go."

"You're prepared for me to add kidnapping charges to whatever I can bring against you?" Surely someone from the gym had noticed. True, Alex might not have called in before he forced this confrontation. Backup might not be on the way. But that didn't mean an honest citizen couldn't step in. Help out.

He just wasn't about to count on that—and not just because Alex could take care of himself, either.

It was more that he had always been forced to do so, and it was just how life seemed to always turn out for him.

The guy took half a step forward and pulled a gun from his waistband. "Drop it on the ground."

On Alex's left, the two others pulled out weapons. Knife guy in front of him let out a pitchy chuckle.

He leveled his gaze on the guy. He couldn't let on that he'd lost the upper hand. And knew it. "You think I know where Javier is?"

"Cop like you? Yeah, I do. I think you know exactly where your brother crashes, and all the places he crawls into to lay low and get high. Spend my boss's money."

"And the boss wants it back? Wants to get paid? That it?"

The man closed in further. "Thirty grand."

Alex winced.

"So either you tell us where he is and come with us to find him, or Dane here carves you up. And I'll let him get *real* creative."

Another pitchy chuckle.

Okay, not good. This whole situation had gone sideways fast. Three guns—not including his—and a guy with a thing for knives?

He didn't want to know what might happen if a civilian tried to get involved right now.

Problem was, he had no idea where Javier had disappeared to this time. Even Javier's own son Mateo, Alex's seventeen-year-old nephew, didn't know. Mama didn't want to know. Alex tried to keep tabs. The pastor kept Javier's situation permanently on the prayer list, just without including his name, only because Mateo's best friend was the pastor's son.

"What if I don't know where he is *or* where to start looking for him?"

"Cop like you? Guess we'll start cutting and see if that's the truth."

"Liars die." Knife guy did that high-pitched chuckle thing again.

Alex's stomach churned. And not just because he'd otherwise be at home making a post-workout smoothie right now.

He'd lowered his gun but wasn't going to set it down anywhere. A cop never disarmed himself when faced with a threat. No matter if that meant the odds were more heavily stacked against him because he refused to give up the only thing he could use to protect himself.

"Can't tell you what I don't know."

"So get on the phone and find out."

Alex's muscles were already fatigued from the deep burn of a hard workout. Still, his stomach continued to tense. "I'm a cop. You think I know where he is? You think Javier would keep me in the loop?"

If his brother did, Alex would arrest him.

"Pretending you're stupid won't get you anywhere." The guy shook his head. "Typical cop. You'll pick up guys for basically nothing and throw them in jail. But your brother? He gets a free pass 'cause he's family." He let out a sound full of derision. "Figures."

"That's not how it works."

"No? Then tell me where he is."

"If I knew Javier's whereabouts, he'd be in an interrogation room right now."

It had been clear for a long time his brother had intel on other players around town, people who were part of the drug trade. Alex'd had several conversations about that very thing with his chief, Conroy Barnes. The chief had cautioned him to go careful if he did pursue it. After all, if things went wrong, it would break Mama's heart more than it had already been broken.

Then everyone would know where Alex came from, and everything he'd had to wade through to be who he was. There wasn't a woman in the world who would contend with all that, and the darkness he had inside him. Analise had proven that when she'd packed all her stuff and left without explanation. Never mind he still had a tiny flicker of hope that he could have everything he wanted.

Even if it would probably never happen.

"You'd arrest your own brother?" He erupted into laughter. "They said you'd be like this, but I didn't believe it."

An interrogation room didn't mean arrested. Alex figured his brother could at least be a confidential informant for the police department, and at best testify against those who supplied the drugs he sold. People he did cash work for.

"You think I'll let you flip him for the sake of *justice*?" The guy laughed some more.

Alex shrugged one shoulder. Turned out that was a bad move since it drew attention to the fact he still held his gun, though by his side. "No. I think you'll kill him before I can make that happen. Because he's what I think he is to you. A liability."

"They said you were smart as well as bullheaded."

Alex figured that was probably accurate but didn't indicate it to these guys. "You're gonna try and make a deal with me?"

"Nah, they said you'd never go for that."

"You tip your hand, indicating he owes your boss money and do it, knowing you'll get nothing from me? How do you expect me to believe that's the whole story?" Alex didn't think that made sense. Except for one thing.

The guy shifted slightly. He wasn't in charge. Alex's hunch had been right—there was a boss above him.

Knife guy half stepped toward him. "I'll get blood."

"One slice of that blade and I put a bullet in you." Never mind that the others would possibly—probably—kill him for it. He looked at the guy to his right and tried to gauge the level of loyalty between these guys. Not to mention whether their orders were different than what they claimed. "I don't know where Javier is. Tell your boss that. And leave now, so this doesn't get more difficult."

It was a reasonable request.

The guy didn't accept it. "I'm leaning toward blood."

Had they been given orders to kill him? Or maybe just cut him up a little?

"You think I'll let it go after that?" Alex shook his head. "Not likely. Unless all of you leave. Now." He could recall enough he'd be able to write detailed descriptions of all four of them. Then he'd spend the rest of the night looking at mug shots on his computer at the office, identifying each of them.

The guy hesitated a second.

That was when Alex knew this was a fishing expedition, not a murder attempt. And not just fishing, but this had been designed to distract him.

The other realization he had was that he was clearly doing well as a police lieutenant if they felt they needed to waylay him so he couldn't respond to…whatever was going on someplace else. Someone was being hurt or taken. A person Alex cared about.

That was a short list if it included whether or not the person could take care of themselves. The vulnerable in his life consisted of Mama and Mateo, though Mama had a shotgun in her hall closet and Mateo was a linebacker on the high school football team. His brother Javier didn't want help.

"This ends now." He swept his gaze through all four of them. "Get out of here."

"Dane." The guy to his right flicked two fingers.

Dane lunged. Before Alex could squeeze the trigger now under his finger, Dane backed off laughing. Nothing but a fake-out.

Alex watched them go and pulled his phone from his pocket. No new texts or calls. Whatever it was, it hadn't been reported yet. He might not be on duty tonight—he'd worked six this morning until eight tonight already—but the new dispatcher would contact him regardless.

He called his mom's number. She didn't pick up.

Mateo did on the second ring, his voice muffled. "Yeah."

"You okay?"

"*Tío* Alex?"

"Yeah. Go check on Mama. Make sure the house is secure."

Mateo groaned, but it sounded like he was only protesting getting up. Totally asleep. Considering it was just after eleven-thirty on a school night, that was a good thing. Or at least it meant the kid didn't have a paper due tomorrow. He lived with Javier on occasion but mostly slept at his Abuela's.

A couple of minutes later, Mateo said, "She's asleep. The house is quiet. All the doors and windows are locked, and no one's messed with the alarm."

"Good. Go back to sleep." Alex hung up.

He slid into the driver's seat of his car and frowned as he tried to figure out who the target was. Someone he would rush in to protect without a second thought.

But not his family.

Was this just about him being a cop and the fact he'd respond to any call about a citizen in danger?

The image of a little boy with bright blue eyes flashed in his mind. A child he'd helped just days ago, along with his mother. Packed them up and took them to Hope Mansion, a refuge in town for women and children.

His phone rang.

Yep. The name on the screen: *Maggie.*

2

Sasha gripped the phone. "I'm not doing it."

"…another job after—wait—what?"

"I'm out." She stared at the curtain hung over the attic window. "I'm not taking any more jobs."

Silence. "For how long?"

"The foreseeable future."

He sounded incredulous. "Babe—"

"Don't. I'm not going to change my mind." Sasha had never liked working side jobs while being fully employed for Millie at the accountant's office. But the pay couldn't be beaten and she was one of only a few people in the world who could—or would—do the type of work they needed. Her retirement accounts were fully funded by now.

For weeks she'd been staying here, at Hope Mansion. Her refuge.

Before this, her job had been working at the accountant's office with Millie and Bridget—and their colleague Clarke, who'd betrayed them all before being arrested.

Considering the company hadn't had anything to do with accounting, the stakes had been high. Their client list consisted of high-level government assets, former spies, and even a few

Special Forces soldiers. People who needed to start over with a clean ID that would keep them safe.

Even though she'd signed a non-compete with her legal employer, Millie Cullings—the wife of an FBI agent—Sasha had still done the side work. Taking government contracts, private contracts, or she-didn't-ask-who contracts had never sat well with her. But only because she didn't like lying to Millie. Considering she didn't have a job right now, it probably wasn't the time to cut all her sources of income. But Sasha was looking for a new path. A fresh start of her own.

After all, this path had put her on the FBI's Most Wanted list.

The feds didn't know half of what she'd done—for Millie, or even before that. Or during those years. Or since.

On top of all that, the fed leading the charge was Special Agent Eric Cullings. Her former boss's *husband*. Talk about complicated.

Sasha sighed. Half the time she didn't even have the mental energy to wade through it all, and yet she'd lived it.

A muffled thud came from downstairs. Sasha strode to the window, which gave her a crow's nest view of the parking area out in front of Hope Mansion. Two trucks had been parked haphazardly on the grass.

"Spread the word," Sasha said. "I'm out until I say otherwise."

She hung up on him. Her "handler" for those jobs. She didn't trust him much farther than she could throw him. Then again, there were only two people in her world she did trust—neither of whom were speaking to her right now. Millie, her former boss, and Bridget, her former colleague. Both came from Last Chance, but Bridget was the only one living here right now.

She was also the one Sasha felt an obligation to make things right with. More than she needed to figure out what she was going to do with her life next.

That was probably the real reason she was still here in town.

Face it. You're a sucker for forgiveness. Friendship had made her soft, and now that they'd discovered the subterfuge she'd perpetrated six years ago? Radio silence.

Sasha passed her cot and opened the trap door. Wooden stairs lowered into the opening so she could climb down to the upstairs hallway. She rarely used them, preferring instead to climb down herself, silently.

"Don't lie to me!" A man's voice rang out, carrying up the stairs and to the hall below her.

Another thud. Someone hit. A woman cried out.

Sasha dropped through the opening into a crouch, then stood. A little boy gasped. Dark hair, dark eyes, and thick brows. He huddled against his mother's side, his face against her abdomen. She stood in the doorway of a room on the second floor which could house up to thirty, though comfortably it was more like twenty-two. Currently, there were sixteen residents: nine women, and seven children. Maggie, the homeowner and manager of Hope Mansion, lived downstairs on the first floor.

The woman in her doorway whimpered. Tears gathered in her eyes, glistening beside the ragged scar down the side of her face. "He hit Maggie with his gun. She's bleeding."

Sasha nodded while her heart twisted at the thought of Maggie being hurt. A woman who did that much good should never have to suffer. "I'll take care of it."

None of these people needed to endure more than they already had. She possessed many scars similar to theirs, and only some couldn't be seen—even in a bathing suit. Because those scars were on the inside.

"Where is he?!"

The little boy started to cry.

Sasha neared them. "Go in your bathroom. Lock the door. Bar it with anything you can find." She turned to the others who'd come out. "Everyone get out of sight. Closets, bathrooms, or under your beds," she whispered. "Hide and don't come out until I tell you the coast is clear."

She headed for the stairs and looked over the railing.

A man trotted up, heavy coat on and a gun in one hand. Sasha stepped to the side. She grabbed a kid's backpack hanging by the wall and tested the weight. Good, there were a couple of books inside.

The man neared the top.

Right as he reached the last step, she swung out, making solid contact with his left shoulder. He tumbled back down the stairs and hit a companion on the way. They both rolled end-over-end to the bottom and landed in a heap with a grunt and a yell.

"There's someone up there."

Before they could race to her, Sasha stepped out. She strode down the stairs as though she had every right to be there, which essentially, she did. Sasha had lived at Hope Mansion for eight months the year she turned seventeen. After she'd given birth to a baby boy, she'd left town and hadn't returned until a few weeks ago.

Now it was like she *couldn't* leave.

She stepped off the bottom stair. "Not someone. Just me."

A big man stood over a woman, holding her by the hair. On her knees. Crying. One eye was already swollen and her face had reddened from being hit.

He shoved her away.

The woman fell to the carpet and curled into a ball.

Sasha looked away, not wishing to remember precisely how that felt. She didn't need to go back there. And yet, given there were five men in the room, how could she not? Five to one wasn't good odds on her best day, armed to the teeth. She had on yoga pants and a tank top, along with running shoes. Not an abundance of places to stow a weapon.

The last time she faced down odds like this?

Yeah. Not a place she wanted to revisit, even being back in Last Chance where all her triggers resided.

"You wanna get involved?" The man took a step toward her.

It was probably supposed to look tough. She was a woman, so cowering was what he'd expect. Instead, she looked around. Maggie wasn't anywhere in sight. Was she somewhere else, bleeding? She returned her gaze to the man like he was nothing to her.

Other than that, Sasha didn't move. She only lifted her chin slightly. "I'm thinking, *yeah*."

He sneered. "Not a good idea. I wish I had time to explain a few things to you, but *she*—" He pointed at the woman on the carpet. "—is gonna go get my son. Then I'll be leaving."

One of the others chuckled.

"You want your son? I'm guessing you should go see a lawyer." After all, there were few reasons a woman and her child would have sought refuge at Hope Mansion. And the reasons this woman had were kind of obvious. "You aren't taking him."

The quicker she could get this resolved, the better. Sasha was on the FBI's Most Wanted list and her physical features currently weren't perfectly disguised as they would be if she were out on the street in Last Chance. Her picture was out there. This guy might've seen it, and she figured he wouldn't mind causing trouble for her.

Or, he wouldn't after she did what she was going to do next.

He took another step.

Two of his guys closed in. Not the two she'd tumbled down the stairs. They were licking their wounds and probably already plotting their revenge.

She swung out and grasped his wrist—the hand holding the gun—and brought up her knee between his legs.

He doubled over. Such a tough guy.

She didn't get the gun in time, so she kicked his face with her tennis shoe. He dropped to the floor unconscious, just as someone grabbed her from behind.

Sasha flung her head back and heard the guy's nose break. Never mind that it hurt the back of her head like few other things did. He let go, so what did she care?

The next guy already had his gun up, but hesitated. Questioning whether or not he wanted to kill a woman he didn't know. She kicked his stomach and grabbed the gun. One of the guys who'd tumbled down the stairs rushed her.

She shot his thigh.

The other pulled up short, hands raised, but she saw the glint in his eye and spun. A knife slashed down from the man behind her.

Boy, it'd been a few weeks since she'd worked out like this. She was kind of rusty. If Zander found out, she'd never live it down. He would put her in a month-long training program until she passed to his satisfaction.

Sasha twisted and felt the fire of the blade as it nicked her shoulder. She hissed out a breath, grabbed his arm and kicked his knee, then slammed the gun down onto his temple. She raised her gun to the only man standing.

A dark blur slammed into her. Sasha hit the wall, and they dropped in a heap together with his shoulder smashed against her cheekbone.

She shoved at his shoulders and chest.

He pulled her under him, and the back of her head slammed onto the bottom step of the stairs. She heard someone laugh.

Hands wrapped around her throat.

Sasha's whole world swallowed down in a rush of memory.

Laughter. Hands. Pain.

She shoved at him and tried to get purchase, not just to push the memories away, either. She tried to fight back. To remember who she was. A grown woman, not a teenage girl with no skill and no training.

She got her feet under him and kicked.

He barely moved, not even slightly dislodged by a ram powered by her strong legs. He was too heavy.

White spots flickered and sparked at the edge of her vision.

Someone screamed. The other woman.

Sasha got her hands up and pressed her thumbs into his eyes. No hesitation.

He cried out and let go enough that she could gasp a breath. And slam her hand into his throat. He coughed, and she scrambled out from under him. Toward the gun.

She brought it up and pointed it at him from her supine position.

"Whoa." He raised both hands, then coughed once. "You got spirit. But you're not why I'm here."

"I'll make it why."

He nodded to one of his buddies. "Get that gun. Then tear this place apart. Bring me my son."

Red and blue lights flashed against the wall through the open curtains.

"*Now*!"

The woman started screaming again. She begged him to leave them alone. To not take her son.

"Shut up!" He turned from her to his wife. Sasha nearly put a bullet in his back. Any other time, or place, she probably would have.

A booted foot kicked her in the head. She rolled, fighting unconsciousness. So that was what that felt like? Yeesh. How many times had she kicked someone in the head? She blinked and realized she'd rolled all the way to the wall.

"Police!"

Hands grasped her.

"Leave it. Let's go." The man added an ugly curse word, referring to the woman. His wife. "This ain't over."

"Last Chance Police!" Pause. "Maggie? You here?"

Sasha pushed off the floor but had no energy to stand. A man was inside, and he was a cop. She had to get out of here before she was seen. There was no time to tell this woman to not mention her presence here. It was going to come out.

Sasha would be discovered.

The woman whimpered. Tears rolled from her one, good

eye. The other was still swollen shut.

"Where is he? Your son?" Sasha could at least make sure the child was all right.

She sucked in a choppy breath. "Upstairs with Marta."

The cop, whoever it was, was in the foyer. She could hear his boots on the wood. Sasha pulled in her feet and stood with one hand braced against the wall.

She could still feel hands on her, the crawl of sweaty palms. A slap. Thick fingers on her throat.

She swallowed against the sensation.

"Ma'am? You okay?"

The other woman was led to a couch and settled there. Sasha's vision blurred. White stripes flashed on the man's workout pants as he made his way to her. Gun in one hand. Broad shoulders. Nausea roiled in her stomach.

He touched her shoulder. "You'll need to get that looked—"

Sasha slapped his hand from her.

"Whoa. Easy."

She lifted her gaze and gasped.

"Sasha Camilero." The way he said her name didn't sound like a good thing.

Memory swallowed her even farther back. Bare feet, racing through a field. Ice cream. Locking their bikes to take a nap in wildflowers. She could still smell them.

"Alex." She said his name on a sigh. Why couldn't she forget it all? Why did she have to remember everything?

He reached for her. "You're under arrest."

Sasha shoved at him.

He stared at her like he had no clue who she was. Like he'd never seen her before.

Sasha turned and raced up the stairs.

OTHER BOOKS IN THE LAST CHANCE COUNTY SERIES

Book 1: Expired Refuge

Book 2: Expired Secrets

Book 3: Expired Cache

Book 4: Expired Hero

Book 5: Expired Game

Book 6: Expired Plot

Book 7: Expired Getaway

Book 8: Expired Betrayal

Book 9: Expired Flight

Book 10: Expired End

Also Available in 2 collections!

Books 1-5

Books 6-10

ABOUT THE AUTHOR

Follow Lisa on social media to find out about new releases and other exciting events!

Visit Lisa's Website to sign up for her mailing list to get FREE books and be the first to learn about new releases and other exciting updates!

https://www.authorlisaphillips.com

Made in the USA
Monee, IL
03 April 2022

94047570R00208